PRAISE FOR *HER BEST SELF*

"*Her Best Self* is a heart-thumping, witty, and deeply layered novel about the things that matter, a can't-put-down thriller with a literary voice. This thrill ride of a novel revolves around the manipulation of memory and the ever-present question at the heart of being human— 'Who am I and what do I believe?' With a seductive landscape and a wide cast of fascinating characters, Friddle's enthralling prose takes us on an addictive, wild, and keep-you-guessing journey. A do not miss."

—Patti Callahan Henry, *New York Times* bestselling author of *The Secret Book of Flora Lea*

"Fast paced, clever, and wickedly compelling, *Her Best Self* grabs you on page 1 and doesn't let go. You simply cannot put it down."

—Michel Stone, author of *The Iguana Tree* and *Border Child*

"Cunning. Unraveling. Sinister and darkly comic. *Her Best Self* is a masterful domestic suspense."

—J.C. Sasser, author of *Gradle Bird*

"In the twists and turns of this quirky, fast-paced novel, Mindy Friddle keeps readers on their toes with a cast of characters who bring humor and heartbreak to the page as they reveal their own secret stories. Surprises abound, down to the perfectly pitched final page."

—Rebecca T. Godwin, author of *Private Parts* and *Keeper of the House*

Praise for Mindy Friddle

"Friddle has a way with the comic yet apt image…funny, down-to-earth and steeped in a sense of place."

—*The Washington Post*

"With fluid prose and telling details, Friddle deftly captures the downward pull of the past and the Southern penchant for mythmaking."

—*Publishers Weekly*

Also by Mindy Friddle

The Garden Angel

Secret Keepers

HER BEST SELF

Mindy Friddle

Regal House Publishing

Published by
Regal House Publishing, LLC
Raleigh, NC 27605
All rights reserved

ISBN -13 (paperback): 9781646034635
ISBN -13 (epub): 9781646034642
Library of Congress Control Number: 2023942879

All efforts were made to determine the copyright holders and obtain their permissions in any circumstance where copyrighted material was used. The publisher apologizes if any errors were made during this process, or if any omissions occurred. If noted, please contact the publisher and all efforts will be made to incorporate permissions in future editions.

Cover images and design by © C. B. Royal
Author photo by Caroline Matheny

Regal House Publishing, LLC
https://regalhousepublishing.com

Printed in the United States of America

For Vito

NOVEMBER 12, 1985

LOCAL WOMAN SERIOUSLY INJURED AFTER CAR PLUNGES INTO RIVER

HAVEN, SC—Wife of local business owner Charles Wolf is in critical condition after her car crashed through a bridge and plunged into a river. Janelle Wolf, 30, reportedly drove off the narrow two-lane bridge on Bremer Road around 9 p.m. Monday. Officials said the mother of two was alone when her station wagon fell six feet from the bridge, floated about 100 yards down Twin River, and began filling with water. Rescuers discovered Wolf unconscious near her submerged vehicle and transported her to Palmetto Memorial Hospital, where she remains in critical condition.

Recently elected PTA president of Haven Elementary School, Janelle Wolf is a community leader and a volunteer, as well as a fundraiser for several Haven charities, according to a family friend who did not wish to be identified.

Charles Wolf said his wife was recovering after undergoing surgery and asked that his family's privacy be respected.

Events that led up to the crash have not yet been determined. As of Tuesday afternoon, police said they don't know whether speed or weather conditions were factors. Heavy rain had washed away tire tracks, authorities said, and the swift current made it hard to determine which direction Janelle Wolf had been heading.

"We don't have a lot of information at this time," Haven Police Chief Bill Tates said. "We need to make sure we get the correct information out."

1

JANELLE

Here I am at the hotel bar again. Barely noon on a Wednesday. Lana will be proud. She says I am making remarkable progress.

I must welcome adventure and court risk. It's part of my treatment plan.

Lana is a gifted healer. She is my counselor, much in demand. She warned me her methods are unorthodox and not for the timid.

I am not timid. Not anymore. But back in the winter, when Lana told me what I must do, I almost refused. Almost.

Then I found myself leaving Haven one Wednesday morning, driving to the Palmetto Hotel—all those bridges to cross! I sat at the bar for two hours and talked to strangers. Those were Lana's orders.

Trust me, Lana said, you need this. Do it and write me a letter. How I love your letters, Janelle.

She was right, of course.

I have come away from all ten of my Wednesday outings feeling invigorated, remembering things. New things, I mean. About the accident. Lana says to write it all down, to stockpile my memories. To prepare.

On our monthly phone calls, Lana talks to me about my letters. She calls them my dispatches. Lana said I am growing empowered, that I am flexing my independence, that I am giving myself permission to remember.

I am so grateful Lana accepted me as a client, even if we can't meet in person. Soon, Lana will make her rounds to clients in the States. I am desperate for her to stop in Haven, to continue our work. She says we will know when the time is right.

On our last call, Lana scolded me. She can be very firm and outspoken. She said I must write more about the people I meet in the hotel bar. She is especially interested in the men.

Today, for example, a young man bought me a drink. He is a consultant in town for business. He is perfectly polite. He listens with interest when I answer his questions.

Lana says I mustn't mistake shyness for reluctance. She says to own my power. She says I am selling myself short, that I must be open to new experiences. Adulteresses are still stoned in nefarious parts of the world, Lana told me. It's women who have always borne the brunt of man's most primitive impulses.

But my proper path is with my husband. I tell her this. I write it in my letters. Charles is the captain of my fate—of our fate. He has always been the love of my life.

That's what he tells me.

I can't always remember.

Lana says we need to EXPLORE this.

She said flirtations are therapeutic and I should not hold back. I must demand to be seen.

Perhaps there are those who would sympathize if my husband philandered. Or if he decided a roll in the hay with me was like a mortgage payment, a tedious monthly duty. Say he was a slob and didn't wash. Or—how did Lana put it?—if he were deep in the closet and lights off so he could pretend I was the pool boy. Or, if he were just not interested in me anymore.

But Charles is none of those things.

The more Lana finds out about Charles, the more she will see just how complicated things are. How tangled it all is. Marriage, I mean.

After all, Charles was married to Janelle Before.

Me, before the accident that sheared away my best self, that left Janelle Before on the far shore of the Twin River.

A different woman altogether.

Janelle Before could have been a star in a Hollywood magazine. Removed and perfect, a woman admired and envied—especially, now, by me.

Oh, how I resent her.

Lana reminds me Janelle Before is not my rival. She says the key to my recovery is welcoming back Janelle Before so I can be whole again. This will be difficult and painful, Lana says, but necessary. Lana knows what to do. Of course she does.

Now I am sitting in the courtyard on this lovely spring day, writing to Lana on the hotel stationery, having myself a nice time, after all. No matter how shameful and sordid—write it down, she says, so you can know, so you can remember, so we can sift through everything, everything.

2

CHARLES

Charles Wolf called his daughter, Mira, from the privacy of his office.

"Daddy? What's wrong?"

Must there always be something wrong when he called? Was he such a harbinger of bad news? Yes. Apparently, he was.

"It's your mother." He cleared his throat.

"Oh." The syllable was heavy with dread.

"Nothing to concern yourself about. But I don't have to tell you how important her birthday dinner will be, to calm her—"

"Yep, Nelson and I will be there."

Charles waited a beat. "Your brother. I haven't heard from him. Would you check to see if he's coming?"

She sighed. "Jeez, Dad. Are you two still not talking? Can't you just get along?"

Charles and his son got along only when they didn't talk. "I have my hands full with the business, Mira," he said. "Very exciting developments." Emitting his own sigh now, Charles was sorry—a little—to resort to the sting of guilt. "And I'm determined to keep your mother on an even keel, especially with your impending wedding—"

"The wedding is no big deal."

No big deal? How like Mira, who eschewed any sort of propriety, to attempt to play down her own wedding. Of course, she had to appease her cheapskate heathen fiancé, but regardless—Charles had his own plan for his daughter's nuptials, Mira just didn't know it yet.

"It is a big deal for us. You're our only daughter—"

"I'm aware."

"Well. You do see how crucial it is that Sunday be a good day for your mother? With all of us there in solidarity? To honor her on her birthday, to set the stage for bigger gatherings? And if Burry and his—" What was the word he was searching for? Burry's longtime girlfriend and her strange child were—

"His family?"

"If they aren't there, if we all aren't gathered around her, think what that will do to your mother."

"Look, Dad. I'll talk to Burry about coming on Sunday but promise me you'll behave yourself."

"Behave myself?"

"Especially around Spec."

"That boy is the one who—"

"'That boy' is essentially your grandson."

He was not essentially or technically any such thing, but Charles knew better than to argue with Mira today. There was too much at stake. He needed Janelle to be well for all that was unfolding. To stand beside him as the family business was reborn.

"—about Mom." Mira's voice cut out.

"What was that?"

Charles's secretary knocked softly on his office door. "Mira, I have to go. Your brother. You'll talk to him?"

"I'll talk to him, but no promises, Dad. You're the one who—"

"Tell him there will be an announcement. Family news."

"Oh…that sounds sort of scary—"

"No, no, good news. Wonderful news."

"Okay, now you've got me curious."

"See you all on Sunday then."

"What should I bring? Foodwise, I mean."

"Nothing. This isn't some sort of shabby potluck. I'm having it catered."

"Wow. That's nice."

"Let me know about your brother."

Charles hung up and turned his attention to his secretary.

"He's here." Arlene peered at Charles from under frizzy bangs, like a wily woodland creature.

"Who?"

"The new consultant? That you hired?" She spoke the word *consultant* as if it were on hooks, filthy evidence to be bagged and sent to forensics.

"Send him in."

The "consultant," Peter something, was meek, bespectacled, swarthy, and too thin, dressed in cheap khakis and knock-off loafers. He sat across from Charles, not meeting his eyes, a bad sign. You hire someone for a job, you want them to have the courage to look at you.

"Sir, I—"

"There's no need to call me 'sir.'"

"Mr. Wolf."

"Charles."

"Charles."

"You have something to report?"

"Yes." He cleared his throat. "I met your wife three hours ago in the hotel bar."

"What happened?"

Defensive. "Nothing. I, uh, I bought her a cocktail. A virgin cocktail. I took careful notes later." He pulled out a notepad from his back pocket. The man's face was purple with embarrassment. Charles almost pitied him. A gumshoe who lacked confidence was going to be an unemployed PI.

Peter glanced down at his notepad. "I think, sir—Charles— she's under the impression you're a captain? She called you the captain of something."

Her fate. Yes. He'd heard that one.

"Did you ask her the questions?"

"I…yes. She didn't want to talk about the senator."

"Nothing? She didn't say anything—anything at all—about Stan or Mary Rex?"

"No. I asked. I asked if she knew them but she acted as if she hadn't heard me, so I asked again, but she ignored the question."

"Tell me. Did she mention anything about her accident?"

"No, sir. Nothing about the accident."

"You did ask her? In a discreet, roundabout way?"

"Yes, sir. I asked her. She changed the subject."

Charles stared up at the ceiling, snapping a rubber band.

"She didn't mention any other names?"

"She did say something about a Lara." He plundered through his notes again. "Lana."

"Lana?" Charles bellowed. That could not be right. "What did she say about Lana?"

"She said, 'I can't wait to tell Lana.'"

Janelle was confused. More confused than he feared. Lana was out of the picture, but that didn't mean Janelle realized it.

"Did she reference me, her husband?"

"No, sir. I'm sorry."

"Don't be. That's good news."

"It is?"

"My wife has a tendency to spin some colorful tales. Occasionally involving me. She has quite an imagination."

"She's…unbalanced due to the accident? Neurological complications or—"

"That's none of your business."

Peter flushed again. "God, I'm sorry. Don't tell Red. I didn't mean to pry. I'm used to, you know, gathering all the facts."

"Apology accepted. I admire curiosity. It indicates empathy."

Red's PI agency hadn't let Charles down yet; the "consultants" he sent were always dewy-faced geeks. But this one was too sensitive.

"It's just—we do so many divorce cases. You see a lot of marriages—" Peter made his small palm into a jet that crashed onto his kneecap. "Kaboom."

"Not this case," Charles said with a tight smile. "No divorce."

"I'm glad to hear it."

"How did my wife appear when you left? Emotionally. Was she confused? Weeping?"

"I think she wanted to be alone."

Now this sad sack across from Charles looked as if he were

about to burst out crying. "Your wife seems like a really nice lady."

Charles cleared his throat. "This might be hard for you to understand, Peter, but the purpose of my hiring you was to monitor my wife's health. It's the responsible thing to do, keeping a careful watch on such a fragile, volatile woman. You and your colleagues provide me with information so that I may be kept abreast of any dangerous delusions she may be entertaining. It's my duty as a husband, as my wife's caregiver. To head things off. Discreetly."

"I—yes. Red told me."

Why did Charles feel the need to justify anything to this cowering ninny? "So that I can make arrangements for my wife's care, if necessary."

"Of course."

For going on three months, since he'd discovered his wife's Wednesday outings to a hotel bar, Charles had discovered this brilliant way to monitor Janelle's state of mind. Who knew what strange notions were churning in Janelle's head? The PIs he hired, that's who! Charles rigorously interrogated them afterward, demanding minute-by-minute reports. If that's what it took to stay abreast of Janelle's volatile state of mind these days, so be it.

"Was there anything else my wife said, Peter? Anything. No matter how silly. My wife usually has more to say. Maybe you didn't record it in your notes?" Charles took out an envelope of cash from his desk drawer and held it up, not handing it over, not yet.

Peter shook his head. "The whole thing didn't take more than twenty minutes, sir."

Charles handed over the envelope of cash.

"Thank you." The PI stood and fumbled around his pockets and pulled out a crumpled receipt. "Here's the bar tab? I think Red told me to go ahead and turn that in since this is a cash-only transaction."

Charles pulled out a twenty and handed it over. "Thank you, Peter."

"My pleasure. I mean not pleasure, really, it was work. But I hope it helped."

"It did."

"We need to meet," Charles told Arlene, after the consultant left. "Close the door behind you."

She looked up at him, curious but pleased. His secretary never felt more appreciated than in moments of crisis. Consequently, Arlene had proven herself valuable all too frequently over the years.

"Heading home, I reckon?" Arlene asked.

Only Arlene knew the lengths Charles had to go to for Janelle. And why.

He nodded. "I should be back in an hour. But first, there is something we need to discuss."

"I'm all ears." She tugged at her dowdy, cheap dress and sat across from him. It was Stan who had advised him to hire Arlene in the first place, all those years ago. Because homely secretaries are so damn grateful.

Arlene's face was peeling, her arms tanned as a shoe, which could only mean one thing. "How is Buddy?" It was Buddy, wasn't it, the name of Arlene's latest boyfriend? Or was it Bobby?

She stabbed the air with her thumb, like a hitchhiker. "Gone. I came home early last week, and lo and behold, there he was fooling around. I told him to git."

Hence, the tanning bed, Arlene's own self-prescribed post-breakup light therapy.

"I'm sorry to hear that."

"Awww, good riddance. He cheated on the computer. Dumbass."

On the computer? Charles shuddered and hastened to change the subject.

"As part of Rex Wolf's new restructuring, there may be some requests to examine our revenue and expenditures." He let that sink in for a minute.

"Okay, you're saying some nosy pencil dick from the government is going to start poking around in my books?"

"Not exactly."

"Not the tax man?"

"This is internal."

"Uh-huh. This is Teddy's idea?"

He shook his head.

"His wife's then. Yeah, that sounds like her."

Yes, it was Reagan's idea. Her request had been almost an aside, so subtle and velvety, Charles did not even feel the pinch of it until later. You won't mind if we have someone look over the books? Just make sure everything is in order? Charles had assured her it was no problem. Nothing would stop the ceremony in August, the announcement that Teddy Rex—Stan's son—was stepping into his late father's shoes, partnering with Charles. Rex Wolf Staffing again, like the old days!

Charles smiled. Arlene narrowed her eyes and scowled.

"It's just a formality," he said. "The point is we must prepare."

"I'm gonna need a whole box of red pens. Teddy's salary and all that marketing stuff—it's bleeding us dry."

That still irritated her, how Charles had cobbled together enough funds to pay Teddy a decent salary so he would come aboard in the first place, to see if he actually wanted to partner with Charles (he did) and if Teddy and Charles were compatible (they were). And now with Teddy's wife, Reagan, in charge of "reinventing and rebranding" Rex Wolf—with new software to install, and plans for expansion—well, as much as he'd explained to Arlene you have to spend money to make money, she remained hostile to the idea. Poor Arlene was old school.

Charles stood and pulled on his suit jacket. "I'll be back shortly."

"Yeah, I know the drill, boss."

Janelle would have returned home from the hotel by now and changed out of some glittery cocktail attire. After the Wednesday PI reports, he rushed home to Janelle's side. Fortunately, she was often in fine spirits afterward, but he wasn't taking any chances. These days his wife was like a grounded zeppelin—quiet, tethered, but combustible.

"Hon," Arlene said in her raspy smoker's whisper, "you're a saint."

3

MIRA

Mira loved mornings at the bar. Before the frantic busyness, the ear-splitting music, the slurred demands of customers, there was this cool, eerie quiet. Ten minutes, twenty if she were lucky, she sensed energy gathering itself around her in the unpeopled rooms, a sort of humming, preparing—like Mira—for the onslaught of humanity. Something to do with the building's old soul, this kinship. She admired its resiliency. A hundred years ago, a cotton broker's office. Then, a hat shop. Now, it was Bar None. And she, the mixologist slash bartender slash manager.

Not a bad gig. She had the perfect boss, after all. As in, never around. Ken Black left Mira in charge of Bar None. Add some cocktails? Help yourself. Hire some help? Long as you manage them.

Of course, bartending wasn't long-term. Nelson pointed out her late hours weren't exactly family friendly. Weren't even boyfriend friendly. After they were married, she'd look around for something else.

Today Mira unlocked the back door of the bar, turned on the lights, made herself a red eye with extra cream, and sat down at one of the high-tops up front, near the window. She took out her notepad. Ten minutes to write down ideas, to-do lists, whatever. Let her rip.

No hometown, no haven. Home again, Haven.

Huh. She hadn't written a poem in months, just scratched out a few lines here and there. Fun to play with the irony, though, that she and her brother had left Haven after high school—face it, they'd fled—and now they were both back, years later. Home again, Haven.

Only it was a different Haven. Pour-over coffee. Hot yoga, a microbrewery. Himalayan salt lamps and dream catchers in the gift shop. Empty storefronts and shabby retail from a decade ago now cafés and tasting rooms.

As for Bar None—the broken penny tiles and concrete floor, rusty tin ceiling, glass block windows, ragged brick and exposed iron water pipes—all the rage. Vintage neglect was de rigueur.

"Morning!"

Crawley. Right on time, unfortunately. She put away her notebook.

"Morning, Crawley."

He lumbered in, reeking of weed. Tied on an apron. "Hey, Mira. I'm here."

"I see that." Mira had hired Crawley last month. He reminded her of the freshmen she used to teach in the second-semester mop-up class, those who failed composition in the fall and were repeating, to be coaxed and coached. Crawley's skill set included that vacant smile, yes, and his imposing six-foot-five height, but also his uncanny ability to stay calm and not take offense when the occasional obnoxious drunk hurled insults. Of course, Crawley didn't often know he'd been insulted. Even better. Every bar needed a pacifist bouncer.

"Uh, Crawley. It's pronounced Meer-uh."

"What is?

"My name. Remember?" Third time was the charm, she thought. Third time this week.

"Okay." He grinned, as if she were teasing. "That's what I said. Mira."

"Not MY-ruh. Meer-uh. Like the looking glass."

"The looking glass?"

She pointed to the mirror above the bar. Crawley followed her finger, and she waited for it. His lightbulb moment didn't flash; it was more of a dimmer switch—

"Ohhhhhhhhh. You mean a mirror."

She nodded. "But drop the last R. Meer-uh."

He beamed, gave a thumbs-up. "Should I bring in the ice?"

"Good plan."

That's when her phone buzzed in her pocket, her father calling, frantic, begging her to talk to Burry—

Mira had to see her brother face to face for this. That meant leaving Crawley in charge. Gulp.

"I need to run an errand, Crawley. You got my phone number, right? Just…let the kitchen guys in, but keep the front door locked until I get back."

"Sure, Mirror."

"Half an hour, tops."

Mira had planned to drop in on Burry anyway, for an overdue talk, but had procrastinated in fact, because it was bad, what she had to tell her brother.

What she'd finally admitted to herself.

"It's open," Burry called. When she stepped inside the duplex, the confession inside her roiled. It wanted out. Burry had that effect on her. A stoic who listened to all the dumb shit she did.

But first—

"Dad called me."

"Hey," he said with a chuckle. "Let's ease into the day, shall we, before we face the darkness?"

She followed her brother down the narrow hall, around stacks of cardboard boxes. Burry and Pansy had bought the duplex a month ago, a shabby colonial with two entrances and a scrubby yard, on the "bad side" of town—the affordable part. They were renting out the other side of the duplex, and Mira thought that was pretty smart, rent to help cover a mortgage, though her father loathed the idea that Burry would live in a shack near the projects.

"You want a sandwich or something?"

"No thanks," she said.

Burry opened the refrigerator. Her brother's back was wide, his T-shirt stretched out. He was getting heavy again. It's all that junk food they eat, Nelson said, pointing out how KFC and Mickey Ds were poisoning her brother and his family, and couldn't she encourage Burry to cook healthy meals? Uh, no. No, because her brother had enough on his plate lately, so to speak, without a lecture on nutrition.

"Pansy has some chablis in here somewhere."

"I have to be back at work in a few minutes."

"And?"

"That's the thing about bartending. You need to be sober."

"My condolences."

"Coffee's fine. Where's Spec?"

"Meeting with his counselor. Pansy will drop him off later."

"How is he?"

"Crushing it. Totally. I've got him reading Twain and Dickens this week."

"He's got a great teacher."

"Aw, shucks."

"Burry. It was the right decision."

"I hope so. For his sake."

"Did you and Pansy meet with that specialist yet?"

"Yeah. Some expert. The diagnosis moved from maybe PDD-NOS to possibly high-functioning Asperger's, now officially collapsed into autism-somewhere-on-the-continuum. Whatever. Spec knows how to self-soothe, he's picking up facial cues. And he knows more about mushrooms than most mycologists."

"He's into mushrooms now?"

"Memorized the fungi chart I gave him last week. But there's ninety thousand species, so that should keep him busy for a bit."

Burry cleared a space for Mira at the kitchen table. The counters were cluttered with junk mail, circulars, Pansy's work schedule. Not a happy kind of mess. Haphazard piles that worried Mira a little, that looked close to chaos, although Burry chalked it up to his "bustling household."

Maybe Mira's tolerance for disarray had been compromised by living with a neat freak like Nelson.

"Had to hit my old physics and chemistry textbooks the other night, you know, actually do lesson plans. In some ways

Spec is so advanced; in other ways, well." He shrugged. "Homeschooling ain't for sissies. But it beats working for Dad."

He handed her a mug of coffee.

"By the way," she said, "you are coming, right? On Sunday?"

"I love your casual aside. But—" Her brother's features clouded. "On the fence."

"Burry! You have to come. It's Mom's birthday."

"Dad sent you as an emissary, huh? To twist my arm? I'm thinking Pansy and Spec and me, we'll celebrate with Mom on another day. Take her out to lunch or—"

"But that won't work! Burry, what's the deal? Did something happen between you and Dad?" Something else, she almost said. Besides their father's obvious discomfort around Spec, there was the six months Burry had worked for their father, had tried to work for their father at Rex Wolf. Epic disaster, as Burry termed it.

"Just the usual unease. I need to avoid Dad for a while. That kind of negativity, it's hard to be around."

"If you're not there, Mom will be— She's having a rough week."

"He told you that? She seemed fine yesterday."

"But not today. I could hear it in Dad's voice, Burry. She's got a headache."

Burry shook his head, a smile playing on his soft, chubby, still-handsome face. "Look, Mira. I know this puts you in a tough spot, always the go-between, but—"

"He wants it to be special, Burry. He's even having lunch catered." She thought of her father's vague promise of good news, an announcement for the family. Maybe it was a business deal, some windfall they could all divide, or maybe he was taking their mother on a world cruise. It could be anything. Or nothing. It didn't sit right with her, and Burry would pick up on that. "He wants us all there, for Mom. I want us all there."

The thing clawed inside her, wanting to escape, to be unloosed, to be told.

She took her empty cup to the kitchen sink and rinsed it. Burry still sat at the table, arms crossed, but there was sympathy in his gaze.

"I need to tell you something," she said. She sat back down at the table, knocking over a bucket. Toy boats, wind-up fish, dinosaurs scattered across the floor. "Sorry!"

"No worries. Spec's old pool stuff. I'm taking the whole thing to Goodwill later."

She kneeled and put the toys back, everything smiling with googly eyes. All that ecstatic, innocent cheer. For some reason, her eyes filled.

"This is the part," her brother said, "where I tell you that you don't have to go through with a certain upcoming event that is freaking you out."

"I'm not."

"You're calling off the wedding?"

"What? No! I'm not freaking out. About that, anyway." She sat back down at the table.

"You don't even have to get hitched. Take your time. Look at Pansy and me. We're shacking up. Always will."

"That's different."

Different because Pansy's child support would be reduced if she and Burry married. Her brother sometimes joked how selfish it would be if they tied the knot.

"Nelson is the one for me. The One. Seriously. I want to have children with him. I want to grow old with him. All that romantic corny stuff…it's true."

"But."

She sighed. "Something weird. Teddy has been coming by the bar a lot."

"Define 'a lot.'"

"Just about every night." No hiding it now, but no relief in the confession. Telling it just made the thing real.

"Okay, I was under the impression you two got that out of your system."

What happened between Mira and Teddy three years ago did not exorcise the lust demons. That night exercised them, Mira thought. The lust demons were stronger.

She'd come away from their brief liaison assuming it meant something, until she learned from a friend's offhand comment that Teddy had a fiancée. Mira ghosted Teddy then, feeling petty and spurned. Also, disappointed in herself. How could she have misread the situation? Teddy was getting on with his life, marriage, a career, and she...wasn't. She was stuck. Until she met Nelson—and, boy, was she ready. Ready to get on with her life too.

"What are we talking about here? Does he just sit on a bar stool and drool over you? Heavy flirting? Light grinding? Down and dirty hook-up?"

"Worse," she said.

"Worse?"

"It's...more of an emotional affair. At this point."

"Ohhhh. What dudes call foreplay?"

"Don't joke. This is a problem."

"So where's Nixon?"

"Reagan. She works long hours at the ad agency."

"He always had a thing for you. But, hey. It's like...imprinting, I guess. Dudes and their babysitters."

"I'm barely three years older than he is!"

"Huh. It's the stress of working with Dad. It can drive a man bonkers." Burry smiled. "That's a joke, sort of. T-Rex still planning to run for office?"

She nodded. It was Burry who came up with Teddy's nickname, T-Rex, back when Teddy was eleven, bulking up already, but skinny, short little arms, like a dinosaur. Teddy Rex, Teddy the Tyrannosaurus Rex. Now Teddy said he was owning it, that name.

"So he's pining away for his favorite bartender right there in the public eye? You'd think a future politician would care about appearances."

"I'm going to tell him to stop coming by the bar. This thing between us cannot be happening, I'm stopping it."

"But telling T-Rex not to hang around anymore? It's like throwing bloody chum in the water for a shark—or whatever T-Rex dinosaurs eat. I'm mixing my metaphors. But dudes like that—they go into overdrive in the face of rejection. Am I right or am I right?"

She buried her face in her hands, then looked up. "What should I do?"

"You're afraid he'll keep coming by—"

"I'm afraid...he won't." Her eyes went shiny again. "I look forward to seeing him way too much. This is crazy. I need advice. I need stern warnings."

"Flames smolder and die down. It's a scientific law. The crush will cool."

Of course it would. But meanwhile, well, that was the rub, wasn't it? The *mean* in the *while*—

Her phone buzzed. Crawley! She had a terrifying vision of Bar None consumed in flames.

"Crawley?"

"Hey, Mirror. Um, it's Crawley."

"What's wrong?"

"There's a guy out here? In a beer truck? Don't worry. I didn't let him in. You said only let the kitchen guys in, right?"

"No, no, that's our beer delivery, Crawley, you need to let him in."

"With the beer?"

"Yes, with the beer."

"I'll be right there, okay? Hello? Crawley?"

"I have to go," she told Burry.

"See you Sunday," he called as she headed to her car.

She stopped, turned around. "You'll be there?"

"We'll be there. For Mom and for you."

"Thank you, thank you, thank you!" She blew him a kiss. But her brother was craning his neck, looking up. "What's wrong?"

"Not a thing. Just admiring this hemlock." She followed his gaze up to the massive evergreen that shaded the narrow clay yard. "Carolina hemlocks have deep taproots. Near threatened. Pretty cool to have one in the front yard. God, I love this tree."

Her brother, who'd studied biology at Emory before dropping out, who lived in what some—what her father and Teddy and even Nelson—would call willful hardship, was the most heroic person Mira knew.

4

TEDDY

The rebranding was Reagan's idea. Starting with the logo and then on to a snazzy new website and "multiple platforms." She was in her element now, charming the hell out of a client, nailing a big, juicy account. Charles was enjoying this. Charles didn't seem to mind. But then... Charles hadn't yet seen the cost. And it would be considerable.

Teddy liked watching his wife work her magic. Reagan, in her pink power suit, the skirt snug around her ass, the collar open just enough to show off her tanned, pencil-thin collarbones. She pulled out a yellow file and held up the logo, the current one: a silhouette of a wolf wearing a crown, howling at the moon.

"So this is the only logo you've had?" she asked Charles.

"Yep. Since we started, back in '79. Janelle was the one who came up with the idea. She liked the play on words—Rex Wolf...king wolf."

Reagan thought the logo looked like a mutt with a halo. Not a wolf king. Like a dog food label, she'd told Teddy last night in bed, under a mound of files, pecking at her laptop.

"Okay, but, Charles?" Reagan bit her lip. "My clients often get sentimental about their logos. They get super attached to them. And I get that. I totally do. But consider your clients. A fresh logo shows Rex Wolf is moving forward. It's part of your new brand. To prove you're modern, not stagnant."

"You mean tweak it?" Charles said.

"Well, I was thinking more of a total revise. Strip it all out, start fresh. I could have my favorite graphics guy come up with some prototypes to run by you?"

Charles nodded. "Sure. I'd like that."

Teddy felt a twinge of guilt. Part of Reagan's talent as a strategist was her infectious enthusiasm, her passionate aggressive vision—for herself, for Teddy, and now for this business, soon to be their business. Charles would go along with it all—the logo, the website, the whole brand identity—Teddy would hardly need to persuade him. Even if Rex Wolf Staffing didn't have the capital on hand. That was the deal, as of today—Teddy had agreed to step into his father's shoes, officially in August, as co-owner of Rex Wolf with Charles, only Reagan had to be in charge of the official announcement, the publicity, the revamping.

"Teddy told me you two drilled down on strategy and came up with ways Rex Wolf is evolving," Reagan said.

Charles glanced at Teddy with a puzzled *we did?* expression. Teddy nodded, having made previous assurances. *Just go with it, she knows what she's doing.*

"So my next deliverable will be an upgraded website to tell the story of Rex Wolf with photos and newspaper clips. You know—this is a family business that is nimble and changes with the times, blah blah. We started out as an executive search firm specializing in the construction and apparel industries." Reagan held her hand up, as if grasping the words, and her long, lush eyelashes quivered as she concentrated. "As the economic climate changed, so did our business. We expanded our focus to include IT recruiting and temporary staffing. As we continued to grow—over X percent since 20XX—you can get those numbers for me, Charles?—we recognized the opportunity to add more value to clients by offering more than just recruiting services. How's that?"

"You make it sound impressive as hell."

"That's my job, Charles." She tilted her head and smiled. "And you are impressive. Okay, so…I'd like to take a look at any collateral materials."

"Old brochures," Teddy translated, when he saw the puzzled look on Charles's face.

"And photographs. Previous media coverage of Rex Wolf, so I can put together a timeline."

"Timeline?"

"On the website?"

"Right."

Reagan threw Teddy a *here it goes* look. This next part was delicate.

"One of my skills is reputation recovery," she said, smooth as satin. "Like after a crisis? I help businesses restore their good names. And, Charles, I'm going to be real here, okay? Rex Wolf Staffing needs a reputation overhaul."

"Ah." Charles looked so wounded, Teddy grabbed the champagne and topped off Charles's glass. They had toasted the new partnership minutes ago, and Teddy hoped the bubbly would cushion this crappy part.

The crappy part about Rex Wolf booming but withering later, under Charles's watch. This was after Teddy's father died, and clients left in droves. Stan had carried Charles for a decade after Janelle's accident; it was Stan running the business, everyone knew. The perception that Charles had his hands full with Janelle, bless her heart, meant clients didn't trust him or warm up to Charles. Some black cloud around Charles and Janelle both, as if it were contagious, what had happened—

"But, Charles? We're going to embrace the history of Rex Wolf," Reagan continued, her comforting tone firm, on the edge of pushy. "You and Stan, now you and Teddy. We're going to craft a new narrative."

It wasn't just the business's reputation that needed scrubbing, Reagan had lamented to Teddy. It was Janelle and Charles. The Wolf family. Reagan had her work cut out for her.

"The new website is a vital channel for reaching customers. And I want to illustrate it with some photos and articles, from the old days, when Rex Wolf started."

"I told Reagan about the pictures you showed me," Teddy piped in. "Of you and Dad."

"And I was so stoked, Charles. I was like, I have to see these."

Charles was beginning to look pleased, wasn't he? "I keep that stuff in a file cabinet in my office. You want to look through it?"

"That would be awesome."

Charles led them out of the conference room, with its outdated office furniture (all shabby, no chic, Reagan told Teddy last night. We have to redecorate ASAP). They made their way to Charles's office, past Teddy's own spacious, windowed wing, past Arlene, Charles's secretary, who appeared both wary and weary, like a tired but loyal—very loyal—guard dog. Her circumspect gaze hardened into suspicion as she watched Reagan's perky tip-toed stride.

In Charles's office, as large as a living room, with a sofa and full bar—photos hung on the back wall. Reagan peered at each picture like an art critic. Charles brought out a box of photographs from a file cabinet and turned it over on his desk: photos in color, and black and white, stacked that way and this, random as memories.

Reagan picked through the photographs, spreading them across Charles's desk as if she were dealing a hand of blackjack.

"I've got some newspaper clippings here too."

"You know what will be super-cool? We'll begin with how you and Stan met, in Vietnam, right? And then…let's see, do you have wedding photos?"

"At home," Charles said. "Somewhere—"

"Your wedding, but Stan's too? Mary didn't keep anything," Reagan said.

"I'm sure I can rustle up a wedding photo of Stan and Mary."

"Teddy would love to have copies of those." She winked at Teddy. "Right, Teddybear? Maybe framed for your office?"

"Sure," Teddy said. Never mind that his own mother hadn't kept any pictures or mementos, or that she hadn't spoken to Charles or Janelle for all those years after she and Teddy moved away, silent about the reasons, even on her deathbed.

"Okay, and when Stan ran for the House? And the Senate?" Reagan asked Charles. "You've got some photos from his campaigns? Personal family glimpses, not the official ones. That will help build credibility on the timeline—a glimpse behind the curtain. People love that."

Reagan stacked the pictures into half a dozen piles, labeling them with sticky notes. "First, we'll have two army buddies who served their country, then your friendship with Stan, and your weddings—I love that you were Stan's best man. Then in 1979, you launch Rex Wolf, here. Then Stan enters politics and wins, wins, wins. Oh, and I'll need a list of your awards, Charles. Rotary and Chamber. Like that."

"I was Rotary president, that was years ago—"

"Perfect." That was sly. Flatter Charles by asking after his pedestrian activities, while it was Stan's shiny story that Reagan was really after, the poor Southern boy made good, wounded veteran, then state representative and senator. She wasn't going to let Charles feel eclipsed.

She picked up a photograph, worn soft. "This…this is gold! Look at Janelle in that hardhat and pearls."

A flushed excitement spread across Charles's fleshy cheeks. "That was the groundbreaking, the official ribbon cutting. Right here, in front of the building—"

"Yes!" Reagan said and snapped her fingers. "This will make great copy. We could have another ribbon cutting, in August. To announce the rebranding, Teddy coming aboard. Play off the history, you see? And, Charles, you and Janelle could pose for photos again. Janelle won't mind, will she?"

"No," he sputtered. "No, of course not."

"Charles," Teddy said, doubling down. "You sure Janelle will be comfortable with this…being in the spotlight?" He searched Charles's face, because face it, Reagan didn't grasp how fragile Janelle was—Teddy had seen it for himself as a kid, had a vague sense of it still. "Do you want to talk to her first, get her buy-in?"

"Janelle will be happy to be part of this."

Charles looked so elated, Teddy didn't have the heart to push any harder.

"I can't tell you how grateful I am," Charles said, "It's brilliant, this, what do you call it? Recasting?"

"Recasting the narrative, Charles," Reagan said.

Charles nodded, and was he choking up? He was. Teddy pretended to study a file.

"So I'll unpack this data dump you're giving me, Charles, and illustrate it," Reagan said. "That's how we'll tell the real story of Rex Wolf—'the people, places, and things that make us what we are today.'"

Charles sniffed, managed to nod.

"We're going to tell it right," Reagan said. "And I'm just getting started."

Teddy appreciated—and occasionally regretted—his marriage to such a ruthlessly motivated woman, who ate ambition for breakfast—or, no, gulped it like the cucumber water she guzzled at dawn after an hour on the treadmill, when Teddy was just waking up. By then, Reagan had run for an hour, and scoured the *Washington Post*, the *New York Times*, and a dozen other news sites, tweets, posts, and wonky blogs. She usually greeted his groggy fumbling for coffee with headlines: guess what, Teddybear? The governor vetoed that gas tax bill.

They'd met at Duke, he majoring in political science—because he had toyed with the idea of law school—and minoring in English—because he couldn't help it, the Irish poets snagged him freshman year, though literature was too whimsical an interest, of course. The whole point of an expensive education was an ensuing lucrative career. Reagan—a public policy and media studies double major—headed the Young Republicans, and recruited him to volunteer for McCain, and the only bright side of working for that doomed presidential campaign was the night Teddy and Reagan commiserated with tequila shots and aerobic sex.

Because sex with Reagan wasn't for the timid. Not at first. Reagan didn't do anything leisurely. Especially in bed. At first that meant ticking off a slew of positions, plundering through her "toy box" of handcuffs, feathers, liquids, vibrators named for animals—the monkey, the rabbit, the unicorn.

These days, Reagan had an ovulation chart, and they had "scheduled sex" because conceiving in the next few weeks meant a baby next spring, and by then she could take four weeks of maternity leave when Teddy's campaign revved up.

When everything revved up.

It was Reagan who'd urged Teddy to relocate to Haven in the first place, once she'd checked out the place for herself. Teddy had visited his hometown throughout the years, driving up from Hilton Head where he and his mother had moved, then later popping in between semesters at Duke. Charles was always happy to wax nostalgic about Stan, and Teddy, hungry to hear about his father, stand-up guy, natural leader, loved people. Teddy occasionally had dinner with the Wolf family; he'd spent Thanksgiving with them the year after his mother died, when Teddy was an official orphan.

But he never planned to move here.

Teddy, through the patina of nostalgia, saw a down-at-the-heels town of five thousand. Reagan spotted growth potential. The legacy of Teddy's father, respected politician—you didn't see those two words together enough, right? Yes, she had a point. Even the low-slung, outdated office building of Rex Wolf, with its empty concrete planters, scattering of cigarette butts, its stable of dejected temp applicants, Reagan envisioned as the best damn staffing firm in the state. The competition now had five offices all over the state, and annual revenues of $24 million. We're going to top that. Talk about job creators. You'll be one, Teddy. Think how that will play.

Teddy was so much further along in his career, thanks to Reagan.

Reagan was rocket fuel.

Not like Mira. So different from Mira.

Sloe-eyed, languid Mira, behind the bar with a bottle opener shoved in the back pocket of her jeans, her wavy brown hair spilling out from its halfhearted twist, anchored with a pencil. God, Mira.

When he moved back to Haven last year, nearly two decades after leaving, he hadn't expected to rekindle his friendship with Mira.

Friendship. Yeah, right.

"Um...Babe?" Reagan said now, meaning I need you to focus.

"What was that?" Teddy said. Charles looked at him patiently, with an older version of Mira's dark eyes.

"I said, do you think you could make it Sunday?" Charles said.

"Only if Janelle won't mind," Reagan said. "We don't want to intrude on a family birthday party."

"You are family," Charles said. "And we can announce to everyone about the website and—you can explain it like no one else, Reagan."

"I'd be happy to."

"You can look through more pictures when you're there. I'll find those albums. I have a lot of old files at the house."

"I can't wait to see them."

Reagan latched on to that. More pictures and albums, a party. Yeah, she was in. She looked at Teddy. "What do you say, Teddybear?" As if the issue hadn't yet been decided. It had.

Never mind that Mira would be there. And Mira's fiancé. Mira would be miffed to see Teddy there, as if he'd blindsided her, planned this.

"Sure," Teddy said. "What time?"

5

August 25, 1983

The Haven Observer

Community Spotlight
Janelle Wolf: Wife, mother, pillar of the community

By Agatha Smook, "Women's Lives" Columnist

Editor's note: This week's spotlight on Janelle Welborne Wolf is the first in a series highlighting "the new woman" in our midst. Every month, columnist Agatha Smook will bring you an interview with a successful woman. It is our aim to both delight and inspire our readers.

Janelle Welborne Wolf met her future husband the night of her debutante party. The problem? Mr. Wolf wasn't Janelle's escort.

He wasn't even invited.

"Charles actually crashed the ball, and I thought Daddy was going to have him arrested," Mrs. Wolf said.

"I stole her away from her date," Charles Wolf added with a laugh. "I was tired of worshipping her from afar."

Mr. Wolf stole something else that night in 1975—Janelle Welborne's heart. After a whirlwind courtship, Mrs. Wolf, then a junior at Vanderbilt, opted not to continue her studies and moved back home to Haven where Mr. Wolf wooed her with flowers and love letters. "I was studying literature, I had starry-eyed notions. Shelley and Keats. The Romantics," she explained.

The two married months later, in a small but resplendent ceremony. Mr. Wolf, who had returned from serving in the Vietnam War in 1970, had recently graduated from the University of South Carolina, and was, he says, "aching to marry the perfect woman." When he first glimpsed

Janelle Welborne, she was outside the Haven post office, helping an elderly gentleman back out his pickup truck. "She finally talked the old guy into getting out—he must have been one hundred years old, little old dried-up farmer, and she got behind the wheel and put that jalopy in reverse and backed it out herself. Old Ford with a stick shift, and Janelle drove it. Well, there was a bunch of folks on the sidewalk watching and clapping."

"Oh my goodness. It was nothing," Mrs. Wolf said with a smile. "I was helping out old Mr. Keller. Everyone knew his eyesight was poor."

"I knew Janelle was the one for me," Mr. Wolf said, gazing at his wife. "The way she comported herself."

The newlyweds set up housekeeping in a small, cramped apartment. There, Mrs. Wolf learned quickly that she was not cut out to be a full-time homemaker. Instead, she went on to engage in a maelstrom of activities, including volunteering for Haven Literacy, heading up the Junior League's new thrift shop, and, most importantly, helping her husband launch a business, Rex Wolf Staffing Solutions.

Eight years later, with two children, a thriving family business, and a household to run, Mrs. Wolf remains a remarkably industrious and energetic woman. As the couple entertains a reporter in their stately home on Welborne Way where Mrs. Wolf grew up, she spoke of her childhood in Haven. She was close to her father, as her mother had died from a burst appendix when Mrs. Wolf was three years old. Her beloved father, Judge Wilbur Welborne, died suddenly in 1978, months away from holding his first grandchild and namesake, Wilbur Wolf. "Daddy was on the bench, instructing a jury, doing what he loved," Mrs. Wolf said. "I wish he could see me now. That he could hold his grandchildren. To see what we've become. He would be so proud."

These days Mrs. Wolf often takes along four-year-old Burry and ten-month-old Mira to Mr. Wolf's office, where her husband and his business partner, Stan Rex, have come to rely on her acumen and strategic thinking.

"Smart as a whip," Mr. Rex said, when asked to describe Mrs. Wolf. "And she's always a step ahead. She had to talk us into setting up one of those newfangled fax machines, and now we can't do without it. Beauty and brains, that's Janelle. There's no one like her."

Other observers agree, pointing out that Mrs. Wolf's business demands and dynamic social schedule have not detracted from her community activities, whether it is volunteering in the church nursery or fundraising for the needy.

The Wolfs are considered lively and enthusiastic guests. He's a chatty conversationalist, with a dry, irreverent wit. She is known to be an intense listener, remarkable for re-membering names and always offering specific personal comments to whomever she is speaking to. Just a week ago, Mrs. Wolf, in flowing yellow silk, charmed guests at the Ha-ven Help Us Ball, dancing with a string of partners.

Now that Sandra Day O'Connor has been appointed to the United States Supreme Court, many women are looking at their life roles differently. There are colleges to attend and career tracks to follow. Opportunities for women—and expectations of them—are elevated. But what sort of woman succeeds at being a wife, a mother, a community volunteer, and a career woman, all at once? Are there heroic women to point the way?

Yes. Janelle Welborne Wolf is one of them, right here in Haven.

6

JANELLE

My favorite valet at the hotel is the rude one. Kip, according to his name tag. Kip! As if he is a border collie who herds. After he brings my car around, this Kip jumps out and snatches my tip in one fluid, bored motion—dismissing me. No thank you, Mrs. Wolf. No have a nice day. His casual disregard gives me confidence. To him, I am just another driver. He doesn't suspect it may take me an hour to navigate the five miles back to Haven. That my circuitous route avoids bridges and certain waterways. After the accident, no one expected me to live, much less drive. Not in Haven, anyway.

The accident happened on a rainy Monday night in November thirty years ago. Just after I crossed over Moore's Bridge, my station wagon plunged into the Twin River, floating, filling with water, then sinking, and me with it.

In my memory, the river is more muscular than menacing, swelling to lift me gently, extricating me from the twisted wreckage of my gurgling, descending car. The gauzy headlights sink into the silty brown river, water fills my mouth like a lover, then the river buoys me, offers me up toward the sky, where the Big Dipper glitters between clouds.

They tell me I was on the way to the home of Stan and Mary Rex. Charles was already there. I'd put the children to bed, the babysitter arrived late. I left my house at quarter to nine. The Rexes' house on Bremer Road was newly constructed, overlooking the river. Mary Rex wanted me there to help plan a housewarming party. Back then, I excelled at such things.

I was lucky: two linemen checking a broken transformer heard my car crash on the bridge. Correction: they heard a car speeding, then the sounds of a collision. In the three minutes it took them to run to the bridge, my car began floating down the Twin River. One of the men called 9-1-1, the other waded in the river toward my car, before he gave up after being nearly swept away. The Haven Police arrived and an ambulance. With heroic efficiency, my rescuers pulled me from the shallows of the river, flushed the water from my lungs, warmed me, revived me. When Charles arrived, I was being strapped onto a gurney. They say I began to scream at him, like a wild river witch, out of her mind, like a woman possessed—descriptions whispered later. Charles assured my rescuers, as well as anyone who would listen, my hysteria was due to my concussion.

I suffered a brain injury, along with three cracked ribs, a fractured femur, terrible lacerations, and dangerous internal bleeding. I nearly died twice that night.

These are the facts.

But questions remain. Why was I driving recklessly? Why did I scream hysterically at Charles when he arrived?

Charles had heard sirens from the Rexes' house half a mile away, and he knew instantly I was in trouble. That is what Stan Rex told the newspaper reporter later, this misguided romantic notion, as if my husband's extraordinary devotion to me included telepathy.

Charles sensed my life was in danger and fled to save me. This version of events, repeated, gave birth to darker notions: that my uxorious husband had already associated me with sirens, that he had concealed my unhappy heart, my unraveling mind.

Nature abhors a vacuum. Oh, but gossipers love it. They fill in the gaps.

To some in Haven, I became the woman who had everything, who dared to be ungrateful, willing to end it all. To others, who averted their eyes at my stunted recovery, I became a shadow of what I once was, a creature to be pitied.

As for me, I cling to what I know.

I know what saved me.

My children. I pictured Burry and Mira that night in my

muddled, bleeding brain, I grabbed at them like floating wreckage in a sea. My children saved me when I nearly drowned in the Twin River, and again later that night as I narrowly escaped bleeding to death on the operating table, in surgery for my ruptured spleen. My children tethered me, kept me here.

Burry and Mira are grown now, yet there are nights I dream I am holding them; a vast wave crests, lifting the three of us, before setting us ever so gently down. Together.

I pull out of the Palmetto Hotel now and merge onto I-26, the highway to Haven. There are three bridges and two overpasses between the Palmetto Hotel and my driveway. Naturally, this entails numerous detours. The Haven Mill water tower, a speck in the distance, is my North Star. If I get turned around or discouraged, I seek it out on the horizon.

My first digression, a quarter of a mile outside of Palmetto, takes me off the highway just before the Booker Bridge, down through the Sans Souci mill neighborhood, where I thread around Twin River until it becomes a stream that runs underground, out of sight. I pass over a short strip of wetlands, but I avoid driving over running water. Mostly.

Lana says rivers divide, they can mark borders. But she reminded me that spirits can't traverse water. I grew up hearing that, though I'm ashamed to say I discounted it as Appalachian superstition. But Lana told me to imagine that when I cross a bridge, malingering shades are left behind, that I am shedding my haunts. A cleansing, crossing the water. That helps.

Today, for instance, as I journey toward Haven, I force myself to drive over another bridge. There is an atrophied stream below, and my heart pounds, but I do it.

Ten Wednesdays at the Palmetto Hotel. Every trip home from the hotel gets shorter.

At the first traffic light in Haven, when the water tower is a few yards away, I loosen my grip on the steering wheel. The Haven Mill tower appears stalwart and imposing in the distance, but up close, at the red light, I am always surprised to see the rust and graffiti, the wrack and ruin.

I drive a block north, to the Haven post office. Today's letter to Lana is deliciously fat, the hotel stationery strains at the corners. I pull up to the blue mailbox, slide in the letter. The greedy metal mouth clangs shut.

I occasionally get carried away in my letters to Lana. On occasion, I embroider my dispatches. I am terrified of boring Lana, of losing her interest. And so I include a few lines about flirtations she is so eager to hear about, dalliances with consultants at the bar that move to hotel rooms. This delights her. I did confess on our last call that I may have exaggerated these torrid seductions, but she says it is perfectly natural to fantasize, that there is nothing false about my pent-up embellishments. She encourages me to let go, to have at it. Fantasies are instructive, the wilder the better. My imaginary experiences, she says, have their own truth.

Last year, Lana and I had two magnificent, powerful sessions together, in person, before she was called away. What a wonderful week that was! Lana just happened to come by my doctor's office to leave some pamphlets about her healing services and there I was in the waiting room. She said my soul cried out to be heard. And she listened.

Lana lives in India now. She instructed me on arranging money orders at a convenience store and mailing these money orders to the post office box in Arizona, separately from my letters. Her assistant sends it all along to her at the ashram. Lana always has a different phone number, and the monthly calls with me must be terribly inconvenient, but she always sounds pleased to talk to me.

I circle behind the Haven post office now and take the side roads. I'm five blocks away from home, and the only bridge left crosses a railroad. There is a family of bicyclists ahead, a woman walking her dog. The old rail line through Haven has been transformed into paths. Rail to trail, they call it. Flocks of hearty people with flushed, intense faces jog by.

As a child, I loved Haven. After the accident, I'm ashamed to say, I detested my hometown. All the joy leached from it, Haven turned colorless, or perhaps just the people in it. Now I have begun to love Haven all over again. Lana says that is a sign our work together is succeeding.

Haven is a place to rest, a stopover before embarking on the narrow, dangerous roads ahead. The Blue Ridge Mountains begin here, Haven at the foot of them, twenty-five miles from the North Carolina border. Once, cattle drivers, headed for markets beyond the mountains, stayed here at Howell's Inn, a shelter for their animals in the basement and in the back barn. More rarefied guests, the wealthy families fleeing the coastal summer heat and sicknesses, lingered here at two splendid establishments—now long gone—en route to their summer manses in Black Mountain and Flat Rock.

I once put together a report about Haven. I strained to see it through a stranger's eyes, an investor's eyes. I can still see the brochure in my mind, the bright photographs of the town square, the proofs from the printer, the smell of fixative. Haven, five square miles, small town charm, on the cusp of explosive growth. That sort of thing. This was after we decided to build the Rex Wolf headquarters here. We? I. I decided I wasn't going anywhere; I was raising my family here, not in Columbia, or even in North Carolina. Of course, I had to convince Charles and Stan.

When my father died, my inheritance footed the bill for Rex Wolf headquarters, here in Haven. That sealed the deal.

Now as I turn onto Randall Street, I catch a glimpse of that slate-gray Rex Wolf building a block up, the overgrown box-woods, the wide black parking lot.

I have a stab of memory. Mary Rex. The suck of slick mud. Drenching rain, her face pinched with humiliation. The picture flickers, and then it is gone.

I turn onto Welborne Way, the last leg of my journey. How it calms me, our house there at the end, a brick Colonial Georgian, staid and stoic among the Victorians, Cape Cods, and Tudors. This was my childhood home, and after Daddy died, Charles and I moved in, with plans to build our own house.

Because Stan and Mary's house smelled like a new car. Fresh paint, white carpet, glass. Modern and sleek, everything seemed so quiet and snowed in. Not like our house on Welborne Way, crumbling mortar and tiny closets, iron tubs, water stains, my grandmother's frumpy sofas, my father's book-filled library—a money pit, Charles called it.

But after my accident, talk of moving stopped. We stayed here on the street named for my father, in this plain two-story brick house he built for my mother. My father had detested frippery and showiness, refused ostentatious porches and Corinthian columns. He had insisted on strict symmetry, shuttered windows five across, a no-nonsense, paneled front door. My father's appreciation for balanced proportions served him well as a judge, but his suspicion of flamboyance is perhaps why he disapproved so of Charles.

When the hospital discharged me here, to our house on Welborne Way, my right leg and arms were in casts, my head shaved and bandaged, my mind muddled from painkillers. It was clear I would have to be looked after. Clara, my father's housekeeper, the capable, tender woman who raised me after my mother died, had long retired. So Charles arranged for his sister, Priscilla, to stay with us for a month.

Priscilla was not the nurturing sort, though she has always been devoted to Charles. She lived in Georgia, married to a military man, but had no children to tend. She was here to fend off visitors, to oversee my speedy recovery.

I snuffled the heads of my children, admired Burry's glittered, green construction picture, and napped with Mira's tiny, hot hand in mine.

Charles said I shouldn't rush things. He said healing would take time.

But Priscilla seethed. "You have to try harder," she told me the day she left. "You have to get well, do you understand?"

Charles hired a young woman, Cora, to come three days a week. Until I felt like myself.

By the spring, six months after my accident, I could amble out to sit in the backyard, though I couldn't yet weed or tend it. Mostly I talked to Cora.

Cora, sit down.

Got this ironing to do, Miss Janelle.

Please sit with me. Let's watch TV. We can watch your stories.

Cora had a man she loved. I liked watching her face when she told me about him, her brown eyes turned tender, and she hummed as she waited for him to pick her up there in my driveway, and I told her he should come inside any time he liked, the two of them were in love—

"You mustn't let the help smoke like that and carry on like dogs in heat in your front yard, it's just not done."

My neighbor Cathy told me this. She and Tina came to visit me one day and sat in my kitchen, pretending to like the chicken salad I made, though I got it all wrong; I think I put sugar in for salt, or cinnamon in for pepper. I had lost my sense of taste as well as decorum.

"It sets a bad example," Tina said. "Cora will think—"

"She'll assume she can take liberties, Janelle," Cathy said. "With all of us. Do you understand?"

I understood my exile from polite society had begun.

I understood my recovery had stalled. I was not my "self."

I needed directions on how to be me.

Or her. Janelle before the accident.

I combed through Janelle Before's calendars, her notes, her recipes, her garden journal, her lists—how to resume? A cruel comfort, seeing how clever she had been, Janelle Before, how good she'd been at everything, everything.

Janelle Before had been PTA president. I wasn't allowed to

drive in the carpool. Janelle Before had kept her house in order, towels in the linen closet folded importantly, like flags. Crisp sheets on beds tight as bandages. Socks mated, toothpaste capped, curtains ironed, rugs ridged in vacuum trails, floors gleaming. Meals planned, freezer stocked, pot roast on Sundays. How had she done it?

Just reading her calendar exhausted me.

Ask Dr. B. about Burry's eye test, tennis doubles next Friday. Prune the hydrangeas on old wood. Line up photographer for Charles and Stan with pipe fitters, pitch to Wanda for feature. PTA fundraiser golf or casino night? Add Timmons et al. to Rolodex, extra chicken divan on Tues., one for Tina and Bill.

Sometimes I plundered through my closet, and I put on Janelle Before's clothes, hoping to slip into her skin.

The yellow suit, the sequined cocktail dress, her fine, polished heels. I still have them.

Janelle Before had an exquisite wardrobe.

There is the sound of a car in the driveway now. I know it is Charles, even before the front door opens and he calls out for me downstairs.

Charles always comes home for lunch after my outings to the Palmetto Hotel. It is uncanny how he knows.

Something has sparked between Charles and me. The first time in many years.

I confessed this to Lana; it was difficult to admit this side effect of my treatment plan, but Lana already knew, of course. She had been waiting for me to tell her.

Lana is aware I lost my love for Charles after the accident. That I awoke in the hospital bed without a flicker of affection for my husband, not even a phantom tickle of fondness. When they scanned my brain, I wanted to ask if my love for Charles was in there somewhere, hidden behind those bursts of colors.

Of course, it's not exactly love I feel for Charles now. I'm a mirror, reflecting his desire for me. The moon beaming sunlight.

But it is better than feeling nothing.

Charles is upstairs now, he opens our bedroom door. His eyes are dancing. He is already loosening his tie.

"There you are," he says, and reaches for me, kissing me on the neck.

Later, in the afterglow, something disturbing. Charles dresses to return to the office, then goes up to the attic and plunders around, and brings down boxes of photograph albums and scrapbooks.

He tells me then about the new plan, the rebirth of Rex Wolf, he calls it; the business we built is being revived. With Teddy here, it will be like the old days. There will be publicity, the right kind. Charles is excited but nervous. He studies my face.

He craves my assurance, though he does not say it. He seeks my promise—that I won't come undone, that trotting this all out won't disturb me.

One of the doctors years ago told me as my brain healed, vivid memories from the past would arise, even as whole days of my life were still obscured. I did not have linear recall, not yet, he said, but he assured me that was perfectly natural for someone like me.

The doctor suggested I look through these picture albums. He said they would help me remember.

But he was wrong.

Janelle Before made me feel worse.

So, I put it all away.

Now Charles has brought it out, the pictures, the clippings, all of it is here, back into the light.

Who is that beautiful, poised woman in seed pearls and candlelight taffeta, whose groom looks at her so adoringly? As if he can't believe his luck? And the woman behind her desk, with a self-assured slant to her head, a pencil behind her ear? Smiling for the camera, always smiling. Janelle Before.

How ashamed Janelle Before would be of me, of the cloud I brought on our name.

I dragged so much down with me.

My love for Charles. My standing. My good name.

Gone.

Black-hearted gossip, cruel rumors have taken root—
Janelle Before would have never allowed such a thing.

After Charles leaves, I sit down on the bed. My vision dims.
A headache approaches. I call Lana's emergency number. A
desperate measure, she has warned me, expensive but always
an option.

I am desperate.

Lana will know what to do. She always does.

7

LANA

Lana O'Shield adored lonely people. The right sort of loneliness. A guarded sense of isolation, a kind of shameful holding back—she had a gift for detecting it—especially in women of a certain age. And income.

Now, as Janelle's blue BMW sedan—ten years old at least, riddled with dents and scrapes, the battle scars of a bad driver—appeared on the road of this small, unpeopled park, Lana congratulated herself on her instincts. Right on the nose, thank God.

This might just work.

Janelle parked, jumped out, and waved. Lana waved back from the picnic table. Meeting here, at Haven Hill State Park, was Janelle's choice. It was important for Janelle to feel in control.

"Am I late?" she called, running up the mulched walking path. "I'm so sorry I'm late."

"There's no rush," Lana said, followed by "Careful!" as Janelle nearly stumbled on a tree root.

"Oh, it's so, so good to see you again." They embraced. Janelle tried to catch her breath and looked a little shy. No wonder, after admitting to such naughty escapades. Turned out, Janelle was one horny hausfrau.

"And it is good to see you, my friend," Lana said.

Janelle wore a lavender linen dress and black leather sandals, and she carried a mauve Coach handbag—none of it matched. Janelle's outfits were ridiculously hodgepodge, but it helped to have exquisite pieces to throw together.

"I'm so grateful you are here!"

"It's lucky I was working with an East Coast client when you called, Janelle. You know, I returned from India just days ago."

"You must be exhausted!"

"You have no idea. The teeming crush of humanity in airports wears one down. But this is a wonderful place to meet," Lana said. "So tranquil."

"I love these woods. I always have." She sat on the picnic bench across from Lana. "Your necklace is lovely."

"Thank you," Lana said. "A client's gift." Sterling silver squash blossom. Vintage. Not that Betty would miss it. Letting this sort of unique piece be snapped up in an estate sale would have been tragic. Lana had saved it. She fingered the silver now, lovingly.

"Have you decided?" Janelle asked, with a childlike eagerness that Lana found both off-putting and encouraging.

"My schedule is overbooked as it is, Janelle. I'm here for a day or so."

Janelle looked crushed, poor woman.

Never had Lana "worked" with someone so motivated and gullible, a winning combination, as far as Lana was concerned.

When she'd first spotted Janelle last year in the psychiatrist's waiting room, Lana knew she was ideal. Dazed, but not too troubled. Reluctant smile but hungry to be listened to, polite but unpretentious, and above all, trusting. Also, sporting a big honking diamond ring, toting a handsome worn designer purse, and wearing scuffed, expensive flats. Only the wealthy displayed such a casual disregard for luxurious accessories. That was Lana's experience, anyway.

A couple of "sessions" with Janelle and Lana knew they were onto something; a bullet was lodged in Janelle's troubled soul.

Then Charles Wolf put a stop to their meetings.

And with such blustering, insulting outrage! Barging into Lana's admittedly shabby rent-by-the-month office and accusing her of trying to "ruin" his "delicate" wife. Claiming Lana trolled for "vulnerable" patients in a psychiatrist's waiting room—well, that part was true enough. But still. It had taken iron will to sit there wordlessly, waiting for the satisfying sound of a check being ripped from a checkbook.

Janelle had no inkling about the covert transaction between her husband and Lana.

It had been pure instinct on Lana's part—before she left Haven—to entreat Janelle to write to her at a post office box in Arizona, where a "friend" would see that Lana got her mail in her "overseas ashram." Just their little secret. Janelle had even set up a post office box of her own in town—Janelle really did love subterfuge, that little sneak. And write Janelle had. She'd mailed Lana fat envelopes stuffed with long, detailed letters.

Lana had set up calls. With advice. Paid, of course. Janelle had followed Lana's long-distance directives to venture out to bars, like a desperate contestant in some risqué scavenger hunt. And what fun. Reading about Janelle's misadventures. So what if Janelle's dispatches were real or fantasy or some combination?

Lana had a playbook now, on how to hustle Charles Wolf.

"I am considering staying a bit longer," Lana told Janelle now. "But it would be a big commitment. So many clients to contact and sessions to postpone, not to mention finding a place to stay—"

"I could help, Lana. I will—"

"That's sweet of you."

"I'm frantic. I have to do something."

Janelle sounded frantic, all right.

Lana couldn't have planned it better. Janelle had "new memories" from her accident, and Lana just had to help her put it all together, before Janelle went cray-cray.

Lana sighed. "Your pain is my pain."

"You said it would be difficult, but I'm ready now. I'm afraid I'm going to ruin everything—Mira's wedding, and the plan for the business."

An important *there, there* moment. Cue soothing voice. "You have so much weighing on you." Lana patted her friend's hand. "What plan for the business?"

"They're going to rescue Rex Wolf. Now with Stan's boy here, they are going to get rid of the dark cloud—that's what Charles calls it. The dark cloud over us."

"That's too much pressure on anyone," Lana said. "You poor thing. I feel as if I know your demons, Janelle. Your letters are riveting. Truly moving. And that notebook you sent—"

"I have more."

"Of course you do. There is so much to talk about..." Your asshole of a husband for starters. Charles Wolf. Wrench in the machine? Or...the payoff? Hard to tell yet.

"Will you come to dinner tomorrow? Meet my family?"

"Are you sure that would be wise?" Poor Janelle still believed her husband and Lana hadn't met. And yet, according to Janelle's letters, when she'd once lamented to Charles how she missed Lana's guidance, that sorry bastard warned his wife away from such a "dangerous kook" who dared to call herself a counselor, who clearly dabbled in the "occult."

"You're my friend, Lana. It's my birthday. Charles will understand."

He wouldn't. But still.

Showing up to Janelle's birthday celebration—a ballsy move. Possibly useful. Lana, with a flash of insight, toyed with the idea. Crash this party, inoculate herself against Charles Wolf. He would rein in his outrage among family and friends when she appeared on his doorstep. Pretend he didn't know her, much less loathe her. Surprise! Lana could hide in plain sight, as the loopy, harmless weirdo friend of Janelle's. Everyone would believe that but Charles, and—really, he was too easy to read—he wouldn't dare challenge her, or risk a scene there, embarrassing his fragile Janelle.

"I'll do my best to make it." Lana's rule: never promise, only promise to try.

"Thank you...thank you." Janelle reached over and squeezed Lana's hand. "I feel stronger already."

8

Unexpected Guests

Judge Wilbur Welborne's portrait was all wrong. He wore a severe expression, the antithesis of his bleeding-heart reputation on the bench. Although Charles had suggested to his wife numerous times throughout the years that she relocate the disturbing painting of her late father to another room in their house (or better yet, the attic), Janelle held firm. Her father deserved to be stationed over their fireplace mantel as he watched over their household.

So the judge stayed, glowering at Charles for decades, holding court in Charles's very own living room.

You mean MY living room, his honor's brush-stroked oily eyes seemed to say. He never let Charles forget that, not for a second.

It irked Charles that the judge had left Janelle, his only child, this house and property, the means to, as he'd put it in his last will and testament, "survive the turbulent years ahead if she insists on remaining with the one with whom she has shackled herself, for Charles Wolf is not a helpmate but a scalawag, a self-deluded man who does not recognize the evil in himself, the most dangerous sort of all."

Charles could occasionally note (after a gin and tonic or two) the irony of Judge Welborne—who liberated criminals!—saving his harshest pronouncement for Charles, his own son-in-law.

Charles rattled the ice in his glass and felt the judge's flat stare bore into the back of his head.

Your hijinks reek of iniquity.

"Shut up, you old bastard."

You're an insufferable cad.

"And you're dead."

Perhaps he shouldn't have that second drink just now.

He cheered himself by walking through the dining room. The starched white tablecloth was set with fine china, crystal, candles, and a centerpiece Arlene had ordered from the florist, all the while griping about the cost, but this was after Charles had invited Teddy and Reagan to Janelle's birthday lunch, and everything had to look good, no cutting corners.

He pushed open the swinging door and entered the spacious kitchen.

"Woo, boy, it smells mighty fine in here. You ladies sure know how to tempt a hungry man."

Elsie had the mixer going. Violet reached over and turned it off. "We're right on schedule. I'll brown the biscuits when everyone gets here."

Elsie and her sister Violet had on matching aprons with V's Vittles embroidered in cursive. Elsie was the chubby sister; Violet, tall and older. Both had on white chef caps, all very professional. They owned a catering business now, with two vans that sported the same V's Vittles across the sides. They did little jobs like this as a favor to Janelle and him, though Lord knows it wasn't free. Elsie and Violet's mother, Clara, had been a housekeeper for Janelle's family and cooked for decades in this very kitchen. Now Clara's daughters were business owners and making a fine living at it, too, thanks to the judge.

"I see you've set the table. I wondered if you could squeeze in two extra places?"

"Squeeze in at that table?" Violet said.

"Yes. For two unexpected guests. It's a surprise." He hadn't told Janelle that Teddy and Reagan were coming by today. Janelle might get worked up. Better they show up unannounced.

Violet and Elsie exchanged a quick glance.

"I know it will be tight, but I'm sure you'll find a way. Is that sweet potato?" he asked, as Elsie turned to take out a bubbling dish from the oven.

"Sweet potato casserole with pecans and brown sugar just

the way Miss Janelle likes it," Violet said. "I know she don't much care for the kind with marshmallows. You want a taste?"

She handed him a spoonful.

"That is heaven, right there, Violet. Heaven." He smacked his lips.

Elsie started up the mixer again. What racket! And frankly, rude, when he was standing there, as if she were dismissing him. Violet should school her sister in etiquette if they expected to run this sort of business.

"I guess I better go check on the birthday girl," he said, but the screaming appliance drowned out his words.

Upstairs, Charles found Janelle at her vanity, wearing an elegant but demure off-white dress with pearls, entirely appropriate for today.

When he'd come home from the office on Wednesday, on the heels of the PI's report, she hadn't yet put the makeup case away or shoved the vampish attire in the back of the closet. After her outings to the hotel bar, his wife was especially affectionate, and he, eager for her attention, acquiesced, a duty he did not shirk, no matter how busy the day.

Still, he'd have to rein in Janelle, put a stop to this indulgence. Hiring the PIs had been a stopgap measure, back in the winter when Janelle began obsessing about her accident. He'd thought she was through with that agony. Revisiting that traumatic night only brought them both grief; hadn't she learned that yet? Her headaches, her hospitalizations—her confabulations, as one of her doctors called them, when Janelle insisted on filling the black-out blanks of her night with outlandish claims.

What had provoked this churn of late?

He blamed himself. If only he hadn't let Janelle drive alone to her doctor's appointments last fall. He'd been pleased, assuming driving herself to an appointment was a sign of progress and not perilous.

But of course, it was perilous. Not the driving, but the doctor's waiting room, where that nauseating parasite Lana O'Shield was lying in wait.

He'd taken care of that problem.

"Ah, you look lovely, my dear," he said now, meeting his wife's eyes in the mirror. "Here, let me zip you up." She nodded. He tugged the zipper up the back of her dress, closing brushed silk over the scar that snaked across her back, ridged like a railroad track.

"Happy birthday." He pulled out a small velvet box from his pocket.

"You shouldn't have, Charles."

"Go ahead. Open it."

It was a thin gold choker with a tiny emerald. Arlene had tried to talk him into something less expensive—reminding him his American Express card was nearly maxed out—but, what the hell. Janelle deserved it. His wife's fine jewelry had been passed down by her grandmother or given by her doting father, whose parsimony never extended to his daughter. They were splendid pieces. The pearl and emerald earrings she wore now, for example, a gift from the judge the night of Janelle's debutante party. Charles had added too few pieces to Janelle's collection.

"It's beautiful. Thank you." Her muted response was disappointing. No doubt she was distracted by the impending dinner.

"Here, let me fasten it for you."

"It will clash with my pearls and my earrings, Charles."

"Don't be silly." He clicked the necklace clasp. "See? Beautiful."

"Something smells wonderful."

"That is your birthday feast." He looked at his watch. A quarter till two.

"I should see if they need me to help."

"I told you. It's your birthday. No helping. How is your headache?"

"I'm all right, Charles. Really."

"I'll let you know when everyone arrives."

She nodded. Agreeable, spookily so. If he were lucky, she would remain this docile, nearly dull, for months to come.

"Why don't you stretch out over there and go back to your reading?"

She sat down on the chintz divan by their bed and picked up the book splayed there among the cushions. *The Wide Sargasso Sea.*

"Nothing like a travel book to get your mind off troubles."

"It's a novel, Charles."

The smile on her face pleased him.

"About the first Mrs. Rochester."

"It's good to see you...so relaxed."

He closed the bedroom door as she reached for the book.

She was always reading fat tomes by dead authors during her recoveries.

After Elsie set two extra place settings in the dining room, she came back into the kitchen and told her sister, "She ain't the crazy one. He is."

"Shhhhh," Violet hissed.

"What? He can't hear me. He's back in the living room again jabbering away, and ain't a soul in there."

Violet slowly shook her head.

"Go ahead. I know what you gonna say. You don't have to like him. It's for the business. You got to do business with all kind of folks." Elsie rolled her eyes.

"That's right."

"Even that crazy cracker-ass out there talking his head off to a picture of the judge?"

"Uh-huh."

"I feel sorry for him. The judge, I mean. Having to listen to that man carrying on."

Violet and her sister had been rather fond of the judge. If it hadn't been for Judge Welborne, Violet might not even be standing there, with her own catering business and a line of credit at the bank and booked-out events for three months. When he died, the judge left money to her mother, Clara—ten thousand in cash delivered by a lawyer along with the deed to

Clara's house. No forms to fill out or lawmen to talk to. Paid-off house, cash in an envelope. And thirty-five years ago, that was a good sum. When Clara passed, she left her house to Violet and Elsie. Five years ago, Violet borrowed against the equity to start V's Vittles. Violet was adding another full-time server at the end of summer. She liked to run the numbers in her head when she cut biscuits. That always got her humming.

But Elsie sulked as she stirred the green beans. Violet knew Charles Wolf got on her sister's last nerve.

"You reckon the judge is trying to talk some sense into him?" Violet said after a minute, and that got the two of them laughing so hard, Violet had to turn on the exhaust fan and the mixer before someone heard.

Someone did.

Janelle slipped into the kitchen in bare feet, holding her heeled shoes in one hand. "It's so nice to hear laughter in the kitchen."

"Miss Janelle! You sure look pretty," Elsie said.

"Thank you, Elsie. So do you."

Elsie guffawed. "I'm sweating like a hog."

"You need anything?" Violet asked.

Janelle whispered, "I believe we may need an extra setting."

"On account of your unexpected guests? Yes. Mr. Wolf told us to set more places."

"He did?"

"Sure did. Few minutes ago."

"Charles knows my friend is coming?"

"He didn't say who exactly. Maybe he wants it to be a surprise. Invited your friend for your birthday in secret."

"Well, I won't spoil it. I'll act shocked when Lana arrives."

Violet took Janelle's hands in hers.

"Don't you worry. We got enough food to feed an army. We'll squeeze in whoever we need to. You go enjoy your special day."

9

MIRA

They were running late. Mira's fault, naturally. She'd forgotten her mother's present, and they'd had to turn around and go back home.

"Actually, we're on time," Nelson said. "It's five minutes after two."

"I know. Not late-late. But I need to get there before Burry. I have to"—she wiggled air quotes—"buffer the awkwardness."

"C'mon, your brother can't handle talking to your father for five minutes?"

Maybe. Maybe not. Nelson didn't grasp how wobbly this whole setup was.

Nelson turned into her parents' driveway.

There was her brother's minivan, one tire in the flower bed.

"Oh, crap. They're already here."

"What's up with the parking?" Nelson asked.

"They're letting Spec practice parking."

"He's a little young for that, isn't he?"

"Cars are another of his obsessions. It calms him."

The front door was open. Mira's father and her aunt Priscilla stood together, watching Mira and Nelson approach. Mira half-hugged her aunt, brittle and unyielding as a hat rack. Her aunt beamed at Nelson. Strapping young men thrilled her.

"Your brother just arrived," her father told Mira. "All of them."

All of them. Her father might as well have said a horde of zombies. "Put the gift down, darlin'. How about a vodka tonic or Bloody Mary?"

"I'll take red wine if you have it," Nelson said, because, hey, if he was going to imbibe this early, antioxidants and flavonoids were a must. That was a Nelson rule.

"We have everything," her father said, closing the door behind them, and gesturing to the living room.

At the far end of the living room, Burry sat on a wing-backed chair. Spec, beside his mother, hunched over a laptop computer on the end table. Spec was fourteen, but he could pass for eighteen, Mira thought. His growth spurt had come on fast. Burry told her he and Spec wore the same size in shoes now. But Spec hated wearing shoes. Today his flip-flops were already off, beside him. He wore his favorite T-shirt, one of Burry's old gray ones from Emory.

"I asked for some help setting up a computer thing," her father said, and Mira thought, *Thank you, Daddy. Thank you.*

"Arlene? Let's open the red."

"I don't see red," Arlene told him, squinting at a wine bottle. "Just a peanut noyr."

"The pinot will be fine," Mira said. "How are you, Arlene?"

"Doing real good, hon," she said, then whispered to Mira, "I drove your aunt Miss Prissy here. She liked to drive me crazy."

Mira's aunt Priscilla scowled. "What was that?"

"Just said how you and me rode together today," Arlene said.

Arlene, her father's aide-de-camp, girl Friday, and, lately, her aunt's driver. Was there nothing the woman wouldn't do for her father?

"Sup, my man?" Nelson asked Spec.

"Hello," Spec said in his usual loud monotone, not looking up. Spec's thick black hair was short now, stylishly shorn, though Mira knew better than to bring up haircuts, even compliments about haircuts. Barbershop equaled battlefield, Burry said, though he had finally persuaded Spec—bribed him with a few hours of Minecraft—to go for a "summer" buzz.

"Spec is setting up a new wireless router for your folks," Pansy said. Pansy's coral-orange dress highlighted her golden skin, and her long beaded braids clicked as she rose to hug

Mira. "Spec, I need you to stand up, shake hands with your uncle Nelson."

Spec stood, taller than his mother, extended his hand, Nelson shook it. "Good grip, little man."

Thank you, Nels, Thank you, thank you. Mira allowed herself a spark of hope. This was going to be a good family day. Finally.

"Pansy brought her own laptop," Burry said. "We thought we'd test the Wi-Fi with it. Then if all goes well, we'll set up Dad's computer."

"You actually use your Wi-Fi now?" Mira asked her father.

"I had the cable company re-install one of those thingamajigs last week," he said, standing behind her, on the periphery, rattling the ice in his drink. He was nervous. Was it her mother?

"Congratulations on joining the twenty-first century."

"It's for the business, so I can work at home on weekends. Teddy convinced me."

Teddy's name jolted her like a cattle prod.

But nothing has happened yet, you idiot, Mira told herself. Yeah? Just you wait. She really needed to sign up for meditation classes. Her thoughts bickered like children in the back seat.

Nelson handed Mira a glass of wine and sat down beside her on the sofa. Her aunt perched on the nearby loveseat, holding an iced tea with both hands, her critical gaze running across the sofa before landing hard on Mira's Birkenstock sandals.

"My goodness, what interesting shoes."

"They're comfortable."

"Yes, I have no doubt. Why else would one wear them? But then you're on your feet all day, aren't you, tending bar? Still?"

Mira nodded and gulped her wine.

"I suppose when you're married, all that will change."

Mira stood up. "Dad, shouldn't we check on Mom?"

"She's fine. Just had a little headache this morning."

"Oh no. Bad?"

"No. She's just taking her time."

"My word. Your father needs to relax," her aunt Priscilla

said, always her father's unwavering defender. "Let your mother primp all she wants. It's her day."

"Everybody's here, right?" Mira looked around. "I'll get Mom to join us."

"It works now," Spec said, turning the laptop around to his mother.

"Hey, Spec. Want to join me outside for a little fresh air?" Nelson said. "I brought a Frisbee." It was just like Nelson to try to pry them all out of the living room. Warning! Sedentary inactivity ran like a news crawl across his face.

"Be right back," Mira said.

She headed up the stairs. Her mother's headache could be a sign she was going to be in bed all day—or all week. It could be the start of a long, blue summer for her mother. That was why her father was so jumpy.

She knocked softly, then slowly opened the bedroom door, bracing herself. Her mother would be in bed, the shades drawn, a cold towel on her face, that sort of thing.

But—what the hell?

Janelle sat in a chair by the window, furiously scribbling in a spiral notebook.

"Mom?"

Her mother looked up and smiled. "Mira!"

She was dressed! Hair done, makeup on, heels!

"Happy birthday. Uh, we're here. All of us, downstairs."

"I must have lost track of time." She looked longingly at the notebook in her lap. "I've been writing."

That was a good sign, wasn't it?

"Writing…what?"

"Letters and things." Her mother stood up and smoothed her dress. She checked herself in the bureau mirror. "I thought I heard your aunt Priscilla's voice."

"Yeah, sorry about that. I know she's not your favorite person. I guess Dad feels obligated to include her. I'll try to block her snark."

"She is honest, though."

"Brutally honest."

"Priscilla was the only one who asked me, 'What on earth were you thinking, driving recklessly that night in that weather? Were you out of your mind?' They were all thinking that. All of them. But Priscilla was the only one who asked."

"You're in reflective mood," Mira said carefully.

Janelle leaned down by the overstuffed chair and looked under it, as if she'd lost something. She pulled out a notebook, then another, and another. Had she hidden them? She stuffed them in a grocery bag.

"I'm giving these to my friend." She stood and put the bag on the bed. "I haven't had a friend in a long, long time."

"Oh, Mom, that's not true. You have friends. The Langleys, and Tina next door, and—"

"Neighbors, but they aren't friends. I've been lonely so long I forgot what it's like not to be lonely. Isn't that funny?"

It wasn't funny. It was awful. "I didn't know you felt that way." You knew, Mira told herself. You knew. That's why you left Haven. And maybe—that's why you came back.

"It's all right. Because I have a friend now. Her name is Lana. I can't wait for you to meet her. I invited her to come today."

"You did? That's good, Mom. Does Daddy know her? Your friend?"

Her mother picked up a tube of lipstick on the bureau and dabbed it on her lips. "Your father despises her."

Something fluttered in Mira's stomach.

"Why?"

"Heaven knows. He thinks Lana is a bad influence on me, and he hasn't even met her! But when he does, I'm sure he'll change his mind."

"Daddy seems on edge today. He said something about some good news. An announcement about the business or something—"

"Oh, that."

"You know what it is?"

"The business. Your father is so happy about it. I wish I

could help him. I used to know the right things to do. Now I just keep out of the way. I don't even like going into that building anymore. And Stan's boy and that girl he married—"

"Reagan."

"Yes. She was over here yesterday."

"What? Why?"

"Something about a website. It makes me nervous. She says things I don't understand. What are deliverables? What is a quality vector?"

Hell if I know. Mira shrugged.

"But she knows what she's doing. That's what your father says. She is collecting our pictures and articles. She says they are going to fix things, to—" Janelle paused. "I'm trying to think what she called it. 'Recast the narrative.'"

"Mom, don't talk about the business if it bothers you. You don't even have to see them, Teddy and Reagan. You don't have to have anything to do with them."

"Your father says they're like family."

"They're not family."

"Your father says this new plan will help us, help me—"

"Help you?"

The doorbell chimed.

Her mother raced past her. Mira followed her to the top of the stairs, where Janelle trilled, "I'll get it!"

Her father looked up as he headed for the door. "Hold on, Janelle. Hold on."

But her mother wasn't listening. Her eyes stayed on the door as Charles opened it. He bellowed, "Welcome!" and then Mira watched her mother's jubilant face change, as if she were the star pupil in an acting class. Here is elation! Here is dejection! Teddy and Reagan.

10

CHARLES

The two of them were dressed impeccably, a proper sign of respect for the occasion. Teddy in a suit and tie, Reagan in a short fuchsia dress, in strappy sandals that flattered her long, thin legs.

"Come in, come in!" Charles boomed, and steered Teddy and Reagan toward the bar. He called for Janelle, then turned to Reagan. "I found more photos, and I think you're going to like them. Even a few pictures of Stan and Mary's wedding."

Reagan clapped. "Oooooh, I can't wait to see."

Janelle floated down the stairs, murmuring hello, distracted civility that stood in for politeness. Mira fled to the backyard to join the others, playing ball or some nonsense, but who cared.

This! The timeline. The rebranding. Recasting the narrative. And a ribbon cutting redux, Reagan called it. Brilliant. Various dignitaries were going to be there, the president of the Chamber of Commerce, two county councilmen, and all the other big-shot windbags Charles could think of so he could gloat. Yes, gloat. Now that Rex Wolf Staffing Solutions was back in business, now that Teddy was working shoulder-to-shoulder with Charles to "invigorate" the company, Charles could hardly contain his glee.

"Have you had a chance to talk to Mira?" Reagan asked.

"No, I thought we'd cover that later," he mumbled, "when I explain it all at lunch. When we're all assembled."

In truth, he was dreading that part. Reagan's brilliant campaign included "leveraging" Mira's wedding, with an impressive guest list, a "soft introduction to the branding kickoff," whatever that meant. But Reagan knew what she was doing. Only Mira would balk, Charles knew she would, it was hard enough to get her to agree to any sort of respectable ceremony. But maybe with a little pressure, the right sort—

"Janelle?" Teddy said. "Happy birthday."

"Thank you, Teddy." She honored him with a faint smile, but her eyes stayed wide and unblinking too long.

"Yes! Happy birthday," Reagan chirped. "Are you excited?"

"Oh yes. I have a dear friend arriving."

Dear God, what was going on now? "Janelle, come see the photographs Reagan selected," Charles said, patting the sofa beside him. "The Rex Wolf groundbreaking. Look what we've got here. Come have a seat."

"No, thank you, Charles." She stared at the front door longingly, her expression unusually alert.

Teddy hadn't taken a seat. He was too polite to sit while Janelle remained standing.

Charles allowed a flash of irritation to pass through him, before drawing from the deep well of patience he reserved for his wife.

"Perhaps you should tell the others to come inside and join us," Charles told her. "They're outside, frolicking."

What was imperative was for Janelle to demonstrate—to Teddy and Reagan if no one else—that she was on an even keel. That a spotlight on her wouldn't result in some sort of meltdown.

"Janelle," Reagan said, "the timing of your fortieth wedding anniversary with Charles is in August. I was—we were thinking we could jump off that occasion for the ribbon cutting redux. Your commitment to each other, from the beginning, that is so, so heartwarming, so vital to our narrative."

Charles was so enthralled with this, he didn't hear the doorbell ring. He remembered thinking it strange that Janelle jumped up and ran—yes, ran—to the front door. And then, the first inkling of trouble, screeches of delight.

Charles placed the photos on the coffee table and rose from

the couch, muttering apologies about the interruption; perhaps a neighbor had dropped by. "Hold that thought," he said. "I'll be right back."

He looked up, and there she stood.

Swaddled in her ethnic getup, her insufferable thin crimson lips smirking.

"I'd like you to meet my dear friend Lana O'Shield," Janelle said, positively giddy as she looked up adoringly at the tall, bizarre creature beside her. "I'm tickled to death she made it."

This isn't happening, Charles thought.

He stared, slack-jawed, as insult muscled through his astonishment. How dare she? How dare that gypsy grifter show up at his house, under his roof. Janelle babbled on, and then Mira and Nelson·and Burry and everyone gathered—talking to that woman!

"Lana, meet my grandson."

Polite exchanges. Charles clenched his fists.

"That's a beautiful sari," Mira said.

"Lana has come from India," Janelle said.

Then Teddy shook hands with her.

"Lana's earrings are from a woman's cooperative of Untouchables, isn't that right, Lana?" Janelle clearly tipping into some sort of crazed agitation, all because of that woman he had banished.

"Hello, Charles," the vile creature said, with that preposterous plummy accent. "It's a pleasure. I've heard so much about you."

He didn't remember extending his hand, only feeling her ringed fingers seize his. She closed her eyes for an instant, then leaned over and whispered something in Janelle's ear.

This was an outrage. Oh, he would not stand for this.

11

Seating Arrangements

Teddy prided himself on his keen observation of nuanced social interactions, a talent one honed with politics in the future. When it came time to gather around the dining room table, the whispered, awkward skirmish that broke out around seating arrangements did not go unnoticed by him. Janelle at the foot, Charles at the head, that was a given. But Mira didn't want to sit across from Reagan and him, and she grimaced as her father tried to seat her.

Charles scowled when Janelle announced to the caterer that they would need another setting at the table for her bizarro friend. Clearly not possible—someone would have to be demoted to the small, wobbly card table. More fierce gestures between Mira and her father.

Burry's girlfriend, Pansy, volunteered to sit at the small table, if no one minded, along with Arlene. "Me too," Nelson said. "Really?" Mira protested, but Nelson said he didn't plan to eat much anyway, something about protein powder and carbs. He'd rather sit at the little table.

Good man, Teddy thought. Better you than me, my friend.

Only, he and Nelson weren't friends. Barely acquaintances. Teddy had scoured Nelson's Facebook page, filled with his nutty crowd of "Bootstrappers," whatever that meant, trying to get a read on such a douchebag. Nelson was one of those Ayn Rand libertarians going on and on about objectivism and the tyranny of rules and regulations. The sneaky evil of non-taxed churches, the need for an "evidence-based life." Pathetic. Teddy had a friend or two from college who were libertarians—mostly because they wanted the freedom to buy and sell weed and screw the government!—no more footing the bill for highways, or hospitals, or schools. But they grew out of it. Nobody took that shit seriously.

Teddy had worked up the courage to ask Mira one night at Bar None about what it was like to live with someone— how had he put it? With a different worldview? Mira told him Nelson was "just what she needed." His self-discipline was apparently awe inspiring, his routine and predictability—she'd never shared an apartment or lived in a household so well run and organized, not with all her nightmare roommates and grad school lean years. She'd come back home last year a "mess," she said, and Nelson's thrift, his strategies for a home together, a "balm for her bohemian screwed-up soul."

The posts that really disgusted him: Nelson's photos of his gym-rat biceps and shorn, soccer-player haircut, the chronicling of his workout routines, whey smoothies, and bare-chested iron-pumping on weight machines that resembled medieval torture instruments. That was ludicrous, not to mention shallow. Pure ego.

Teddy had said as much to Reagan, when they'd first met Nelson months ago. Total wack job. But Reagan had said, "I know, Teddybear. But with those pecs, who cares? The guy is ripped."

And that had stung.

"How long did you live in India?" Mira asked her mother's friend. Lana's kohl-lined eyes and hennaed hair gave her an exotic air, but up close, she had waxy, freckly skin.

"Not long enough. It is a powerful land."

"Your accent. New Zealand?"

Lana smiled. "How did you guess?"

"I'm pretty good with accents. I studied linguistics for a while."

Mira sensed Reagan trying to get her attention across the table, so she focused like a laser on Lana. As for Teddy—she was too livid to trust herself to even glance his way. He probably wormed an invitation from her father to show up today. Telling T-Rex they should cool it; it was nothing but a dare, an invitation. No wonder she could feel his eyes on her now, he probably had that amused look he got—

"How did you and Mom meet?"

"Lana is a soul tender," Janelle piped in.

"I'm a spiritual counselor," Lana added. "I help unlock people's hearts."

Really? Mira thought. I'd like to padlock mine.

"My spirit guide is a sea turtle," her mother whispered.

Mira studied her mother. There was something off here. Her mother seemed too cheerful. Was she that lonely? Would that explain her alliance with this odd bird Lana? Mira felt a wave of guilt. She had to carve out more time with her mother.

"Your mother's guide, I saw that right away," Lana said. "Sometimes that happens when the image is strong. Your father's too. His spirit guide is a vulture."

Aunt Priscilla twirled her hearing aid. "What…was that?" she sputtered. "What did she say…about Charles?"

"Not an insult by any means. They are vital to the life cycle, you know. Vultures."

"Thanks to Lana, I am making such progress," her mother said, beaming at her friend.

"That's great, Mom." Did her father know about this? Did he approve? He was always so protective of her mother. But judging from his glare in their direction—yes. Yes, he knew, and, no, he didn't approve.

Charles strained to hear the grifter, disturbed that he couldn't make out a word of Lana's conversation. What was that woman plotting? How in hell did Janelle track her down? Did she actually invite her here?

When he'd first caught a glimpse of that repulsive charlatan last year—with her veils and tiny bells and garish attire, her lipsticked gash of a mouth—he'd assumed she was a patient of Janelle's psychiatrist.

That was after he'd followed his wife to Lana's dingy cubby-hole of an office. Thank God, he'd picked up on Janelle's off-hand comment over breakfast about her "new friend." Janelle didn't have new friends.

By the time he'd discovered that Janelle had been lured into sessions with Lana, a "counselor" who specialized in "lucid dreaming," "magic hand" writing, and hypnosis, which frankly smacked of the occult, it was nearly too late. Janelle was already talking of "recovered memories." She no longer enjoyed cooking or conversing with him after a long day. She scratched furtively half the night in notebook after notebook, "recording her dreams," as she put it, and not sharing a word of it with him.

Charles paid a visit to that crank and found Lana fluent in a language he knew well.

Money. He'd written her a check for ten grand. The deal? Leave.

And so she had, concocting some story, telling Janelle that a famous teacher—a terrorist, judging by the name—had invited her to study with him in India, "an opportunity of a lifetime."

Ashram, commune, wigwam—he couldn't care less. Shack up with a snake charmer. Leave Janelle alone. That was the deal. Just go.

He didn't tell Janelle he'd met that fly-by-night flake, much less confess it had been his generous "donation" that had afforded that nut job the opportunity of a lifetime.

He'd cashed out his life insurance policy for that one. It had been worth every penny.

But she was back. No doubt for another payoff. Did she think he was a fool? He was not. He was not an ATM either. Most of all, he was not a man who would let his wife be toyed with.

"Can you believe this young man is driving now?" Janelle told Mira, winking at Spec. "Isn't that fabulous!"

"Yes," Spec said, looking at a space just above Janelle's ear. "But only on driveways."

Mira passed the basket of cornbread and biscuits, her eyes down or up, anywhere but straight across at Reagan, like a comical scene in an improv class. "You must be so busy right now planning for the wedding?" Reagan said loudly. "Three months out can get just crrraaazy."

"Oh, well, I'm not worried." Mira squinted at Reagan, willing tunnel vision, cutting out Teddy. Most of him. She could see his arm, his hand, his ring. "Nelson and I—we want to scale it back, to tell you the truth. I mean, who needs the stress?"

"Oh, I get that," Reagan said. "I so, so get that."

"A lot of Nelson's friends are foodies. So, I'm thinking a locally sourced menu." Why did Mira feel the need to even talk about it? Just shut up, she told herself. Talk to the dream tender.

"Right, right, right. Boho weddings are hot now. Have you ordered your cake?"

Had she? Of course not. A bone of contention between her and Nelson. Ridiculous to pay so much money for some decorative confection that will be eaten and forgotten, he'd said.

"Because there's this bakery in Charlotte? They're geniuses. Gluten-free, vegan, and regular fat-filled sugar, you name it. My college roommate's sister runs it, so full disclosure. Hey, why don't you meet me tomorrow and we'll go by there?"

"Oh, I wouldn't want to take your time. I know you're busy."

"I can squeeze in an hour. Let's do lunch."

"Lunch? Where?" Teddy said, muscling into Mira's frame of vision.

"Don't butt in, Teddybear," Reagan said. "This is a girls' thing."

Mira studied her plate.

Her father said, "For God's sake, Mira. Reagan's time is valuable. You have no idea how valuable. Of course you should have lunch."

"Some other time, maybe," Mira mumbled.

"Sure. Let me know when you're free," Reagan said, and then her hand fluttered up to cover her pink-mouthed yawn, so precious, like a baby panda sneezing. "Excuse me. I'm so excited about Rex Wolf. I stayed up wayyyy too late last night working." She poked Teddy beside her with one long pearly fingernail. "While this guy snored like a bear. What is it with guys and their beauty sleep? You totally know how that is, right?"

"Yeah," Mira said, her face flushing. "Totally."

Charles had kept his head. He took Reagan aside shortly before they'd sat in the dining room and told her he'd like to keep a lid on announcing their Rex Wolf plans to the family until later, perhaps after dessert. Not with a stranger in their midst. He couldn't bear to think Reagan could see his humiliation; it was all he could do to pretend that this repulsive interloper sitting beside his wife, eating his food, didn't outrage him.

And look at Reagan and Teddy, attractive, gifted conversationalists—pretending not to notice how Spec was staring at a spot on the wall. The boy had refused to sit at the small table and sat by Burry. An outrage, really, not to teach children the most basic manners. The way Burry coddled him—at Easter, letting the kid, as big as a linebacker—hide eggs here with the neighborhood children—well, Charles couldn't think about it; it would make him angry all over again.

Elsie came out of the kitchen and brought in more platters of fried chicken, potatoes, squash casserole, green beans, and biscuits.

"Elsie?" Burry said, "Come sit down with us and enjoy all the food you cooked."

That boy! Charles shook his head. Inviting the help to join them. No head for business. The disastrous months Burry had worked with Charles—letting job applicants skip drug tests, believing every sob story he heard—

Well. Those disappointments were bad enough.

But this gypsy grifter showing up out of the blue!

"Spec," Grandmother's friend said. "I hear you are a computer wiz."

When Grandmother's friend talked to Spec, she didn't look at him. She looked across the room, and that was good. That's what Mrs. Lee, Spec's counselor, did. It made him NOT NERVOUS.

"Your grandmother said you are good with animals too. You had a cat."

"Domino."

"Yes. Domino."

Domino had died in the winter. He was old and Dad said it was Domino's time. Spec missed Domino every day. The sadness did not fade, it was not a line. The sadness was a circle, it moved around and around, coiled, like a spring.

"Domino wants you to know he is happy where he is." Grandmother's friend had such a soft voice that Spec had to listen carefully. He wanted to hear about Domino.

"In cat heaven?"

"Of a sort. Domino…" Grandmother's friend closed her eyes for a minute, then opened them. "He wants you to be happy. He wants you to have pets. I saw Domino, just for a second. Oh, he's adorable."

Grandmother's friend said this and still did not look at him.

But Grandfather stared. Maybe he knew Grandmother's friend could see cat ghosts.

"Spec. What a wonderful name," Grandmother's friend said. "You do know that, don't you?"

When Spec was growing inside his mother, she saw a picture of him on the sonogram, she said he was a speck of precious. His mother called him a speck of precious over and over, she said nothing would change that, she knew from the start. His real name was Edward but he called himself Spec on the first day of kindergarten. That boy last year, the mean one on the school bus, said "Spec" meant on the spectrum, "Spec" meant Special Ed, and that's when they started calling him that, Spec Ed; and he tried to explain, but they wouldn't listen.

"Names are powerful," Grandmother's friend said now. "Especially when you choose them yourself."

"Charles," Reagan said. "Do you know anything about that photo of Teddy's grandmother? There was a photo of her in the file you gave us from your office."

"The squaw?"

Mira gasped. "Daddy, really? That's an offensive term!"

"Okay, well, an Indian woman. Cherokee."

"Oh my god, Teddy," Reagan said. "Did you know your grandmother was Native American?"

Teddy, mouth full, managed a shrug.

"That's fantastic! You can explore your roots and reach out to the Native American community. That's gold, Teddybear."

"That's not right," Mira said, meeting Teddy's eyes for the first time that day. Exactly the wrong thing to say, because it was a dare. Teddy smiled. Oh, why couldn't she just shut up around him? "I mean, yes, explore your roots, but surely you're not thinking of appropriating the culture—"

"Why not?" her father said. "Back when Stan and I were coming up, well, you didn't advertise such things. But these days, if Teddy has kin in the tribe, the Eastern band or whatever it is, hell, yes, he should use that. Stan would be proud."

"Use that? For your business? Like in a political campaign? That's appalling."

Mira looked at Teddy again, hard this time, spotting a hint of discomfort.

"How about we table this discussion?" Teddy said. "Written any new poems, Mira?"

"Nope."

She looked longingly over at Nelson. He and Pansy were talking and laughing. Outsiders, marginalized, stuck in the cheap seats, and having a high old time. She should have insisted on sitting with them.

Mira stood and cleared her plate.

"What are you doing?" her father demanded, irritated just as she knew he'd be. "Let Elsie and Violet do that."

A burst of laughter arose, her mother and her friend, Lana, whooping it up. But an inverse to the levity was her father's menacing glare, like a light sweeping from a guard tower. "What's so funny?" her father snapped. "Lana, isn't it?" He speared a chunk of meat and pointed his fork at her. "You are returning to India soon?"

Lana didn't answer. Didn't even nod. Met her father's eyes, though, and offered her own scythe of a smile.

"Daddy," Mira hissed. "Stop."

Janelle grabbed her friend's arm. "I hope not."

"I'm sure her visit here is coming to a close. You shouldn't pester her, Janelle. And you have so many other guests to talk to today."

There was a predatory glint in her father's eye.

"I can't imagine what brought you here, Lana," her father continued. As her mother's friend sat right there, looking, well, damn unflappable, Mira had to give the woman credit. "But I'm sure you are needed back there."

"Charles," her mother pleaded, "please don't—"

"You know what, Reagan? How's tomorrow look?" Mira said this loudly before she leaned across the table in front of her father, drawing away his hostile attention—here, here! "It's my day off. If that's good for you."

"I'll make that work," Reagan said.

"Dad, Reagan and I are meeting tomorrow for lunch—"

"Excellent." Charles nodded at Mira; the storm clouds passed. He smiled.

12

TEDDY

When Teddy woke up in a sweat, gasping, his heart pounding, he did not tell Reagan. Not last night, not the other times either. A dozen night terrors this month. Not that he was counting. Well, yes, he was counting. Still, he kept it to himself. Reagan would send him for tests, she'd end up taking control of whatever this was.

Waking from nightmares, failure clinging to him like cobwebs. He would lose everything. Disgrace his father's memory. All of it gone, if he didn't watch himself.

And there it was again, his heart cantering—was this a cardiac event? He slipped out of bed and drank a glass of water in the kitchen, trying to calm down, but he just worked himself up, worrying about his panic.

So, after Reagan left for work he made a doctor's appointment, because you didn't mess around with chest pains. Especially if your father had heart disease and diabetes. (Of course, Teddy was only thirty-two, and it was cancer that got his father and his mother too. Another affliction to dodge! Tracers, like a video game.)

They worked him in at ten o'clock that morning. The nurse—a cute redhead with bee-stung lips—took his pulse and blood pressure, flirting with him, calling him Mr. T-Rex in that coy *meet-me-for-a-drink?* way. She followed him on Facebook and loved his "articles."

He undressed in the examining room, sat in the humiliating paper gown, chastising himself for giving into middle-of-the-night fear. Seeing a doctor in the harsh fluorescent light. Ridiculous.

His heart demanded to be tended to, plied with promises. Doctor-patient confidentiality. That was tempting. Maybe unburden himself, placate his heavy heart—that tyrant—demanding things from him, impossible things. The heart, yeah, and let's not forget that most fickle organ—shrinking now between his legs, in the cold, sterile examining room, cowering and stupid, one-eyed dictator—DICKtator—did not dare rear its head. Thanks, buddy.

Dr. Crumley shuffled in. Near retirement, he'd signed off on Teddy's peewee football physical form back when Teddy was ten. Doc had seen some things. A family doctor saw the whole range of human foibles and heartaches, like Chekhov. Or was it Tolstoy who'd been the doctor? One of the Russians. Mira would know.

Dr. Crumley was going over Teddy's family history, clicking his ballpoint pen. Asking questions about his symptoms. Examining him, his cold stethoscope on Teddy's chest, pleased by the regular, robust heartbeats, Teddy's ideal blood pressure.

"We can discuss referring you to a specialist."

"A specialist?" A shrink. Jesus. No way. That's all he needed, rumors that he was certified. He shook his head.

"A cardiologist."

"Oh, so there is something wrong?"

"No, no sign of it that I can detect."

"I'd rather not."

"Been under a lot of stress lately?"

"Helping run my dad's old business. You may have heard."

Doc nodded. Already signing off on something, closing Teddy's file.

And planning to run for office and carrying on with my business partner's daughter. Yeah, Doc, stress level is code red.

"Here's an order for the lab, basic blood work. Might relieve your mind. Anything else I can do for you, Teddy?"

Teddy smiled. "I'm good." Now that he wasn't dying.

Teddy returned to his office relieved, a smidge more confident. His heart was a robust drama queen.

Not even Arlene's glowering mug dampened his spirits.

Reagan called and reminded him to pick up the dry cleaning, his good suit he'd need sometime soon—for something something something—and then, almost as an aside, she mentioned lunch with Mira.

"What?" but he reeled it in just as fast, his surprise. "I thought you said she canceled." That was last night, after Janelle's birthday dinner. Mira texted Reagan and "flaked out."

"She changed her mind again. This morning."

"Oh, right." Thinking, this can't be good. Those two.

"Hopefully, she goes for it."

"For…what?"

"Oh my God, Teddy, are you…you aren't playing online poker again, are you? Pay attention, mister."

"I…am."

"To amp up the wedding, so we can tie it into…everything." She yawned. "Crap. I need espresso. God, I will be so glad to drink caffeine again."

"Call me later," he said. "Let me know how it goes."

"K. Love you."

"Love you."

But she didn't call. After lunch. All that afternoon.

Just what the hell had the two of them discussed? Mira and his wife? They barely knew each other.

It would be like Mira to break down and cry. She was so emotional. No hiding those soulful eyes, and she'd confess, she'd tell Reagan she didn't love Nelson, that she was in love with someone else—

Sudden panic. Holy shit. His blast of confidence gone, his optimism seeping away. His heart hammered.

By the end of the day, heading home, Teddy was useless. He wanted a drink. A drink at Bar None, with his favorite bartender, who was not working today anyway, since she had driven all the way to Charlotte to meet his wife for lunch.

Reagan still hadn't responded to his texts. Well, just a terse "can't talk, back 2 back meetings now."

What had the two of them talked about? More importantly, what had the two of them said about him?

He picked up the dry cleaning, nuked a frozen pizza at home, changed into saggy sweats, too revolting to wear outside, much less to a bar. His own insurance policy: make it hard to leave your living room.

That was how it started. He'd be alone in the evenings, waiting for Reagan, and he'd convince himself he could drop by Bar None and have ONE beer and stay THIRTY MINUTES and talk to, maybe, a future constituent or two...and, oh yeah, SEE MIRA. And that turned into three, then four nights a week. And the other nights he wasn't there? All he thought about was how he wanted to be at Bar None.

It was like being twelve again. That was the last time he remembered being consumed with such tormented yearning. The week Teddy practically moved in with the Wolf family because his father was in hospice and his mother had stationed herself by Stan's bedside in the hospital. Teddy hadn't realized his father was dying, not at that point. He hadn't been allowed to visit Stan on his deathbed, hadn't seen how bad it was. He remembered his mother dropping him in front of the Wolfs' house on Welborne Way, not even getting out of the car, just watching him go to the front door as he lugged his sleeping bag and backpack. He plopped it all down in the guest room Mira led him to.

That week, Charles was mostly away—at the office or the hospital. Janelle stayed home, though looking back, Teddy could see she wasn't exactly the adult in the room. Mira and Burry whipped together meals of frozen lasagna and salad and sandwiches and cheeseburgers, while Janelle set the table, humming to herself, holding up each piece of silverware to the light, setting it down on the linen napkins she'd insisted upon.

There was something off about Janelle, but she'd always

been kind to Teddy. Sometimes she'd gaze at him and whisper, you poor thing. And she'd let him skip basketball practice that week after school, didn't even take his temperature or ask where it hurt, just nodded, not suspecting he didn't want to spend one minute away from Mira, who would be home at three on the dot. Janelle made him a grilled cheese, which turned out to be inedible, what with the maple syrup and peanut butter and pickle relish, then he had to sit in the dim living room with her and watch old movies. He pretended to be comforted. But on the couch, he and Miffles, Mira's beloved mutt, both had their eyes glued to the door, waiting for Mira.

What a stroke of luck. Mira, a fifteen-year-old goddess, charged with keeping an eye on Teddy, though it was Teddy who kept his eyes on her, of course. She'd welcomed him into the sanctum of her black and purple room, which smelled deliciously of Mira—chapstick, the gummy bears she binged on, sandalwood candles. The girls his age were into the Backstreet Boys and the Spice Girls, but Mira played CDs of singers, mostly women in pain. Jewel, Natalie Merchant, Sarah McLachlan. Plaintive tunes with lyrics she said meant something. Mira was saving her babysitting money to go to something called Lilith Fair, and he asked if he could tag along because a fair—fun, right? Like a carnival? She just smiled. She did her homework at her desk, and he pretended to do his on her unmade bed, on top of clean laundry and fat, furry black pillows, beside a sprawled-out, snoring Miffles. Then they'd go to the living room to watch *Seinfeld* and *The Simpsons*, funny stuff, he realized later, that Mira insisted upon. Because his father was dying.

Once during a commercial, Mira took his sweaty, wart-blighted hand and squeezed it.

"Hey. You okay?"

"Yeah." No.

At night, zipped up in his cowboy sleeping bag on the Wolfs' guest bed, Teddy's eyes would sting with tears, but not before he'd feel a twinge of guilt for the opportunity his father's illness had delivered, to be under the same roof with Mira.

God, what a week. The rapture of his first crush and then, wham. Hello, death.

His father died on Sunday. Teddy and his mother moved away a few weeks later, Teddy's heart bleeding for Mira. His heart still bled for her. Despite that night three years ago. The week between Christmas and New Year's when Teddy blew through Haven and dropped in on Charles, who insisted Teddy have dinner with the Wolfs. Mira had come home for winter break. Surprise! Only it wasn't, really. Teddy had hoped she'd be home for the holidays.

She was teaching then, bored, but dreading going back to Baltimore with her noisy roommates, boxed wine, and ridiculous teaching load.

Teddy still worked in development at a private college in North Carolina. Planned giving, he told Mira over drinks later that evening after dinner, in the lobby of the Palmetto Hotel where he was staying "on business," arranging to talk to an ailing rich widow the next day. A cinch, really, lots of golf with geezers, working up to the Ask, nudging them to add a clause in their wills, endowments to the college. But look at her! Professor and poet, he was impressed. "Don't be," she said.

Later that night, he confessed his was a "just-kill-me-now job." He hated it.

She admitted that going for a PhD was nuts these days; no tenure, unless you were a nuclear physicist. She didn't know what she was going to do, really. Anyway, they had that in common. At the crossroads of life.

"You want go upstairs and see my room?" he'd asked. They both laughed at that lame line. Then—

Mira in his hotel room, finally! It was the sort of fantasy-come-true that was supposed to cauterize a lovesick heart. It was supposed to finish things, not start them.

Later, they kept in touch. Flirty emails. Late night phone calls. Dancing around their next meet-up.

One day he quit his soul-sucking job without notice. He had no idea what to do next. He worked up the courage to tell

Reagan, knowing this rash move was his version of forcing a breakup. Because souls lacking direction were, for Reagan, lost souls. Hopeless wraiths without purpose, floating on the outer ring of hell.

Only, Reagan surprised him. She praised him for having the balls to quit a job that wasn't getting him where he needed to be. Then she laid out a vision—moving to Haven, approaching Charles about joining Rex Wolf, running for office. Stan's legacy was waiting for Teddy. The best kind of inheritance, right? Teddy found himself agreeing with her. He actually grew excited about the possibilities. That was the thing about Reagan. She could persuade the devil himself.

They were engaged a few weeks later.

He could never bring himself to tell Mira he had a girlfriend—much less a fiancée. That would have involved calling Mira, hearing her voice, and…doubting his decision. He hated excruciating uncertainty. So, he put it off.

Then Mira heard he was engaged.

No more emails or calls. She ghosted him. Fine. He deserved it.

But sometimes he second-guessed himself anyway. He should have tried harder. He should have wooed Mira.

He married Reagan a year later. A woman he was lucky to have, as she often reminded him. Reagan had their life on track. Mira doodled on cocktail napkins.

Marrying Reagan was the right choice.

So why, when Mira served him a frosty mug of pilsner the other night, did a line from Yeats float up to him? Something about a pearl-pale hand, and binding up her long hair and sighing.

Teddy rubbed his solar plexus now, wielded a chair and a whip at his heart, get back, get back.

He poured himself another beer and called Reagan again. Straight to voicemail. Where in the hell was she? Driving home, hosting a conference call, listening to a podcast, maybe all at once. Unless. Unless she was pissed off at Teddy.

Maybe Mira wasn't going to marry that musclehead after all. He decided to text Mira. Verboten, sure. He'd promised Mira he wouldn't call or text her anymore. But he had to know what was going on, for Pete's sake. He typed out a sentence and then deleted it. Typed and deleted. On and on. Until finally he pecked out—So r u good with all this? Perfect. Nebulous enough to avoid mischief. He sent it.

Waited.

Then—Don't contact me, I'm blocking U.

Blocking him? He tried again. Nothing. Mira had blocked him?

Teddy's chest hurt again.

13

MIRA

She could handle a friendly, superficial lunch, right?

Because, hey, what better way to deflate an almost-affair than having lunch with your almost-lover's wife? And it would send a message to that almost-lover that she, Mira, was serious when she said no more. The fling is flung. We're done here, T-Rex. Seriously.

The sick curiosity, though. That was unexpected. She'd never talked to Reagan alone.

"Take my car," Nelson said now, and handed her the keys.

"Aw, thanks, Nels. That's nice."

"I don't want you stranded out there alone on the highway. And we really don't need car repair bills right now."

Ouch. That was for the money she'd "blown" at the vet. On Yeats, the alley cat that hung out in the back of the bar, that she'd finally coaxed into her car—yeah, with Teddy's help—and then took him in for shots, to clear up an abscess, and to be neutered. Nelson said, you spent one hundred bucks on a stray cat? He wasn't a stray anymore, she said. He's our cat. And then they'd quarreled but then they made up, and he said, as they lay in bed naked and sweaty, "The thing about money, it takes discipline. Sticking to a budget. It's like a muscle you exercise."

Obviously, her money muscle was flaccid.

So, she drove Nelson's Honda Civic the forty miles to Charlotte because her own creaky Kia was unreliable (only four car payments left!) and shook like a Maytag when it hit sixty on the highway.

She pulled into the parking deck behind Ideas Ink and found a space among the BMWs, Mercedes, and Audis. She looked at her puffy, tired eyes in the car mirror. You really want to do this? On your day off? She fumbled around her big cloth handbag for lipstick or eyeliner—any cosmetic—and pulled out an old Clinique sample, empty, alas, but then she found lip balm, fuzzy with lint. There's still time to leave. Call her, tell her you had a dead battery or you're sick—

Her phone rang.

"Hi there!" Reagan said.

"Oh, hey. Listen, Reagan—"

"When you park, come up one flight of stairs and you'll see the receptionist's desk. Just ask for me. Oh, and I almost forgot—bring your parking ticket. I'll have it validated. I'm so excited! This will be fun."

The silvery lines of the elevator door took on a slight wave, the hint of warp like a funhouse mirror. Not fun, though, not fun at all. Reagan, petite and put together in fuchsia, peep-toed tan pumps (Italian designer—Mira had asked, and the name had trilled off Reagan's tongue). Beside her Mira felt sloppy and overeager, a St. Bernard towering over the delicate, sleek, narrow-faced Reagan, who was built for racing, like a whippet. Reagan hadn't stopped talking since Mira met her in the lobby; she was describing some sort of presentation, a "deck" she'd managed to slap together at the last minute. They stepped off the elevator.

"I just love that," Reagan said, peering at Mira's purse, big as a feedbag.

"Oh, thanks. It was handmade in Ecuador."

"Peasant things are so in right now."

Reagan's heels echoed like shots across the gleaming marble floor, as Mira padded beside her in espadrilles, her peasant shoes.

"I thought we'd head to the bakery first, up the street? Then grab some lunch? I know this great little place around the corner."

Reagan had quite a pace on her, doubly impressive because

she was half-jogging on the sidewalk in stiletto Italian designer-what's-his-name heels. Mira kept up. Thanks to the punishing hiking and biking treks Nelson planned for them on weekends, she was in good shape, aerobically speaking.

"Here we are." Reagan stopped, pointing to a striped green awning, Piece a Cake, in gold-leaf cursive across the shop window.

The place smelled heavenly, of sugar and flour, the well-lit shelves brimming with tarts and cupcakes and confections. Something about a bakery was so damn comforting.

"Hey there. Can you tell Anna Rose I'm here?" Reagan asked a bored-looking teenage girl behind the counter.

"This place is amazing," Mira said, eyeing a chocolate espresso layer cake.

"It totally is. But I'm not much of a sweets person, to tell you the truth."

No, Mira thought. No, I bet you're not. Meanwhile, her own mouth watered and her stomach growled like a squalling tomcat.

"I called ahead and talked to Anna Rose so she'll have everything ready."

"Reagan! So, so good to see you," an elegant, tall woman gushed as she came out of the back, embracing Reagan, the two of them squealing. "It's been forever!"

"I know, Anna Rose, I am so sorry. I have been working eighty hours a week. Some days, I barely have time for lunch at my desk."

"How's Teddy?"

"He loved that peach tart. Too much. I made him do some serious treadmill time." They chuckled, while Mira tried not to picture Teddy sweating like a galley slave while Reagan cracked a whip. "My friend Mira is getting married, and I told her Piece of Cake was the best bakery around. Mira, meet Anna Rose."

"Oh, the bride. Congratulations!" she said, clasping Mira's hand. Anna Rose wore a crisp frilled apron over a silky blouse and a pencil skirt with a daring slit—a chic, middle-aged, rail-thin woman who owned a bakery and looked as if she didn't eat a crumb.

"You should see the groom," Reagan told her friend, then winked at Mira. "Bet you don't have to bitch at Nelson about going to the gym, huh?"

"I have your sample plate all ready," Anna Rose called out to the girl behind the counter, who brought out a large platter and set it down on one of the bistro tables. Half a dozen squares of cake, labeled with little paper flags.

"Reagan said y'all are going to have some picky eaters, right?"

"Picky?"

"Sugar-free, vegan, gluten-free? Honey, we got it all right here. You'll need a groom cake and then the—"

"Groom cake? I think I just need the one wedding cake. Real basic...wedding cake," she mumbled.

A quick exchange between Reagan and Anna Rose, telegraphing an eye roll, maybe?

"Let's back up for a minute. What's your theme and your colors?"

"Theme? We don't really have one, we..." Mira trailed off.

"They are being super casual," Reagan said.

"Oh dear," Anna Rose said.

"Mira, why don't you sample the cake and decide your favorites," Reagan said. "Anna Rose will email you photos and an order form. Done and done. Right?"

You couldn't help but admire that kind of antic energy, that get-shit-done attitude.

After Mira dutifully sampled cake, she tried to beg off lunch, but Reagan wouldn't take no for an answer. They walked—sprinted—another block, this time to an ugly cinderblock building with a full parking lot. A local meat-and-three, where everything was oversalted, breaded, deep-fried, and therefore delicious, the kind of place Nelson—and therefore Mira—avoided. "I'll have my usual, Dee Dee," Reagan told the waitress.

"I'm full, from all that cake. Maybe just tea?" Mira said.

"Don't be silly. This is on me," Reagan said with mock outrage, as if the idea of a free lunch would be too much for Mira to refuse. "Besides, the macaroni and cheese is out of this world. And the fried okra? Oh my God, I have no words."

Mira ordered the mac and cheese, the okra, and green beans. Technically vegetables, right? A deep-fried, meat-seasoned vegetable plate.

"You know what? Your daddy is so great. I really do love having him as a client. And he and Teddy, they work so well together. They have big plans."

Mira nodded. After her mother's friend, Lana, had left after yesterday's dinner, no doubt driven away by her father's appalling rudeness, he had visibly relaxed, announcing that Teddy was coming aboard, that there were big plans for Rex Wolf. "Charles and your mother, I admire them so much. You know, their marriage. Through sickness and in health. Teddy told me how hard it was."

What exactly had Teddy told her?

"Yes, they've been through a lot," Mira managed. She nibbled at a biscuit, then took a big bite because it was insanely delicious and if her mouth was full, she wouldn't have to talk.

At the table beside them, four utility linemen put down their menus, their eyes rolling over Mira before raking slowly, slowly over Reagan.

"I vote for the lemon buttercream, by the way. For your wedding cake? Let me know what you decide."

Mira held up a finger, swallowed. "Yeah, about that. Thank you for taking me to the bakery. But those cakes are a little fancy for what Nelson and I have in mind."

Reagan winced. "You don't want some common wedding cake. It's a vital set piece."

"We don't plan to spend a lot on things like cake. I'd love to"—Mira paused to smile and soften the blow—"but I can't."

This did not faze Reagan. "Did your dad not talk to you about amping up your wedding?"

"Amping up?"

"Hmmm. We were supposed to hash this all out yesterday at your mother's birthday lunch, but I don't think Charles will mind if I give you the deets."

"What…deets?"

"Your wedding is pivotal, Mira. It's an opportunity to leverage goodwill before we announce the rebranding of Rex Wolf. Two bank presidents, the mayor, company brass—like really important decision-makers, they could be on your guest list."

Mira laughed, because come on, Reagan couldn't be serious. "It's a wedding, not a Chamber of Commerce meeting."

This did not insult Reagan so much as ignite her. There was a flinty sheen in her eyes as she leaned forward, pushing the salt and pepper out of the way. "I'm going to be honest, Mira. Okay? I have curated a guest list to die for because this—your wedding—is for your family. You, your father, and especially your mother. Because, Mira—okay, I'm just—I'm just going to say it. Your wedding is the first step in correcting the narrative."

"What narrative?" Though of course Mira knew. The one that said her mother, with two children at home, had struck out alone one night on the way to meet her husband at Stan and Mary's and in some sort of reckless, inscrutable lunacy, had come to a bridge and ended up in the river. Accidentally. Or maybe not.

"It's terrible, the whole tragic thing," Reagan said. "And how people reacted. Ugh. Some of them assumed Charles had his hands full with…everything and didn't have his head in the business. And after Stan passed away—God, another tragedy, right? Cancer just when Stan was kicking ass as a senator—the business shed clients like crazy. Stan was always so good with people, the sales guy, right? I don't have to tell you how scary that must have been for your dad."

"The business hit some lean years, yes."

"Some people said Charles was all hat and no cattle. He tried to keep up appearances, bless his heart. The business came close to closing a few years ago, you know that, right? Your dad kept it afloat, but, as Teddy says, Rex Wolf is one hell of a leaky ship."

Hearing "the narrative" distilled and recited, so clinically—the whole tragic thing. It hurt. The saltshaker in front of Mira began to swim.

Reagan pretended not to notice, but her voice softened. "I know, I know. It's not fair. Charles deserves to be admired. And your mother, she deserves—"

"Friends," Mira said.

"Believe me, all those snooty ladies? Those town bitches will be begging your mother for lunch dates."

Mira sipped her iced tea, so sweet it made her teeth hurt. "How?"

"We're going to paper over that old story and craft a new narrative. New website, of course. I'm working on coverage with some long-lead regional glossies. A big spread on Charles and Janelle. How they coped, how they came out on the other side of a traumatic brain injury. People eat that stuff up. And your wedding is an opportunity to have this select powerful group there to witness your parents at the top of their game again. The optics will be brilliant." Reagan sipped her water. "So what do you think?"

Mira didn't care about optics or rebranding or guest lists. It was the papering over the old story that got her. Crafting a new narrative. She thought of her mother, yesterday. They're going to fix everything.

"What about—"

"Oh my God, hold that thought. My phone is exploding."

Mira found herself apologizing. Reagan was in demand! She was a marketing genius! People were clamoring for her decks and vortexes and recast narratives.

"Anyway." Reagan looked up from her phone. "You should definitely order one of those wedding cakes pronto. Think simple but stunning. Memorable. Your whole wedding, I mean."

"I'll talk to Nelson." Mira sighed. "He's not going to like it. He hates big weddings. He's very budget conscious." The

rip-off wedding industry, he called it. Nelson would bleed from
the eyeballs if he saw the price of cake.

"Tell Nelson this is a return on investment. You're launching
your life together."

Mira would have to provide Nelson with some context.
Convince him that this amped-up wedding wasn't for her—it
was for her parents. Mostly for her mother.

Those town bitches will be begging your mother for lunch dates.

"So, Mira, I need you to be all in. I know you're stuck with
that farm as the venue for the wedding. But you can accessorize
with cake, flowers, music. Gussy it up."

Mira nodded. A terrible thought occurred to her. Had her
mother assumed Mira didn't want a big wedding because Mira
was ashamed? Embarrassed of her own mother?

"It will be totally worth it," Reagan said. "A wedding is once
in a lifetime…hopefully."

The waitress set down Mira's plate, a hunk of ham on the
green beans, the okra deep-fried, more flour and cornmeal than
vegetable, the macaroni traffic-cone orange.

Reagan's "usual" turned out to be half a baked chicken
breast and a steamed carrot.

"Want to hear something funny? I joke with Teddy sometimes," Reagan said. "I call him my first husband. Especially
when he screws up."

Mira stabbed a clump of soggy green beans.

"Last month he screwed up big time. He almost forgot our
wedding anniversary."

"That's terrible," Mira said, still not looking up.

"I know. But he's not going to forget next year's anniversary,
I guaran-damn-tee you. I can roll out some punishing shit when
I need to." She cut up her chicken into tiny pieces, as if feeding
a child. "Anyway, Teddy needs reminding. The man does not
have a romantic bone in his body."

Mira pressed her napkin to her mouth to hide her astonishment. Because Teddy? Teddy was the most sentimental,
poetry-reciting, starry-eyed, sappy romantic—

"But I didn't marry him for romance anyway." Reagan lowered her voice. "Hey, I don't mean to pry, but are you and Nelson planning on starting a family soon?"

"Yes. Not right away, but soon."

"Nature is a bitch. You have to be young to have babies, right when your career peaks. I mean, I could wait, but I don't want to take my chances with old eggs. And all that in-vitro stuff." She shuddered. "Ugh."

Mira swallowed a clump of breaded okra. "Mmmm," she said. "Delicious."

"I told you."

"Here, have some."

"Oh, no thanks. I'm having to be super strict with myself right now. No wine, no coffee or tea, no fried or fatty stuff, just this healthy food that is sooo boring." She lowered her voice. "I shouldn't say anything yet…but…Teddy and I are planning on a late winter or early spring baby. So that leaves me with a window of about six weeks here."

A spring baby.

Mira choked on her biscuit. Her face burned, she coughed into her napkin.

"Oh my gosh, are you okay?" Reagan's face was going out of focus. Mira's eyes watered. She was hacking away like a sick dog!

The table of linemen stared from the next table. One of them shouted, "Y'all need the Highlick?"

Mira waved, shook her head. "I'm fine," she croaked. "Really."

14

LANA

Janelle arrived pink-cheeked after sprinting up the trail from the parking lot and wore an expression of fervent elation. "You look radiant," Lana said. The truth. "I'm glad I could tell you goodbye in person." The lie.

Janelle gasped. "Lana, you can't leave. Is it Charles? I don't know why he was so impolite. It's not like him."

"I can see Charles is overly protective. That sort of family dynamic isn't unusual."

"I told him he was rude to you, just plain hateful. No one else noticed, I'm sure, but I did."

Lana had enjoyed it too much, the outrage on Charles's florid, well-fed face.

Charles had handed over her "hush and go away" money.

Well, Lana had hushed. And gone away.

But now she was back.

And what fun. To witness his blustering outrage. His hatred was palpable. Lana had bathed in it.

She had to be more cautious.

What she was about to do was risky as hell.

"I'm sorry to have caused a rift between you and your husband. That sort of turmoil you don't need. Not on my account."

"I already told Charles you were going back to India. I had a go-to-pieces, I was so upset with him. He thinks you left today."

"He does?" Lana managed to look shocked. "But you had to fib."

"When I'm well, he'll understand. I'll explain about our sessions. After."

Lana folded her hands in front of her and smiled sadly.

There was a beat of silence. Waterfowl honked and quacked in the nearby pond.

"Here. Here, I brought—" Janelle dug around in her purse—"this." She set a black velvet sack on the picnic table between them. Something jangled and clanged. "Since I can't pay you properly today. I mean, not what you deserve, Lana. But I do have these. Take them."

Lana opened the sack and let out a soft gasp. "Not your jewelry?"

"They were my grandmother's jewels. I don't know how much they're worth. Maybe you can sell them?"

Two necklaces, a ring, earrings, a broach. Emerald. Pearls. Rubies. Gold. Three grand. Four grand, maybe.

"And here." Janelle took out a clutch of papers that looked alarmingly official. Lana's eyes ran over them, put off by legal papers that resembled subpoenas or summons.

"Is this a lease?"

"I dressed up in disguise and I pretended to be your aunt. I said my niece was coming in for the summer! I said you'd come by to sign it. I paid the deposit and one month's rent. In cash. From my household account. It was all I could manage now, but later—"

"A rental?"

"Just over the hill. Near my father's property."

"Your father? You said he had passed."

"Yes, he has."

"Your property."

Janelle looked perplexed. "I think of it as Daddy's land. It's in case I need it. To be looked after, I mean."

Lana let that tantalizing bit of news go by for now.

"This is a cabin?"

"They showed me pictures."

"They?"

"The vacation rental office. People rent cabins there now. They told me it's small but clean."

It would have to be small, for the rent. Probably a dump. Household account? Charles controlled this poor woman like a 1950s housewife.

"You've been quite the whirlwind today, Janelle."

Janelle didn't say it, but her eyes were pleading with Lana to stay. One of Lana's terse reminders to Janelle was how off-putting neediness was...in anyone.

"Say I did stay, Janelle. If—big IF—I agreed to take you on as my sole client, it wouldn't be because of this"—she pointed to the black velvet sack and the lease—"but because of this."

Lana reached into her purse and took out Janelle's spiral notebooks. "This. Is. Powerful."

Janelle's eyes watered, but she sucked it up. Good girl. "You are staying then? To help me?"

"A few weeks, at the most."

"The wedding...if I can be well by the wedding." Janelle's voice cracked with emotion.

"Not a lot of time for our work. Very intense sessions. My methods are not for the fainthearted, as you know. But I have many arrows in my quiver, Janelle."

"And I won't...come undone?"

"I will serve as your spiritual midwife. There will be pain, that is expected, but in the end, a miracle."

Lana ran the numbers in her head. Last year she'd tended to the soul of Betty Finkle in Arizona. That was a sweet deal. Hard to top that one. Betty's cognitive befuddlement elicited opportunity. She'd invited Lana to stay in the guest cottage. Poolside crystal readings. Three meals a day, gym membership...until the sons arrived.

Now she'd have to stay in a crappy rental and pawn off this booty—jewel by jewel if she had to.

But it would be worth it.

"Does this rental have internet service? Because I need a way to communicate with my clients, virtually, at least."

"Oh, I didn't think to ask about computers."

"I'll need help setting up the Wi-Fi. Your grandson? He's a techie, isn't he?" Lana had homed in on that kid at Janelle's birthday dinner, already vetting him for the task—

"Spec is good with computers."

"And can he keep a secret? Because no one else can know, Janelle. About our work together."

"Yes, Spec is very shy."

"You will find it necessary to fib to Charles again. He can't know I am here. I must insist on that. Our sessions are between you and me."

"Yes, of course. I promise."

"There is something you wrote in your notebook, Janelle. One of those pieces of memory, something the senator said?"

"Stan. Yes. I hear his voice, he's saying it, I know it's him—"

"I must stop you there. We'll take this up in a proper session. And I need to record you, of course. Let's go look at this cabin and work out a schedule."

This senator tidbit was not a lodged bullet, it was unexploded ordnance. Removing it would be a tricky business. Too bad Janelle had to suffer. It might even destroy her. It would definitely destroy Charles.

"And keep filling your notebooks. I will read every word."

The look on Janelle's face! Such raw reverence. Even Lana had to turn away.

15

DECEMBER 18, 1996

The Haven Observer

Community Spotlight
Mary Rex: A Politician's Wife Avoids the Limelight

By Agatha Smook, "Women's Lives" Columnist

Mary Rex may soon be a senator's wife, but you won't find the stay-at-home mother on the campaign trail.

"Being in the public eye has never been easy for me," she said recently, beside a crackling fire in the couple's living room. "That's Stan's talent. I've got my hands full being a mother and wife."

After serving three terms in the South Carolina House of Representatives, Stan Rex announced Friday he will run for the South Carolina state senate seat vacated by Eddie Duncan.

"The election is already difficult, very time consuming for our family," Mrs. Rex said. "But Stan is dedicated to people. He's a natural leader. My job is to support my husband so he can run his business and serve his constituents. And I take care of Teddy. I could never let someone else do that for me."

As if on cue, eight-year-old Teddy Rex runs into the room and greets a visitor. The third grader left a trail of muddy footprints from the front door, but his mother did not scold him. She laughed. "We started out with white carpet in the house. Can you believe it? That was before our Teddy."

Born in a small town in the Tennessee mountains, Mrs. Rex was raised by her grandparents after her parents died.

She is not comfortable talking about herself, or her child-hood, she said, stressing that "my grandparents raised me in a church-going home. Not much money, but it didn't matter."

After high school Mrs. Rex longed to travel. She moved to Atlanta and worked as an airline stewardess.

"I thought it would be a glamorous way to see the world," she said. "Silly me."

A photograph shows a twenty-year-old Mary among her stewardess graduating class, wearing a pillbox hat cocked to the side and white gloves, a knotted scarf at her throat, and black pumps.

"Our sleeves and hemlines had to be a certain distance from our wrists and knees," she explained. "Later, the uni-forms changed with the fashion. Short skirts and go-go boots."

In 1970, airline stewardesses had to be between the ages of eighteen and twenty-six, from five feet to five feet nine inches, and weigh no more than 135 pounds. Mrs. Rex said it never occurred to her to be bothered by the rules.

"Yes, we were measured and weighed," she said, "be-cause you had to be, back then."

"Like a cut of beef?"

"Like a model," Mrs. Rex insisted. "It was just how they did business. I wasn't insulted like girls these days. I was glad to have the job. Anyway, it's different now. They even hire men."

Another requirement from back then: flight attendants had to be single.

"That was the rule that got me," she said with a smile. "You couldn't marry. And when I met Stan, that was that."

Mrs. Rex recounts the evening her future husband's flight was delayed on the tarmac after landing. The passen-gers were restless, she said, demanding to get off the plane. "You just had to smile and bear it. Part of the job was learning to deal with rude and impatient people." But Stan

Rex wasn't rude or impatient, she said. He introduced himself and offered to buy her dinner. She turned him down, but he waited for her afterward, watching her deplane and meeting her with a rose he'd bought at an airport kiosk. "It was very sweet," she said. "How could I turn him down?"

The couple married a year later and moved to Haven, where her husband joined forces with his friend Charles Wolf to open Rex Wolf Staffing.

"It was Stan who brought me here to Haven. I thought it was a beautiful town. I still do."

Although she didn't plan on marrying a career politician, Mrs. Rex said she knew Stan would be the sort of husband who would put in long, grueling hours at work. "I knew from the first day the business started just how involved Stan would be. Sometimes he works half the night." Rex Wolf Staffing has expanded, with offices in Columbia, Charlotte, and Aiken, with more locations planned, she said.

But it hasn't always been smooth sailing. The recession that began in 1981 shortly after the business started was "scary," Mrs. Rex said. "But Stan kept his head. He said turbulent market forces were normal, we would just ride them out. And he was right."

The other "turbulence" occurred in 1985 when Charles Wolf's wife was involved in an accident that left her seriously injured. Janelle Wolf was on the way to the Rexes' house when her car ran off a bridge and into a river. Mrs. Wolf nearly drowned.

"Yes, it was a tragedy, but Mrs. Wolf's recovery is a miracle. We almost lost her. We're blessed."

And that is all Mrs. Rex will say about her friend's accident, again stressing how she values privacy.

The spotlight, she says, should shine on her husband.

PART II

JUNE 2015

16

Spec

Grandmother violated three traffic laws in seven minutes. When she pulled onto the side of the road (no blinker!) and asked him to drive, Spec said yes.

"I know you don't even have your license yet, but I detest driving."

Dad had warned Spec never to drive without him or Mom, but Grandmother was not a good driver. Spec would be careful. He would obey the traffic laws. He had memorized them.

Spec got out of the car and sat behind the wheel and waited for Grandmother to fasten her seat belt. Dad said Spec could call her Grandmother if he wanted to, as she wanted him to, even though she wasn't really his grandmother. But then Dad wasn't technically his father, either. It was confusing—the names, the rules—if you thought about it. So, Spec decided not to think about it.

He put the car into drive. It was a BMW 328i sedan. The engine was quiet and good. He pulled onto the road. He felt Grandmother's eyes on him, but he looked straight ahead. He liked that part about driving—eyes on the road, not on the person trying to talk to you.

"Spec, in a few minutes, there will be a bridge."

"Okay."

"I don't like bridges. I can't drive over them. But I can ride over them if I don't look. Tell me when you see the bridge."

Spec looked at the mountain range in the distance. It looked like a cardboard cutout.

"I'll explain to Burry," she said. "About today. About what we're doing."

"All right."

"I'm not asking you to tell a story."

"I don't know any."

He thought she was blowing her nose, but she was laughing.

"You're a wit."

"What is a wit?"

"You're humorous. By story, I mean a falsehood. A lie. I'm not asking you to lie. I'll explain that we deviated from our plan to go to the mall." She was quiet for a minute, and Spec relaxed. He wanted the silence to stretch on and on. Then she said, "But I don't think he'll be very cross with us, do you? Burry is a patient, good soul. A good dad. Just as my father was. His namesake. You see, Burry is named after Judge Wilbur Welborne. He hated to be called Wilbur, your dad. So, we settled on the nickname."

Spec thought Dad should go by "Judge." It was a better name.

"We'll have a little snack later. Are you hungry?"

Spec was always hungry.

"Here is the bridge," he said.

Grandmother closed her eyes and leaned over in her seat. "Tell me when we are over it."

She was afraid, and that made Spec sad. He drove over the narrow stone bridge. The car bounced on a hump as they exited and slammed back down to the asphalt.

Grandmother screamed.

"All right, Grandmother," Spec said. He kept his eyes on the road. "We are over the bridge."

"Oh, thank goodness. I thought something was wrong." She sat up.

"Do you want me to keep driving?"

"Yes, please."

"I will be careful and slow."

She got a tissue out of her purse and dabbed at her face and then offered him a piece of gum. He didn't look at it, but he could smell it.

"I don't like wintergreen."

They drove up the foot of the mountain. The road began to wind, to coil like a snake, and little streams of water splashed down over the boulders.

The engine kicked up, revving with the incline. Spec kept both hands on the wheel, at two and ten o'clock.

"We'll need to take a right soon."

"How many miles?" he asked.

"Oh, I don't know. Just a bit more."

A bit could be a yard, a mile!

"Right there, see?"

He put on the blinker and turned onto a dirt road with potholes. He slowed down to eight miles per hour.

She told him to drive up ahead. "See, under the trees? The driveway."

He pulled behind a green Chevy Sebring convertible. The beige top was up. It was dirty and torn. There was a small house behind the trees. A woman came out on the deck, raised her arm, waved.

Spec turned off the ignition. "I will wait here."

"Spec, please come inside."

He shook his head. "No, thank you."

The woman was barefooted, she wore a long beige dress—was it a nightgown? The sleeves were wide as wings. She looked like a butterfly. Or a moth. Yes, a moth, tan and brown, to blend into bark.

Grandmother got out of the car and hugged the Moth-woman. She was Grandmother's friend, the one who had talked to Spec at Grandmother's birthday party, the one who could see ghost cats. Grandmother knocked on the car window, until Spec got out.

"You remember Lana?" Grandmother asked.

Spec nodded but looked straight ahead, not seeing Grandmother, or her friend.

"You can't stay out here in the sweltering heat," Grandmother whispered. "Come join us. You don't want to hurt our feelings, do you?"

No. No, Spec didn't want to hurt their feelings. He didn't want to hurt anyone's feelings, but it was tricky, because he did that a lot, without meaning to. Mrs. Lee, his counselor, said he could learn to be considerate, he could memorize the rules for talking, the faces people make. Only it wasn't as easy as memorizing traffic laws and signs or even maps of mountain ranges and ocean topography. It was the hardest thing he'd ever done.

There was a flicker of movement at the side of the driveway. A chicken. Then another, then three. Grandmother's friend bent down and picked one up. "Come meet the hens," she told Spec. "These ladies love to be petted."

He got out and held a hen. She felt airy and plump, and she was shy and kind. She mumbled and settled into his arms. The other hen zigzagged around his feet, the third one took a dirt bath.

"Spec, come inside. Lana has made us refreshments," Grandmother said.

The hen in his arms had eyes like tiny buttons; her small head twitched, looking at him, then not looking.

"I know you love pets," Grandmother's friend said. Lana, Spec thought. Lana. Knowing people's names was an important rule. "I have a puppy too. Would you like to meet her?"

A puppy? "Yes."

"And Lana has a tortoise," Grandmother said. "In a tank."

"An Eastern Box Turtle," Lana said.

And that helped Spec like the woman, Lana, because it was important to use correct terms.

The cabin had a main room with wooden floors and an oval rug, a couch, and a desk. There was a stone fireplace. The other rooms—the kitchen, the bathroom, and the bedroom—were very small. Spec walked through the rooms first thing, because he liked to see how a place was laid out, to have a map in his head. The desk in the big room had a new Apple computer—a MacBook Pro laptop—still in the box. There was no television.

The kitchen had a plastic floor, linoleum, Lana called it, so that's where the puppy stayed until she could learn to do her business outside, she said.

Spec fed worms to Shelly the turtle. Then he played with the puppy.

Then he ate five chocolate cookies and drank a glass of lemonade.

Grandmother and her friend sat at the kitchen table, which looked old-timey with iron chairs and plastic cushions. They were looking at pieces of glass spread across the table. For a while Spec listened to them because he loved puzzles. Lana told Grandmother they would label each piece of the puzzle and soon they could put it together. But Spec didn't think they could, because it was just a pile of shiny, broken things, parts of a mirror, and not like any kind of puzzle he'd ever seen. Maybe he said that out loud because Grandmother said, "He's very literal. I adore that."

Lana said, "Yes, we all have our strengths, don't we?" Spec felt his face warm the way it did when someone looked hard at him. "This is a symbolic puzzle, Spec. A metaphorical way to find the truth." Then she said she needed him to keep the puppy quiet, and she was going to turn out the lights, because Grandmother was going to be in a trance.

"But before we begin," Lana said. "I wonder if you could help me with something, Spec."

"The computer," Grandmother said. "Burry says you are so smart about computers."

"I was hoping you could help me set it up, the router, too," Lana said. "And I have a new video camera."

He took the computer and the camera out of the boxes.

"Do you think you could load the software on my computer?"

He sat at the computer. He held the puppy on his lap.

"Thank you, Spec. How long do you think it will take?"

"Ten minutes."

She didn't leave. She stood behind him and watched.

Grandmother drove most of the way home, except for the bridge part. Spec drove over the bridge, but slowly this time. They stopped at a produce stand. Grandmother let Spec pick out anything he wanted. He chose a bag of boiled peanuts. Grandmother bought a jar of honey and some tomatoes and peaches.

Although the air conditioning was blowing icy and hard, Grandmother rolled down her window, and that bothered Spec because it wasted energy.

"One time I played hooky up here with your dad and Aunt Mira. What do they call playing hooky these days?"

"Skipping," Spec said. Spec had wanted to skip school every single day.

Grandmother didn't say anything for a few minutes. She had a smile on her face. Smiles didn't mean people were happy, though. Some people could smile and be mad.

"Do you want me to drive now?" Spec asked. Because they were going twenty-seven miles per hour. A car honked and passed them, then another.

"Oh, for goodness' sake," she said and made a sound like she'd been hurt. "I got distracted." She sped up.

"Did you get in trouble?" Spec asked.

"When I played hooky? Oh yes, I did get in trouble." Grandmother dabbed at her wet eyes with her knuckle.

Grandmother told him there were napkins in the glove compartment. He found one under some mustard and relish packets and handed it to her.

"I'm sorry," she said. She used the napkin to dry her eyes. "I'll try not to come undone."

At home, Dad smiled about the peaches and tomatoes. He said he was proud of Spec for keeping Grandmother company when she went shopping. Dad said computer camp started soon, but until then, Spec could help Grandmother all he wanted.

"It's always harder in the summer," Dad told Grandmother

in a whispery voice. That was because Spec's other dad didn't want to see him in the summer anymore. But Dad said Spec had to get out into the world.

Spec didn't tell Dad about Grandmother's friend or even about the puppy, the turtle, or the hens. Dad didn't ask. If he did, Spec wouldn't lie. If Dad asked Spec if he drove Grandmother over bridges, Spec would say yes. If Dad asked if Spec took care of a puppy and a turtle and the hen ladies, he would say yes. But Dad didn't ask those questions. If Spec tried to tell a little bit, a lot of it might come out like shaving cream, globs of it when you barely pressed the top of the can. So Spec did not talk about his afternoon with Grandmother.

After Grandmother left, Dad said Spec had earned the right to play video games for one hour. Then Mom got home and told him to wash up for dinner. Spec's hands still smelled like the puppy, and he didn't want to wash them. He just pretended to. He tried to keep his hands dry even when he had to help with the dishes, even when he brushed his teeth. But at night in bed, as he held his hands over his face and breathed in as hard as he could, he couldn't smell the puppy at all, not even a little bit.

17

JANELLE

Mira and Burry are looking through the photographs and old newspaper clippings Charles brought down from the attic. Sometimes Mira reads aloud things, shaking her head. "'Judge Welborne's daughter injured. Charles Wolf says doctors cautiously optimistic.' Mom, do you notice how they defined you through men? No mention of your marketing and PR role at Rex Wolf, not one freaking word about your career, not to mention all the community volunteering you did."

She calls it the patriarchal lens. "You were the dead judge's daughter and the businessman's wife. You'd think it was the 1880s, not the 1980s."

Now that Mira has a degree in women's studies and poetry, she likes to point out how backward "those days" were. I like that. Janelle Before had grit and ambition. I feel a flicker of pride. Lana says my resentment of Janelle Before is waning.

"Now this—oh my God, this is more like it. Burry, look." Mira holds up a yellowed newspaper article.

"That was the groundbreaking," I tell them. "The official opening of Rex Wolf."

"You're all muddy," Burry says, squinting.

"But you're in a hard hat," Mira says. "That's what's interesting. You and Mary both."

"It rained that day. Terrible storms."

Mira and Burry look at each other, then Mira looks at me. Her face gives nothing away, but something unsettled hangs between us.

"What's wrong?" They look startled when I ask, perhaps because I can sense such things now. I am no longer in a fog; I pay attention. I am aware they have "dropped by" here to talk when Charles is at the office, perhaps to impart some difficult request. My heart pounds. "Is it Spec? You don't approve of our afternoons together?"

"No, no," Burry says. "It's great, you two spending time together."

"Is it bad news?"

"No, Mom," Mira says. "It's actually good."

My children believe I am fragile. I am not. Lana says I'm a rock. I have hidden reserves of enormous power, she says, and then she leads me through a meditation as I hold her lava stone.

Mira says she wants to make sure I'm good with all this. The publicity around the business, the interviews of Charles and me; the coverage might not be easy, she says. The spotlight on me.

"For T-Rex's campaign, let's not lose sight of the end game here," Burry says.

"Well. But it's for us too," Mira says. "Our family."

"Recasting the narrative," I say, and they are astonished again. I smile.

"My wedding is…it might be bigger than I thought," Mira says. "Daddy says you're fine with that. But are you, Mom? Fine with it? More guests and sort of amped up."

"Amped up," Burry whispers. "Jesus." His hands cover his face.

Not long ago this sort of announcement would have sent me to bed. Any formal gathering, Haven's eyes on me—I would have hidden. But not anymore. In a few weeks Lana says my old confidence will be restored. I am bursting to share this with Burry and Mira, my excellent progress and how brilliant Lana is, but I gave my word that our sessions will stay secret. Except from Spec. Fortunately, keeping secrets comes naturally to sweet Spec. Lana said she would sense at once if I told anyone, she would feel it, the cracks in our confidentiality, like a cabin in an airplane that loses pressure, when oxygen thins, and people panic. Lana said she would have no choice but to leave at once if I broke my promise, and I don't blame her. I completely understand.

Lana said the cleverest thing yesterday. She told me to remember my debutante ball, how revered I was, how I commanded the room. Mira's wedding reception, she said, is my second debut. My coming out to Haven. Janelle Before reintroduced.

I will not embarrass my children or bring shame onto them. Charles will be proud again to have me by his side. I must have said this aloud.

"Mom, I would never, ever be ashamed of you." Mira looks so hurt I reach out to pat her arm.

I remember the Rex Wolf groundbreaking. How nearly disastrous it was, how Janelle Before saved that day.

First, the weather. Fat raindrops splattered onto the gauged raw dirt, and not an umbrella in sight.

Charles and Stan wore hard hats and their best Sunday suits, holding shovels. Mary and I, well-heeled fashionable wives, were to look on, clapping, smiling, proud of our men.

A boring ceremony, destined for a newspaper's back pages. The cub reporter with a cheap camera and rain-soaked notepad knew this.

Then the heavens opened. The rain pounded. My own crisp yellow suit soon mud-splattered, my hair sodden and flat.

"Sweetheart," Stan called to Mary. "Sweetheart, where do you think you're going?"

She was getting out of the rain, she said, before she ruined her good clothes.

"But we don't have the photo yet."

"We'll look like drowned rats!" Mary's heels stabbed mud and sloshed puddles. Stan followed her to the car, pleading.

"Mary, for God's sake. I'll buy you another dress," Stan told her, his voice tight with anger. And if Mary's face hadn't been slick with rain, you might suspect she'd been crying.

They quarreled in the car. Mary trudged back, nearly slipped, then did slip, her beautiful bone-white dress, her dove-gray shoes smeared with red Carolina clay.

"What do I have to do, Janelle?"

I handed her Stan's hard hat. I blocked the scene. Like a choreographer, a movie director. Husbands, there. Wives, here.

"Like this, Mary."

I wielded the shovel—me, in a hard hat and pearls.

Stan said, "Yes. Goddamn brilliant, Janelle." He would have to clean up his cursing habit before he ran for office.

The reporter snapped the photograph.

It wasn't buried.

The Rex Wolf groundbreaking made the front page.

Comical, yes, the muddy, silly fun of it.

But the women looked in charge, digging in the mud, intrepid and fierce, while the men looked on from the sidelines, clapping, deferential.

Lana warns me before each session that my memories, unloosed, may burst like broken glass and scatter. Our job is to collect them.

The margins of my recall are widening, and she is pleased. After a few more sessions, Lana says I will remember everything. There were weeks around my accident I didn't remember for the longest time, but now it's coming back to me.

I tried to leave Charles, for example. I'd forgotten.

This was a few years after the accident. I wasn't angry but numb. And it hurt to feel nothing. I couldn't pretend I loved Charles. It was too hard. And so, one morning I convinced myself it was a kind of mercy, what I was going to do.

When my children were at school and Charles left for his office, I walked down the street to ask my neighbor, Tina, for a ride to the grocery store.

Tina answered the door wearing her tennis dress, crisp and white as paper, her tanned face betraying a flash of irritation. She did not have time to take me to the store, but good manners prevailed. I didn't drive. Everyone in the neighborhood knew of my "tragedy" and my need to be ferried around and looked after.

Inside Winn-Dixie, while Tina examined tray after tray of cellophaned chicken parts, I pretended to study the frozen dinners.

I darted through the back "employees only" door, into a room full of boxes and then out the double doors, behind the dumpsters, around the mounds of rotted fruit back there, sparkling with flies.

Behind me, the grocery store's back door squawked open, a man called, "Ma'am? Ma'am?" but I didn't turn around. I hurried across the vacant lot. Tina would be right behind me, I was certain. Two streets over, the houses grew smaller and shabbier, weedy yards dirt-packed inside chain-link fences, snapping dogs, dead cars. I knew where I was going.

The Gaslight, in a strip mall at the bottom of the hill. The kind of tavern that was open at quarter to eleven in the morning. In the back alleyway I peeled off my denim shirt and stepped out of my dowdy beige skirt. Janelle Before's closet was full of stylish, smart frocks, and in the back that morning, I'd found a cocktail dress. I slipped it on now and crammed my clothes in my purse.

Inside the tavern, the black cinderblock walls sucked up the sunlight. The stench of old grease, beer, the chemical waft of soap cakes, a whiff of urine managed to penetrate even my blunted sense of smell.

A middle-aged man emptied a bucket of something into a drain on the floor. His gray hair was in a ponytail and he wore a tank top. At first, until my eyes adjusted to the dimness, I thought he was a woman. He looked up at me.

"Ma'am, you lost?"

"Why, no. I'd like a drink, please."

He stood and wiped his hands on his jeans. "What'll it be?"

As I sat on the barstool in tight red sequins, I wondered, What would Janelle Before's drink of choice be on a Tuesday morning?

"I'll have a dirty martini, please. With extra olives."

His hooded eyes went hard. "Martinis we ain't got, sorry to say."

The sign above the cash register advertised a Miller High Life special. I put a twenty on the bar and ordered it. A plastic pitcher of beer arrived with a dirty glass.

Two men wandered in then and sat at the end of the bar. One of them, thin as a wire hanger, with a hard face. The other, younger, with the careless eagerness of a puppy.

The bartender turned on a radio. Loud. Rock music.

Good, I thought. Tina will be horrified.

That was the plan, you see. For Tina, panicked at losing me, to find me here. Disgraced.

But Tina didn't show up.

That fact began to bother me less and less as the pitcher grew lighter. "May I have a clean glass, please?" I asked. My words came out thick and slow. My sight narrowed and blurred. But other senses grew sharp. The knowledge I was being studied, for example.

The two men at the end of the bar had been discussing "sales quotas." It became evident they worked at the satellite dish store in the shopping center, and that "the assholes at cable" were "killing them." But they grew quiet after a while, watching me.

I stood up beside the barstool. The room went swimmy. The music, the ranting guitar riffs, I began to love it. Something about a free bird, a bird that can't be tamed.

"The facilities?" I asked.

The bartender looked up from his bucket of filthy water, and said, "Straight back yonder. The door with the dubbya."

The women's room, filthy. I squatted over a clogged toilet. No hand soap. Empty paper towel dispenser. I rinsed my hands and dried them on my sequins, scraping like fish scales. In the wavy metal over the sink, Janelle Before's glittery costume winked. I remembered the sling-back stilettos I'd stuffed in my purse that morning. I took them out and slipped them on, shoved my sneakers in the trash can. I wobbled across the cracked tiles.

When I opened the door, he was waiting for me. The cute one. The puppy. "You okay? Looks like you could use some help." He held out his hand, and I took it, steadied myself. There was decency in his brown eyes, well-bred consideration.

"Thank you," I said. He nodded. He wore khaki pants and a royal-blue golf shirt with a name tag that said Timmy Your Sales Associate.

"Could I call someone for you?"

I shook my head and then, still holding his hand, I pulled him to me.

I did.

"Whoa there," he said and laughed, and that's when I felt it. A surge. I was her, in her skin, or rather, she was in my skin. Janelle Before. She had come across the river, for just a few seconds, a minute or two, and as I pressed my mouth over his bristly chin, his soft, sweet beery mouth, his startled reluctance gave way. I imagined the look of shock and disgust on Tina's face. She would be here any minute, surely! She'd tell Charles right away and—well, even a man known as a devoted caretaker wouldn't stand for this sort of behavior. What man would? Pride. His pride. I was giving him an excuse (the only excuse everyone would approve of) to leave me. You see, I was setting Charles free.

Timmy Your Sales Associate's hands began to wander up my thighs, under the red sequins. He buried his face in my neck.

I looked over his shoulder just as my husband came toward me.

Charles did not say a word as he drove me home. Inside the car, the cruel noonday sunlight made the skin on my legs look as mottled and ugly as Tina's shrink-wrapped trays of chicken thighs. That had been an hour before. Just an hour. And now my life was going to be very different.

I massaged my ankle. I had twisted it as Charles pulled me out of the tavern, and I'd left one of Janelle Before's shoes behind in the parking lot.

When we pulled into our driveway, the garage door opened like a mouth, swallowing us, car and all, before it roared closed, sealing us inside the dark, secret cave, away from prying eyes, from neighbors. Later I discovered that Tina had called Charles and told him I had "slipped out" of the grocery store. At Tina's behest, one of the employees had followed me on foot until I disappeared into the tavern.

Charles turned off the ignition. We sat in silence as the engine ticked. Finally, he looked at me. "What were you thinking, Janelle?"

There was something sharp as a blade in his eyes, and I thought here it comes, the hate. Here is the hate.

"I know you're going to leave me, Charles. I don't blame you." I got out of the car and walked upstairs to the bedroom.

My purse bulged with my dowdy skirt and blouse. I threw it on the floor. I began to unzip the red dress. It would have to be dry cleaned before I donated it to Goodwill.

Charles appeared in the doorway. I hadn't heard him come up the stairs. He moved quietly.

"What were you thinking, Janelle?" he said again, but his voice was soft.

"I wasn't."

"Drinking alone in a dive bar? Do you know how dangerous that is?"

Where was the outrage? His humiliation? I turned my back to him, slid off the dress. "I only drank a little."

"Were you trying to punish me?"

"Oh, Charles, no. I don't want to punish you." I put on my ancient nubby robe. I found my courage. "I want you to leave me."

And what I saw on his face when I turned back around? It wasn't rage or hate. It wasn't love, not exactly. Not the kind of glowing love he'd beamed at Janelle Before in our old wedding photos, the smitten way he'd looked at her that broke my heart. There was a fervent look in his eyes now, a hunger. He cupped my face in his hands. "My God, I've missed you."

How odd, I thought. How bewildering. It was Janelle Before he missed, you see. The dress and the derring-do had reminded him.

"Leave you?" Charles looked into my eyes. His tender smile unsettled me. "Oh, darlin'." He tucked my hair behind my ears, and my heart sank. "I'm not going anywhere."

So perhaps I was the one who needed to leave.

Leave Charles, leave Haven.

But take my children, of course.

This occurred to me one morning as I watched Burry and Mira climb into Lesley Moore's Mercedes station wagon.

The mothers didn't trust me to drive.

I had my license back by then. I drove to the store, to the hair salon, to the school to volunteer in the children's classrooms. But the mothers didn't allow me to join the carpool. They had a meeting and decided; I don't know how I knew that, but I did. They made excuses at first—they "had it covered," no need to "stress" myself. Every morning when a minivan or station wagon would pull into our driveway, Mira and Burry would run outside and get into the back seat, and whoever was driving, one of four mothers, would give me an okay sign or a thumbs-up, and they would wave me away, as if to say, Go lie down and rest, honey.

I volunteered to be a room mother in Mira's classroom. She was seven that year.

Dee Hines, the principal, spoke to me privately and said—because the teacher was too shy—that it wouldn't do to be a room mother, because I had to be alone with the children for short periods—and would I mind spending an hour to work with the children on crafts instead? Potatoes and toothpicks, paper towel rolls and fingerpaint, that sort of thing. Surely I understood? Some of the parents…

I stood up and left Mrs. Hines in her excruciating silence. I left the school, but I returned later to pick up Mira and Burry. I drove them up the mountain. I told them we were playing hooky. Daddy left me a little piece of land up there. There was an old hunting cabin. There was no power or running water inside the cabin. But it was still there. How peaceful it was. Just the three of us. No carpools or reprimands. I asked Mira and Burry if they wanted to live there.

"Where would we go to school?" Burry asked me.

"You could learn everything here," I said. "I will teach you. Like a one-room schoolhouse. All about birds and insects, and experiments for science, and your numbers. And we can read books together."

He seemed to mull it over. "Okay." My boy, always on my side. He was six when I almost died. Even today I wonder if his life is stunted, atrophied like mine, because of the accident.

"Is Daddy coming too?" Mira, not on my side, or her father's, really, but on the side of the marriage. Together. Family. Four of us. Maybe the age. Seven-year-olds are idealists.

"I don't think so."

Raising my children there, though! The memories of my own father made me feel safe.

We walked down the trail, to a little stream, and beyond, the belly laugh of the waterfall. The children made leaf boats and skipped rocks. We ate a bag of chips and a box of cookies. Burry found a turkey feather.

Darkness was coming, but it felt velvety, a comfort.

Fireflies flashed like paparazzi. Then I showed them the fairies. The field farther away, at dusk, turned magical. A carpet of tiny, glowing blue lights floating there, so luminous, so beautiful, it hurt me. Mira asked, Are they really fairies, Mommy? Burry told her they were insects. Maybe a special kind of lightning bug, and he showed her one in his hand, no bigger than a grain of rice.

Night fell there, at the river.

Ah, the river. That's where they found us.

That night, the sheriff took my children.

Mira and Burry were beside me, and the next instant, they weren't.

A deputy with his gun and his crackling radio told me to step aside, an ambulance was on the way.

I told him I wasn't sick. That we had a place to stay here.

"You mean that shed?" He pointed up the hill, to the old hunting cabin, nothing but a kudzu-covered ruin, a collapsed porch...

They took my children.

"Where are they?" I screamed. "Where are my children?"

He said, "Ma'am, ma'am, you need to calm yourself."

And then, the sound of tires on the dirt road. Charles.

Charles got out of the car and talked to the deputies alone, and then he led the children to me, holding their hands.

Charles embraced me and announced to the deputy, to the children, that everything was fine, it was just a mix-up. He told me, "You know I wouldn't let anything happen to you."

He whispered, "Next time, you will lose the children."

Lana leads me into a calm state after each session. She gives me smooth stones from the Twin River to keep in my pocket, talismans to run my fingers over at the slightest distress. I admit that when I leave the cabin, I'm often a tad agitated. But by the time Spec and I arrive in Haven proper, the turbulence has subsided, just as Lana assured me.

I do fret about compensating her. I pay her in dribs and drabs, as much as I can, but she assures me we will settle up later. Because our work together is so vital, she says, so fulfilling.

I am smiling more. I wave to Tina at the mailbox. Everyone seems friendlier somehow. Charles is pleased.

Only at night do I feel the old fear come over me. But Lana says that is expected. She tells me it may get worse before it gets better. She says I am making excellent progress.

18

CHARLES

"I got my invite," Arlene said. "Real nice paper, thick as a playing card."

"Yes," Charles said. "The invitations were mailed out this week." He smiled. How odd to feel proud. He'd nearly forgotten what that felt like.

"Never been to a wedding at a farm before."

"It will be dignified, Mira assures me. With all the right touches. Reagan has been advising her."

"Yeah, I bet."

"Arlene."

"Yeah, bossman?" She closed his office door and sat across from him. "You want to clean my clock, you go right ahead. But this don't sit right with me, all these fancy plans they're cooking up."

They, Reagan and Teddy, had yet to win over Arlene. But this rift must heal. Charles would hate to force Arlene into early retirement.

"To just hijack Mira's wedding like that."

"Hijack? It's all part of—"

"I know, I know. The branding rollout shindig or whatever." She made a retching sound.

"Look at this," he said. "And you'll change your mind." He pointed to his monitor and clicked on the link Reagan had emailed him that morning. Arlene came around, stood peering over Charles's shoulder as the Rex Wolf website opened, a "draft," Reagan had said, not yet "live," but look, it was magnificent.

"There, see—that picture is from our first year," Charles

said. "Someone from the newspaper came and took it. Stan and me, we'd deliver the paychecks to welders and electricians out in the field, take them Krispy Kreme donuts and Gatorade. To shore up morale and build relationships."

"Before direct deposit."

"That ruined things."

"If you ask me, you need your own lawyer to eyeball the deal with them. Just giving up half your company—"

"Arlene," he said with a sigh.

"You need to see how it's broke down and what all goes into it. You're giving up too much, if you ask me."

"I didn't ask. Rest assured I'm giving up half my owner-ship. It is my honor to do so. Teddy will capitalize. We will be co-owners."

"So owning half but not ponying up any cash just because his name is Rex?"

"He is Stan's boy. That's gold."

"I just don't want you up shit creek without a leg to stand on."

"It's already working. Reagan's plan." He cleared his throat. "Janelle is a regular social butterfly."

His wife now had a calendar filled with social events, as other wives did. A garden club meeting last week. A women's luncheon for some sort of wife-beating charity. Neighbors who waved. Unfortunately, she had also devoted herself to that strange child, Spec, the two of them with their picnics and drives in the country and whatnot. That boy with his vacant stare, his chubby, girlish stomach, his mottled caramel skin, his tippy-toed loping along with Janelle...the two of them together, well, not a pretty picture. They could be mistaken for a couple of loonies. Cruel, but perceptions often were. Still, it seemed a worthy compromise, as long as they stayed in the parks and out of sight.

"Well, that's hunky-dory, but maybe it's the calm before—"

"There is no storm, Arlene. Not this time."

"Uh-huh. And that pal of Janelle's you wanted to run out of town? That kooky foreigner?"

"I took care of that problem." That repulsive fraud had apparently hightailed it back to India. Janelle did not speak of her, did not dare say her name. Janelle knew he was right to protect her, to nip that sort of outrageous behavior in the bud.

"Janelle is...better." She took to her mother-of-the-bride role better than even he expected. No more PIs, for one thing, as she had ceased her ventures to the hotel bar. And that saved a bundle.

Arlene stood. "I hope you're right. Lord knows you deserve it."

Of course, he was right. Charles had learned to monitor his wife as vigilantly as a seismologist studying tremors on the Richter scale. And now, it was quiet. A new kind of quiet.

Janelle had dressed for lunch with Mira that very morning. They were going to a boutique to select a mother-of-the-bride dress for Janelle. He'd replenished Janelle's household account for that, of course, although she seemed lately to spend her allotted funds at an alarming rate, but he couldn't, he wouldn't, complain—not with the splendid turn of events. Not with Janelle finally, finally on the mend.

19

MIRA

It was barely noon on a Tuesday when Reagan walked into a nearly empty Bar None, shoved her oversized sunglasses on her head, squinted in the dimness until she spotted Mira, restocking wine glasses. Mira's first instinct had been to duck and hide behind the counter, but Reagan was too quick for her.

"Hey there. Can we talk?"

This isn't good, Mira thought.

Surely this was about the spreadsheet Reagan had emailed Mira weeks ago, an intricate, intimidating To Do list for the wedding that Mira hadn't updated, not in any timely way. Had to be it.

Because Teddy hadn't been in the bar in weeks. Banished and blocked.

"I have a few minutes before I head to my office. I thought I'd drop in for a face-to-face." Reagan in pale green linen, crisp and thin as a stalk of celery. Was she…could she possibly be pregnant? No, Reagan wouldn't sit on that news, surely. She'd tell Mira, gushing with happiness, Teddy and I are expecting!… wouldn't she?

"Sure. What did I forget?" Mira asked. Hours would go by, days sometimes, before she would respond to Reagan's nudges. Did you call the florist for a quote? Order the cakes? "I meant to text you."

"We can hash out all those deliverables now. No worries."

"Can I get you a drink?"

"Club soda with lime, thanks."

They sat at the high-top by the window.

Reagan had been in Bar None only once that Mira knew of.

A jam-packed Friday night back in the fall when Reagan and Teddy dropped by and Mira had been so slammed, she'd barely had time to acknowledge them. Thank God.

So why did Teddy appear now in her mind's eye, with his wide, craggy, almost handsome face and his dry-cleaned starched shirt, already loosening the noose of his royal blue tie as he took his usual seat? Damn him. Mira's cheeks burned, remembering Teddy's searching mouth, as if he wanted to devour her, his neck meaty and sweet, she'd nearly bit it—

"About the guest list," Reagan said. "The invitations have already gone out. The A-list is up to fifty. But things were a little tight, so we have a B-list. For any cancellations. And there are people who know this. Who want to be invited. News spreads fast."

"Is that good?" Mira asked.

"Oh, hell yeah. It's about creating demand." Reagan squeezed her lime into her water, then nibbled at the shriveled pulp. "These guests at your wedding. The 'movers-and-shakers' of Haven, as your dad calls them. It will be great for your career too. It doesn't hurt to know these people on a first-name basis, let me tell you."

But Mira was stuck on—"my career?"

"You are going to have one, right? I figured you and Nelson were settling in Haven."

This made a strange sort of sense. This was weirdly inspiring. Her career.

"You've got a master's degree?"

"I have an MFA in poetry."

"Hmmm." Reagan sipped her water. "I assumed you were planning to buy the bar."

"Bar None? No, I just bartend here."

"Listen to you. 'Just bartend.'"

"Sorry."

"Stop apologizing. Lean in, sister. You already run it, right? Why not own it?"

"I guess I never thought about it."

"Didn't I hear the owner was thinking of selling?"

"Kenny? He's selling Bar None?"

"Circling back to the tasks, Mira."

"Yeah?"

"There are some serious To-Dos this week. Like, ASAP tasks."

Mira nodded.

"Would Nelson mind wearing a tux?"

"Ummm." Nelson would mind paying for a tux.

"He'll be sooo adorable, a boho groom, suspenders, boutonniere, vest. I know a shop, a manager. I'll send you the address."

According to Reagan, Mira's theme was Rustic Bohemian. She and Nelson were having a boho country wedding.

"Also, catering. The catering manager at the club, could you meet with him this week? To review the menu I suggested? And Janelle's mother-of-the-bride dress. I made an appointment for that too."

"You've done a lot," Mira said. "I'm sorry I've been such a slacker. I'm on it. I promise."

Reagan took out her phone. "Texting you the deets."

She came home from work at midnight. Nelson was in bed. He'd be at the gym at dawn. She hated to wake him, especially for this—

She sat on the edge of the bed, felt him stir. He turned on the lamp.

"I want to talk to you about something important," she said. He yawned.

"Tomorrow you're going to need to rent a tux for the wedding, Nels."

His eyes went small and hard as pencil points. "And why did you realize this today?"

"Reagan came by the bar."

"Right. Okay, well. I get it now."

"Get what?"

"She sells. For a living. We can't have a wedding on steroids.

Remember the steps? We agreed to pay off all debt. Your student loans. Save for a house. Start a family. Five-year plan."

Yeah, five-year plan, she thought. Like Stalin.

Last month, Mira had pitched to him—yes, pitched—the idea of their wedding as a public display of healing and acceptance, with her father back in the loop, her mother back into the fold—

Nelson had balked. At first. "Mira, your mother's accident was decades ago. Who cares? Aren't most of those people dead anyway?"

"That's not how it works in Haven. The rumors…it's vicious."

She'd appealed to his personal motto of reinventing himself. Because…lard ass. That was one of the kinder nicknames flung at Nelson in high school. On their third date, he'd brought out his high school yearbook, kept on the shelf to illustrate his heroic tale, and pointed out to Mira the picture of a chubby-faced kid. Nelson's blue eyes, now one of his best features were, at sixteen, deep-set and hidden, like two glass marbles shoved into a ball of dough. Back then he was north of two hundred pounds, six feet tall, and flunking out of school because he missed so many days—to avoid the daily humiliations. LARD ASS! painted on his locker. Crisco cans left on his doorstep—that sort of thing. Mira had been moved to tears. "I can't believe you were the victim of such cruel bullying."

And he'd stopped her there. "Not a victim. Survivor. And stronger for it."

The best revenge was success, hadn't he said that? Well then, they were helping her parents succeed.

It was a stretch, but it worked. In the end, Nelson had reluctantly gone along with Mira's idea of a wedding with some "nice touches."

"But slippery slope," he said. "A few hours of fancy decorations."

A truce. And then she'd accidentally left out a receipt on the printer, the wedding cake estimate. How could you let your father be ripped off like that? Insane! Hundreds of dollars for CAKE?

That was a rough weekend.

Now Mira said the only thing that would work, but, God, she hated to—

"The cost of the tux will be covered, Nels."

"And we're still getting the wedding present from your parents, right? The whole ten grand?"

"Yes." Maybe. Probably. Mira didn't know yet. But no need to panic Nelson. Her father had offered the cash for a wedding present in lieu of a ceremony, back when she and Nelson were going to have a no-frills thing. But now that her father was pushing her for a bigger wedding, that changed things. Didn't it?

"Because, hey, I don't want us saddled with those 'special touches' or whatever you call them."

"You want it in writing? You want my dad to throw in a milking cow, a goat, and an acre? Like a real dowry?"

"Dowry." Nelson chuckled. "That's funny." He turned off the lamp.

Mira stepped into the bathroom to brush her teeth and calm down. When she was occasionally put off by Nelson's single-minded interest in fitness—physical and fiscal—she reminded herself how he had untangled her snarled, messy life. How he'd straightened out her credit report, advised her to consolidate her student loans (she'd been too proud to hit up her parents for all the tuition bills she'd racked up). How he was a stickler for checking expiration dates on food, so there was nothing fuzzy and rotting in the refrigerator. How he bought her vitamins, how he'd shared his hacks for a healthy lifestyle—and she was feeling good. Mostly.

It was almost cute, he'd told her once, how naive she was about the metrics of the world.

She and Nelson were opposites in some ways. Okay, a lot of ways. But, hey, that was a sign of a healthy relationship, that's what couples did—they cultivated their own individual interests; she read that somewhere. And if you were lucky, your partner in life could offset your own weaknesses.

It always cheered her to recall the serendipity of their first meeting, that day last summer, her first day back in Haven, visiting her parents. What if she hadn't been filling up her dusty Kia at a gas station as a group of teenagers with wilted posters fruitlessly begged motorists to submit to a five-dollar car wash, a fundraiser for their field trip to Dollywood? Mira, champion of underdogs, had yelled over, "Sure, I'd love a car wash." Then she'd emptied out the coins in her ashtray and found she was a dollar short.

"Hey, no problem. I got you," beamed the good-looking guy beside her, holding out a crisp fiver. Nelson.

Thirty minutes later, she had a clean car—and a date for dinner. She assumed at first Nelson was gay. A fit, clean guy like that with a certain GQ vanity—but she realized she'd just dated too many scruffy, insalubrious, broke academics. Nelson was straight, neat, and gainfully employed.

Every Saturday Nelson filled up her car with gas, threw out a week's worth of clutter that piled up on the floorboard and back seat, and washed her car. He organized her glove compartment, her proof of insurance and car registration on top of her owner's manual. That warmed her heart, because talk was cheap, but taking on these tedious errands? They were acts of love.

After she flossed her teeth, Mira took out her engagement ring from the medicine cabinet and slid it onto her finger. She never wore it to the bar; she was afraid she'd lose it. It was modest but striking, an opal in gold, and a little loose. Six months ago, Nelson had left the ring dangling on a pine tree air freshener in her car, his way of popping the question. She appreciated his attempt at cleverness, a way to make the moment memorable, a story we can tell our grandchildren, he'd said.

When she came back into the bedroom, Nelson was awake. He'd turned on the lamp again, his face half hidden in the shadows, the light illuminating his bare torso like a piece of Greek statuary. Her irritation fell away. She was lucky to have this man in her life.

"Come to bed," he said, patting the space beside him. "I missed you."

Mira pulled up to her parents' house the next morning. Her mother stood waiting.

"Are we going straight to the dress shop?" her mother asked when she got in the car.

"Lunch first," Mira said. "Then the boutique at two." It was good to feel in charge, like a daughter who had it together.

Never mind that the Kia's air conditioning turned from lukewarm to blow-dryer hot. Mira turned it off. It was one hundred degrees at high noon. Her mother fanned herself with a yoga brochure she found on the floorboard.

The dining room in the Haven Country Club was cold as a morgue. She and her mother stood there for a minute, their drenched clothes sticking to them, as if someone had hosed them off.

"We look a sight, don't we?" her mother said with a smile.

"We're dewy and glowing."

Her mother wore a lovely dress, the same one from her birthday weeks before. So what if she wore a floppy sun hat and white clogs, the kind nurses wear?

Today's tasks: sign off on the catering menu for the wedding reception and then off to the boutique to select a dress for Janelle and don't forget shoes, purse, accessories, etc. That prod from Reagan because Janelle could use some help coordinating an outfit; at least that's how Mira read it.

Mira asked for the catering manager. She was going to sign whatever they put in front of her. The club would cater the wedding reception at the farm. It had all been decided by Reagan and her father anyway.

The waiter led them to a table.

Mira ordered tuna salad with pickled peaches. Her mother, chicken salad. For a starter, pimento cheese and house chippers.

Then the waiter brought Mira and her mother two glasses of champagne. Compliments of Mrs. Moore.

"Who?" Mira asked.

"Is that Lesley Moore?" her mother said, peering at someone across the club's dining room, waving at them. A small woman with a silver bob and glasses. Mira recognized Mrs. Moore, mother of Cleo, who had been a year ahead of Mira in high school.

"And here she comes," Mira said under her breath.

"Janelle! I declare. I thought that was you." Mrs. Moore wore an expression of forced chumminess. "Mira—your engagement picture in Sunday's paper was lovely. Such a handsome young man you've landed."

Landed, Mira thought. As if I'd wrestled him down and roped him like a calf.

Mira thanked her for the champagne. She tried to remember if Mrs. Moore was on the wedding guest list. Maybe the B list? How embarrassing not to know.

"Janelle, you must be over the moon about the wedding. It seems like yesterday when I was driving you and Cleo in the carpool, Mira, picking you and Burry up in our station wagon every Friday—" Mrs. Moore sputtered to a stop, oops, and Mira could swear she saw Mrs. Moore's cheeks redden. "Janelle, we must get together for lunch soon."

Her mother nodded. "Yes." Hats off to Mom, for holding her own here, Mira thought.

"How about next week? Thursday?" Mrs. Moore persisted.

"I will check my calendar."

"I'll call you later."

Mira took a long sip of champagne.

"Mom," she whispered after Mrs. Moore left. "Was she one of the mean moms?"

"One of the…what?" her mother said, looking up from her menu.

"Was she one of those women who stopped inviting you to things…afterward?"

"Oh no, Lesley Moore wasn't one of them. They all were like that. Anyway. Bygones."

"Are you going to have lunch with her?"

"I will have to check my calendar."

Mira laughed. Good one. Then realized her mother was serious.

Her mother didn't look sad. A little pensive maybe, but her eyes flashed. "I suppose it would make your father happy, having lunch with Lesley Moore."

"Mom, you should have lunch with her if you want to. I mean, what's the big deal?"

"Oh, honey, in marriage, everything like this is a big deal."

"What do you mean, 'like this'?"

"One of those things you just can't agree on. You ignore it, mostly, but it stays and gets bigger, it swells, and everything else recedes. And then you can't see the thing the way it is anymore. The lens of marriage can magnify. It can warp."

Message received, Mira thought. Marriage is not easy. Carve out your own life. Navigate around those things. That's what her mother was telling her. Wasn't she?

"But you and Daddy are happy together."

"Yes." Her mother's dreamy, distracted look was back. "Everyone says so."

When they were back inside Mira's blistering sweat lodge of a car, she gave her mother an out. "Maybe we should just go for ice cream this afternoon. We'll do the bridal shop thing some other time."

"But we have to find your wedding gown."

"I already have my dress, Mom. I told you, this is for you. A mother-of-the-bride dress."

The thing was, Mira wanted the day to end on a high note. The Mrs. Moore thing, her mother so eerily self-possessed, that was oddly encouraging.

But her mother insisted on going to the shop. The heat

didn't bother her, she said, nothing bothered her, not today, didn't Mira see?

Her father would have given Mira a heads-up if something were amiss. Wouldn't he?

We have to handle your mother with kid gloves, as he used to put it. When Janelle took to her bed or wasn't making sense. This was when Mira was a child, obsessed with the Grimm fairy tales her mother read aloud to her. Mira thought kid gloves were made from the skin of children. Naughty, dead children. Today, Janelle seemed weirdly loquacious. No kid gloves needed.

"We're only going because Reagan arranged it."

"Is it far away? This shop?"

"No, it's just a few blocks away. Magnolia Bridal Boutique."

"Does Nancy Brown still own it?"

"Who's Nancy Brown?"

"She opened that boutique ages ago. Back when everyone wore Jackie Kennedy hats. Nancy Brown is married to Doug Brown, who was a great admirer of your grandfather. He was always on the other side of things. In the courtroom, I mean. He said Daddy always ruled against him. But they sent such a lovely flower arrangement to his funeral."

A few minutes later, they walked inside Magnolia Bridal Boutique. A wall of mirrors glittered like ice. The whispery white taffeta and silk dresses rustled in the small showroom, as the door closed behind them.

"Janelle Wolf!" a crackly voice boomed from the corner. "What a pleasure!"

"Nancy," her mother said as the elderly woman limped over, leaning on a cane.

Nancy leaned in and bestowed an air kiss on Janelle's cheeks. More warm greetings for Mom!

"I haven't seen you in years."

"Not since Stan's election night," her mother said.

Stan? Elections? Her mother never spoke of such things.

"We have the dresses ready," Nancy Brown said. "Right this way. Erica! Erica, they're here."

The back of the shop was one large fitting room. In the center, a round velvet couch, pocked with gold buttons. On a small table, a pitcher of lemonade with mint sprigs and citrus slices and a plate of gingersnaps arranged in a daisy pattern. Also, Mira and Nelson's engagement announcement from the newspaper, laminated and framed, along with a display of the wedding invitation. Holy moly, these people went all out.

Erica, Mrs. Brown's granddaughter, a former runway model, gangly but adorable as a baby giraffe, was going to take over the shop after what Mrs. Brown called her "imminent demise." Mrs. Brown would probably keel over right there if she knew Mira had ordered her own wedding dress on eBay.

"You know," Erica told Mira, "Reagan dropped by." Of course, she did. "She told us all about the plans for Rex Wolf, and Teddy is running for his daddy's seat. Oh my God. So exciting."

Yes, Mira admitted it was.

Erica said, "We have five gorgeous dresses we thought we'd start with, Miss Janelle." She pointed to a portable rack.

Her mother went straight to the blue one. "This one. It's heavenly."

"That cerulean hue is fabulous," Erica said.

Mira helped her mother try on the dress, behind a creamy velvet curtain.

"I'll take this one. I'm sure."

"But, Mom, you haven't tried on the others. Don't you think you should just—"

"I love this one. The blue. It's the color of porch ceilings."

"Okay, easy peasy. I'll let them know."

"Mira?" Her mother clutched her arm and looked frantic for the first time that day.

Uh-oh. "What's wrong?"

"How much is this dress?"

"That's a good question." Mira looked for a price tag

and didn't find one. Would it be super tacky to call over Erica-the-adorable-baby-giraffe and ask? Yes, it would. It definitely would.

"I don't know how much it is, Mom." Sticker shock, that was a given for a woman who still wore clothes from decades ago. "We're going to need to get your shoes and purse while we're here too. We'll get them to total it all up."

"I'll ask them to hold it. Or maybe I can put it on layaway."

"Mom, no. God, no. You can't lay it away like it's Sears or something."

Her mother began to slide the dress off.

"Wait. They're going to want to see it on you."

"I don't know if I can pay for it."

"What do you mean? You don't have your wallet?"

"I only have twenty dollars," her mother said. "I don't want to pester your father again about the household expenses."

Not following, but okay, Mira thought. Her father had told Mira he'd replenished her mother's account. Money is no object. See to it your mother selects the fanciest dress there. Perhaps her mother had forgotten? This would be embarrassing if they walked out without buying anything.

"I'll cover it, Mom. I'll square it with Dad later."

"Oh, honey. Are you sure?"

"Hey, it's all from the same pot." Pulling out the expression that Nelson detested. Let's just pool our money and pay the bills out of one pot. You'd think she'd suggested they join a nudist colony. Are you crazy? He pointed out there was no one pot but many cups. Categories. Line items. That's how budgets worked.

"You won't tell your father, will you?" her mother whispered. "He'll be cross with me. About the household account. About not managing it."

Yeah, Mira got that. Boy, did she. Another one of those "things" in marriage her mother had warned her about. Nelson would be more than cross if he saw charges from a bridal shop, even if she did discreetly hit up her dad for reimbursement.

Erica helped her mother select shoes, which they would send out to be dyed to match the cerulean blue of her dress. Also, a cute, exorbitantly expensive clutch purse. Mira put it all on her new Visa—for "emergencies," like this one.

"Janelle, you will come and see me again? Humor an old friend?" Mrs. Brown said as they left.

"Certainly," her mother said. "I will check my calendar."

"Mom, you're popular," Mira said in the car.

"It appears the cloud is lifting," her mother said. "Doesn't it?"

Mira had Reagan to thank for this. Her mother wasn't lonely anymore!

That pretty much made up for the fight with Nelson later, and what happened that night at the bar with Teddy.

She sent Reagan a text: BIG thank you. Tasks done. Everything went great.

Reagan texted back a few minutes later: GR8. Finalizing interview 4 magazine, 4 Janelle & Charles. Yr mom up for it?

Up for it? Her mother was "up for it," all right. Janelle was just fine. Better than fine.

Better than Mira.

20

TEDDY

Teddy arrived at Bar None expecting Mira's ire. Looking forward to it. Sure, she'd claim to be pissed off—but Mira could never hide that I've-missed-you longing in her eyes.

What he didn't expect was this—Mira, all business with a neutral smile, as if he were any old customer.

"It's been weeks since I've entered the portals of this fine establishment," he announced when he finally caught her eye. "I've served my sentence. I was hoping to catch a break for good behavior."

That's when she said, "What'll it be, T-Rex?"

First off. T-Rex? No one called him that now but wonks, pundits, and sarcastic bloggers. Second—pilsner on draft. His drink without having to be asked. Always.

"Pilsner," he said.

When she set the beer in front of him, he glimpsed a shimmery powder on her eyelids, some blush on her cheeks. Not like her to wear the stuff. She had on a belt tonight with her jeans, the bottle opener peeking out of one back pocket, the rectangle of her phone in the other. A little baggy, those jeans, on that exquisitely soft heart-shaped ass. Was she losing weight? Maybe, and his heart leapt at this. Maybe she'd lost her appetite because she was sick about the wedding. The thought of getting hitched to that asshole pretty boy was making her nauseated.

It was making Teddy nauseated.

He checked Nelson's feed on Facebook occasionally. Maybe five or six times a day. Just last night—Teddy checked his phone in bed, scrolled through and gah!—Nelson's shirtless selfies, another of his bizarre peppy posts: *I was sleepwalking for eighteen years, ignorant of my own willpower, stuffing my face, always broke, going along, believing the world "out there" owed me something. Then I started to measure and manage my own life. To take responsibility. People really need to know about the sovereign right of the individual. They need to wake the hell up.* He'd actually had this ridiculous "philosophy"—*If you can measure it*—tattooed on his left arm. *You can manage it,* on his right. Apparently, the dumbass needed his life philosophy inked—so he wouldn't forget it.

Teddy had caught himself grunting in disgust. Reagan, tapping out some midnight directive on her iPad, mumbled, "What's wrong?"

"That narcissistic ass-wipe."

"Which one?"

"What's-his-face. Nelson." And then in a deft move, shifting the conversation ever so slightly to the issue Reagan would latch on to, "Can you believe that libertarian crap he's spouting? Can you imagine him talking to Caldwell Pinkershine or Townes Gardenwell at the…" Wedding. But Teddy couldn't bring himself to say it. "The reception?"

"Don't worry, babe. I'm handling it."

Reagan said she'd already told Mira that Nelson's role was to stand like a "super-buff mannequin" in his tuxedo. That's all he needed to do, "stand there and not say a word, except 'I do,' and he'll be a hit."

A hit. Really. "Aren't you objectifying him? That thing you women are always bitching about?"

Reagan stopped typing and honored him with an amused glance. Then her fingers resumed their tap-tap-tapping. "Nothing wrong about being admired," she said. "You know I'm not the type to complain about that."

A few more people wandered into Bar None now, straggly, tired, after-work types, clearly there to suck up the cheap draft and free boiled peanuts. Crawley sauntered over with a bucket of ice. Not much help, he moved with the speed of a tranquilized sloth, but a giant sloth, which was the point. Security. What was it about Mira, that she surrounded herself with dumbass knuckle-draggers? No wonder she liked talking to Teddy. She craved intellectual stimulation.

"Another?" Mira asked him, after he made a big show of slurping up the last drops of his beer.

"Yep. And can you just—"

She didn't look at him as she filled his glass, but she was within earshot.

"Drop this robotic shit? The polite tone is killing me."

"Here you go," she said with courtesy as frosty as the mug of beer she slid in front of him. Quick as a flash, he touched her wrist.

"Hey, tear me a new one if you want. I'll take a little steam over this businesslike act."

"It's not an act," she hissed.

"Thank you. See, that's better. I'm warming myself in the heat of your fury."

She ignored him. After his next beer, he played the ace up his sleeve.

"Actually, I came here seeking your autograph." He pulled out a copy of her poetry chapbook, *All My Previous Lives*. That stopped her.

"I ordered it online," he said proudly.

"Why? I have a whole box of them in my apartment."

"So you said, but you never honored me with a copy of your book, as much as I begged."

"I guess you bought one of twelve copies sold."

"I not only bought it, I read it. Numerous times, as a matter of fact."

"And?"

The collection was about a reincarnated woman who finally achieves enlightenment and becomes a powerful, beloved world leader. Each poem was about one of the woman's previous lives as an antebellum slave trader, an oil baron, a serial killer, and a hedge fund manager. Teddy appreciated the narrative arc. He was tempted to tell Mira he found her book "crisply imagined and startlingly inventive," as one fancy-pants critic called the collection (of course he researched and read the few reviews), but she might assume he was toying with her. He couldn't risk offending Mira now that he had her full attention.

"It blew me away."

There. He caught the faintest flutter of excitement in her eyes, a little ping of eagerness. Something she wanted to talk to him about. Get his opinion. Like the old days. Like last month.

"Alas," she said. "There's no money in poetry."

"And no poetry in money, as some famous luminary whose name I can't remember once said."

Her laugh, how he missed it. They were hitting their old rhythm.

"Maybe I'll buy the bar."

Teddy tried to look surprised. Reagan had filled him in on this curious angle. "I don't think it even occurred to Mira to buy Bar None. Can you believe it?" Reagan told him. Souls lacking direction were, for Reagan, hopeless wraiths without purpose, floating on the outer ring of hell. "She's so disorganized. A real shit show."

"About the wedding?" he'd asked Reagan.

"About her life. And I just don't have the time right now to advise her, as much as she wants it. I mean, I did what I could. We talked a little about careers. I planted a seed, that she should buy the bar. It never occurred to her, can you believe it? Anyway. Her wedding to-do list—get on it. That was my main point. And I tried to be nice about it."

"Maybe," he'd said carefully, "Mira doesn't want the wedding?"

"Teddybear!" Reagan laughed. "Don't panic." Reagan had made a pistol with her index finger, blew it, tucked it back into her pretend holster. "I got Mira back on track. Mission accomplished."

Now, Teddy looked at the ceiling of Bar None, appraising. "Good bones. Tin ceiling under that paint—"

"I know. I love the building."

He raised his eyebrows, interested—in watching the play of light on her thick black curls, half captured in a ponytail.

"You could make it a great pub," he said. "Rescue this dive."

"Shhhh," she said. They both looked over at Crawley, dreamily wiping down a high-top table in large, loopy circles, as if he were demonstrating slo-mo tai chi. "I don't want anyone to get the wrong idea."

"No danger there," Teddy said, head tipping toward Crawley. Ideas? As if. "What would you call it?"

"The Get Lit Pub. And it wouldn't be a bar. More of a speakeasy...and a bookstore."

"Okay, that's brilliant right there," he said. "I mean how many bookstore-slash-bars are there?"

After a few minutes of settling tabs and slicing limes and oranges, she came back. The eagerness in her eyes killed him. Killed him. Did she even know the bar wasn't for sale?

She somehow spotted his reluctance, though he tried like hell to hide it. "So," he asked. "Kenny is selling?"

"No, Kenny's not selling. Are you kidding? Never here, and yet the man must be raking in some cash. Why would he want to mess up a good thing?" She sighed. "It was just fun to work on the idea, a new project. To pretend. I just wanted the challenge, the distraction of...never mind."

"So, do it somewhere else. Down the street. Run Kenny out of business."

"Yeah, like that's going to happen." She slid an olive into her mouth in a practiced, furtive gesture that never failed to arouse him.

"Why not? You nailed the vision."

"Apparently there are liability issues and risk—there is a high rate of failure for bars and restaurants...I've been told."

By Nelson, Teddy thought. Of course. Mr. Manage It And Measure It.

"Well, yeah, but it's a great idea, the Get Lit Pub. And, of course, you can do it."

Something fell in her face; the excitement drained away.

"What's wrong?"

She shook her head, grabbed a clutch of empty wine glasses, dunked them in the small sink.

He waited. He studied the back of her neck. Finally—

"This," she said, turning around. "This is wrong."

She whispered something to Crawley, then disappeared in the back.

Teddy waited a respectable four minutes. Then followed.

She stood in the alley.

He kicked away the empty glass crate wedged in the back door. It clanged shut.

"This has to stop," she said, meeting his eyes. "Whatever it is. This…keening lust."

He let that statement go, let it rise above the smells of cigarette butts and garbage around them and float off like a rogue balloon.

"I thought I was having a heart attack again the other night."

The concern on her face was a gift.

"Thirty-year-old guys don't have heart attacks," she said. "Do they?"

"Just heartbreaks."

"Stop."

Any second now she would turn to go back inside, any second. And he had so much to tell her—

She put her hand on the door handle and for the second time that night he touched her wrist, this time letting his fingers linger, and just that strip of her warm skin jolted him, jolted her, too, he could tell. She closed her eyes for an instant, as if gathering her strength.

"I miss talking to you. I miss…this."

"This?" she said. "Standing in a back alley that smells like piss and garbage?"

"We have something here. Admit it, Mira. I think about you all the time. Since that night—"

"That night was three years ago, Teddy."

"That's my point. I still think about—"

"And in those three years you A, got engaged and B, married. And married well, by the way. You made the right choice."

"You cut me off. I called, remember? I emailed. You iced me out."

"You were engaged."

"I should have tried harder. I admit it. I should have tracked you down. I'm paying for it now. My mistake." He held a hand over his heart. "You think I'm making this up?"

She laughed. Laughed! "You know what's funny? I don't. I don't doubt your sincerity, Teddy. I think you believe you're telling the truth. You have this uncanny ability to believe yourself. Whatever tale you come up with. Your capacity for self-deception is breathtaking."

"Now, see. That's what I love. Who else is going to insult me so eloquently?"

"Plenty. Legions."

"But I won't love it."

"This can't continue."

"What, talking? Can't we just talk?"

"But we can't just talk. These intimate chats, they just fan the flames."

"We haven't talked like this for weeks, Mira. I stayed away. Like you asked. But come on, you didn't miss this?" Miss me, is what he meant. You didn't miss me?

"Look. You're married," she said. "And I'm about to be. So, yeah, the fling has flung. It's over, Teddy. So don't show up here anymore. Please."

The door behind them burst open, the cacophony of bar noises poured out. One of the kitchen guys brought out a bulging bag of trash, threw it in the dumpster. Mira said something to him in Spanish, he said something back, and they both laughed. No doubt at Teddy's expense. Teddy didn't mind.

When they were alone again, he said, "I'm definitely going

to run for the House next year. Republican primary. Which is essentially the same thing, since there won't likely be a Democrat on the ticket."

"You want my blessing?"

"Right now, I'd settle for a handshake."

"Well, I'm not voting for you."

"I'd be shocked if you did."

"You're lucky to know what you're good at, though. Going confidently in the direction of your dreams."

"I never thought of myself as a Transcendentalist, but thanks. I'll take even faint praise."

She smiled at that, and he felt a rush of happiness. He'd made her smile, even if she pretended to be furious at him.

"I'm going now," he said.

She nodded. "You should."

He didn't move.

He leaned over and kissed her, her warm mouth opened, and she kissed him back, hard.

Now her hands were running up his arms, his hands moving inside her blouse. This is happening, he told himself, this is happening, they were going to—

She pushed him away. He stepped back, lost his balance, knocked over a stack of empty crates.

"We have to stop! Stay away from Bar None, Teddy. Promise me."

"I promise to try."

"Not good enough."

His shrug infuriated her.

"I will tell her, T-Rex, so help me. I'll tell Reagan."

"I'm not carousing at a bar for cheap thrills, Mira. I'm in love."

"Love?"

The word echoed, ricocheting in the narrow alley, bouncing merrily on the old bricks. Love, love, love. Even in the dimness, he could see the red splotches on her cheeks, as if she'd been slapped.

"I have something to say," she said finally, "and you need to hear it."

"But—"

"Listen!"

"Okay. Okay, I'm listening."

"I spent the afternoon with my mother," she said, and again he sensed her pent-up desire to talk to him, to discuss, to share. "We had lunch at the club and then we went shopping. Average, boring, wonderful day. I used to feel like my mom and me, like we'd reversed roles. I was the mother, and she was the scandalized bullied child with no one to sit with in the lunchroom. You know how ashamed I am for finally realizing how sad and shunned my mother has been all these years? But not anymore. For the first time, people she's known for years are friendly."

"I'm glad," he said. What a lame thing to say. Ridiculous. Where was his verbal dexterity when he needed it the most?

"You're glad? You don't know what this means to me, Teddy. To have a normal day with my mother." Her eyes were bright with tears.

"Oh yeah, yeah, I do know. Christ, Mira, I was at your house the week my father died. With your mother. You and Burry were running the household. I remember. I know what that means. I get it."

"You do. Yes. And that's even worse."

"I don't—"

"My father—he worships you. Like your father came back from the dead. Stan again, his best friend. The new Rex Wolf, that's all he can talk about, and so-and-so bigwigs are coming to my wedding—"

"Yes, but—"

"Let me finish. And this 'reinvention' of Rex Wolf. The plan to wrest control of the narrative or whatever? The website, the timeline, the press campaign. It's brilliant. And Reagan put it together, and hats off to her. Your wife. She has more talent and smarts in her little finger than you have—"

"No argument there."

She gave a sad little laugh. "You don't want the life you've chosen, your marriage, your bright, shiny, perfect political future? Fine. Torpedo it all. That's on you. But leave me out of it."

"You think I haven't tried?"

"I'm not the pin in your grenade, Teddy."

She stormed back inside. Teddy followed and sat at the bar. It took a good ten minutes before she got close enough to pretend not to hear him. "You can't throw your life away for Janelle and Charles," he said in a frantic whisper. "Your mother wouldn't want that, for you to go through with a wedding just because—"

She stacked dirty plates, not even a glance his way, and took them to the kitchen.

When she returned with a tray of clean glasses he said, "Mira, don't marry that guy."

She didn't ignore him that time.

"I am marrying a man who isn't perfect." Her voice was quiet but furious. "But he isn't complicated. He is practical and rational, and I need that. He doesn't yearn like some lovesick twelve-year-old and wallow in misery. You're not going to screw it up, T-Rex."

The bar mirror behind the rows of liquor bottles reflected an idiot staring back at her, stunned and desperate. Teddy wasn't used to seeing desperation on his own face. He opened his mouth to…what? To beg? He closed it.

"Now go home, T-Rex. To your wife. Go work on your spring baby."

"Crawley, I'm going home," she announced. She went to the back and Teddy followed, calling to her. Ignored again.

She came back out with her purse and told Crawley she was sick. "Is it the wings?" Crawley told her. "Because I just ate a whole bowl of them. I feel sorta sick too."

"Not my problem," she said. "Let Kenny worry about it."

Crawley, the big galoot, managing the bar for the night? Mira couldn't be serious. Teddy stood beside him watching Mira go. "But what should I tell the boss?" Crawley asked.

"Tell him I left early. To be with the man I love."

Go work on your spring baby. In bed that night, nursing his broken heart, Teddy would seize upon those words, turn them over and over in his sleep-deprived mind. Your spring baby. He wrung out that phrase until he squeezed out a green glint of jealousy, and he found some tiny comfort in it. Mira had held that tidbit back, but blurted it out anyway, horrified at herself. Teddy smiled to himself in the dark. She loved him.

21

LANA

Lana Skyped with Petya as soon as she got back to the cabin, trusting that his face—and the rest of him—would lift her mood. There he was, tanned and scrubbed, the shabby apartment wall with its dented drywall, like a cheap movie set, behind him. It was still light in Las Vegas, different time zone, yes, but then it was never dark there. Unlike this creepy place, surrounded by inky-black woods and the eerie drones of cicadas.

"Lana! Baby! I am waiting all day until I see you." A bit effusive for her taste, but never mind, she was paying plenty for it.

"Petya, you're my tonic."

"You are my gin."

God help us. Don't talk, honey. Just smile and listen and nod.

Petya's boyish, eager face distorted, then froze, and she nearly lost the connection.

"Are you there?" she said, as he flickered back. "You have no idea what I've been through. I am sick of living in the sticks."

"What is 'sticks'?" he murmured, turning the term erotic.

"A place with wonky internet and skunk weed."

"You want feel better?" he said and tore off his tank top.

"Keep your shirt on for now, Petya. Literally."

"Now you. Take off."

"Later, my sweet. Business first, okay? Did you check on that Yak-Yak app?"

"Yes. Will work. Mask IP address. Latva says good for a non moose."

"Anonymous. Thank God. Well, all the pieces are falling into place, then."

And what glorious pieces they were.

Haven was the kind of hidebound town that besmirched people like Janelle. An accident on a bridge, decades ago, not adequately explained. Plenty of envious ignoramuses invented tragic, dark intentions. Poor Janelle. Lana had plundered through the trove of online archived newspaper articles. And then—another benefit of crashing Janelle's birthday—witnessed the senator's son and that wife of his…all their plans, their spinning, like spiders. No wonder Charles hated Lana with every cell of his body.

Sometimes Lana humored herself, thinking she and Janelle were in this together, that Lana was on the cusp of liberating that poor soul from Charles Wolf and his ilk. She had become rather fond of Janelle. The warmest she felt toward any of her clients.

"This is my biggest project ever," she told Petya. "If I pull this off, we'll be in high cotton, my love."

"Where is high cotton?"

"It means we'll hit the jackpot." She had to remember to scrub the idioms with Petya—it was tiring having to explain. She wasn't a language tutor, for God's sake. But "jackpot" he understood. There were dollar signs in his dazzling blue eyes.

"When we together?"

"Soon. I almost have what I need. Just a little more."

"Lana, my lady love, Luka and Vlad asking again."

Lana poured herself a shot of tequila and bolted it. "I don't need this shit right now."

"But you said tell you—"

"Yes, yes. Tell me. I mean their bullshit, Petya. Those goons hang on like a bad case of the clap."

"What is clap?"

"Just…what did they say?"

"No thing. They ask where are you. They ask many, many where are yous. I say who, do not know. They want what is O."

"I don't owe them a cent."

"You are hero. For me."

"Thank you, sweet buns."

Getting sex workers a little kickback, that was noble of her, if she did say so herself. Lucrative, too. While it worked. A little research on her part, then targeting some higher-up executives in Vegas, from cereal companies to tire manufacturers—"on business" in Vegas—and voilà! A few call girls and boys with hidden cameras, a ten-second video of naughty business, a well-placed email, and a whole lot of loot. She'd split the proceeds with her "contractors," of course, but she cut out their pimps. And what nasty goons they were. She'd had to slip out of Vegas when it all got out of hand.

And then to Arizona with Betty—chump change.

But this.

This project. Janelle had given Lana so much material—

And more, always more. The latest from Janelle, about Mary Rex, another kink Lana had to explore.

This tale had more layers than baklava. More nuts too.

And Spec, pure luck to have him, too, a boy whose singular channels and obsessions were almost too easy to leverage. Yeah, she'd had to take in some stray mutt and lucked out to "adopt" that turtle from a gas station. But it was all shaping up. Oh, it was a beautiful thing.

"Lana, I love you now?"

"Knock yourself out, Boy Toy."

She took another shot of tequila. "Hey, Petya, you know what?" She'd slipped into her native tongue, her hometown accent muscling through. She had to watch that, reel it in.

"What is to know?"

"The world would be a better place if all men were like you."

He showed his dazzling bleached teeth.

Luscious, dim, and compliant.

22

JANELLE

Mary visited me alone after my accident. Once.

This was early spring, when I spent the days on a hospital bed in my living room. Every day the physical therapist arrived to torture me. I looked at picture books with Mira. Reading was still hard, so I made up stories about wicked queens and unicorns. I was learning words again, right along with Mira.

I woke up one afternoon and there was Mary, sitting across from me. She held a vase of gladiolas and carnations—joyless, stiff flowers, a bouquet for funerals.

"Janelle, I would have come sooner. Charles said you weren't up for visitors."

Mary wasn't adept at social graces. Not at first. Her grandparents raised her on a small farm in Tennessee. Her mother had run off after Mary was born, and never told anyone who Mary's father was. Mary told me once that her grandparents never forgave her for her mother's sins. They didn't allow her to wear shorts or pants, she couldn't watch television or go to movies, she couldn't be alone with boys. The day she turned eighteen, she ran away to Atlanta.

But she couldn't leave behind the burden of her upbringing, because she was ashamed of it—being abandoned by her mother, being born into sin and out of wedlock, as she called it. She cut off all communication with her grandparents, not even attending their funerals later. Not that they expected her to. They left the farm and property to their church. She wouldn't discuss her childhood with anyone besides me and Stan, she said. But I told her she had to find a way to talk about it.

She had to learn how to be in the public eye.

She got better at decorum. She had to.

But on that day when she visited me after my accident, she couldn't hide the horror of seeing me, the scar down my arm, the bandages, my poor shaved head, with patches of hair just growing back.

She said, "How are you?"

How was I? She could see for herself.

"Is there anything I can do for you?"

"Yes. I want to know what happened."

But it came out slowly, sound by sound. My speech was recovering—so my doctor claimed—I didn't even sound drunk anymore, just thoughtful. That...night. What...happened? Like that.

She looked down and after a while she said, "It was heartbreaking. By the time we heard the sirens..."

Then she cried a little. That made me angry. How could she come here and bring her pity!

She stood and put the flower arrangement on the coffee table and then I saw.

She was expecting.

That's why she hadn't come before to visit me. Not because I wasn't up for visitors. Mary was expecting a child. And there was a glow about her she tried to conceal, yet the light leaked out from her eyes, melted her frozen smile. She couldn't hide her happiness.

She saw my astonishment through the bruised wounds on my face. I know she did.

"Janelle, I'm sorry. This must be hard for you."

She was radiant. And yet she visited me. Mary, swollen with that new life, and I was...

Wrecked.

Lana, I can make the pictures come alive now. Did you know that? I see episodes from the life of Janelle Before.

I remember, I remember. I gather it all together, I recompose.

The paper in my notebook is damp from my bath, the ink blurs, the pages warp and yellow like parchment in a museum, a sacred document that changes things. You told me don't let up, we will sift through it all, and that gives me strength. The words are coming so fast now, Lana. A portal is open.

The election returns are coming in. Stan is on stage, giving his victory speech. But something he says—

It's fun.

My headache comes on so hard and fast, I think I am dying.

Honored to serve the voters…supporting strong family values…working to keep your tax dollars here at home, not in Washington…I do this for you, the voters, and it's hard work. But tonight, my friends, you make it worth it. Let's celebrate. It's time for some fun.

Just a little fun.

There is a retching sound and it's coming from me. Right here, in the crowded first row.

Stan doesn't pause. People pretend they don't see me. Maybe they don't.

When I am invisible, I am glad.

A sour stream of broccoli, ranch dressing, cheese, and grapes fills my mouth. I hold it back with my fist.

Someone spirits me away. Priscilla. She takes my elbow and leads me through the crowd, whispering *My goodness, are you all right?* My goodness. And then we are alone in the ladies' room.

Did you do that on purpose?

I go into the stall and throw up while Priscilla waits. I come out and splash water on my face.

Don't do that! Now your makeup is going to be—good Lord, Janelle, you look like a drunk raccoon.

I wipe off my makeup. Priscilla warns me how terrible I look.

She tells me to use her lipstick and rouge and eyeliner. She always carries an emergency makeup kit; she learned that trick from me…before.

I don't want to think about Janelle Before.

Priscilla tells me I am staying put, as if I wanted to go back out there.

I go into a stall and tell her to leave me alone. I ask for aspirin. She complains and then goes in search of some.

The door opens, the sounds of applause and music squeeze in, then the door closes.

And then it opens again, revelry and cheers, before the door shuts it off.

Footsteps.

I recognize Mary's shoes. She wears red stilettos with a drab, demure lace-collared dress. She stood beside Stan on the stage, and now she is here.

I step onto the toilet lid, to hide myself. I sense her eyes sweeping the tiled room like a flashlight. Is she looking for me?

The door swings open again. My minder swoops in. With aspirin. Announces that poor Janelle has some awful bug that's going around.

There is nothing to do but come out, where Priscilla and Mary wait. If Mary were thoughtful, another kind of woman, she would leave. Spare me. But no. She stands there. To make sure I'm "all right."

Mary says Burry is such a nice young man. "And Mira is so good with little Teddy. He adores her. I hope you don't mind, I slipped her a little cash tonight. For keeping an eye on Teddy. He's a handful."

Priscilla thinks Mary is being so considerate.

More women come into the ladies' room. They distract Priscilla. Mary leans in, her breath warm and moist on my ear. She whispers, "I still hate him."

In my living room all those years before, when she'd brought her funeral bouquet and her swollen belly and her happiness to my sickbed to witness my disfigurement, she'd looked at me, appalled. Now she wore a different expression in that crowded restroom, a sort of weary resentment that she quickly tucked away behind her practiced, empty mask of a smile.

I slip out of the ladies' room. It is important that I see my children when I lose myself. There is Mira, her hand on little Teddy's shoulder, scolding him, handing him a glass of punch. And outside, Burry is sneaking a cigarette with the kitchen boys. Mira and Burry. Mira and Burry. My mantra. My children! My children calm me, center me, remind me...to stay.

Charles finds me in the parking lot. I tried to disappear, but he finds me. He always does.

It is awful, how he is riding on the coattails of Stan. Parading me around when everyone pictures Janelle Before and how SHE would have done things right. I feel their icy pity. The carpool mothers. Our neighbors. Mira is old enough to bear the burden, and Burry, his eyes flashing anger at Charles.

"I can't go back inside, Charles. I can't. My headache...it's very bad tonight, Charles."

He says I have made a scene. He says I must go back in. They will talk if I don't. I have to, for the family. Just a brief appearance. A quick photo. "Janelle, listen to me. Someone might call an ambulance. If they take you to the hospital, you'll have to stay there. What will I tell the children? They will keep you this time."

I must pose for one picture, for the newspaper. Then we can leave.

I go back inside and pretend I am happy to be a shadow of Janelle Before. For the business and to save Charles's dignity, for the sake of our family, our good name, though he doesn't say that. He doesn't have to.

Inside, the newspaperman takes our pictures. I don't remember posing with Charles and the children, but I must have. We gather and smile, all of us with Stan and Mary and little Teddy, the two wholesome families, the two men behind Rex Wolf—

I have the clipping. Here we are, see? Front page news. There I am, perfectly normal.

Mary and Stan are the only people not looking at me.

PART III

JULY 2015

23

SPEC

A grumpy man ran the produce stand. The man always sat on a lawn chair and followed Spec with his eyes. He thought Spec would steal something small like a peach or a pecan. The man didn't have a cash register or a calculator or even a pencil. He did the numbers in his head and told Grandmother how much it cost. It was always hot in there, with just one fan, and a lot of flies. That was probably why the man was grouchy.

Spec put newspapers across the leather back seat of Grandmother's car, and then he loaded the plants and cartons of fruit.

"We'll need to drive slowly around the curves," she told him. "Those tomato plants are delicate. They're rather spindly, aren't they? I hope they're healthy. It's late in the season, but Lana wants to grow tomatoes. The big, meaty kinds, the yellow ones, the ugly heirlooms, and the tiny ones. She wants to make salsa and sauce. She has all sorts of plans for a fall garden. I'm so relieved she's staying. That's what a garden is, Spec. It's for optimists. It means you're putting down roots."

Grandmother talked like this to Spec, talked and talked, but he didn't have to pay attention if he didn't want to.

They turned off the curvy, steep highway. And then it was time for Spec to drive over the bridge and up the rutted dirt road. He knew now where the big holes were. He parked in the driveway and his grandmother took out some plants and he took the rest, and they went to the back of the cabin. Spec picked up Biscuit the puppy and she licked his face. The chicken ladies scratched in the thick brown dirt. Lana waited there. She was wearing a bikini top and cutoffs and a cowboy hat. She waved them over and pointed. "This is the sunniest spot."

"We've brought tomatoes, basil, and rosemary," Grandmother said. "You're going to have a bumper crop."

"Janelle, you're going to ruin another pair of sandals," she said, looking down at Grandmother's shoes.

"It doesn't matter. I have more."

"Here, take these. Just slip them on." Lana stepped right out of her tall plastic rainbow boots, then handed over her garden gloves.

"But what will you wear?"

"I'll find something else. I've got to go inside, and I need Spec's assistance. Here, my hat. You don't want a sunburn."

"Are you sure?"

"Yes. You look smashing."

Grandmother wore the cowboy hat slanted over her large round sunglasses; the boots came up to the edge of her dress. "Spec, your grandmother is the cat's pajamas, isn't she?"

Spec shook his head because cats didn't wear pajamas. Unless she meant cartoon ones.

"We'll be right back. This way, Spec."

Spec carried Biscuit inside and checked on Shelly in her glass house.

"The turtle is fine, okay?" Lana said. "You can feed it worms later." Lana led him to the desk. "We have to work fast." Her voice turned hard and fast now, like she was a different person. "It's important."

He sat down in front of her computer. She always complained about the internet, how it was so freaking awful up here. She typed for a minute. "Do you know what a contingency plan is?"

"I don't like vocabulary and spelling."

"It means a backup plan. If something doesn't turn out the way you want it to, then you have another plan. A contingency plan."

Grandmother's voice floated over to them from the screened window in the kitchen. She was talking to someone. Lana said, "Who in the hell...?" She stood up and watched Grandmother.

"Oh, thank God, she's talking to the hens again." Then Lana said, "I have a job for you, Spec. I think you'll like it." Her eyes ran over his face like fingers touching him. "Let's back up for a minute. I need your help to keep Biscuit and Shelly and the hens safe."

"Safe from what?"

"You know about bullies, right? I know you do. I heard. There is a bully after me, Spec. And I may have to leave for a while. I'm worried about Shelly and Puppy and the hens. So that's part of the contingency plan. You may need to rescue them. Take care of them, feed them, but only after you do something for me, here, on the computer. Do you understand?"

"Rescue Biscuit and—"

"Yes, yes. Rescue the pets, but after you do the thing on the computer for me. I'm going to go over the directions, every step. Okay? But do not tell your grandmother. Or anyone." She looked into his eyes, hard, so he couldn't look away, and touched his shoulder and he cringed. "Sorry, I know I'm violating your personal space, but I need you to repeat that, so it's clear you understand. Don't tell anyone. This is between you and me."

"Don't tell anyone. This is between you and me."

"If you told anyone, you would endanger Biscuit and Shelly and the ladies."

That scared him.

"Hopefully, you won't have to do this contingency plan. It's just…it's for your grandmother. But she can't know. It would be very bad for her to know."

"Hello? What's keeping you two?" Grandmother came in; the screen door slammed like a shot behind her, and she fanned herself with Lana's cowboy hat. "I'd love a glass of water."

"Sit down, Janelle, here, by the fan. It's not often I have a tech genius around. I got carried away." Lana's voice changed again, back into the other person's kind of voice, slow and easy. "Here, I've got iced tea and brownies."

Grandmother used a fork to eat her brownie. Spec swallowed his in two bites. Lana didn't eat at all.

There was a green tattoo of a praying mantis on Lana's back. You could see one of the insect's eyes and antennae on her shoulder. Lana told Spec the praying mantis was a sexual carnivore, and that meant the female devours the male.

"How are the wedding plans coming?" she asked Grandmother.

"Charles said we must prepare for one hundred people or more."

"Exciting."

"You are coming, Lana?"

"I haven't received an invitation."

Grandmother made a *pfft* sound with her lips. "I'm inviting you."

"I love weddings, Janelle. A time for decisions. The road taken…and not taken."

"Mira deserves a good day. I am holding everything together. I am determined."

Lana reached over and handed Grandmother a tissue. Grandmother was crying for some reason. Why? Spec had no idea. He poured himself another glass of tea.

Spec waited for them to go to the other room, to the table with the pieces of broken glass and the candles and the camera on its tripod. That's when Spec usually took the puppy outside and fed the hens. Lana scared him sometimes. She raised her voice at Grandmother, because she said she was a coach, but Lana sounded like the strict kind of teacher who yelled a lot and sent you to detention.

"I've decided to make this our last session."

"Whaaat?" Grandmother made a hurt sound like someone had punched her.

"We'll continue after the wedding," Lana told Grandmother and patted her hand.

"But that's two weeks away. That's too long to go without—"

"We are cauterizing the wound, Janelle. When we continue our work, you'll be reenergized."

"I know you have other clients to tend to, Lana, but—"

"I do, and I will be away to see them in person. I have so many I've neglected."

"But, Lana, what if I can't manage—what if I can't get through it?"

"You'll record everything in your notebook, Janelle. And I mean everything. That's your safety valve. And it will be so, so tremendously valuable, this respite. To step back—and allow your memories to steep. I haven't been wrong yet, have I? Trust me. This will work. I expect a great breakthrough...after the wedding."

"But...I will see you there, at the wedding, Lana? If I know you'll be there, that will get me through—"

"Yes. Yes, and we'll schedule our next sessions, at the wedding."

Then Grandmother said Janelle B4 was getting stronger.

"Well, let's make today's session a good one, then," Lana said, "since we'll be on hiatus for a while."

Spec stood up and put his plate in the sink. He hooked the puppy's leash on her collar. "I'm going to take Biscuit for a walk. We're going to dig up worms for Shelly," he said, but they didn't look up. Lana lit the candles. They were starting Grandmother's session, and they didn't hear him. They never did.

Later, Spec drove over the bridge. Then they switched places and Grandmother got behind the wheel.

"It won't do for Burry to fret about your driving me," she said, what she said every time. Maybe Grandmother needed to remind herself.

Grandmother parked on Spec's street, crooked, too close to the mailbox, but when he told her, Grandmother said, "Sometimes it's good to see other people make mistakes."

Dad met them at the door. "What's this? More goodies? Peaches. Wow. Mom, you got some sun today on your arms."

"I should have put on sunblock."

"You look good. Healthy." Dad looked at him. "Did you remind your grandmother, Spec? Computer camp next week?"

"No." He sat behind the desktop computer in the corner of the living room.

"He'll be tied up most days during computer camp. The camp director was impressed with Spec. Right, buddy? He's going to help the younger kids this time."

"Spec, you didn't tell me that," Grandmother said. "That's quite an accomplishment."

"Don't get too comfortable over there, man," Dad said. "We're meeting your mom at the outlet mall soon."

"I don't want to go."

"That makes two of us." Then he told Grandmother it was for The Wedding. "Pansy is insisting on new threads for Spec and me."

"Burry? Is your sister nervous about the wedding?" Grandmother asked.

"Why don't you ask her, Mom?"

"She'll be afraid to upset me. But I know you two are close."

And here, another conversation lost to Spec, a code he hadn't cracked, around The Wedding. The very important date on the calendar he needed to circle, Lana said. But it already was circled, right on the family calendar, on the refrigerator by the computer camp brochure.

"Oh, heavens, is it four-thirty? I have to go. Your father will be home soon."

"So what if he has to wait a few minutes for you? C'mon, Mom. You want a glass of wine?"

"No, he gets anxious if I'm late. And don't you have to meet Pansy?"

Dad walked Grandmother to her car, and when he came back inside, he turned the chair so Spec faced him and said, "How about you go off-line for a few minutes. Look at me."

Spec didn't. He looked down.

"What have you and your grandmother been up to lately?"

"Up to."

"What did you do?"

"I let her talk to me."

"What did you do today, for example?"

Dad leaned over and turned off the computer. He hardly ever did mean stuff like that.

Spec looked over at the television. It was on mute, but there were people talking at a desk, angry people, their faces scrunched up—

"Dude. Come on, focus. I know you don't want to watch CNN, right?"

In Spec's mouth, words. Stuck like hard candy, but he couldn't get them out. What was he supposed to say? Or not say? Grandmother said not to tell anyone that he drove her over the bridge, that Burry would have a hissy fit. And Lana told him to keep the Contingency Plan a secret. He might have to rescue Biscuit and Shelly and the hens and he would have to save them by himself. He wanted to keep them safe from the bullies.

Dad sighed. "Look, I don't have a problem with your excursions, but I just need to know the two of you are safe. Sometimes Grandmother's judgment is…a little off. All right?"

"All right."

"So, what did you two do today?"

Spec and Grandmother always stopped by the produce stand. They bought blackberries and peaches and boiled peanuts and honey for Spec to bring home, so Dad wouldn't mind when Spec spent the afternoon with Grandmother, driving Grandmother over the bridge. Only Dad didn't know Spec was driving; he thought Spec was just keeping Grandmother company and lifting heavy things when she shopped. It was hard to keep up with what everyone knew and didn't know, so Spec tried not to talk about his afternoons with Grandmother.

"You've got be more forthcoming about your afternoons with Grandmother if you expect them to continue."

Spec couldn't decide the parts to leave out or to keep in and so he said the only thing he could think of that mattered.

"We visited the lady on the mountain."

"The lady?"

"Grandmother's friend."

"What's the name of this friend?"

"Lana."

Dad gave a little laugh like a hiccup. "Well, that explains some things. Why Grandma is being so hush-hush."

"Hush-hush."

"Grandfather hates Grandmother's friend. Anyway, that's a relief. Visiting Grandmother's friend. It's not like you're doing anything dangerous."

Spec's mother waited for them in the outlet mall. She came straight from her important job being a boss at Office Depot and she was dressed up and tired. She said her feet hurt and Dad told her to take off her pointy shoes and go get a foot massage in the mall and he would buy her some flip-flops or sneakers, and that made Mom laugh. But Dad said he was serious.

"How was your day, baby?" Mom asked Spec.

Spec said it was excellent.

Mom laughed. "Excellent, huh?" And she looked at Burry and she was HAPPY.

Mom was in the National Guard and then she wasn't. That was when Spec was a baby and they lived in Atlanta. His other grandmother took care of him sometimes, but she was old and she got sick and passed away. Then he and Mom moved into an apartment with a swimming pool. There were unsupervised kids who cussed on the playground. Spec had to go to daycare a lot and it was very noisy and bad. When Spec was in fourth grade, Mom got happy. Spec knew she was happy because she told him. She said she was in love with a good man. That was Burry. One day, Burry picked Spec up after school in fourth grade and said Spec didn't have to go to daycare anymore. Then Spec was happy.

The next year he and Mom and Dad moved to Haven. No one told Spec to call Burry "Dad." It just happened because Spec wanted a dad like other kids. Mom stayed home with Spec in sixth grade to get him adjusted and Dad worked for

Grandfather until Dad couldn't take working for that egomaniac anymore.

Mom and Dad held hands now as they walked in the outlet mall. Spec hated the mall, but Mom told him he could have a pretzel, the big kind with salt and butter, after he tried on pants and a shirt. Spec walked beside Mom and she patted his shoulder, a love pat.

In the food court later, Mom had a salad and Dad ordered a Chinese dinner. Spec ate his pretzel.

"Can we have a puppy?" Spec asked them. "And a turtle and chickens?"

"What, you're a budding zoologist now?" Dad asked. "It's up to your mom. She's got allergies."

Mom said, "Uh, you're kicking the can to me?"

"You're the boss," Dad said.

Mom said, "We'll see."

"But if I am good?" Spec said. "If I am perfect?"

"You are good, Spec," Mom said. "You are perfect to us."

Inside Spec it hurt. Sadness. It was invisible but Mom and Dad saw it.

Back when Perry Akers started calling him Special Ed, Spec held the sadness inside, but then the bad part happened. Perry Akers got all the eighth graders to call Spec retard, nutjob, schizo, and the sadness inside him exploded like when you shake up a can of Coke; and he was UPSET and he punched Perry Akers, he punched and punched Perry Aker's stomach over and over.

Spec's mother cried and Dad got UPSET inside the principal's office, and Dad raised his voice and told Mr. Timmons the principal, Where were you for our boy when he was bullied? Where was your zero-tolerance then?

They expelled Spec and he liked it because he didn't have to ride the bus and go to school anymore with the bullies. Dad said Spec could have school at home now. Bullies are hell, Dad said, and are best avoided and walked away from, and now that you've hit your growth spurt? You're a big guy now, and you're going to get bigger. Yeah, you could take out that wuss-faced clown, but you don't have to.

Spec's mother said, "Know your own strength and don't get pulled in. Walk away."

After Spec ate his pretzel, Dad told Mom that he was going to BRAG about Spec, how he was proud Spec helped out Grandmother all summer, and now Spec was going to computer camp too. That's when Spec knew Dad wanted a pet too.

Mom said they could talk about a pet. A dog would need a fenced yard. They would find a solution. That was Mom's favorite thing to say—find a solution. "How's that, baby?"

Spec nodded.

Now Spec needed to stop, not to talk anymore. Not to explain how he was going to rescue the pets. Build a pen for the hens in their backyard. Clear a space on his dresser for Shelly's aquarium. Buy a dish for the puppy.

And send out that message on Lana's computer.

24

CHARLES

"Sorry, but like I said, you don't have an appointment, and Mr. Wolf is a busy man."

Charles was on a phone call when he overheard Arlene. He strained to listen. His secretary's ornery deflections often pleased him.

"I sense you're in pain, Arlene," came the venomous reply. "If you release your trapped energy, you'll feel so much calmer."

"Not that it's any of your business, but my energy is going to be released tonight just fine thank you, with a six-pack and a fellow named Booster."

Charles hung up on his caller, an important caller, the vice president of the Haven Chamber of Commerce, because, dear God, who was Arlene talking to? He got up and peered out of his office door. Arlene's face pinched in irritation, and no, no, no, it couldn't be—

Those black-lined eyes, that smug smile.

"It's all right, Arlene," he said.

But it wasn't all right.

Lana. What a goddamn fool he was! To believe that charlatan wouldn't come back again and again. The enemy had slithered out and shown herself, but he would not give her the satisfaction of seeing his surprise. Tempting, to close his office door and let Arlene send that devious quack on her way, but he couldn't. She was too dangerous. And such arrogance. Did she really think she could traipse right into his office? She was a vampire—and you didn't invite them in.

"There is an urgent, confidential matter we need to discuss." That oily voice!

"Five minutes," he said. "And not a second more."

Lana sauntered into his office, her filmy scarlet scarf fluttering over a long, shapeless purple dress. Her brash attire—flamboyance designed to radiate confidence, he had no doubt. He threw Arlene an I'll-explain-later look and closed the door.

He sat down behind his desk. He did not ask the vampire to have a seat. Never in his life had he so relished impudence as when he was around this hideous scofflaw. Finally she sat down, flicking something invisible off her shoulder, slyly settling herself, the way a cat does.

"It is rather unseemly of me to barge in, as your lovely assistant pointed out. But I assumed you wouldn't take my calls, much less allow me to make an appointment."

He didn't trust himself to speak, not just yet.

"I suppose you're wondering what brought me here?"

"Not for another handout," he said finally, pleased his voice was smooth, his ragged anger, hidden. "I'm not running a travel agency."

"A handout?" She laughed. Laughed.

"I assumed you understood it was a one-way ticket to India I sponsored. Not a round trip."

"No. No more travel for me. Not for a while."

There was something subtle about this woman that changed each time he saw her, beyond her bizarre wardrobe and her tacky makeup. In some nearly imperceptible manner she seemed different, the way identical twins weren't exactly duplicate people. Dear God, he hoped this woman didn't have a doppelgänger, for the good of the world.

"The confidential matter I spoke of," she continued. "It's deadly serious."

Charles seethed. His chair creaked, as if straining from the weight of his rage. He gripped the armrests and managed to smile.

"You have no idea how Janelle is hurting," she said.

His wife's name emerging from that wide vulgar mouth! Janelle's name, a hostage.

"Janelle is..." thriving, he nearly said. His favorite description. But he held himself back, just in time. He would not be lured into discussing his wife with this infuriating monster, who sighed as if she had hauled in the weight of the world with her, to deliver it here, a bag of shit dumped in Charles's office. Did she know how hideous she appeared? With her carousel horse eyes rolling, her ethnic getup?

He longed to demand she leave, but the rational side of him clamped down, took over. "You are not her counselor," he said slowly. "You are to have no further contact with her. I made that clear."

"Oh, Charles, you have no idea, do you?"

The realization hit him then, a punch in the gut. Had his wife slipped off to meet this woman? Not a word, not a hint of guilt from Janelle about a surreptitious afternoon? Or two? He'd allowed himself such hope, with Janelle's lunch dates now and shopping with Mira and normal days. "If you tricked her into meeting you—" It came out louder than he intended. "I warned you, no more of your crackpot sessions with my wife. I told you I'd get the law—"

"Your wife is not under house arrest," she said with a chuckle. "As much as you might hope. Janelle is on the cusp of some powerful revelations after all her suffering."

"What do you want?" Deflate her warm-up act, cut through her psychobabble with a pinprick. Yet his mind raced. How had Janelle managed to keep this from him? Janelle said she'd gone back to India...had his wife lied to him? When he'd pushed Janelle about how she'd invited that monster to her birthday dinner, Janelle had remained evasive and seemingly befuddled, her refrain, ringing in his ears even now—*Oh, but it was so good of her to come, wasn't it? It made my birthday special, and it worked out, didn't it?*

His outrage, he had to hide it, she could see it. He couldn't afford to appear weak, not with this loathsome cretin studying him.

"I want Janelle to heal," she said, "and to stop hurting."

"Do you think I'm going to just sit back and let you take advantage of my wife?" he sputtered. "She's under the care of a doctor."

"I know all about your buddy, the shrink, who will write any scrip for anesthetizing, controlling chemicals."

He held on to his rage, held it, held it by the tail, barely, as it snapped and snarled. "Why are you doing this to me?"

"To you?" There was the clinking of bracelets, a tinkling of laughter. "To you. Oh, Charles. It is always about you, isn't it?"

He stood, leaned across his desk, loomed over her. "You will not see Janelle anymore…you're dangerous. I'll go to the police. I'll get a restraining order. Don't think I won't. I can. I will."

"You don't want me to leave," she said in a silken whisper. "Not until you have what I've come to deliver." She held out something, a flash of silver—a weapon? A blade? Some reptilian primitive part of his brain reeled—

"Take it. It's yours." She dropped the thing on his desk.

He picked it up. The metal was warm. She must have been holding it the entire time.

"Put that flash drive in your computer."

"Flash drive?" he repeated numbly.

"I'm not leaving until you see."

And still he stood, because what was happening? When had he lost control?

"There is a single file on that drive, an MP4 video. You plug it in there." She pointed to a place on his computer.

"I…I know that." He didn't. He had to get his bearings.

"Click on the media player," she said, with a bemused smile. "And I'll be on my merry way."

His hands shook with anger as he shoved the metal nub in. He clicked. The Windows Media Player opened; the video buffered, then played.

Janelle! Looking at the camera, at him—

All right, Janelle, you are recalling events that have been buried, memories that have come to you? Lana's toxic whisper, off camera. *That's right.* His wife's face dreamy, her pale green eyes focusing. *And you are telling this of your own free will, with no interference from anyone?* Yes. *When there are painful parts of your narrative, you may want to pause. Just let the memories come. We can take as long as you need. All right. Let's begin with that night. The evening of your accident. It was rainy that night. The babysitter was late—*

Charles tried to stop the video, clicking here and there, pounding the keyboard, and yet Janelle's voice continued—*I told Charles to go on without me*—and finally, finally he turned the computer off.

"This...this is a crime," he sputtered. "My wife is a vulnerable adult and you've been subjecting her to—"

"Maybe you should finish watching before you cast aspersions."

"Leave. Now. I'm...I'm calling the police."

"Mr. Loyal Loving Husband. What a crock of shit, Charles. You're the sick one. The poor woman has been held captive by you long enough."

"You tricked her. You made her meet you," he sputtered. "I won't tolerate it."

"Watch. You can't afford not to."

"She's better now! She's better and you're trying to unbalance her again."

"Better? Because she stopped her outings to hotel bars?" She laughed. "Oh yes. Charles, I have more bad news. For a few weeks there in the spring, your wife was making the rounds. Discreetly, of course. Secretly enjoying herself in a plush hotel bar."

"I do know," he found himself saying—reflexive, defensive. He did know! He was trying to take it in, this sickening development. What had Janelle told this woman? "I do know," he repeated.

There—a fleeting shadow crossed Lana's face: surprise.

"You're lying."

He'd landed a blow. He wanted to pump his fist in the air. "I made sure she was safe there—at the hotel."

Now it was she who sputtered, knocked off her game. The vampire hadn't expected that, had she? He was so elated at her surprise, he had to pull himself back. Those men were PIs, he wanted to say, to yell, trained professionals! But he couldn't overplay his hand. Better to seal off any more information. This savage crank would tell Janelle, she would use it against him, she would use anything against him—

She sat back in her chair, coiled, reassessing.

Charles knew his wife better than anyone, better than this grifter did, and now she knew it too.

"You followed her? Had her followed? How overbearing, Charles. How creepy."

She raised her arms, stretched, and…yawned. "Let's return to the subject at hand. What you're about to watch? It's a rough cut. Just a tease. A minute of Janelle telling enough to sink you. But this is still a work in progress, Charles. Because I have so much on the cutting room floor, so much of Janelle's dark tale. I'm putting together a video about Janelle, and it's smoking hot, Charles. Genius. But no one has to see the final product. Well, except for you and me. It's up to you. Take some deep breaths, Charles. You look like you've seen a ghost."

"What do you mean, up to me?"

"Your daughter's wedding is right around the corner. What a shame if my polished video is shared with the family. Just in time for your sweet forty-year anniversary too. Just when Janelle is welcomed back into this village of idiots, just when this business"—and here she looked around Charles's office, indicating with a nod the photographs on the wall—"this nostalgic tale is being trotted out, the senator and on and on. Turns out it's a sordid story. And just as you're set to walk your daughter down the aisle. What a pall on the festivities."

Charles heard ragged gasps, his own. "I will not be threatened."

"And yet you are."

She fixed her hard, painted eyes on him. "One hundred grand to stop this family movie from being broadcast. Cash. It's not much, in the scheme of things. I've done my due diligence. Researched property records and such. You are overextended, but there's your new business with an influx of capital."

"You evil, greedy—"

He stood ramrod straight, his hands balled into fists, Mr. Levelheaded Businessman long gone. He wanted to strangle this infuriating harpy, wrap that scarlet scarf around her neck—

"I'll need the money by next Thursday. Six p.m. That will give you ample time. I'll be in touch with you soon to discuss the transfer." She took a step toward the door but stopped and turned to face him. "Oh, and, Charles? I've made arrangements to distribute the little family movie should plans go awry. If you were to panic, say, and contact the authorities, I have a contingency plan."

She closed the door behind her.

He was left with the nauseating stench of her vile, peppery scent and his own incinerating rage. He collapsed in his chair, buried his face in his hands.

The door opened. "You all right, bossman?" Arlene asked. He didn't bother to look up. "I know a crazy bitch when I see one."

"She…threatened…she is dangerous, very dangerous for Janelle."

"Lord, Charles." Arlene closed his door. "That witch is back in Haven to mess with Janelle's head?"

"She's going to ruin her…ruin me."

He couldn't tell Arlene all of it, though he longed to—

"You know Booster is a bugman."

"Who?"

"Booster? My guy. He can throw some flea bombs at her—she won't know what hit her. That'll run her out of town."

Boyfriend. Extermination. Flea bombs, poisonous clouds. Charles shook his head. This situation was worse than even Arlene imagined, beyond the reach of a prank.

"Got some Jack Daniel's in my desk drawer for emergencies, better than nerve pills. How about a shot?"

He declined. He had to have his wits about him.

"Why don't you call your PI guy? Get some dirt on that loon. Scrape this shit off your shoe."

Arlene had a point. He allowed himself a tiny flicker of hope. Call Red's PI agency, tell him to send over the best investigator in his agency. Or better yet, ask Red himself to dig up dirt on this criminal. Yes. Of course—

He wanted to rush home, confront Janelle, but…he had to think this through. All the angles.

Arlene left for her Jack Daniel's. Closed his door.

Charles called Red, left a message that he needed an investigator, no one but Red himself would do.

And then Charles got the thumb drive, plugged the thing back into his computer.

He clicked on the video. And he watched.

Let's begin with that night. The evening of your accident. It is Monday, November 11, 1985. Take your time, Janelle. Follow your memories.

Suffering through that vile woman's voice was bad enough, Charles thought. But Janelle's face! Watching his wife's earnest, frightened face meeting the camera's eye pained him even more. How could he have let this happen? He'd let that vampire prey on his wife!

That night I made crab dip. I carried the dishes and put them in the back seat of the station wagon. It was raining hard. The babysitter was late. She was a high school girl who had cheerleading practice, and so I told Charles to go on.

To go on where?

To Stan and Mary's new house. I was going to join him there.

This is important, Janelle. You remember now, don't you? The night of your accident, you were there. You arrived at Stan and Mary's house, didn't you?

Yes. Yes, I was there.

But something traumatic happened there. Something that upset you terribly. You fled the home of Stan and Mary Rex. Your accident happened after you left.

Yes. Yes, I was trying to get home.

Why? Go on, Janelle. What do you remember? What shocking thing happened that night at the home of Stan and Mary Rex?

The video stuttered to a close. Charles buried his face in his hands.

Just a tease. I have so much more on the cutting room floor. But what, what?

Because no telling what else Janelle had told this woman. Did Janelle even know what she said? Dear God, if he could only ask Janelle, but it was Russian roulette—even bringing up the accident, especially now, with the wedding, with the business rebranding—

But what if there was nothing more there? The grifter... bluffing. Janelle recalling that she'd arrived that night at Stan and Mary's, that was bad, very bad. Then leaving because of something traumatic. But...maybe that was all Janelle remembered. And he could explain that, talk to Janelle about it, couldn't he?

But the grifter, what fun she would have twisting Janelle's words into some sort of outrageous scandal. With that polished video of hers, that work in progress—hinting at claims he couldn't explain.

A sneak preview, she'd called it—just to torture him! Because it was bad, this tease, yes...but perhaps not...the worst.

That vile woman with her sleight of hand, she knew how to make him desperate enough to imagine all sorts of horrible things. All part of her hoax.

But Charles couldn't take any chances. She knew that too.

25

TEDDY

It started the night Reagan happened to mention the wedding present. It wasn't like Mira and Nelson were registered at the good places, she said, and Reagan needed ideas. She was waiting for Mira to text her.

This was Monday, another evening of Teddy's solitary take-out Thai. Reagan came home after an exercise class—rumba? zumba?—swigging water and gunning for an argument. Why hadn't Charles called her back? What was the deal? The new Rex Wolf website was going live this week, and the interview she'd set up for Charles and Janelle was still a go, right? This week was no time for Charles to hit a wall.

Teddy told her to chill. Everything was fine.

But Teddy wondered if Charles might be having a slight freak-out. He'd slipped out of the office on Friday, without a word to Teddy. Not like him to do that. And this morning, he was MIA again. Arlene, that gargoyle, was not forthcoming about when the bossman would be in. Teddy had explained that an accountant would need to come in soon, tossing it off casually as a no-big-deal look at the books and payroll, shouldn't take long. Arlene's eyes narrowed into slits; she reared back in her chair. "No way, T-Rex. Not going to happen. Not on my watch. Not now." She added that Charles "had a lot on him this week" and Teddy should cut him some slack, "what with the wedding and all."

"The wedding?" Teddy said. "Is there some kind of...complication?" He waited, stared, let the silence do the work.

Finally, Arlene told Teddy she was going outside for a smoke while it was still a free country.

Cold feet. That's what popped into his head. Mira's got cold feet and Charles is panicking about how it will look if she called off the wedding. Mira's got cold feet. Like a line from a song, playing in his head, over and over.

Reagan's phone buzzed now on the kitchen counter. She was in the shower. Teddy found himself reading Mira's text, a flash of vicarious contact.

—You've done so much, no gift really just yr presence! Thx.

Teddy scrolled up, to read the previous thread.

—Where u registered?

—We r not. Celebrate no frills no worries.

—?! U crazy? Wedding = cleanup :D

And then Reagan had tried again.

—Vitamix? We love ours.

—No 2 much but thanx U have done so much already with all the deets!

—Surprise u then :)

That was today's exchange. How paltry. What a tantalizing but disappointing exchange that could have been so...revealing.

Teddy, his heart knocking hard in his chest, typed:

—u got 2nd thoughts a/b the big day?

He waited. Interminable seconds. The shower was still on. Then dot dot dot and ding!

—Full speed ahead!

—Cmon girl u can tell me, u nervous?

That didn't even sound like Reagan, but he couldn't help himself.

—All good here thx CU Sat.

And what did he expect? That Mira would even hint at what she really felt to Reagan, by text?

The shower stopped. He frantically deleted the texts.

Reagan came into the kitchen, swaddled in her pink robe. He liked her like this, scrubbed bare face wimpled in a towel, plain and just a little...vulnerable. She checked her phone.

"What's wrong?"

She looked up. "Nothing," then her face crumpled and... Oh, hell.

"Hey." He took her in his arms. Did she know? Her body was damp from her shower, the towel loosening and falling away from her hair. "What's wrong?" Had some rogue text bounced back from Mira? Or—

"I started my period."

Huge relief. Big honking wave of relief...which he could not show. He commanded his face to look shocked and disappointed.

"Okay. So, we'll try again."

"We missed the window. The timing will be all wrong. We have to wait another year, remember?"

A chart, a calendar, yes. He remembered. "I am your stud-for-hire. Just say the word." Joking, but not really.

"It's so frustrating. We did everything right."

"It is biology we're talking here. Sometimes bodies do what they want."

He led her to bed. Tucked her in. "You want Advil?"

"Thanks, Teddybear."

He brought her a glass of her favorite pinot grigio. "At least you can drink with me now."

"Cheers," she said with a sad smile. He sat on the bed beside her. Stroked her cheek. How nice to comfort her. He was about to suggest they curl up and catch a Netflix show on his laptop—

"I'm missing something," she said. "I know it. And I can't put my finger on it."

"Missing something?"

"About Rex Wolf, about the wedding, the rebranding. Something is off."

On to the next thing. How was it Reagan could redirect her emotions, by sheer will, better than he could? Better than anyone he knew. He envied it, begrudged it too.

He pulled away.

"Did I tell you Mark called?" she asked, sitting up. "He wants to move up the audit—"

"Audit? Do we have to call it that?"

"I told him tomorrow would work."

"Tomorrow? Whoa. I think we need to push it up to next week. I need to discuss this with Charles before Mark just shows up."

"What's there to discuss? Mark has done this hundreds of times. This week he'll look over the books and review the business plan." She went on and on, about outsourcing the back-office piece, low-cost disrupters that have emerged in the human cloud… God, where did she get this stuff?

Teddy yawned. Reagan got out of bed.

"But you did remind Charles, right? About the audit?"

"Yeah, I mentioned it." Technically to Arlene, but she'd tell Charles. Wouldn't she? "It's a little awkward. Mark marches in there, nosing around. I need to talk to Charles again beforehand. I owe him that."

"Teddybear, it's not complicated. Intense due diligence here. Charles still owes us a list of outstanding debts and copies of all the insurance policies. No hidden liability or liens, that's all. Done and done. If there are problems, we'll get out in front of them. No surprises."

Reagan's phone dinged with a text. She didn't look at it. She dropped it into the large velvety pocket of her robe, where it dinged again, smothered and lost to him.

—Yes have 2nd thoughts. Don't want to go thru this don't love him help!

He could see the text in his head. He had to check! He wouldn't get a minute of sleep.

An excruciating hour later, when Reagan brushed her teeth, Teddy managed to peek at her phone, at the text—from the auditor. He would be at Rex Wolf no later than Wednesday.

26

JANELLE

I wasn't on my way to Stan and Mary's house that night.
I was there.
I was trying to leave.
Start with that, Lana says. Every day, start with that.
For years I had no memory of my accident, or even the days around it. A whole month of my life was lost to me, days and nights the doctors said I would never recall. But Lana says that is nonsense. My blackout is shrinking from days to hours, and now to minutes.

I must keep the pictures in my mind, even if they are scattered and scary. When Lana returns, I will be ready.

So, I am writing by candlelight, because I do love candlelight, a tiny comfort when the pictures are sharp and cutting. Also, I am in the kitchen pantry, and it is two in the morning. Charles won't find me here.

I arrived. I was there. I was trying to leave.

The morning before my accident, Mary sat in my kitchen crying.

She announced her life had come to a dead end. A dead end, that's what she called it, over and over.

Her new house was ugly she said. Horrible, cold, empty.

Stan was never happy with her anymore, complaining because she'd dropped out of the Junior League, she detested office work, she dreaded entertaining. On and on.

It was true Mary hadn't found her niche. But Mary never admitted such a thing. She'd emerged resolute from a hardscrabble childhood, then flew the friendly skies as a glamorous stewardess, before being swept off her feet, rescued, by Stan.

Such an idyllic tale required careful construction and reinvention, after all. Mary was polished but brittle. Her pride could be misconstrued as chilly reserve.

But her misery, once acknowledged, flooded into my kitchen. Her shoulders shook with sobs.

She'd assumed she and Stan would end up in a city, Charlotte or Atlanta—not this petty-minded town. Also, Mary wanted a big family. She and Stan had no children, but it wasn't for lack of trying, and he refused to talk about it.

She had sought solace at a small church in the hills, having wandered in one day, but Stan said it didn't look right, her affiliation with a bunch of snake handlers. Then Mary began jogging alone for miles, for hours, advertising her solitary rebellion. Stan said running by herself like that was heedless, dangerous.

Mary had taken to wearing glasses, large tortoiseshell frames that dwarfed her small, pert face, that hid her mascaraed, dun-colored eyes. She took off her glasses and wiped her face with the scented, warm cloth I handed her.

I used to think that when I had children, she said, all this wouldn't matter. I'll be a mother, like you, like the other mothers. I'll find a way to stay, with a family. To make Haven home. But I'm nearly thirty-two, Janelle. Thirty-two! Before you know it—I'll be stuck. In Haven. In that big empty house. With him. And I can't. There, I said it. I want to leave Stan.

I see my hands pouring her coffee. I hear my hollow, stupid words. This will blow over. Every marriage has its storms.

Mary said she had talked to a lawyer, over in Palmetto. She was leaving Stan.

Mary had rarely asked me for anything. Even advice. But now, now she was asking for a favor.

Tonight, I am going to tell him, she said. I can't do it alone. You know how he gets, Janelle. He won't stand for it.

She needed someone in her corner. He'll listen to you, Janelle. He respects you. How he talks about you! He trusts your judgment.

About the business, I said.

About everything.

I walked her outside, to her car in my driveway. Fat drops of rain plunked down as Mary cried. How often I remember Mary and the rain, together. Twinned. Lana says this is a remarkable observation, a telling pattern.

I'll say we're planning a housewarming party, Mary said. And when you get there, I'll tell him.

In the back seat of Mary's car, her luggage.

I'm going back home, she said. I panicked. This is a better plan, isn't it?

Her slumped shoulders, her smeared makeup—my heart ached for her. I'm sure it did.

Her long embrace startled me.

Mary called me her only friend, yet I'm certain we weren't particularly close.

I will see you tonight.

Yes, I said. Tonight.

27

CHARLES

Charles rushed home from his office Friday afternoon, but when he pulled into his garage, he sat. Didn't even get out of the car.

He tried to collect himself before—before what? Before he lost his temper with Janelle and triggered a crack-up, or worse—would she flee to that scheming reprobate? Inside his pocket was the thing. *The thing she had given him, just the rough cut, I have so much more.* He couldn't leave it at the office, or even inside his own house. But the garage... He walked over to the corner storage cabinet and fumbled for the metal box at the top. He opened the combination lock and dropped the thing in there, beside his old service revolver. Allowed himself a pinch of satisfaction for completing at least one rational step—

Think, think, think. How to talk to Janelle about this? How to diffuse this dirty bomb?

Dear God. A sob racked his chest. How had he let this happen? Extortion! But if he went to the police, they would confiscate the thing and...then there was Lana's threat, *I have a contingency plan...*

He had to keep his head. He couldn't lose his temper. As much as he yearned to tell Janelle—to scream—*that criminal has duped you!*—he had to proceed carefully. How to broach the topic with Janelle without playing into the hands of that smirking, infuriating Svengali? There would be accusations; there might very well be ugly, warped notions...

Hence, dinner at the club.

The old trick of broaching inflammatory topics in a public place.

"Janelle! I'm taking you out to dinner," he called from the bottom of the stairs.

There, he would get to the bottom of this. And more importantly, inform his wife what needed to be done. Unfortunately, it required both her knowledge and her signature.

They ran into a few acquaintances at the club. Janelle comfortable with surface chatter when she wanted to be, her socialite-trained charm threadbare but useful.

He ordered a shrimp cocktail because he knew she liked it. But when the plump pink shellfish arrived, curled like commas around a dot of blood-red sauce, she barely touched it.

"I'm not very hungry, Charles. I'm sorry. You eat them."

But she knew he hated shrimp, those antennaed sea roaches. Had she forgotten?

She ordered a grilled cheese sandwich and soup. He, the porterhouse steak, rare, with a baked potato, and another bourbon.

"I want to discuss something important, Janelle. Something vital to our family."

She took a sip of water. "About the wedding?"

"Yes. Well, in part." A dangerous course he was on. Teetering, it could go either way.

"Our family needs shoring up. Financially."

"Oh dear. Why?" She looked concerned, and he needed her to be concerned. Not excessively, but enough.

"Well, there's Mira's wedding, of course, and we're still paying off a number of expenses. Rex Wolf is positioned for growth, but that will be down the road. And then"—here he played his ace—"on top of everything, there are those medical bills." Not much left on her private hospital stay three years ago, but still.

She looked down at her lap. "I'm sorry."

"Don't be. There is nothing to be sorry about. We have a remedy." He waited until she met his eyes.

"The property. We need to sell it, Janelle."

"You mean…Daddy's land?"

"Your father has been dead for many years. It's our land now."

"Is that what the children want?"

"I haven't talked to them about this, Janelle. This is between you and me."

Her eyes shiny, but alert. "What about our house? Isn't there…equity?"

He nearly choked on his drink. How sharp she could be sometimes.

"Yes, but we…unfortunately, we have already tapped into that."

"I promised Daddy I would keep the mountain property. He loved it so up there."

"I know." He reached over and squeezed her hand. "But things change, my dear. It's a different world. And we aren't really using it, are we? It's vacant land."

"I…excuse me. I'm going to the powder room."

Would she cry? Come back baby-bawling, red-faced, insisting on leaving? Perhaps it was the memory of her father that had upset her. The very idea of making Janelle promise to keep the mountain property in the family, with Janelle as the sole owner on the deed, why, really, imposing a burden like that on your only child, it was outrageous.

Janelle returned, dry-eyed and composed. Charles stood, pulled out her chair. He told her how very lovely she looked.

"To whom?" she said when he sat back down.

"Why, to me," he said with an uneasy chuckle.

"No, I mean…who are we selling the land to, Charles?"

"There are interested parties who will pay a generous amount. I will be bringing some papers for you to sign, so that we'll both be…well, so I can proceed."

"Let me think about it."

"Let you…what?" Charles barked, more sharply than he intended. The waiter flinched as he served their entrées.

Charles slowly carved a slice of cool bloody meat, but he could no longer hold himself back. It was Janelle's doing—allowing that grifter to swindle them—and now she refused the only remedy!

"That Lana is in town, isn't she?" He lobbed that and watched Janelle's expression turn from surprise to something inscrutable. What happened? He couldn't read his own wife's thoughts anymore.

"She's here somewhere…isn't she?"

"Charles, I know you don't care for her."

He put his fork and knife down. "Your alliance with that woman has to stop."

"She's my friend." This said with the puzzled innocence of a child. Infuriating!

"She's no such thing," he hissed. "She's a parasite!"

"But, Charles," she said softly, "I'm remembering."

He took a long swig of bourbon before he trusted himself to respond. "Her poisonous flimflam has confused you, as I said it would."

"She said you would be angry with me."

"When did you see that criminal? Where? I…I can't allow you to be traumatized by that woman—you must promise me, Janelle, promise you'll not talk to her—"

"Charles, please calm down. You don't look well."

He yearned to tell Janelle what her "friend" the scam artist was doing to them, making them sell Janelle's precious property—blackmailing them! With Janelle's own words! Because no telling what sick tale she'd persuaded Janelle to recite. He'd make Janelle understand—unless…she wouldn't. Unless she refused to understand. Unless Janelle accused him, turned on him, her own husband. Because he didn't know what she recalled now, did he?

He was certain Lana had planned for that, it was another trap she'd set, vaguely alluded to. The poor woman has been held captive by you long enough.

"No more sneaking off and meeting with that dangerous woman, do you hear me? I insist, Janelle. Promise me."

He sensed a few stares. He forced what he hoped was a

patient grin, illustrating a harmless kerfuffle. He signaled to the waiter, ordered the chocolate mousse, Janelle's favorite, to show curious onlookers they were having a perfectly normal evening out, but then she hardly touched that dish either.

She was silent, shut down. He'd failed.

He ordered another drink and ate the mousse himself, though he disliked anything so soft.

Janelle, the designated driver as usual, drove them home in her agonizingly sluggish fashion, barely breaking forty miles an hour. He rolled his window down, the night air perfumed with honeysuckle and gardenia. He said carefully, "No need to worry about any of this, Janelle. We've discussed our options. I'll take care of it."

"I'm not worried."

When they pulled into the garage, he added, "I'm going to bring the papers home next week for you to sign."

She killed the ignition.

"What papers?"

"To sell the land, remember?"

"Charles, we can't sell Daddy's land."

"Janelle, my darling." His voice shook with frustration. "I am begging you. Begging you. Would you do this for me? Sign it over and let me take care of what needs to be done. Haven't I always taken care of you?"

"I know it's hard on you, Charles, but you'll see—"

"Do you know what's hard on me? You—sneaking around behind my back and meeting that woman!"

She didn't deny it.

"She's not a counselor. She's a fraud! She's disturbing you before Mira's wedding and our anniversary and everyone... watching and—" He was grasping for words, not making sense, not daring to make sense. "She knows how to traumatize you."

"I'll make you another drink or...would you like hot tea?"

That's how it went all weekend, the longest two days of his life. Never letting Janelle out of his sight, coming close to telling her more, but not daring to. She, putting him off, murmuring, and treating him as if he were the patient. Just her filmy gaze, what could he do with that? No firm yes, no firm denial either. He was no better off than he'd been on Friday, when the nightmare had begun.

He arrived at his office brutally early on Monday, a raw-faced, bleary-eyed, weekend insomniac.

He wanted coffee, but Arlene hadn't come in yet, and he couldn't begin to figure out that newfangled coffee maker with those pods. The day stretched out in front of him gun-metal gray, heavy with despair. At his age, life should be easy, not this shit pit.

When Arlene arrived, he called her into his office and closed the door. "We have to figure out how to access some quick capital."

"You broke again?" Arlene's jocular tone pained him. How he longed to laugh. He grimaced to show the gravity of the situation.

"For a short period of time—a week, maybe two—I'm going to need to access some cash. Not overly long, you understand. Just until I can replace it."

"How much scratch we talking about?"

"One hundred."

"I got that in petty cash." Then her eyes bugged out. "Christ on a stick. One hundred grand? That's going to be hard, Charles. You'd have to tap into the account for vendor payments, maybe even payroll."

Silence.

"You know T-Rex and Reagan are supposed to have that accountant nosing around any day now. What if they get wind of this?"

"I'll put that off," Charles said. "I'll talk to Teddy. I'll think of something."

"Is this moolah for the wedding? I thought you said Mira wasn't going to have one of those fancy shindigs—"

"Yes. Well."

"Lord. I know. Girls these days—they all want big ones. They think they're entitled."

"It's not just...Mira." He felt the need to deflect Arlene's criticism away from his daughter. In fact, Mira claimed she was learning to abide by a budget, or some sort of horseshit.

"Uh-huh. Is it...is it Janelle again? She heading to the nervous hospital?"

He sighed and let Arlene draw her own conclusions. There were things even Arlene mustn't know. For now.

She tapped her pen on her legal pad and screwed up her mouth, thinking hard.

"Rest assured there will be an influx of funds to replace it," he said. "Shortly."

"When's it coming in? These funds?"

"I'm—we're—selling Janelle's property. On the mountain." She didn't blink. "Hell, yeah. It's about time. Not doing nobody any good just setting up there."

"Why don't you go check the accounts on your computer?"

"I don't need to. I got all the numbers right up here." She pointed to her forehead. "And I can tell you there isn't a dime to squeeze until it hollers. The law will be beating down our door."

"Why don't you let me worry about that?"

She fell silent and looked pensive, which vaguely alarmed him. He rarely saw Arlene crestfallen. So, it really was that bad?

"Bring in the checkbook."

Arlene was the kind of old-fashioned secretary who kept a ledger and checkbook and balked at the software and digital upgrades Teddy pushed. Thank God. Good ol' Arlene.

"Okay, but—" She put her hands over her ears. "I don't want to know nothing more about it. It's better that way."

Left in the quiet of his office, Charles wondered if taking a swig of whiskey at nine in the morning was so bad. He would have to ask for some of Arlene's breath mints.

Then the phone rang. His private investigator.

"Red, here. I dug up some real interesting stuff on that grift-er gal."

"Interesting?" Charles echoed, savoring the promise of that word. "When can we meet?"

"You free now?"

"Waffle House, exit thirteen?"

"You got it."

28

JANELLE

Charles knows about Lana. He is beside himself. He raises his voice, he accuses me of lying. He says I am going to ruin the wedding and the business, ruin us. Then he apologizes for losing his temper before he yells again.

Lana prepared me. We rehearsed what to say in the face of such accusations. Charles is overprotective and can't see what progress Lana and I have made. But I won't say a word. I gave my word. Lana is my spiritual midwife, and she warned me there could be complications. When our sessions are complete, when Janelle Before stands before Charles again, he will understand.

This hiatus between our sessions is so very difficult. But Lana says we had a breakthrough. I only have to close my eyes now, and the pictures in my mind gather, they beam and connect, they play.

I arrive at Stan and Mary's. Charles's car is at the end of the driveway. I park my station wagon behind it. The rain pounds on the roof of my car. I run to the front door. The door opens. Stan.

His house smells like a new car.

Where is Charles? Stan doesn't answer.

There is food on the coffee table. A slab of cheese, a row of crackers, meatballs on toothpicks, a cluster of purple grapes, nothing touched. Like a wax display in a shop window.

Stan tells me to come sit by the fire. He says he's been waiting for me. He hands me a drink.

He puts a log on the fire. The sparks scatter but they don't touch the white carpet.

Tell me, Stan says. He pokes at the fire. What kind of hare-brained scheme were you two gals cooking up?

Stan's hand, it is large and strong, like a laborer's. Calloused. He chops his own wood. He is a big man, with a square face and pockmarked cheeks.

Where is Charles? I ask again. And again. Stan says, Oh, he's around here somewhere. Then his hand covers my own. My palm is a tiny bird, snake-swallowed. The brandy leaves a hot trail down my throat. I set the glass on the table.

Don't worry, Stan says. It's just a little fun.

And then...

It is later. I am running.

The film has jumped. That's what Lana says.

Lana says we are closing in on that stubborn void. It will require fortitude and courage to recover this lost precious piece, when we continue our sessions.

I wonder if it would comfort Charles. If I told him just a bit of what I know? If I said, Charles, I was at Stan and Mary's that night, and you tried to stop me from leaving, you begged me not to leave, I was in no state of mind to drive.

But no. I am holding everything inside. As Lana insists.

Now it is my husband who is coming undone.

He yearns for my reassurance, craves my affection. His desperation is touching and sad.

Today, for example, Charles wants to woo me, in the middle of the day. Meet me for afternoon cocktails.

There on the bed, a new dress Charles bought for me. A tasteless frock. Nothing Janelle Before would wear.

29

CHARLES

Charles had no appetite for breakfast. He couldn't think of once in his marriage when he'd pushed away a plate of eggs. Steam curls rose from his coffee. Janelle arranged bruised gardenias in a jelly jar. On the counter, the file Red had handed him, should he need it.

"I have the papers for you to sign."

"About Daddy's land, you mean? I thought we weren't—"

He banged his fist on his table. "It's our property, Janelle. And the time has come to sell it. We have to. We have no choice. That's what I need you to understand. We have to. Today."

Arlene awaited his call. She would come here, to witness and notarize Janelle's signature.

"I'm at my wit's end, Janelle." He waited for her tears. To his surprise, his own eyes filled. "Do you want to see us ruined? Do you want our family business to tank? Do you want to deprive Mira and Nelson of their wedding, their gift from us?"

She looked stunned, witnessing his raw emotion. "Charles, my goodness. I just…I don't understand why. I'm not going to need to be looked after anymore. I promise. And you know I told Daddy I wouldn't sell the—"

"Janelle." He stood, trying to regain his composure, sneaking a sideways look at her. Would she really refuse him? He was overreaching. At some point, he had to move on and take this in the proper direction, but first…first, one more try.

"Has she talked to you about this? About our…our business?"

Janelle pressed her lips together.

He scraped his untouched breakfast into the trash can.

Janelle sat at the kitchen table squinting at him as sunlight filled the kitchen. He closed the blinds above the sink, then sat back down beside her. "Lana isn't even her name," he said quietly. "Did you know that?"

"Lana has a stage name."

"She's a big phony. Her real name is Martha Jean Dipple. That accent? Phony. Everything about her is phony. She was born in West Virginia! She's a fraud."

He waited for her reaction. He thought he was prepared for it.

He wasn't.

She knows. Janelle did not look shocked, or even bothered. She shrugged.

Shrugged.

The question now, which stung like a poisonous dart: Were they in cahoots? It hadn't occurred to him. Did Janelle know about Lana's scheme to extort money from the business? Had she approved? Was Janelle's intractable insistence on independence from him—her refusal to sign the damn forms!—genuine or a symptom of her brain-fogged gullibility? What a powerful hold that scheming scofflaw had on her.

"There's no crime in reinventing yourself," Janelle said, parroting Lana, reciting! He could see those painted eyes, as if that woman were in his very kitchen, peering at him beyond Janelle's implacable expression. That vile harpy!

"Did she tell you how she ripped off a grandmother? How last year in Arizona the sons of a poor woman with dementia ran your friend out of town? She was trying to trick that elderly woman into signing over her property and her bank accounts and—"

"Lana is an outsider. She made her peace with it, and now she helps other outsiders."

"Is that what she told you to say? She scams trusting women like you! You! She…she tricks them and steals from them—"

He buried his face in his hands. Janelle fluttered over to him, clutching him to her pillowy, familiar chest, stroking what was left of his hair, murmuring, "Poor Charles."

He didn't want to do this. To veer off in this other direction. Well, nothing to do but proceed. She'd forced his hand.

He pulled away from her and allowed her to dab his face with a dishcloth.

"I'm sorry I got angry. I am lucky to have you," he said. "You know that. It's just…I want to keep you safe. All of us, safe."

The slightest pause now, a pulling back, looking away, biting her lip, hesitation barely perceptible.

"I have a gift for you," he said. "Upstairs."

"Charles. You shouldn't. You have enough on your mind."

"But that's exactly why. It always makes me feel better…to make you happy."

He rose, took her hand, led her up the stairs. In the bedroom, he pulled out the dress, hidden between his winter suits.

"You will look beautiful in this," he said, as he laid the dress on the bed. "Try it on. Go on. It will do me good to see you in it."

"I already have my dress—"

"This isn't for the wedding. This is for us. For today…just… just try it on."

She took the dress into the bathroom. Five minutes, ten— what was the holdup? "Janelle?"

"I'll be right out."

She modeled it for him—ridiculous—tight, mauve-hued knit. From Walmart, apparently. He had cut off the tags after Arlene—overjoyed with such a vital errand—delivered the purchase to him.

He searched Janelle's face; he could always see in her frantic eyes the spell in the distance, gathering energy, like the green menacing blur of a storm on radar.

Infuriating to have to resort to this, to conjure up this complication so near Mira's wedding day.

He took her hands in his. "I want to take you to lunch. You will be decked out and stunning. It will help me get though the morning, thinking of you, waiting."

"Oh, Charles. I don't think so, not today."

"Your social calendar is too busy for lunch with your husband?"

"Mira said something about a picnic, with Burry and Spec. I forget if it's today or tomorrow. She's going to call me—"

"Mira will understand."

She nodded. Not eager, but…willing.

"Let's meet at the Palmetto Hotel lounge," he said. "I happen to have a young colleague, I'll ask him to join us for a few minutes. Well, I should say *possible* colleague. I am considering hiring him. If you get there before me, you can help vet him. See if he's sociable, likable. You know that's important in our business."

He kissed her on the cheek and dressed for work.

He left her at her makeup mirror pulling out all manner of bottles, powdery palettes, and brushes.

He should know soon if it took.

After he pulled out of the driveway, he parked half a block away, behind a clump of hedges. He called Red, told him to get his PI ready, another fresh-faced dolt willing to make some easy cash. To engage Janelle in conversation…

Charles had to time it right. No use paying for a PI sitting on his ass for hours in a bar.

What was taking her so long? Just as he despaired, Janelle drove past him. He pulled out slowly, tailing her.

Outrageous, hiring a PI this week—but he had no choice. Charles had to know what was going on behind those sea-glass eyes of his wife. Something was. Surely, she would pour it out to today's PI. Perhaps Charles could get an inkling of just what Janelle had told the grifter, so Charles might get some sense of what his wife knew. What she claimed to know.

If nothing else, Red's PI could serve as a witness to Janelle's unbalanced behavior. Because Charles was prepared to activate his durable power of attorney. Yes, it had come this. And if anyone questioned why, he had the evidence. His wife, not of sound mind, was in no shape to sign papers, to run her affairs, to meet developers about mountain property.

How tragic. What unnecessary grief. All because of that odious charlatan.

Janelle pulled onto the main road. Really, she was an atrocious driver.

As soon as she took the highway toward Palmetto, he would call Red.

Only she didn't.

She headed away from the city, took a back road. He cursed. Was she headed to that grifter? But would that be so bad? Charles could barge right in and put a stop to it—

Janelle turned suddenly, pulled into what looked like a small storefront, a shed. He drove past, then made a U-turn out of sight. Was this some sort of juke joint? Some shabby tavern? He'd have to call Red, tell him to send his boy here.

It was a produce stand. He drove by slowly. He couldn't park there without her seeing him. He found a dirt road around the bend, and through the trees he could just see the parking lot. He let the engine idle and blasted the AC, sweat soaking his collar.

Then she tottered out to her car. Wearing high heels, that tight dress, like a hooker carrying a basket of…corn? What the hell?

She drove back toward downtown Haven. He followed. It was nearly lunchtime. Surely she would exit onto the highway to Palmetto, head to the hotel—

But no. No, with crushing disappointment he followed her home. She parked in the driveway and wobbled to the door, carrying her heap of vegetables.

A few minutes later he went inside, claiming he'd forgotten some important files. She looked up at him in the kitchen—tomatoes, corn, squash, eggplant, okra, peaches—spread across the kitchen island.

"Look," she said, "aren't they beautiful? The colors. Like a painting."

"Where did you go?" he said, probing with the care of a surgeon. She was often effusive with her praise about beauty on the cusp of a fugue, seeing art wherever she looked. "To a wonderful place that calms me." She picked up a clutch of leaves. "Lavender." She inhaled, smiled. A peaceful smile.

"I—I won't be long. Just need to drop these files off at work…and I'll meet you in an hour?" He kissed her powdery, perfumed cheek and he wondered what the local yokels at that produce stand thought of his wife, decked out like a lady-of-the-night, traipsing in, scooping up tomatoes.

"Meet me…where?"

"Where? For lunch. At the hotel, as we discussed."

She grimaced and stepped out of her shoes. "I don't think so, Charles. My feet hurt and I'm tired of…all that."

"Huh?" he grunted, as if he'd been punched, because this… this could not be right. "Tired of what?" he managed.

She held her high heels in one hand. "I'm going upstairs to change."

"No!" It came out loud, too harsh. "Janelle, please." He hated the wheedling tone in his own voice, hated it. "Janelle, you can't. Remember? The interview, the job candidate—"

Her face softened. "I can make us tomato sandwiches here. Fresh white bread and Duke's mayonnaise, your favorite." She headed up the stairs, not waiting for his answer.

He called Red, called it off. Called Arlene, told her not today, not now.

"I've been trying to get ahold of you all morning," Arlene said in a hoarse whisper.

"Which is why I told you to hold all my calls. It's important I am not disturbed." Not that it mattered now. He was plenty disturbed.

"T-Rex and that suit are in here nosing around the books."

"Suit?" Something in his gut curdled. "An audit? You mean the IRS?"

"No, it's that numbers man T-Rex told you about, remember? He's looking at things like payroll and all the things he's got no business looking into," she added, each word coated in disgust.

"Tell Teddy to stop him!"

"You don't think I tried? I had a hissy fit when he came in here. I've been stalling them all morning. T-Rex said he's been trying to call you."

"Tell him to stop, tell him I'm on the way."

"Hurry."

But when he hung up, he did not hurry.

He went into the garage.

How dark his life was. How hopeless. Never had he felt so burdened, not even those weeks Janelle was in the hospital recovering and he had a business to run and two children to raise. Did anyone appreciate just how bleak that time was, how he had held everything together?

In the garage, he reached for the metal box at the top of the shelf. He popped open the combination lock. The thing. He had to make sure it was there. It was. Beside his revolver. He hadn't held it for years; the chamber was empty. What was the use of a gun without ammunition? He sighed and put the firearm back inside the box and locked it. He'd pick up some bullets on the way to the office.

30

MIRA

Something was wrong with Spec.

"He's regressing," Burry told Mira that morning on the phone. "Something's going on but he's locked up tighter than Fort Knox. And, man, I can't get a read on it."

They met at Haven Hill State Park, her suggestion. Mira brought a thermos of lemonade and peanut-butter sandwiches. Swimming, a paddleboat, something different. Spec would like it, wouldn't he?

Nope. Spec stood ankle deep at the edge of the lake, his back to Mira and Burry.

"Sorry," Mira told her brother. "I thought he'd get a kick out of this place."

When she and Burry were kids, the park had been their refuge. They'd spent summer days here as teenagers, Burry as a lifeguard and Mira tagging along, packing their lunch, bringing Burry ice-cold Cokes and salty peanuts from the vending machine, ice cream cones from the camp store. She'd spent hours—so many glorious hours—in the lake with friends frolicking like playful dolphins, with an occasional sharp whistle from Burry when they swam out too far. Back then, the narrow sandy beach had been teeming with families. Now the place looked desolate and shabby. No more lifeguard or ice cream. A flotilla of battered, faded paddle boats, once glittery blue as eyeshadow. A rack of overturned muddy kayaks and a "help yourself" life-jacket loaner station.

"No competing with the new water park," Burry said. "But it's nice, having the place all to ourselves."

They lazed on the dock. Burry, his feet dangling in the water, watched Spec in that squint-eyed responsible way, looking like a lifeguard again. Mira lay across the dock, just as she had when she was fourteen.

"Is it lunchtime?" Spec asked.

Burry shook his head. "Dude, it's ten in the morning."

After a few minutes, Mira called out to Spec, asked if he was ready for a paddle boat ride, but he ignored her.

"He's sulking," Burry said. "The computer camp hasn't worked out. Rough week."

"But he was doing so well. What happened?"

"It's what didn't happen. He and Mom stopped their afternoons together last week. He's waiting for them to start up again, that's my take."

"What do they do? Go to movies?"

"Shopping, driving around—"

"Is that wise? Maybe you should drop them off at the mall instead."

"Right. Like two twelve-year-old girls? Nah. I think part of the thrill is the two of them sneaking off."

"Sneaking off where?"

"They visited Mom's friend for one thing, the one who came to her birthday—"

Mira gasped. "What? Mom told you that?"

"No. No, Spec did. The only information I could pull from him. Before he shut down."

"Lana, right? The soul tender?"

Burry nodded.

Mira had checked out her website. Lots of woo-woo language, but pretty harmless. We will delve into the underworld of your psyche unearthing the hidden and elusive pieces of your soul.

"Where does she live? Mom's friend? I thought she was just passing through."

"I assume she stayed somewhere nearby. Maybe on vacation."

"You didn't ask Mom?"

"Nope. She deserves some privacy."

"We should tell Dad."

"Yeah, right. Tell him what? That Mom dares to have her own friend?" He chuckled. "That would drive Dad bonkers. He's such a control freak."

Ugh! This old rift. Mira couldn't deal, not today. Pivot, dammit!

"Remember that time Mom took us to see those weird lightning bugs? It was somewhere in the mountains. I was little, second grade, I think...it's sort of fuzzy, but I can still picture it—this weird carpet of blue lights."

"*Phausis reticulata*. Blue ghosts. Extremely rare firefly."

Her brother looked pleased to riff on the natural world. Mission accomplished.

"Mom called them fairies," she said. "There were millions of them."

"The males emit this steady blue glow. We happen to be near one of the few pockets in the Appalachians where they breed."

"How about we take Mom and Spec to see them?"

"Next year." He yawned, wiped his eyes. "You can only catch the blue ghost show in the spring."

"Take a nap, Burry. I'll watch Spec."

"Thanks. I'm wiped." He stretched out on the warm dock, pulled his hat over his face.

Mira walked over to Spec, still standing at the edge of the lake.

Dragonflies skimmed the water, tiger swallowtails wing-waving on the joe-pye weed. A blue heron on the far dock, a regal sentinel. There was such busyness behind the serenity, Mira thought. Like her own body, which felt like a hive of activity. Marshaling resources, braiding genetic coils. Her breasts were sore, and she felt...swollen. She was building a new human! Possibly.

"Hey, Spec, come here." She pointed to the shallows.

The salamander was the size of her finger, sunset red,

black-spotted, moving dreamily in the cold stream of spring water, as if floating in space. "They like it here, where the stream runs into the lake," she said. Spec bent down and stared. "You better put on more sunscreen," Burry told Mira after a while when he joined them.

"Later," she said. "It's in the car."

"You're going to make one hell of a blushing bride."

She made the trek back to her car. Squirted suntan lotion in her hands, rubbed it on her chest and arms and stinging face, ow, ow, ow, oh crap. Burry was right.

She pulled out her phone from under the seat and checked it. Missed calls, voicemails, all from Teddy? From his office number, the landline. She deleted them, proud of herself. Not going to listen to his caterwauling, nope. She shoved the phone back under the seat.

"What's wrong?" Burry asked, when she returned. Of course, Burry would pick up on it. Her exasperation.

"Teddy."

"Cut him off, huh?"

"Yep."

"You're surprised he can't take no for an answer?"

She shrugged.

"And you and Nixon are still buddies, right?"

Buddies? Not the right word. Mira was a lackey, intimidated by a brilliant taskmaster. Only, Reagan had recently texted Mira in the middle of the night with bizarre questions. "I think Reagan is worried I'm going to be some scandalous runaway bride or something. She texted me this week to ask if I'm getting cold feet. I mean, who does that?"

"Huh. Maybe she gets sloshed at night. Drunk texting."

"Anyway, I don't have cold feet."

"Good to know."

They found a picnic table in the cool, fragrant shade of pines and sweetgums. Mira spread a beach towel over the splintered, warped wood. She unwrapped sandwiches and watermelon slices. Spec still watched the salamander. She and Burry ate in silence for a few minutes. Then Mira said, "Nels and I might be adding to our family sooner than we thought."

"What?" Burry took off his sunglasses and stared at her.

"Might be. Slight possibility."

"Whoa. Back up. Adding…on purpose?"

"Accidentally on purpose."

"Congratulations! Right? You both good with it?"

"We're excited."

"So, you got symptoms yet? Like barfing?"

"No, this isn't a sure thing by any means. I'm almost late. It's just—"

"Conceivable?"

"Yeah, smart-ass." She grinned.

"You take a pregnancy test?"

"No, not yet. I mean, I'm probably not. Right now I want to, you know, just savor the possibility."

"Huh. Okay, when did this possibility arise?"

"Monday."

Monday evening, to be exact, after Nelson had arrived from work. He'd hung up his keys, flipped through the mail. She kissed him and then blurted it all out. "I'm a day late for my period, maybe three? Not that I'm regular, I'm not, so probably false alarm but—" Bracing herself, because really this was on her. Technically. As the user of the diaphragm, which was extremely effective if used correctly and definitely iffy if not.

Nelson's wordless astonishment almost comical. Almost.

"You're…?" All he could manage.

"It's possible," she muttered. "Slightly possible. But say I am, Nels, that we're expecting. Would that be such a bad thing, to move up our goal of starting a family?"

"We decided to wait three years," he said numbly. "When we have a house and yard and…we're prepared for a baby."

"In three years, I'll be thirty-six. Do you know they call that a geriatric pregnancy? Infertility spikes at thirty-five, with risks of complications. And in vitro—that's twenty grand a pop. Unless

we decide to bank my eggs, and that's even more expensive."
Numbers, money, statistics, she was talking Nelson's language.
"Twenty grand?" he'd said. "You're kidding."
"Check it yourself, Nels. Look up 'geriatric pregnancy.'"
When he started googling on his phone, she went into the
bedroom and lit some candles.
In a few minutes he joined her. Oh God, she thought, here it
comes. He sat beside her on the bed and then...he took her in
his arms. His hand moved across her belly. In his amber-flecked
brown eyes, a look of such tenderness, Mira felt her own eyes
fill.
"We'll need a nursery, a house of our own. You'll need to find
a desk job or something. You can't be a pregnant bartender."
"I can't?"
"I'll do some consulting on the side."
"Oh, Nels, we'll figure it out."
She kissed his shoulder, rubbed his knotty, beautiful arms.
No more diaphragm, full speed ahead.
"There will be three of us," he said. "We'll recalibrate."
Recalibrate. Like GPS when you're lost. What a glorious
word. A word that meant yes.
Now, as Mira fished out frozen Milky Way candy bars from
the bottom of the cooler, she sensed her brother studying her.
"It's probably just a big bad case of PMS."
"So take a pregnancy test already!"
"I will. After the wedding."
"Is this some kind of superstition I don't know about?"
"I don't want to be disappointed. I just...I want to savor the
suspense."
"Uh-huh."
"What? Go ahead," she said. "You have a theory."
"You maybe floating a trial balloon?"
"Explain."
"No second thoughts with a bambino on the way, right?"
She shook her head, but she was glad to hide her watery eyes
behind sunglasses.

"Sorry, that was cynical, wasn't it?"

"It was, yes."

"Hey, I can't wait to be an uncle. I'm happy if you're happy."

"I'm happy."

After Burry and Spec left, Mira got into her car, her cutoffs crunchy dry, smelling of funky lake water. She looked into the car mirror, dabbed lotion across her sunburn-slapped cheeks. You need structure and limitations, she told herself.

She would not lose this life with Nelson, this best version of herself. This newly forming family. She needed to be held in check, secured, kept close.

She started the car. Pulled out her phone. A text, from Reagan.

—Gotta talk! Meet me at Ox & Hound 2 today? Will be out of reach so don't text or call b/c confidential! Just B there plz plz plz.

31

TEDDY

Teddy had taken a big risk.

While he waited, he came up with a list of excuses, should he need them, all of them lame, but hey. Desperate times, desperate measures.

Like—I must have grabbed your phone by mistake. And—I meant to text Milo, the contacts are screwed up on my phone.

For all Teddy knew, Mira had called Reagan, was calling her right now, trying to beg off from meeting at the 'Ox & Hound, and...Reagan's sharp, *What meeting? I don't know what you're talking about...*

He'd managed to grab Reagan's phone for a minute that afternoon, during the intense meeting with Mark, the accountant, shortly after they'd begun to get an inkling of just how fried the books were. Totally cooked. Reagan, incredulous, frazzled, hanging on to every word Mark said, didn't see Teddy slide her phone onto his lap and tap out that SOS text to Mira.

Yesterday Teddy had a preview of how bad it might be. He'd managed to pull up the accounts on his own when Arlene darted out for lunch—you could tell she didn't want to go, but apparently she had to run some errand—that's when Teddy unlocked her desk drawer and found the checkbook ledger.

"You're going to be the face of that business," Reagan had reminded Teddy last night. As if he needed reminding. He needed consoling. He and Reagan had met at a tapas bar near her office, trendy, crowded, tiny plates, guaranteed to leave you hungry. They'd been waiting for Sylvia, the campaign strategist. Who was running late, thank God.

Over briny olives and drifts of hummus and a bottle of

red, Teddy admitted that the business was in trouble. He felt wounded, pissed off at Charles. The business Teddy's father had started was going down in flames.

"At least we know," Reagan said. "Remember, I said no surprises."

"Yeah, we flushed out the surprises, all right." Why hadn't Charles confided in him? Did he not trust him? "Charles should never have approved your marketing campaign. Rex Wolf can't afford it."

"My marketing campaign? It's for you and the business. And it's a done deal, Teddy. No way am I walking that back. Then my job at the agency is on the rocks? Nope."

He shrugged, eyed the exposed brick wall and an acrylic painting of an eggplant.

"You're going to have to leave or fix it."

"Tell me something I don't know," he said.

"Okay," she said brightly, and he saw she wasn't being flip. She had that gleam in her eye, the tilt of her head, zeroing in on some new target. She'd been waiting to tell him…

"We are going to fix it," she said. "After we meet with Mark tomorrow and assess the damage, but—big but—if this is pointing to anything faintly illegal, well, we're going to have to be proactive."

"Yeah, yeah, I know."

"Spoiler alert, Teddybear. It's not going to be pretty."

"It's just…Charles is—"

"Like a father, like a father, oh my God, Teddy. One-note song, okay? Not helpful."

Teddy hadn't told Reagan that Charles had been out most of the week, and the few times Teddy had seen him, Charles made excuses, always leaving. Avoiding him. And that fantasy Teddy had let himself indulge in—maybe Charles was bent out of shape about Mira trying to get out of marrying that musclehead? Warped pipe dream. Totally. Charles was hurting, yep. And now Teddy knew why. Money problems. And the guy had so much pride. Teddy got that. He really did.

Reagan waved toward the doorway. "Oh, look! Sylvia is here."

Teddy stood. Reagan leaned over to him, murmuring, "No matter how the meeting with Mark goes tomorrow, we'll confront Charles after the wedding. No worries, Teddybear. We're not monsters."

Then the meeting today with Mark. Plenty of worries, all right, boatloads of worries.

Charles avoiding them. Missed the meeting, didn't return calls, while Arlene glared and snarled. And man, the fallout could be...bad. Legally, financially. For Charles, for the family. Mira would never forgive Teddy. She'd blame him.

Inside the 'Ox & Hound—technically the Fox & Hound, the F had been missing forever on the sign outside—Teddy found himself the sole customer. A down-at-the-heels bar on a mangy golf course on the edge of an aged-out suburb, Pebble Run. Practically empty. Perfect for his purpose.

He ordered a beer and staked out a barstool with a view of the parking lot. After ten minutes, he pacified his disappointment with a vodka soda. She wouldn't come, of course she wouldn't. What kind of Hail Mary move was this, adding to his own problems? He was his own worst enemy. What Reagan told him.

Just as he squeezed the lime into his drink, the front doors swung open. She didn't see him. Not at first. Her eyes skittered across the empty tables, the long mahogany bar. She wore a T-shirt, cutoff jeans, flip-flops, her hair wet, sunglasses shoved on her head. He slid off the stool and approached her, with the pleasure of watching her eyes widen.

"What are you doing here?"

"Waiting for a beautiful woman." Stupid. Wrong way to start off, like this was some kind of sneaky ambush when his intentions were sincere and serious.

"Where's Reagan?"

Clever. How she deflected the compliment.

He lowered his voice and touched her elbow. "Let's grab a booth. We need to talk."

"Is it Mom? The magazine interview with Dad? I was just going over there, to talk—"

"No. It's not Janelle."

Her eyes moved beyond him, to the restroom. "Is Reagan—"

"She's…not here yet."

"She sent you?"

His tie was wadded up in his pocket; he felt disheveled, a slouch, lost. "Look," he said. "This isn't about your mother, it's about Charles. Something serious you should know about."

"Know what? What? Just tell me."

"Let's sit down, just for a minute."

"I'm not staying."

"This is complicated."

"Are you bullshitting me?"

"Hear me out and judge for yourself." He stepped over to a booth, hoping she'd follow. She did.

"What can I get you to drink?"

"Water."

"Water and—?"

"Ice."

Teddy ordered himself another vodka soda, and the ice water. He didn't allow himself to take long looks at her, just glances. The pink skin around the frayed collar of her T-shirt—

"You're sunburned."

"No kidding." She ran a hand through her hair, found the sunglasses, and shoved them into her purse. "Burry and I took Spec to the park." She drifted off, then sat up straight. "Anyway. Spill it, T-Rex."

"Your father is…the business is in trouble."

"That's it? I don't pay attention to that stuff, Teddy. You know that."

The bartender brought over her water. She drank it, all of it, and rattled the ice chips. "Daddy runs Rex Wolf the way he wants to."

"This is different."

"Isn't that what you're there for? To take over?"

She still didn't get it.

"Yes. Eventually. Maybe. If there's still a business to run."

She sat back in the studded leather booth. "Okay, now you're just trying to scare me."

He dropped his voice. "It looks like he may be doing some questionable things off the books. Hiding money or…I don't know yet. Some dicey shell game."

"Sloppy bookkeeping isn't a crime—"

"This could be."

The bartender set down Teddy's drink and a bowl of nuts. He plucked out two Brazil nuts, Mira's favorite. "Here."

She ate them absently, while he shook out a handful of peanuts, cashews, and those little round ones. He was starving. He hadn't eaten a bite of the barbecue lunch; his appetite had vanished sometime around the time he discovered the payroll taxes were missing.

"You want me to talk to Daddy—"

"No. No, God no. Not with…"—your wedding—"…not now. I don't want to burden him with this until…when we have all the facts. Next week."

"Then why are you telling me this now?"

"I admit the timing sucks."

"You think?"

Music blared; the bartender scrambled to turn it down. Teddy recognized "Hurt," Johnny Cash's gravelly baritone covering Nine Inch Nails. The freaking perfect soundtrack for his afternoon.

"I don't want you blindsided, is all."

"But what am I supposed to do with this? Are you telling me to cover your ass? Or to upset me?"

Did she really suspect he took any pleasure in this?

"No, I'm telling you—"

"—so when it all goes to shit and Dad loses the business or worse…you can say you warned me. So I won't blame you."

She shook out the silverware from a napkin and swiped her wet eyes; her nose was running. He slid around in the booth beside her.

"Look, I don't have the answers right now. I haven't even talked to Charles yet…maybe he has some reasonable explanation, or even if he doesn't…you know I'll do everything in my power to help him."

"You're going to talk to him about this today?"

"God, no. Not until next week. I'll find a way to keep it under wraps…and then I'll do my damnedest to clean it up—"

"Clean it up."

"If I can, yes. I…you have to understand, I can't be swept up in anything that's…if there's evidence of malfeasance."

And now—what an icy glare stung him from that red, tender face.

"That won't help…anyone," he added weakly.

Silence.

"Is that what she says?"

"She?"

"Your wife." She drank more water, her pinkie wiggling a little air quote. Wife. "Reagan does know you're telling me all this, right? Or were you supposed to wait for her?"

"This all just happened today, Mira."

"She would have a strategy. To keep your hands clean. A plan with bullet points."

He put his arm around her now. He could smell suntan lotion on her skin—

"What are you, crazy?" she said. "Get back over there in your seat, Teddy."

"Don't…it's okay. She's not coming."

"She's not? How do you know?"

"I promise you—she's not."

She searched his face. "Let me out."

He stood. She slid out of the booth and headed for the restroom.

He checked his phone. Nothing new, just more where RU? texts, over and over, from Reagan. Would Mira even come back out here with him? Or slip out the back?

But she returned. Slid back into the booth. She'd splashed water on her puffy, angry, wonderful face. She stared at him with narrowed eyes.

"I'm such an idiot," she said.

"No, you're not."

"Yeah, I am."

He didn't understand.

Until he did.

"You pretended to be her today...you texted me, you set up this little tête-à-tête." What torture. To see her look at him with such hurt. "Oh my God, Teddy. I am so stupid...of course it was you, demanding I meet you. You tricked me."

"I didn't trick you. It's not like that—I tried to reach you. You blocked me."

"It was you," she said slowly. "It was you all along," her voice so loud, the bartender looked over. "About the...the cold feet the other night, that was you, you pretending to be her!"

"Look, I admit to a couple of dark moments when I—"

"At one in the morning, that was you, asking if I had second thoughts and—"

"Yes. Yes, it was me. Okay? Hey, listen, I know it was stupid. Mira, listen—" She stood up, shook his hand off her elbow. "Mira, look, I'm sorry."

"Stop apologizing, T-Rex. You don't do sympathy. You just come off sounding like a jerk."

"Okay, I deserve that."

The double doors opened, and he strained to see who was arriving. Two old men in plaid pants shambled in, just off the links.

She slung her purse over her shoulder.

"Wait." He followed her to the door. "Don't do anything

rash. Be careful about talking about this, Mira. I am trying to
protect them—Charles and your mother. You do know that,
right?"

She grabbed the door handle, a brass fox's head, and he put
his hand on hers.

"Do me a favor?" she said, not looking at him. "Promise me
you won't come Saturday."

"To the wedding? You're kidding, right?"

"No."

"But...I have to."

She gave a sad laugh. "Seriously?" They were in the tiny
vestibule now; the doors clanked behind them. "Make up
something. You're good at that. Just don't come to my wedding.
Please, as a gift to me—Do. Not. Come."

"You don't really mean that," he said slowly. "Do you?"

"I do. I DO, I DO!"

"Mira—" His fingers left bleached prints on her warm, red
arms. And for a few seconds they were pressed there together,
not an embrace, just a sort of leaning into each other, and he
inhaled her coconut-scented hot skin, her damp, musky hair—
before she pushed away and opened the door, the clapping of
her flip-flops fading as she ran to her car.

She peeled out of the parking lot, burned some rubber.

He knew exactly where she was going.

32

JANELLE

Mira has come looking for her father.

"I have just the thing for that sunburn," I tell her. Buttermilk and mint leaves. Clara used to make it for me, a salve. I remember her cool fingers smoothing my stinging skin. I don't have buttermilk. But I have yogurt and fresh mint. I dab it on Mira's face.

"Arlene says Daddy isn't at the office," Mira says. "But she won't tell me where he is. I called her three times on the way over here. Does Dad seem worried about anything lately?"

Mira wants to know if her father and I are "having problems."

"Doesn't everyone?"

"But are you having money troubles?"

That's when I know Charles has riled up Mira too. Honestly, the two of them stewing over me! "Your father is getting worked up over nothing. We don't need to sell the land. I don't need to be looked after."

And that's when the doorbell rings. "I bet that's the Girl Scout cookies I ordered."

But it's not the Girl Scouts. It is Teddy.

He wants to talk to Charles.

Teddy just stands there, looking pitiful, after I tell him Charles isn't home. I invite him in. He is well mannered, he greets me, he always asks how I am, and he waits for my answer. I like that about him, his politeness, even if it is more duty than kindness.

Teddy steps inside and looks beyond me. "Was that Mira's car in the driveway?"

"She's in the kitchen with a terrible sunburn."

He asks if I have any idea where Charles is, or when he might be back?

And from behind me—"What is this? The third degree, T-Rex?" Mira is very cross with him.

"I'm sorry to interrupt," he says.

She has a washcloth in her hand and she is wiping off the yogurt. "Spare me."

They stare at each other.

I can't help but laugh. "My goodness, you two are acting like you're kids again."

I ask Teddy if he'd like a bite to eat or a drink.

"No," Mira says. "He was just leaving. Right, T-Rex?"

He turns and leaves like a scolded dog. I see him to the door. "Will you tell Charles to call me, Janelle? As soon as he returns, no matter how late?"

After he leaves, Mira says, "What nerve to show up here like that."

"You must have the jitters."

"If one more person tells me I have cold feet, I swear I'm going to scream." And then she says she is sorry, she doesn't mean to fuss.

There are dings and rings coming from her purse on the floor. "That's probably Nelson," she says. But she just sits there, her eyes closed.

I take a warm cloth and wipe off her face. Gently, as if she is a little girl again.

"Don't worry about your father or me. Go home to Nelson. Sometimes love is hard. Sometimes it makes life harder."

Now it is after midnight. Charles is still not home.

Perhaps he won't return tonight. To punish me. He is so angry with me. He knows I'm waiting.

But waiting is a kind of love, isn't it?

I have come down to the garage. To drive, to go in search of Charles. I get inside my car, but I just sit.

I sit here in the garage, behind the wheel, writing, writing, writing.

The film jumped, but I see it now.

I am running, I am opening the door of my station wagon. I am inside it. I lock the doors. Charles presses his face against the window and his mouth is opening and closing and opening, he yells at me to unlock the doors. Don't you dare leave—don't you leave!

Then...the river swallows my car. I am inside it while inside me, floating—a baby, barely begun. When I woke up in the hospital bed, I was empty, scraped out like a jack-o'-lantern. That amphibious curl, that big-eyed, stemmed, sacred bud of a child. Gone. They wouldn't talk to me about it, not the doctors, not Charles.

A terrible thing has come loose in me; it wants to announce itself. I keep it contained, a venomous spider in a jar.

33

CHARLES

"I have the funds." The hardest words Charles had ever uttered. He avoided "your money"—even worse.

"I knew you would," she purred. She was enjoying this, bringing him to his knees.

"I'll deliver it to you within the hour."

"No, you won't." The sound of her long exhale. She was smoking.

"I don't understand," Charles whispered. He was calling from a phone in the florist's shop. He didn't want a trace of that grifter on him, not in his phone logs, or emails, especially not in person.

"We will meet in a well-lit, public place of my choosing. The Pines Motel Coffee Shop. On Highway 26—"

"I know where that is."

"In…hmmm…let's say two hours."

"No, I—"

She hung up.

He was so furious he stormed out and nearly forgot Janelle's flowers.

She was inside the coffee shop when he arrived, her profile in the corner window—tawdry hennaed hair covered with a baseball cap. He stood there beside his car, hoping the criminal would come outside to meet him, conduct their hideous business in the parking lot.

But no. Her wan face, tapered like an ax, found him. She motioned, a quick gesture, a command. Come here.

Inside, under the harsh fluorescent diner lights, he sat across

from her in the orange booth. Her gray sweatshirt and camou-
flage baseball cap—clearly another costume, that of the weary
local, after second shift. The waitress appeared.

"Nothing for me," he said.

"You might as well have coffee," Lana said. "You'll be here
five minutes. Starting now."

The waitress took that as a yes, that this woman ordered on
his behalf. She filled his cup.

"It's in the trunk," he said when the waitress left.

"Is it?" She smiled. "Before the exchange, a reminder. I have
a plan in place. If you renege, if there are any unforeseen kinks,
if I am inconvenienced or incapacitated in any way? The video
goes out, right in time for the wedding."

He stared, mute with fury.

"You look half dead, Charles." She stood, as if to leave.

"Not so fast, Martha Jean Dipple."

She would make a scene. Even if there was just a waitress,
a short-order cook, a tired truck driver shoving in eggs who
would turn and watch the show. She would make a scene, but
that didn't stop him.

"Martha Jean from West Virginia," he said, finally enjoying
himself.

She sat down.

"Dirt poor. College scholarship for theater, then dropped
out, knocked up by a rich boy. Toy Farreaux. And that family
didn't want any part of you, the white-trash girl, not in their
gene pool, did they? Paid you off, to get rid of it, to get the hell
away from their son. Guess the acting career didn't turn out,
though. Seeing as how you bilked some poor widow woman in
a certain Podunk town in Arizona."

Her eyes narrowed, but that smile lingered, the same gash in
her face that passed for a smile.

"You think I'm shocked? What took you so long?"

"A widow, though." He shook his head.

"Her sons were greedy tyrants."

"Tell that to the law. I'm sure a certain sheriff in Arizona would jump at the chance to help our locals bag a scam artist like you." He had her on the defensive—surely he did—and that energized him. "I can make a phone call and—" he snapped his fingers "—have you arrested by morning."

She sighed. "Charles, you insult me. Of course, you could play that card. But if I am arrested, my contingency plan kicks in. Your family movie will be sent and shared—"

"Stop calling it that!"

"—unless I call it off."

"You are a vicious, wicked woman."

"I've been called worse by better people."

"You...you want to ruin us—our family. You want to destroy Janelle."

"It will ruin you, Charles. She'll be better off without you."

"You got her to say things, didn't you? She's...gullible. She imagines things and she...she played right into your hands—everyone will know that! They will blame you, because you got her to say crazy things!"

"Crazy? Au contraire. It's beautiful, how the pieces fit, how this tale has come together."

"What do you mean...what pieces?"

"Ahhhh. I see what you're doing. Trying to trick me into divulging the highlights of my polished little movie. No spoilers, Charles. Didn't that sneak preview I slipped you disturb you enough?"

"You're bluffing. You don't have anything."

"You're welcome to find out."

His last move, desperate, but he played it.

"I'm going to tell them, then. All of it. When the family is together tomorrow."

"All of it. Really?" She ripped open two packets of sugar and stirred her coffee.

"I protect her, everyone knows I look after my wife—for all these years I've kept her safe."

"You keep her safe? Is that what you tell yourself? You're possessive, overbearing, and sneaky as hell, Charles. You spied on her when she dared to venture out for a few afternoons in a hotel bar for some harmless flirtations. You admitted as much."

"Those…those were private investigators." His voice shook. "They were lawmen, experienced, and I hired them to protect her."

"Your capacity for self-delusion is impressive, Charles." She chuckled. "Protect her? Aren't you the sly one. Did they give you blow-by-blow reports?"

"Shut up!"

The cook looked up from his fry basket.

"You twist everything," he said, quieter now.

"You hired a few hunks to monitor Janelle because you're terrified she'll remember—"

"No, no—"

"—what a lousy bastard you are."

She leaned in closer over the table and whispered. "What is so delicious is how you let him spin those lies. The up-and-coming senator claiming Janelle never arrived that night, and then, oh my, how the rumors flew."

"Pure gossip!"

"But how did you manage to keep it out of the papers, about Janelle's being"—she smirked—"shall we say, in the family way? Now that is a very dark tale. A mother driving off a bridge is one thing, a mother-to-be is…unforgivable, no matter how you spin it. Was it polite censorship or did you have to threaten a newspaper editor?"

"Janelle wasn't pregnant." His hands curled into fists under the table. His heart was a racehorse.

She barked a laugh. "Oh, please."

"She dreamed it up. She only thought she was. It was a con-fabulation, the doctors said."

Lana tried to hide her astonishment, but the mask fell for an instant, and he saw behind that cool insouciance. He'd landed a blow.

"And of course you trusted those doctors?" Lana said, try-ing to recover, but she was wounded. Yes.

"There was no medical evidence of a pregnancy. She dreamed it up." He smiled and pointed at her. "You didn't figure that one out, did you?" A sort of unseemly delight, watching the vampire squirm.

"Get your finger out of my face," she said quietly, "before I scream."

"You believed it, just because she told you. You see? You don't know anything about my wife."

She looked at the clock behind him. "Your time is up."

Outside in the parking lot he opened the trunk and pulled out the dusty bowling bag.

"You will leave Haven," he said. "Immediately."

"You don't get to tell me what I'll do." She opened the bag, looked inside, and zipped it back up. "We are no longer negotiating."

"If I see you around my family—"

She opened her car door and threw in the bag.

"See ya."

34

LANA

She deserved a vacation.

There had been so many details, so much careful arranging. Now the endgame was in sight. Her spirits should be soaring. So why this deflated lag? Was she such an adrenaline junkie? Lana wouldn't blow all the cash this time. She'd funnel it into under-the-radar investments and offshore accounts, the sort of things people with means did.

But, holy ,other—first, Lana needed a vacation.

"Lana, my darling. I am not seeing you now."

Lana adjusted the computer screen. "Better?"

"Oh yes. Yes. I am seeing you."

Petya stood to unzip his jeans.

"No, not tonight," she said.

"Novirtuallove?" he said, running the words into one syrupy glop.

"Tempting, but let's save it for our physical meeting."

She wanted to review their plans again, because Petya wasn't the brightest bulb on the makeup mirror. Meet in Jacksonville, ditch her car for cash, then on to Miami. Yes, yes, yes, he said. Once there—though she didn't share it with Petya, of course—she would arrange the offshore account and make their island resort reservations: St. Kitts, maybe, or the Bahamas. Also, find storage to stash her jewelry.

Stressful. All this shit left to do. She lit a joint. She'd bought weed from a kid at the gas station who claimed it was "kick-ass."

"You haven't told a soul of our plans?"

"No," he said. "No, no. To no one. Luka and Vlad know not thing."

"We don't need those goons on our tails."

"My poor baby," Petya said. "You wait. I will relax you. We will have fun."

Yes, he would. Yes, they would.

But until then—more steps to take, more missteps to avoid.

"I need to pack," she said. "You're all set?"

Petya—counting down the seconds when he could take her in his arms, murmuring about tearing off her clothes et cetera, et cetera—in a roundabout way wanting assurances that the price of his rental car would be refunded. And if he happened to arrive before she did, the cost of the hotel room, where of course he would be waiting. Counting down the seconds.

She would cover it all, she told him. But she'd need his receipts "for tax purposes." As for the car rental—piece of shit Ford Fiesta, fine. No Escalades or Benz. Not on her dime.

"I can hardly wait, baby—"

Buffering, buffering, he blipped off. Just as well.

There was still so much to do.

The video was in the can, though. You'd think she'd be relieved. She'd planned all along to slap something together in case that tease on the ol' thumb-drive trick didn't scare Charles enough. An exposé, credible and damaging...enough. Three minutes, tops. But then she found herself editing, tweaking, polishing this lurid family movie. Enjoying herself. Her own rage at Charles Wolf—frankly, it fueled her creativity.

She'd miss tormenting him.

She admitted that to herself as she filled a suitcase. She'd leave most of this crap behind, buy a new wardrobe, enough with the New Age chiffon and cheap saris. Take the computer, of course, her camera, the jewels. Janelle's jewels.

Maybe it was the weed, a delayed ass-kick, after all, but she sat in the kitchen laughing. Poured a shot of tequila, a toast to herself. She was hysterical imagining it: showing up at the wedding, the look on his face. Charles—

Because, really, how dare that bastard? Throwing Toy

Farreaux in her face...dredging up her sole heartbreak, flinging it at her like a bucket of sewage. Charles thought he'd found her weak spot, but she'd shut it down, hadn't she? Shut him up. She was the one with the nuclear code.

Oh, Charles Wolf thought he was so clever. Every dumbass with a smart phone could dig up dirt. Toy Farreaux was ancient history, but it still hurt like hell twenty years later, what happened there in the cocoon of her sophomore year in college. A theater scholarship had catapulted her out of a dying West Virginia town and into the lap of luxury for a few months, doted on by Toy, until they got careless, and his pearl-clutching family, appalled at the idea that their precious heir would even consider marrying a plebe from the hills of a coal-mining town, much less allow progeny from the hillbilly...

They'd thrown money at the problem: her. First, insisting she go through "the procedure."

That was her first influx of cash. Then the dean called her into his office, into the Farreaux administration building, because they were a "generous" family whose name graced a dozen campus buildings, donors for generations, who were "considerate and understanding" about "the situation," and the dean had paused then, perhaps decent enough to feel humiliated about his smarmy duties as a hired gun. In those few seconds, the iron smell of blood floated up to her, and she worried the maxi pad she wore from "the procedure" would leak and ruin the dean's velvet sofa. He cleared his throat and told her she would no longer see or talk to Toy. Another clot of cash...to soften the blow.

But it didn't soften anything.

Another warning to leave Toy alone, but she couldn't, and before the term *stalker* came into vogue, her scholarship mysteriously evaporated, and they served papers on her between classes, setting a hearing for the restraining order; it almost broke her. Almost. Sweet, dewy-eyed Martha Jean Dipple perished in the flames of humiliation, but Lana O'Shield rose from the ashes strong, resilient, vengeful, honing a talent for knocking down crass, entitled men from their pedestals when they dared to look down on her.

What delicious revenge it would be, to pop in at the wedding reception and watch Charles Wolf choke on his champagne.

He deserved to choke.

She deserved to see it.

Lana walked into the bathroom. Nothing to pack there. She'd buy toiletries on the road. And not that crappy store-brand shampoo, either, she'd get the good stuff at a salon—high-end soaps and masks and lotions. Maybe a hot-stone massage, too, while she waited for Petya.

In the kitchen she rummaged through the refrigerator, found the last of the eggs, thanks to the hens, and made herself an omelet. She was baked—that was good weed—and starving. She used the remaining ketchup and a heel of hardened cheese. Not much else in the fridge, which was good. She hated to waste food; it had something to do with her childhood.

She set her dirty dishes in the sink.

If, big IF, she dared to drop by the wedding reception on her way out of town, she could touch base with Janelle. The poor soul was bat-shit crazy, and counting on their continued "sessions," so Lana would placate her, tell her she had to leave for an urgent matter, and no doubt relieve Janelle of a new pallet of notebooks, the woman wrote like a freaking son of a bitch.

There was no need to burn bridges—Lana chuckled at that. Keep the "friendship" with Janelle, as her mole. Yes, she'd capped this well; Charles Wolf was tapped out. But the field was rich in possibilities. That T-Rex, for example. In a few years when he was a senator, or governor, or…who knows? Bigger idiots had headed to the White House—she could circle back. Trot out this video, because surely he would be running on the coattails of his heroic father, the senator, who, it turns out, was no saint. Not even close. Easy enough to lay down a few more lines of voiceover—freshen it up. That would bag some cash. If not from T-Rex, then one of the tabloids.

On the other hand, Lana could—should—play it safe, hit the road as soon as she was sober enough to drive, find a way to contact Janelle later, after an appropriate period of time, of course. Arrange for another post office box to exchange letters. As wily as Janelle turned out to be about such things, surely the two of them could come up with a way to continue their "chats."

Provided Janelle didn't wig out totally or get royally pissed off at Lana. For standing her up. For not showing up at the wedding after all. Not likely, but Janelle wasn't entirely predictable, was she?

You don't know her. That insult Charles had lobbed at Lana at the diner still irked her. His relishing that she, Lana, got it wrong, that Janelle hadn't been knocked up the night of her accident. Lana failed to hide the surprise on her face, but that was the cost of emotive talent and method acting. Anyway, why should she believe anything Charles Wolf said?

Only she did. A gut feeling.

Confabulation. She dreamed it up. What a load of bullshit. Really? Surely Janelle had figured out that her phantom pregnancy shtick was over by now, so why hadn't she confided as much to Lana? Why would Janelle lie to Lana? That was the sort of loose thread that niggled Lana, that really irritated the hell out of her. Lana didn't like to be played, was the thing. By anyone. Not even a client. Especially a client.

Lana sat at her computer and pulled up a video clip of Janelle's whispery confession:

And so, I call out to him. Charles! Louder and louder. Charles, Charles, Charles!

Stan tells me, Now, don't be like that.

Stan pushes the hair out of my face. His hand swallows mine again. He says my name over and over, Janelle, Janelle.

I am leaving. I tell him, I am leaving.

Stan says, I can't stand to see a beautiful woman cry. He says, Darlin', it has nothing to do with love—it's a little fun. Just a little fun.

What a perfect, scandalous, sordid little video! Lana began

to laugh again. Her face streamed with tears. Lana recalled Charles Wolf's swollen, enraged face across from her in that coffee shop. *I see how you warp things with your filthy mind. Right.* This from a man who paid PIs to flirt and spy on his wife in hotel bars.

Of course, Lana had taken some creative license, tarted it up. Easy peasy to weave Janelle's bits and pieces into a juicy clip. Damn shame not to share this, her best work. Oh, well. Thems the breaks.

So, what would it be?

Just a brief stop, on her way out of town? Appease Janelle with ten minutes, a swig of champagne. Take Janelle's load of notebooks, with an appropriate sacred air, promising to read every word. Then shove them into a circular file at the first highway rest area.

And Lana would be sure to wear Janelle's garnet and diamond set, the necklace and earrings. Delight Janelle and royally piss off Charles. But Charles couldn't touch Lana—she would arrive strapped with explosives, so to speak, with the threat of the family movie.

Throw Charles Wolf a kiss—Ta-ta!

Or play it safe and get the hell out?

Into the arms of Petya, her luscious bodyguard. Because, seriously, she couldn't risk it. Not with the jackpot stuffed in a bowling bag.

"I'll sleep on it, how's that?" she asked the puppy.

It was curled up on a chair but snapped to attention and wagged its tail.

When she left, she'd leave newspapers on the floor, kibble, a bowl of water, but otherwise this mutt was on its own. "Sorry, it's a dog-eat-dog world, as you'll soon discover," she told the puppy. She never called it by name, that only complicated things. The cleaning crew would come in a few days, after the rental company realized she'd left. Let them deal with the animals, the dirty dishes.

Not her problem.

"Try to look adorable," she told the puppy.

Lana snapped a photo with her phone.

She had one of the turtle, even the hens roosting. She sent a text to Spec.

—Remember the plan, I will text U & then U DON'T DO IT.

Yes, she was taking this contingency plan to the brink, but she had to explore every scenario. Remain vigilant. Because men like Charles Wolf did not like losing. If he got desperate and stupid enough to send some Barney Fife to hassle her on the way out of Haven, she would at least know from the back seat of a police cruiser that she might be handcuffed, but her hands weren't tied. That the backup plan was kicking in.

The kid would send out the video—unless she called it off. God knows she'd drilled that into his skull.

She would text Spec a few hours before the wedding to stand down, of course.

Provided she was unimpeded, unpissed off, and sober.

She texted: R U standing by?

—Yes.

Good boy.

She sent him photos of the puppy, the turtle, the hens. A reminder, if they needed to be "rescued."

—I am ready, he texted.

As he had been all week.

35

TEDDY

Teddy strained to sound nonchalant when he told Reagan he wasn't going to the office. "Thought I'd take the day off," he said, in his practiced off-the-cuff voice. "Feeling a little logy."

"Teddybear. You have to go in." She was on the final stretch of her treadmill session, the cool-down. Her eyes flashed with excitement; her sinewy skin gleamed. He stood in shorts, unshaven, his voice thick with sleep.

"I was up half the night," she said. "Totally nailed it."

"Nailed...what?"

"The solution. I figured it out." She stepped off the treadmill.

What a change from the night before, when they were still reeling from the news that Rex Wolf wasn't just a leaky ship listing out at sea but sinking fast. A shipwreck without lifeboats. So how to exit...gracefully?

"We confront Charles," she said now. "Tell him we'll solve the money problems before this leaks and gets into the wrong hands, so he won't be exposed or arrested."

"And how," Teddy asked, "will we 'solve the money problems'?"

"We take out a second mortgage. I ran the numbers. Only because we'll be making a sweet profit in a couple of years."

"You're saying we buy out Charles?"

"Buy him out?" She laughed. "No, Teddybear. Buy the assets. It will be a fire sale. He'll sign over all of it, because we're saving his skin." She guzzled her cucumber water, looked at him, and sighed. "What?"

He's been like a father to me. He swallowed the words. Yeah, he was pissed off at Charles, but now there was this enormous sadness settling in.

"You're rescuing his business and letting him leave quietly, without a scandal. And with a restored reputation by the way. So, you have to go in today, Teddybear. I mean, come on. Next week you'll be running the place."

"That's the point. I'll take a day off now, when I have the time."

He followed her into the bathroom, where she peeled off her running shorts and jogging bra.

"You just don't want to face Charles," she said as she stepped into the shower, blasted the water, and closed the glass door with a clang, shutting him out.

The room filled with steam and the sharp, clean smell of shampoo.

"You don't need to do or say anything different." Her voice echoed on the tiles. "Just carry on like normal."

"Until next week, you mean? Just pretend until *Et tu, Brute?*"

"This isn't a tragedy. You're saving his ass. It's business. Jesus."

The thing was, it did feel like a tragedy.

"You're going to have to pretend everything is normal tomorrow at the wedding anyway," she said.

She was right. He didn't want to face Charles. Or Mira. Mira who'd begged him not to come to her wedding, his "gift" to her, and, man, that killed him. But when it came down to it, he didn't relish the thought of witnessing Mira chaining herself to that lunkhead anyway. That was past awkward and well into agonizing. Could he possibly get out of going? Come down with some ailment today, head off a Saturday of humiliation? Fortunately, he was feeling sick just thinking about it.

Reagan stepped out of the shower. He handed her a towel and followed her to the bedroom walk-in closet. "Why don't you take the day off and hang with me?" he said. "We'll go somewhere, anywhere. You name it."

He came up behind her. She was naked, running a hand across her clothes, plucking out a red dress, then a blue one.

"Which one?" She held both up.

"Neither."

"Ha, ha."

"I'm serious. Let's take off somewhere. Let's do it."

"I thought you were feeling sick?"

"Yeah, I am."

"Which is it? You want to skip work or you're sick? Because this is not cool. Do not wimp out on me, Teddy. Anyway, you'd insult Charles if you didn't make an appearance at the office today. Did that occur to you? Plus, Arlene would definitely suspect something was up."

Teddy didn't dress—donning a shirt and tie would mean he'd lost the argument. Reagan was back in the steamed-up bathroom, wearing a black bra and panties, slender as a stem, leaning toward the mirror, putting on her makeup.

He tried again. "If my symptoms were to worsen, let's say, hypothetically, and develop into some sort of projectile-vomiting contagion...you could represent me, right? Tomorrow. Tell them I caught a bug?"

"What the hell, Teddy? This wedding is freaking you out."

"What do you mean?" Cold dread. She...could she be onto him?

"Okay, what, you're trying to pick a fight with me? Because all this work? All the contacts and networking? I did it for you. The Rex Wolf website goes live today. The guest list is crème de la crème, you know that. And I hired a photographer for tomorrow, a good one, an expensive one, because Mira is so ditzed out she probably forgot or has some art student doing it for free. He'll be taking lots of shots with you in the crowd, okay? Of you. Rex Wolf is paying for it. So play along, and smile."

"The business is paying for a photographer tomorrow? I don't think Rex Wolf needs to pay for anything else right now. You should have asked me before—"

"If I ran every decision by you, I'd never get anything done."
She had a point. Reagan wielded her mascara wand at him.
"The spotlight will be on all of us. Tomorrow is your day too,
Teddy."

She blow-dried her hair while he pondered. What in the hell
just happened? He was being carried away by this turbulent
plan of Reagan's, and unless he did something desperate like—
drink cod liver oil? Or eat a bag of prunes?—he'd have to face
Charles…and Mira….

"The spotlight shouldn't be on me," he said. "It's her day.
Mira's wedding day, for Christ's sake."

Reagan's pep talk had turned torturous, and her uncanny
ability to deflate him made him desperate.

"Uh-huh. Right."

She smiled at him in the mirror, then turned around. Ran her
hands down his chest, plundered in his shorts, grabbed his—

"Ouch!"

"Just checking. Thought you'd lost them."

Teddy went to the office. But what a relief! Charles wasn't there.
Hopefully, he wouldn't show up at all. Teddy breezed past Arlene's empty (thank God!) desk. He closed his door.

Teddy could cut out early. Why not? Hang out…somewhere.
Back to the old 'Ox and Hound.

He sat back in his chair and closed his eyes. Oh God, what
to do, what to do?

Because how could Charles be so stupid? Cooking the
books? Reagan was right—they could end up saving Charles
from another scandal. This fire-sale plan was merciful if you
thought about it.

Teddy didn't want to think about it. He wanted to get the
hell out of town.

If Teddy showed up tomorrow at the wedding, Mira would
be mad as hell. She'd never talk to him again. Not that she
would talk to him anyway. She'd not only ignored his calls and

texts and emails, she'd blocked him again on social media. And, man, that was low.

But Nelson hadn't. Teddy got on his computer now and pulled up Nelson's Facebook posts...scrolled past photos of hipsters with douche knots, scouring Nelson's posts for news of Mira, of pictures...there, Mira, outdoor shot, baggy T-shirt and straw hat: my wife in two days!

Teddy logged off and picked up a legal pad.

Come on, focus. Notes on a new op-ed. Raising the gas tax is no way to fix roads.

A soft knock. He looked up as the door opened.

"Just wanted to let you know I'm in today," Charles said.

Oh, shit. "Good to hear."

"You busy?"

Not this. Not now.

Charles didn't wait for an answer. He sat down across from Teddy's desk.

Had Janelle even told Charles that Teddy had come looking for him? Probably not. Surely not. She'd forgotten to tell Charles to call. Or...or maybe she hadn't forgotten, maybe she was protecting Charles, from work, from Teddy, because the truth was, Charles looked exhausted.

"Arlene told me about the mix-up," Charles said with an uneasy chuckle. "I'm sorry you got a scare. But it's all there now."

"What's...all there?"

"The funds in the operating account. All there." He shifted, pulled out his wallet, handed over a slip of paper to Teddy.

A deposit slip. One hundred thousand. Dated today, this morning.

"I learned my lesson. I know it's no way to run a business. Just a little error. Won't happen again."

Teddy murmured something...did he actually say "no problem"? So, the money was back, no need to cover it, Reagan would be relieved, wouldn't she? No. No way to run a business. Charles had said that. Surely, he knew...this wouldn't work.

Operating account disappearing and reappearing, it opened them up to liens and lawsuits. Even if it was all there now.

He pictured Charles, dangling from Reagan's prong of a solution, swinging in the wind—

"You look...beat," Teddy said when he finally met Charles's bloodshot eyes, shocked by his grayish skin, the slump of his shoulders.

"Got a lot going on."

Charles knew the shell game wasn't going to cut it, didn't he? That the shit would hit the fan. He did know, but that didn't make things easier—not on Teddy.

"Go home and grab a nap. Take the day off."

"That interview for the magazine is today. Janelle and I have to get gussied up and talk about our anniversary. I have my sister coming in; Arlene went to get her. I'm taking Mira and the family to the club tonight." He grimaced, trying to smile. "No rest for the weary."

He stood, anguished, Atlas with the world on his shoulders. As he opened Teddy's office door, Charles hesitated. "I just want to say," he said, "how good it is to have someone in my corner, Teddy. Finally. Thank you, for being here and taking the reins and, well, you brought new blood and new life into this place. And Reagan, she's a whip-smart girl. You married well, son. The two of you...mean so much..." His voice broke.

Teddy had to look away. He had to get out of here.

"So," Charles said, with a fake cough, pulling himself together. "See you tomorrow."

Teddy hesitated, just a second or two, considering...how he could plant the seed, of how he was coming down with something, hope it's nothing.

"Later," Teddy managed.

That was before Mira called, and Teddy decided nothing would keep him away from that wedding.

36

MIRA

Nelson woke her before dawn with his version of breakfast in bed: swampy goop in a tall glass.

"Kale, carrots, beets, banana. Just juiced."

It was sweet, how attentive he was. She took a sip, tried not to gag.

"Folic acid, tons of vitamins. Bottoms up."

"It's an acquired taste. I'm trying."

He turned on the lamp.

"Your face," he said, and not in a good way. Was he—wincing?

"What's wrong with my—?" She set the glass down, jumped out of bed, and peered into the bureau mirror. "Oh my God." Her cheeks. Her baboon-butt red face.

"I can cover this with makeup." Couldn't she?

The wedding was tomorrow.

"I hope you learned your lesson. About sunscreen." He put his hands on her shoulders. "I bought a couple of bottles yesterday, one hundred SPF. Keep one in the car, one in your purse."

"Thanks, Nels."

He watched with pleasure as she finished the glass of glop. If you thought of it as tequila, that helped. Don't taste, just throw it back...

"Ready?" he asked.

"Well, I'm sort of nervous about all the details. And I have to revise my vows—"

"No, I mean, ready for our ride?"

Our ride. Oh, that. The daybreak bicycle ride she'd promised him last night. She was out of her mind to agree to something like that.

"It's the day before our wedding, Nels. I mean, there are things to do—"

"Health first, remember? Put on sunscreen. Hydrate. I'll pour you more juice in a takeout cup."

"Ummm..."

"You can't let these kinds of things derail your workout routine."

These kinds of things. Like weddings? Like vows to revise and print out and revise and print out? Like a big family dinner tonight? Like wondering if your tits were swollen and sore because of PMS and nerves? Like trying not to think of Teddy at the 'Ox & Hound? Like agonizing over your father's stoic suffering, on the precipice of fiscal disaster, of malfeasance...

"I've already loaded the bikes," Nelson said. "Let's hit it."

Ah, but this was her best self. So empowering to be reminded. The old Mira would still be in bed, insisting she was a night owl, and missing this gorgeous pink new-day sky, this gentle wind rustling the cattails in the ditches, the red-winged blackbirds, the rousing of the morning before the hiss of traffic...

The cattails rustle
like a taffeta bustle.

The old Mira would scratch down that silly line, playing with it, worrying it, ruminating over syllables and sounds for hours—days—a worthless arrangement of words no one cared about, that made no difference in a world of commerce and practical endeavors.

Nelson rode just ahead of her now, leisurely for him, leading her patiently around the defunct Air Force base, a popular spot for flocks of cyclists. Only they were the proficient kind—in their gleaming tight fluorescent shorts and shirts, their arthropod helmets, their clicking pedals—whizzing by her like clouds of locusts.

Mira pumped hard to keep up with Nelson—a metaphor for the new Mira, pushed in new directions!

But then she screwed up.

Maybe because her endorphins were surging, her legs floaty from an hour of aerobic bike riding on such a stunning morning. Or maybe it was the surge of love for the man sitting across from her. Her husband. Tomorrow. Jeez, she was getting sentimental.

Probably it was the decaf coffee Nelson brought her (you should cut out caffeine cold turkey) because without real coffee, she was foggy as London.

Maybe it was all those things.

But as they sat on a bench outside the coffee shop, Mira said, "Nels, I'm going to tell my parents we can't accept their wedding gift. The money."

"You're what?" Nelson looked as if he wore dime-store joke glasses, comic eyeballs on springs.

"They can't really afford it. And I just can't—"

"And you know this how?"

"Well, I get the feeling my father is under pressure..."

"You get the feeling?" Nelson shook his head, then dug in. "Feelings, Mira? What are the facts? Did they tell you that?"

"Not...explicitly."

She was dancing around the topic—Rex Wolf, the business—she couldn't find a way to talk about it without bringing in Teddy, and his confiding to her. Even now, her stomach clenched like a fist at Teddy's words, the concern on his face—

"My father has been stressed lately. Mom told me."

"Your mother? Would she even know about your family's fiscal affairs?"

Well, no. Blunt statement, but true.

"And second. Your father is rolling out the new business model. All the hoopla around that—could be tense, right? Lot of late nights. Not to mention the wedding-on-steroids he insisted on."

"I just—I don't think this is a good time for my folks to fork over cash to us. Okay? Can we leave it at that?"

"We have our own family to think about, Mira. And if we have kids coming sooner rather than later? We're going to need that nest egg!"

There was panic in his voice. Nelson was terrified. Mira reminded herself this was Nelson's version of love—ensuring they were solvent and prepared for their own little family.

"I started retooling the plans this week," he said. "I took another look at the budget—"

"I know, I know."

"So why don't you just straight out ask your father if he's stressed about his finances?"

She almost laughed. Almost. You don't get it, is what she wanted to say. Only Teddy knew how fragile her father was behind all that bluster, maybe better than she did. "He'd be insulted."

"We have to know the facts before we make a decision. Numbers add up. Balance sheets don't lie. This isn't complicated."

Oh, but it was.

She arrived at her parents' house a few hours later. "You need another yogurt mask," her mother said. She led Mira into the kitchen. "Sit down. I'll mix it up."

"Mom, it's okay. My cheeks don't even feel hot anymore. I'll cover it up with makeup."

Her mother tied on an apron.

"You're all dressed up," Mira said.

"The magazine lady was here."

"The magazine—oh, the interview." Yikes. Mira had forgotten. "Did it go okay? What did the reporter want to know?"

"She was very sweet. Right out of college. She asked a lot of questions, and your father answered them."

"Questions like what?"

"Oh, like, 'What is the secret to being married for so long? Was it love at first sight?' That sort of thing."

"Is Dad still here?"

"He's upstairs."

"Is he okay?" Mira whispered.

"Why wouldn't he be?" Her mother looked perplexed. "I believe we're out of yogurt."

"Mom, let's skip the face mask."

Her mother nodded absently. She had a faraway gaze that made Mira's stomach hurt. Maybe the magazine interview hadn't gone well. Her father's footsteps overhead jarred her mother out of her daze; she looked up, following them with her eyes. Then she leaned close to Mira and said, "How does a phone mailbox get full?"

"A phone mailbox? Oh, you mean voicemail? How does voicemail fill up?"

"Yes. How?"

"Well, it just means someone's voicemails on their phone piled up, and they ran out of space, so the phone can't accept any more messages. Why? Is it Daddy's phone?"

"No. But how can voices fill up invisible message boxes?"

"Mom, are you getting a headache?" Mira asked, because Janelle was rubbing her temples.

Her mother shook her head. "I don't understand."

"I don't either. It's an interesting question, though. You'd have to talk to a computer scientist about something like that." Mira pretended, no, prayed, that Janelle really was curious about software technology and not...fixated with voices and messages. Oh God, how were they all going to get through the next twenty-four hours?

Her father burst into the kitchen. "Ah, the bride. I thought I heard you." He was knotting his tie, freshly shaven, but wan, a little slump to his shoulders, and was that a sleep crease on his face?

"Daddy, were you resting? I didn't mean to wake you."

"Resting? I don't nap, you know that. Did your mother tell you about the nice girl who interviewed us for the magazine?"

"Woman, Dad. Magazine writers aren't usually girls."

Her mother reached over and straightened her father's collar and smoothed his tie, a tender gesture that brought a lump to Mira's throat.

"So, the interview went well?"

"We knocked it out of the park," he said, and turned to Janelle. "Didn't we, sweetheart?" He leaned over to kiss her on the cheek.

"Your father brought me flowers," Janelle said, and pointed to a vase in the sink, jam-packed with voluptuous pink lilies.

"Wow. Very nice."

"But I don't think the lilies would mind sharing the vase with some of my peonies. I'm going to cut a few. I'll be right back."

Her mother headed out the back door, and Mira thought, Okay, here it comes, the real story.

"How did it go?" she asked her father.

"We knocked it out of the park."

"So you said."

"Well? You have your answer. Good God," her father said, looking hard at Mira for the first time. "Did you go to a tanning booth?"

"Seriously, Dad? Tanning booths are cancer coffins. I mean, who does that anymore?"

"Arlene does. She highly recommends tanning booths." He seemed to perk up. "Follow me. I know exactly what you need."

"What's that?" she said, as they moved to the living room.

"A drink. I have the bar set up."

"No, thanks. I have to keep a clear head."

"One Bloody Mary?"

"Only if it's a virgin Bloody Mary."

He chuckled.

"Really."

"Fine, fine. By the way, the reservation at the club is for seven o'clock tonight."

"Yeah, about that. I was thinking it might be better to keep it casual tonight. Not a fancy sit-down dinner."

"It's all arranged."

"But...that's a lot of people."

"Ten people is not a big party. I reserved the small banquet room." He handed her a Bloody Mary in a stemmed glass, garnished with celery, speared olives, and a lime wedge.

"Beautifully executed," she said. "I guess I got my bartending talent from you."

He gave her a tight smile. He despised being reminded that she was "underemployed."

She took a sip and the tangy heat was delicious, even without a vodka kick. It occurred to her that the two important men in her life today were foisting their carefully crafted beverages on her—juiced vegetables and virgin Bloody Marys.

"Let's just hang out here tonight and order pizza."

"Are you out of your mind?" he said.

"It's a lot of money. A dinner like that."

"Peanuts," he sputtered. "Chump change."

"Daddy, look. Nelson and I talked about it (true) and we agreed (yeah, right!) that we'd rather not accept the wedding gift, the money, from you and Mom. At least not yet."

He stirred his bourbon, added another ice cube. "You're joking."

"Not on top of the expenses. The wedding tomorrow and the dinner tonight. I don't want you to feel obligated is all. Not if you have other...demands."

He grabbed her elbow. "Lower your voice." He stared toward the kitchen. The sound of water being turned on and off, her mother humming.

"With the Rex Wolf rollout and everything," Mira said quietly, "I'm sure there could be challenges with cash flow—"

"What on earth are you talking about?" He'd forgotten to whisper, his face flushed.

"I mean...the business. If you need to concentrate resources on Rex Wolf." And that was as close as she was going to get to Teddy's confession.

"No," he hissed, "there are no cash flow challenges. So don't create problems and start rumors. I don't want your mother to be alarmed."

"Daddy I just…I want you to be all right."

"I am all right. Your mother is all right. Stay here. I'll be right back."

She sat on the sofa. From the kitchen, more sounds of her mother puttering around.

Was she avoiding Mira and her father on purpose?

When her father returned he handed Mira an envelope. "Open it."

Inside, a cashier's check written out to her for ten thousand dollars. She gasped.

"Put that away someplace safe," he murmured. "I was planning on presenting it to you tomorrow, but you forced my hand."

She mustered up her nerve, one more time. She wouldn't lie awake tonight aching from guilt.

"I can only accept this if you promise you don't need it. For you and Mom, or for the business."

"It's yours. We don't. And the business has never been better."

"Really?"

"Teddy is a wonder. Like his father. Rex Wolf is…it's a rebirth, that's the truth." He smiled now and looked close to happiness. "Business is booming."

She stuffed the check back into the envelope.

"Thank you."

"You are welcome."

When she left, Mira slid the envelope into the glove compartment of her car. She sat there for a minute in her parents' driveway, trying to talk herself out of what she was about to do.

She called Teddy. He picked up on the first ring.

"You low-down bastard."

"Mira?"

"You made it all up to freak me out. To make me worried sick about my father…embezzling? In handcuffs? You spewed that scary shit to screw up my wedding day."

Teddy tried to interrupt, but she didn't let him; she was practically screaming now. "And to think I believed you! While you pretended to…to comfort me. That's crazy and mean as hell! And you lie so easily, T-Rex. You lie."

37

SPEC

"And for the young man?"

Spec shrugged.

The waiter was a Black man with silver hair, wearing a bow tie and a vest. The man did not lose his patience with Spec. The waiter had good manners.

"Hey, Spec? You know what you want to order for dinner?" Aunt Mira whispered to Spec and held up a menu. "Want me to help you decide?"

The waiter's vest was white and clean. How could the waiter be dressed up and serve food without getting stains? Spec had already ruined his good shirt with a smear of cocktail sauce.

"I will have the Cord on Blue," Spec told the waiter man. He did not know what a Cord on Blue was, but when Grandmother had ordered it, he thought of a song, a guitar strum like Dad played some days.

Spec's mother, sitting across from him, cleared her throat, to tell him he was forgetting something. "Please," Spec added. "Thank you."

The waiter wrote something down. Then Aunt Mira ordered a vegetable plate.

When his mother started talking to Aunt Mira and Dad, Spec looked down at his lap and slipped the phone out of his pocket and checked it. It was a secret flip phone. Grandmother's friend called it a burner phone when she gave it to him at the cabin.

He did not feel the buzz of a message yet, but sometimes if you weren't paying attention, you could miss things, like your phone was playing tricks on you. On bad days, a phone could sneak things past you, but on good days, it could be the best friend you ever had; it could deliver pictures and tell you things, like a good robot.

But there was nothing. His secret phone told him that it was seven twenty-seven on a Friday night. He sat back in his chair and looked around, then up, above the faces and all the mouths talking. The room had swirly red wallpaper with a big mirror, edged in gold, like in a castle. The chair he sat in was cushioned and heavy with no arms.

"Hey, Spec, let's get some air," Dad said, and that's when Spec felt the chair move under him and realized he himself was rocking it, side to side.

Spec stood. Something stung him. It was Grandfather's stare. Then Spec felt something warm on the back of his neck, Dad's hand. "Come on. I want to show you something."

Spec and Dad went outside, to the back of the Club. The cement steps there did not have a railing. There were two green dumpsters, three parked cars, and a rusty basketball goal without a net.

Dad sat down on the top step. "Oh God, the memories." He patted a place beside him, hoping Spec would sit with him, but Spec didn't.

"I would sneak out here sometimes, shoot a few baskets. Anything to get out of dinner…in there." Dad cleared his throat. "My point is, don't worry about him."

"Who?"

"Your grandfather."

"I'm not worried about him."

"No, I mean, don't let him worry you. Don't let him get under your skin. And I can tell he did, man. You feel judged." Dad sighed. "Go ahead, pace."

Spec walked down the steps, back up, and down. But he was not pacing because of Grandfather. He was pacing because his secret phone was quiet and did not buzz in his pocket. And he had four hours and twenty-five minutes left. If he did not get the next message by midnight…

"Spec, look at me. See, you can't pick your parents…or

your grandparents. So, you learn to live with them. Ignore him.
That's what I've learned. You hearing this?"
    A boy came out from another door, down by the dumpster.
He was wearing a white shirt but no bow tie. Black pants and an
apron covered in stains. He took out a cigarette.
    "Hey, man, you don't happen to have a basketball?" Dad
called out.
    The boy nodded. Put out the cigarette. Disappeared behind
the dumpster, came out dribbling a ball.
    "Now we're talking." Dad walked over to the boy, shook his
hand. Introduced himself.
    "Spec, this is Carlos. You wanna play?"
    Spec shook his head.
    "Okay, how about you keep score?"
    Dad handed Spec his phone so he could use the calculator
on it if he wanted to.
    Dad didn't know Spec had the secret phone, pushed deep
down in his pocket. No one did. Except Grandmother's friend.
    Another boy came out of the kitchen. He was smaller than
the other one, and his apron was dirtier. Spec wondered if the
old man in the bow tie would get mad at them for staining
their white aprons. Dad aimed the ball, took a shot, missed. The
Carlos boy caught it, made a basket.
    The door opened behind Spec. He did not have to turn
around to know who it was. He smelled her lavender body lotion and heard the click-clack of her special dress-up church
shoes. His mother. Dad stopped dribbling. "Hey, baby love."
    "Really? Basketball? Don't *baby love* me." But his mother was
NOT MAD, because her face was smiling in a good way.
    "You guys need to come on back in. They're about to serve
dinner. You're going to get all sweaty."
    "Nope. I smell good." Dad bounced the ball behind him,
jogged up the steps, and kissed Spec's mother, acting like he
was going to pick her up, and they laughed. Spec handed Dad's
phone to him, and his mother fussed at Dad for letting Spec
play on a phone because Spec was to be on no devices tonight.

"He was keeping score," Dad said.

"Keeping score? Uh-huh."

Spec could keep score in his head. Dad knew Spec would play Angry Birds and it would make him feel better.

Spec said he wasn't going inside again.

"Yes, you are," his mother said. "We've already compromised tonight, remember?"

They had compromised about Spec wearing his cargo pants that were not appropriate for tonight. His mother said his cargo pants were old and faded and what was wrong with his new pants? But his new pants were stiff and did not have good pockets to hide his secret phone. Dad took Spec's side. He's wearing a shirt and tie at the table. Who cares what the kid wears from the waist down?

"No," he said, and it came out loud. The boys stopped playing basketball to stare at him.

"Calm yourself." She took Dad's phone, then shut it off. "Now don't let me see you with it again. I mean it. Or I will confiscate it."

"And you," she said to Dad, "leaving me alone in there."

"You looked like you were having fun."

"I was. I am."

They went back inside, and when Spec sat down, the nice dressed-up waiter put Spec's plate of food in front of him.

Cord on Blue was just chicken. Beside it a thin slice of cantaloupe curved like a smile on a green leaf, so Spec turned his plate around, to turn the slice into a frown. He hated cantaloupe, the slimy way it felt.

"That leaf, that's kale," Uncle Nelson told him. "Most nutritious thing on your plate. You should eat it."

But he didn't have to eat anything. His mother told him that. He could have mac 'n' cheese when they got home. The waiter man did not know Spec hated the way the chicken and the potatoes and the green beans touched.

Grandmother stood up and excused herself. Spec jumped

up and told Dad he had to go to the bathroom. Grandmother told Dad she would help Spec find the restroom.

Out in the hall Grandmother said, "Spec, come here. I haven't had a chance to talk with you all evening." Her face looked soft, like she wanted to put her arms around him, but she didn't. Spec did not want to be hugged. "I'm sorry. This isn't fun for you, is it? Of course not. What boy your age wouldn't want to leave?"

Spec could not say things, the words weren't there to explain, it was getting mixed up in his head, the plan, Lana said, don't tell anyone, don't tell Grandmother—

"The puppy might need water," he said.

"Oh, you sweet boy. You miss Lana, don't you? She heals. She lights up the dark path of self-discovery. Yes, she does wonders. I've been trying to call her, but her phone mailbox is full."

Dad appeared at the end of the hallway. "You okay, man?"

"He's splendid," Grandmother told him, and waved him away.

In the bathroom, Spec peeked at the secret phone. It said nothing but seven fifty-nine.

Grandmother waited for him out in the hallway. She leaned in close and said, "I can't wait until we see Lana tomorrow at the wedding."

"With Biscuit?"

Grandmother did not hear him. She was talking fast the way she did on their car drives, when she said things were building up inside her.

Three hours and fifty-five minutes. Then it would be midnight. Then Spec would know if he should follow the plan.

He would rescue Biscuit and Shelly and the ladies. He would send out the message.

He was ready.

PART IV

THE WEDDING

38

MIRA

The third floor of the renovated farmhouse, once an attic, was stifling hot and smelled of cedar. The fans whirred around Mira, stirring the oppressive air, as she sat at a vanity. She walked over to the small round window and looked for Burry's car. She needed to talk ASAP. He'd texted he was on the way.

Gorgeous up here on the top floor, she had to admit. You might die from heatstroke, but you got to see the lay of the land.

Below her, white tablecloths lifted in the breeze, anchored with Mason jars stuffed with sunflowers, cosmos, and zinnias—the florist's super-casual-loosely-arranged pricey centerpieces. The band was still setting up.

She spotted Burry's car winding up the unpaved lane. He parked, glanced at his phone, then looked up, his eyes scaling the house until he saw her in the alcove window, waving.

She wore a tank top, cutoffs, and flip-flops. Her wedding dress, plain as paper, hung in the corner. The dress was all wrong, she saw that now. The idea had been to cloak herself in severe elegance, a blank page that gave a middle finger to lace and pearls. But it was a drab and homely choice.

Or…maybe not. She was second-guessing herself about everything today.

A few minutes later there was a soft knock. Burry stepped inside.

"SOS received. Wilbur Wolf reporting for duty."

"I forgot my vows!"

"You're not even married yet."

"No, I mean…I forgot to bring them. I worked on them for

weeks and weeks. Every word was perfect. Then, I don't know, I had all these different versions on my laptop at the apartment and I printed out the wrong one."

"Okay, let's…first let's take a deep breath."

"—and look at my sunburned face!"

"Breathe in with me, count to three—come on. It will calm you."

So she inhaled though the nose, counted to three, exhaled…

"Better?"

"Better. But what am I going to do?"

"You're a bride. Wear a veil." Burry, teasing out any humor he could find.

"No. I mean, about my vows."

"Iambic pentameter? Sonnet?"

"Brother, you know me so well."

He laughed, but she meant it.

"I chiseled out some gorgeous phrases, but I worked in the practical stuff, too, for Nelson."

"You want me to go get your laptop?"

"By the time you go and come back, it would take an hour."

"You want me to ask Pansy to go by your place? You got a key hidden somewhere?"

"No…no key. Just forget it. When I realized I had the wrong version, we were almost here. Nelson warned me to get everything ready last night and load the car. He said I was the most disorganized person on the planet. He's right. That makes it harder. He's always right."

Burry winced. "Well, yeah. But chock it up to a wedding day freak-out. Let it go."

"I did. Then we pulled up…here…and the band was setting up, and the tables were so beautiful, the linens and flowers, and the beer truck was ready, and it was all so bucolic, so picturesque, and I realized it was really happening, our day, and—"

"Quite a spread."

"Nelson really let me have it. He said, 'What the hell is all this? A band? A beer truck? Two wedding cakes? We can't afford this. What happened?'"

"Okay, you two didn't talk about all this stuff? Beer and cake and bands and whatnot?"

"Yes, we talked. Nelson always thought it was too expensive. Even after I worked hard at getting deals—like the craft beer guys. They said they're doing it for half off, and they really need the business. And the band—"

"Sick Cooter, right?"

"Yeah, I told you about that, they cut a deal because they're trying to land some wedding gigs—"

"So, you did a friend or two a solid."

"But he said I'd blown the budget. His budget. He doesn't get that this isn't about him. Or me. It's about Mom and Dad. This is their day, not mine. And that makes me happy."

Burry stood at the window, looking down.

What she didn't tell Nelson was that her "dowry" was still in her glove compartment. She wanted to hold on to it a little longer, before sending it along to be sliced and diced by a budget. Their budget. Plus, well, she couldn't tell Burry either because it wasn't fair, was it? That Burry missed out on some wedding loot just because he and Pansy didn't officially tie the knot. But if she split her father's check with Burry, that would really set off Nelson.

"How's Spec today?"

"Rough night," he said.

"God, I'm sorry, Burry. And here I am bitching and moaning. What happened?"

"He didn't sleep. Pansy and I took shifts to check on him. We locked up Pansy's laptop in the minivan. Never had to do that before."

Mira sighed. "Crap. Someone told me there are baby goats in the barn…he'll like that, right?"

"Couldn't hurt. Pansy was trying to bribe him into wearing his new pants when I left. I'll let her know."

"And you had to leave early because of me? You should have told me, Burry. I'm a total asshole."

"You're a total asshole."

"Thanks for coming. Talking to you always makes me feel better."

"I'd hug you but we'd both be drenched." He took off his jacket, loosened his tie. "Jeez. You could cure hams in here. Before I go..." He pulled out a plastic bag from his jacket pocket. "An early wedding present."

"Aw, thanks." She took the drugstore bag. Opened it. A pregnancy test.

Burry wore his enigmatic Buddha smile.

"Is this you being funny—"

"Pansy said you can take it the day you're late. And you are, right?"

"—or is this you sending a message?"

"This is me being whatever you'd like me to be. Jokester or sage adviser."

"So, you're advising me to pee on this stick today?"

"Nope. I'm not advising you to do anything."

"What should I do?"

He laughed. "Come on. That's on you."

"Really! What do you think I should do?"

"Right now? Scratch out some vows on a sticky note. Maybe not poetry. Just the basics. You promise to love, honor, and obey—"

She laughed. "Good one. Obey!"

"—and put on that fancy dress."

"Yeah, well. First, I've got my work cut out for me, with this"—she waved her hand in front of her red face—"disaster."

"Hey, who predicted you'd be a blushing bride?"

"You did, brother."

"Just don't forget to wear a smile."

39

JANELLE

The morning of the wedding, we quarreled because I wouldn't lie.

I wore the dress from the boutique. Porch-ceiling blue. It was time to leave.

Charles stood in the hallway, jiggling his car keys, waiting. He held up his hands to me, like a surgeon after scrubbing, so I could see.

He wore his monogrammed cuff links.

The cuff links I gave him years ago, for our first anniversary. He said they would be perfect today, for the wedding photographs. But he looked furious. "Have you given your jewelry to Mira?"

He'd found my empty jewelry box, you see. Nothing but his cuff links in that black velvet.

"I think that's a fine idea, passing down your heirlooms," he said. "The wedding is a good occasion for it. Was Mira pleased?"

I could have lied. Perhaps I should have. Just a nod. To cover it all up, for the day—Mira's wedding day.

But I didn't lie. I didn't say anything. And in the silence, his anger grew.

Then the tirade. "Not her. Dear God, not that criminal. You did not give your jewelry to her!"

Her. A grunt. HER. He would not say your name.

Neither would I.

And yet you were there, my friend, as if I'd summoned you.

Soon I will see you, milling around with the guests, and then we can talk, you will be desperate to know what I've recalled...

"I know I was trying to leave you that night, Charles, wasn't I?"

That stopped his words, his anger too.

"Not now, Janelle, not today. Our daughter is getting married."

"But that night, Charles. You were begging me not to leave you. I remember. You were yelling, 'Don't you leave ME.'"

Me—a tiny word, perilous as a blood clot. I hear it now, Lana. And it leads to all of it, the parts you said DON'T. Lana, you said don't breathe a word, but it is poisoning me.

"I was trying to leave you, Charles. I was so angry with you. I believe I may have hated you." Don't be angry, Lana. Please. I had to tell it, just that part...just to him.

"Janelle. My God, Janelle."

He reached for me, and held me close, very close, I could hardly breathe.

He said he was sorry for upsetting me. He said he was selfish for arguing with me, especially now. When so much was at stake. When Mira's day could be ruined.

"You know how you distort things, Janelle. You don't see things right when you are tipping into a spell."

He said if I had a headache tomorrow, that was all right. Tomorrow.

But today. Today I mustn't spoil things. Mira's day. "Your day too," he said. "This day is for Mira, for you, for the Wolf family. You can't be unmoored."

Unmoored. Water, and I'm the boat, tied, docked, anchored. I mustn't become unmoored.

40

TEDDY

"Please tell me those aren't hay bales," Reagan said, as they drove up the dirt road past barbed-wire pastures. Teddy followed the signs—Wedding This Way!—stuck in—yes, those were indeed hay bales.

"So wrong," she said. "More hee-haw than boho."

They parked on grass near the farmhouse, alongside a dozen cars. They were early. Reagan had insisted. Teddy's job today was to glad-hand and smile as if he were having the time of his life and pretend he wasn't about to screw over Charles next week.

But his mission? Talk to Mira.

Mira might blow up at him, or worse—ignore him—but he had to see her again, to explain that she had it all wrong, that he hadn't concocted some story about her father's financial troubles just to torment her. They had to at least feign friendship and talk, right? If that meant pretending, fine. He was good at pretending.

He opened Reagan's door and offered his elbow, and she took it, wobbling on her high heels, then stepping high-kneed like a heron through the mud-soaked field. "Is that a camel?" Reagan said, squinting ahead.

"Llama." There were children around it, feeding it.

"Ugh. Like a petting zoo."

"Yep." He made a show of inhaling. "Smell that fresh bull-shit?"

"Teddybear. Get a drink."

There was a country-fair feel about the day, what with kids running around herding a pair of dogs (or were the dogs herding the kids?). And a few people here in denim and khaki—had to be from the groom's side. No sign of Charles or Janelle or even the groom. The families were huddling somewhere, maybe? But what was this, a beer truck? Crawley from Bar None, pouring? And a band—was that Sick Cooter, that sad clutch of wispy-chinned wannabe musicians he recognized from the bar, cranking out some off-key Bon Jovi?

"Impressive, isn't it?" Reagan said, and it was good to see her pleased.

"It is," he said wistfully.

"The wedding cakes, over there," Reagan gasped. "Stunning."

"I'm hitting the beer truck. You want white wine?"

"Remember, photographer, councilmen. So, network, Teddy. Network like a son of a bitch. Don't just stand around."

"I thought you wanted me to be outstanding in the field."

"What field?"

"Out standing...in the field? Get it?"

Big eye roll and she trotted off, while Teddy ordered himself a craft brew.

In her peach sleeveless sheath of a dress, Reagan resembled a rare tropical bloom among these common field daisies. She passed the band and a gaggle of young fathers, all of whom did comical double takes to watch her. Well, that was fun. Watching. Reminding himself how lucky he was...to go home with such a prize.

He polished off his beer. Ordered another. Something lighter. A Belgian ale. Had to keep his head. He recognized a few people arriving, some contacts, a few geezers, Charles's friends, but he kept to himself, did not mingle or look up from his beer, just nursed his wound. His broken heart. Because that's what it was, right? What was it Mira accused him of being? A jaded romantic? A warped idealist? He had to hold on to that sensitive part, she said, keep that vein of empathy open or he would turn...hard. And screw up a lot of people's lives, politically speaking. That was a few weeks before…when they were still talking.

"Make that two," said a raspy voice behind him. Teddy winced but turned around with a smile. "Arlene. Good to see you. You look lovely." Two easy lies, thanks to the brews.

She frowned and looked down at her silver dress—did she know she resembled a foil-wrapped burrito, the kind you get at gas stations? "I tried to get all dolled up. TJ Max—you never know what they'll get in. But what the hell. Thing is, polyester don't breathe. I'm sweating like a whore in church. And they won't let you smoke here. I'm old enough to remember when they grew a field of tobacco over yonder. Now you can't have a damn cigarette."

Arlene was in a foul mood, as usual, but she seemed even more on edge. Did she know more about the audit scare? Suspect next week's coup? "You seen Charles?"

"No," Teddy said. "I just got here."

"You talk to him yet?"

"Talk—?" Teddy swallowed. She knows, she knows I'm about to screw over her bossman. "About what?"

She took a gulp of beer.

"Guess they're holed up somewhere," she said. "The family."

Teddy made his excuses and went inside, in search of a bathroom. Now that he'd had a few beers, he could handle the congratulations so happy for you and…maybe just catch a glimpse of Mira.

He liked the renovated farmhouse decor more than he had expected to, exposed beams and oak floors, stone fireplace. Nice. But dark. Hot too. In the hall, a line of wiggly kids and chatting mothers waited for the restroom. No way was he standing in that line. He took a sharp right and climbed the stairs.

On the second floor, he darted into a bathroom off the hallway. Took off his tie when he finished, stuffed it in his pocket. Then took off the jacket too. When he stepped out into the hallway again—smelling like that weird cake of soap with sprigs and leaves that looked more like something to eat than to lather—he paused.

He heard her. He listened hard, two voices now. Directly overhead. He took a step back and darted into a side room. A chuckle. Burry? Had to be. Then Mira. "What should I do?" Mira, a reluctant bride after all. Don't do it! Teddy thought. I'd give my left nut to tell you that.

Heavy footsteps plodded down the narrow flight of stairs. When Burry was out of sight, Teddy waited a few minutes, darted up the stairs. A closed door met him. He raised his knuckle, ready to knock. Then didn't.

He turned the glass doorknob and opened the door.

She sat at a vanity, her back to him.

"I'm fine, really. I promise. Can you—" She turned.

He expected her to lose it. He shut the door behind him, held a hand up, universal gesture for hear me out.

She blinked, then shook her head. Her face, God. Tender with sunburn, yes, but emotions, too, roiling—astonishment, naked outrage—before she could stop them. Or not. She couldn't rein them in, and that moved him.

"Why am I surprised?" she said. "After I begged you not to come, of course you charge in here like some badass." She reached for a tissue on the vanity and blotted her eyes. "Crap, my mascara. I just fixed it."

"I just, I want us to be friends," he said. "Not some icy estrangement that would frankly hurt...everyone."

She made that sound, that exasperated little laugh he missed. "Save the spin, T-Rex. This is me you're talking to."

"I know that, Mira. I got an earful yesterday on the phone." She narrowed her eyes. "You deserved it. That story you made up about Daddy. Legal issues? Money problems?"

"Mira, I didn't make it up."

She turned her back to him, faced the mirror. "You'll make a wonderful senator. Unfortunately."

"I wish it weren't true, about your father."

"Oh my God, there you go again!"

"Look, I would never lie to you about that...but, okay, okay...let's leave it for now, that's not why I came up here."

She dabbed pink powder on her face, with a little brush, careless moves, just going through the motions, really, he could tell.

"I miss you, Mira. It's been hell, being cut off from you. I just want to talk to you. I need to talk to you. Can we just settle on that? A truce?"

That breathy laugh again. "I need to get ready. You need to leave." She stood up, smoothing her dress—he'd thought it was a slip or some underthing—but it was her wedding dress, thin straps, creased now, from her sitting. Vaguely disheveled, hint of cleavage, sexy as hell. Her hair twisted up, her elfin ears. He met her dark eyes—morose, weren't they? Or was he projecting? She looked away.

"You're sweating," she said.

It was true. The back of his shirt was soaked. A trickle of perspiration ran down the side of his face.

She sighed. Took one of her tissues, came over to him. "Here," she whispered. Blotted his cheek.

Then her other arm was around him, around his neck, as if they were dancing, and he drew her close, both of them clammy. Something broke loose inside him, some slag of ice sheared away. He braced himself for the pushback. Get out of here. Get out of my sight.

But she did not let go.

41

SPEC

Grandmother found him behind the barn.

Spec stood alone by the pasture fence, watching five cows eat grass. They had drowsy eyes that made Spec feel peaceful. They chewed their food slowly the way you are supposed to, and they didn't seem to mind things, not him standing there, not the heat, not even the flies.

Grandmother said, "Spec, thank goodness you're here." Grandmother scared him. She was UPSET.

He wanted to tell Grandmother he was upset too.

Lana had not texted him at midnight. If she DID NOT text him at midnight, that meant he had to start THE PLAN.

The plan had two steps. First, you send out the message. Then you rescue the pets.

But Spec couldn't start the plan.

Because Dad took away Spec's computer privileges.

Mom locked up her laptop in the minivan so Spec wouldn't sneak and use it when they were asleep.

Spec couldn't log on to the site with the password that Lana set up for him. He couldn't send out the message. He kept thinking of the puppy and Shelly and the ladies. They were waiting for him to save them. So, he had screamed and pounded the floor. Then he yelled and threw his mother's favorite bowl and broke it and had to go to his room and keep the door open so Dad could watch him. It had been a bad night and nothing good had happened until now, until he watched the cows.

Dad said he could pet the goats in the barn. But there were too many people in there. So he stayed behind the barn, with the cows.

Grandmother closed her eyes for a minute and then opened them. "I need Lana."

This morning in the bathroom, Spec had texted Lana three times on the secret phone. But she did not text back. That meant start the plan.

First you send out the message. Then you rescue the pets.

Grandmother said she was hurting; it was like labor pains. She said something wanted to emerge, to be born, and Grandmother couldn't let it. Not yet. Not without Lana to guide her. She did not want to come undone, especially not today.

Then she said, "I'm afraid, Spec. I'm afraid Lana isn't coming. I feel it. I can't explain how I know, but I do. We have a special connection."

Spec was afraid too. He was afraid Lana was mad at him. Maybe that's why she wouldn't come to the wedding. Maybe that's why she didn't answer his texts. She was mad he didn't follow the PLAN.

"I told Burry I would check on you," Grandmother said. "I'll tell him you're fine, out here with the cows."

Grandmother tried to smile, but she was not happy. Grandmother said she had pains and she missed her friend.

Spec couldn't tell Grandmother he was the reason her friend wouldn't come.

Or—and this made his stomach hurt—maybe the bullies were punishing Lana, and maybe Biscuit and Shelly and the hens had to be rescued. Maybe they were all waiting for him.

Grandmother left and walked through the crowd. Spec watched her. The music was loud. His mother and dad were dancing.

The music hurt his ears, and there were so many faces and talking and laughing, it was not easy to walk there, but Spec did. His mother's purse and Dad's jacket were on a chair. They were dancing and they were laughing. His mother's car keys were in the side of her purse. He slipped them into his pocket.

He turned around and pretended to go to the barn.

His mother's minivan was at the end of a row of cars far away on the grass.

Her laptop was still in the very back, hidden beside the spare tire and the jumper cables.

First you send out the message.

But if he took the laptop inside the farmhouse to use the Wi-Fi, someone might see him. Mom would take it away and she would be UPSET. Mom and Dad would stop him from sending out the message and rescuing the pets.

First, he would check on the pets. Then he would send out the message.

He got into the driver's seat. He put on his mother's big round sunglasses that she'd left on the dashboard. He put on his seat belt. He turned the key in the ignition and put the van in reverse. Then he drove away.

The cabin was two miles away. Spec could see the map in his head. Turn off this lane, then the main road, and there was the produce stand, and another turn. He would have to drive carefully, but fast too. He thought of Biscuit, waiting for him. Maybe she didn't have water. A puppy needs fresh water.

He drove up the bumpy dirt road, then he pulled up to the cabin. Lana's car wasn't there. She wasn't home. She was gone, maybe to the wedding. Maybe Lana had passed him on the way, and he didn't see. Or maybe the bullies had kidnapped her.

The front door was locked. Spec stood there, trying to decide what to do. Then he heard Biscuit bark. From inside. He went to the backyard. The glass on the back door was broken. The door was unlocked. Spec went inside. He knelt and petted Biscuit in the kitchen, away from all the pieces of glass on the floor. She licked him over and over. Spec told Biscuit not to worry; he said he was going to take care of her. She had pooped on the floor. She was out of food, and she was thirsty. He filled her water bowl and she drank it. He fed Shelly some dried mealworms. He looked around the house. He knew no one was there because he could feel the nice emptiness, without people.

The fan was on in the bedroom. But it was messy in there. The mattress was sliced open, and the springs showed. A lamp was broken. There was an open suitcase. Clothes on the floor. He told Biscuit he was going to rescue her and Shelly. They would go back to the farm with him. Maybe Lana had run away from the bullies. She'd told Spec to look out for Biscuit and Shelly and the ladies, and that was what he was doing.

He found Biscuit's leash.

He brought the laptop from the minivan inside, to the corner of the kitchen where the internet was strong. He logged on. It was all there, the account Grandmother's friend had set up, the list of emails and the video clip. She had it all ready, and she must be very mad at him for not following the PLAN and sending it out. He had promised. Now the bullies were after her and she had to escape.

He could send out the message now. He could follow the plan and Lana would be proud of him. When she escaped from the bullies and came back, he would ask her if could keep Biscuit and Shelly and the hens forever.

He pressed send.

42

JANELLE

This is our day of redemption. My second debut.

I tell myself that, over and over.

The wedding guests smile, they kiss me on the cheek, they shake hands with Charles.

Charles is in his element. His high-pitched laugh like a cymbal over the band's songs. He circulates, but I stay rooted.

I am a cardboard cutout, a life-size photo of Janelle Welborne Wolf. My smile is flat. I do not hold glances, I deflect them. This way I can stand it, minute by minute.

But I am looking for Lana. I'm beginning to panic. I can bear this thing—if she is here.

This is our day of redemption. My second debut.

I should take comfort in seeing Charles, unburdened by me. Our scandal overwritten by the new tale, a tale of a happy marriage.

I want to go back behind the barn with Spec, to watch the cows. To be away from this laughing, chattering crowd. Then the band starts up again, and Burry and Pansy dance and it gives me strength. Because the look on my boy's face, how he loves to dance—

Priscilla is at my elbow.

I don't need a minder.

I turn away from her and leave.

"Janelle, where are you off to?"

"To be with Mira." I am the mother of the bride, after all. Priscilla watches me go into the farmhouse.

This is Mira's day, and I will not wreck it.

I climb the stairs of the farmhouse. At the top, I knock. I open the door.

There is a fluttering sound, like wings. Mira's dress.

The sound of it sliding.

The two of them, like hands clasped in prayer—they fall away—

Mira.

And Teddy.

"Mom," she says.

There is shame in the room, something unsaid.

"We...uh...I...It's not—" Teddy stutters.

"He was just leaving," Mira says.

Teddy opens his mouth, then closes it. He leaves. We listen to his footsteps fade down the stairs.

"Mom, it was nothing."

But I understand—it is everything.

We sit down together on a narrow bench in front of the vanity.

She says, "That was stupid."

I put my arm on her shoulder. It is important to hold her now, as I had when she was a child, smelling the top of her head. She is weeping, quietly. She looks in the mirror. "I keep ruining my makeup."

Teddy's stricken expression. How oddly defenseless he'd looked for an instant, before the softness vanished.

Like his mother's face.

Mary. In my kitchen, her raw red eyes, her startling vulnerability. How moving, to watch someone committed to self-control lose herself so utterly. I'm going to leave him.

Only she didn't. Not that night.

"Something terrible," I tell Mira. "I remember something terrible."

Then footsteps pounding, like a drum, hard, and the door bursts open, hits the wall.

Burry. Gasping, out of breath.

Mira jumps up. "What happened? Burry, what's wrong?"

Burry holds out his phone to us. "Watch."

43

THE VIDEO

The camera pans over newspaper headline: River Nearly Claims Life.

[Off-camera voice]:

"On the evening of November 11, 1985, Janelle Welborne Wolf experienced a grave injustice. That night her car ran off Bremer bridge and into the Twin River. She nearly drowned. She suffered a traumatic brain injury. But when she awoke later in a hospital bed, she faced the cruelest injury of all."

[The camera lingers on a photo of Janelle with baby Mira and toddler Burry.]

"Lies. Lies that would rob her of her dignity. Lies about what really happened that night at the home of Stan and Mary Rex. Lies that her husband and the future senator concocted to cover up their own disgusting behavior."

[Photo of Stan Rex and Charles Wolf the night of Stan's election.]

"The truth is, Janelle Wolf was not on the way to Stan and Mary Rex's house that night. She was trying to leave."

[The camera opens to Janelle's face now, close up, panning out as she speaks.]

"When you arrived that night, Stan Rex opened the door. What happened next?"

"Stan said he was waiting for me. We sat there together. I kept asking where Charles was. His car was there."

"And what did Stan Rex—the decorated veteran, respected businessman, and future senator—tell you? About your husband, Charles Wolf?"

"He told me not to worry about Charles. Stan said…he was having a little fun."

"A little fun. And did you know what he meant?"

[Janelle shakes her head, overcome.]

"Until now. Finally, you can tell it, the truth. Mary Rex wanted to leave her sorry excuse of a husband. Her marriage was a sham. She told you that, didn't she?"

"Mary said Stan won't stand for a divorce. She said, 'You know how he gets.'"

"Janelle, that night Stan pressed himself on you, didn't he? Made a pass. But this was nothing new. Stan Rex pursued you for years, didn't he? Pining away, not bothering to hide his lust for you, his own business partner's wife."

"Stan often said inappropriate things to me. Charles said it was just the way Stan was. He told me to ignore it, that I should be flattered. He said Stan just...he wanted what he couldn't have."

"In fact, on that night, Stan Rex and Charles Wolf had planned a night of perversion, hadn't they? And when you arrived late, Stan told you that your husband and Mary Rex were 'having a little fun' down the hall. Was Stan shocked about his business partner and his wife carrying on?"

"It wasn't love. That's...Stan said it wasn't love. It was just a little fun."

"Take your time, Janelle. Revisiting this trauma must be so hard."

[Janelle dabs at her eyes with a tissue, nods.]

"You didn't go along with it, did you? You were sickened and repulsed. And when you insisted on leaving; when you caused a scene, that's when your husband appeared?"

"I ran outside. It was raining hard, but I started up the station wagon and he...Charles ran to me. I locked the car doors. He pounded on the window. He was so angry. He screamed, 'Don't leave. Don't you dare leave me.'"

"But you did leave, didn't you, Janelle?"

"I drove too fast. I stopped at the bridge to wipe my eyes, to wipe my windshield. It was so, so dark, the river was full, the road nearly washed out."

"Janelle, you were driving away from Stan and Mary Rex's house in a panic the night of your accident, weren't you? You were trying to get away."

"Yes."

[Janelle sobs.]

"You did not drive your car into the river on purpose, did you? As the rumors claim?"

"I...I don't know why anyone would say such a thing. It confused me...for a long time."

"To hide the facts. To discredit you, Janelle, when you remembered."

[A newspaper photo of Janelle, her children, and her husband, Charles Wolf, with Stan and Mary Rex, the night of Stan's state senate election win. The camera focuses on a distraught Janelle, the only one not looking into the camera.]

"The night of November 11, 1985, Janelle Wolf's car slid off the Bremer Bridge as she rushed home, away from betrayal and perversion, to safety. To her home, to her children. Only she didn't make it. Janelle Wolf was a victim that night. A victim of vicious rumors the senator planted and spread. A victim whose husband masked his warnings about sending her to the loony bin with phony declarations of love. No wonder Janelle began to distrust her own memories. But not anymore."

[Janelle gazes at the camera now. She looks startled, and the light in her sea-green eyes dims for a second and then comes back on again. She nods.]

"Thank you. For helping me remember."

"Thank YOU, Janelle. You are a survivor. For too long, you have been unfairly shunned. Now you know the truth. It's time everyone does."

[Fade to black.]

44

AMBUSHED

That sorry excuse for a band was finally playing a song Charles recognized, an off-key version of "Love the One You're With." Shortly the ceremony would commence, and he and Janelle would escort Mira through the crowd—she'd insisted both he and her mother escort her and "give her away." Fine. Charles could live with such unorthodox quirks.

Because—chic guests, in twos and threes, bursts of laughter, dancing. Charles no longer needed to impress, he was there to mingle, to nod tight little hellos, to be embraced in clouds of perfume.

But what was this? Reagan's stormy expression marred her pretty face. That was a damn shame. Was something wrong?

Something was wrong. Reagan met Charles's eyes across the lawn and began to approach, teetering on her high heels, veering around clumps of chatting guests, a wobbly missile heading right for him. Ordinarily he would be thrilled to be her target of attention—good or bad—but she looked...ferocious.

She gripped his arm; he could barely mumble an excuse to Hal Perkins, as she dragged him away.

"Oh my God, Charles. Have you seen this?" She shoved her phone into his ribs as if it were a gun. He squinted and fumbled for his reading glasses. "Of course you haven't. Well, it's messed up, Charles. It's...bad."

"What is...bad, exactly?" he muttered, pasting on a smile.

"Come inside," Reagan hissed, grinning angelically, waving to someone.

Reagan led him inside the farmhouse, into the side office, near the ancient fireplace. She closed the door and shoved her phone at him. "Watch."

He fumbled for his glasses again and squinted at the little screen on Reagan's phone. But he heard it, before he saw—

That voice.

Surely it wasn't…it couldn't be—

Lana.

On Reagan's phone?

"What is…this?" he croaked, but he knew. Oh, he knew. This is a nightmare, Charles thought. I'm going to wake up—

"It's a video, Charles. That's what it is."

He watched, stunned. The vampire's vulgar capacity to come up with such filth—a planned night of perversion? The grifter had overplayed her hand. No one would believe such sinister, warped accusations! Charles welcomed the fireball of rage rising in him, anger that eclipsed the hazy, spectral emotions that lingered like shades on the periphery of his mind—remorse and despair. Because it was what Janelle told the camera, her calm, painful words—that haunted him. Janelle's words were… true, weren't they? Charles shook his head, no, no, because… the shame of it. His shame. His disgrace. "I don't know how—"

"How? How is a cinch. Someone grabbed a video clip of your wife spouting this crazy shit and posted it, and emailed the link along with a freaking transcript, just so no one misses a word."

Reagan played it again. On her phone. He put his hands over his ears.

"For God's sake…please turn that off," he said. The grifter—with her preview of coming attractions, her contingency plan. He would not let her win. He would not.

Reagan walked over to the window, peering out with the steely squint of a sniper.

"Oh no. No, no, no. It's going viral."

"Viral?"

"Everyone's phone is blowing up with this. It's spreading."

Like an infection, Charles thought. Like an epidemic, a viral epidemic, only this would kill him.

"We need Janelle in here," she said.

"It's not true," he mumbled. "That crank—she made Janelle believe things. She…that woman wanted to turn my own wife against me—"

"What woman? You know who dropped this?"

"She tried to corrupt Janelle, she was at Janelle's birthday dinner. That nutjob in the sari. I warned her. I told her to stay away from Janelle."

"She's the woman who did this? And you knew this could happen? And you didn't tell me? After all I've done for you, for you and Janelle, and the business, and you didn't bother to tell me this asshat with a camera wanted to smear you?"

"I thought I…took care of it."

"How did that woman get the email list? The freaking wedding guest list?"

He didn't know. He didn't know how any of this had happened.

"Janelle's not out there, right?" she said, looking out of the window again.

Where was Janelle? There was no sign of her on the lawn, just more people glued to their phones. The other ones looking around, whispering…

"We have to get her in here. We've got to prepare. This will leak to the press."

"The press? But it's not news," he bleated. "It's…personal."

"It's personal, and it's news, a nasty story like this about you. And this is on you, Charles. Not Teddy. This is not about Teddy. You are not going to ruin him. That bullshit about Stan… you have to say it was a cruel joke. I've got to find Teddy."

Teddy was in the bathroom on the second floor. He'd washed up, but he needed a shower. Love chemicals pumped through his system. He savored each second, knowing he'd be plummeting soon; despondency beckoned, crooking her wicked finger at him. But not yet. Not yet. He could think about Mira for a minute longer even as he rinsed away her musky behind-the-ear scent.

He dried his hands on the pristine linen towel, checked his phone, turned the ringer back on. Reagan had texted him... about a hundred times—WHERE R U???? WTF IS THIS?!! He clicked on the link. And watched.

Nelson, eyes full of pity, wandered into the office.

"Charles, I don't know if you're aware—"

"A sick joke," Charles muttered.

Jesus, what Charles would have given to summon up a thunderstorm that took out the power and the internet for the day. Or an hour. These people were sick. Addicted to their metal rectangles—

Then Teddy burst into the room, flushed out from wherever he'd been hiding. Teddy looked destroyed.

"This is...I need to explain," Charles told Teddy. "Janelle has been taken advantage of...a dangerous criminal has tricked her."

"This isn't true, right? This story about...about my mother and you?"

"Pure bunk!" Charles said. His voice shook. "The woman is a con artist, she concocted these smears and you...you know Janelle, how gullible she is, how susceptible—"

"Okay, did you find Janelle?" Reagan asked Charles.

"No," he said with a flash of irritation. A no-brainer, as the kids say. This woman nipped at your ankles. For the first time, he felt sorry for Teddy. To be shackled to a nipper like that.

"Janelle went upstairs to help Mira get ready," Arlene said. She had come in with the stealth of a cat. Charles met her eyes. The only friend in the room.

"Arlene," Reagan said. "Go to the band. Tell them to start playing again until we tell them to stop. I don't care what they play. I don't care if it's 'Highway to Hell.' Just play, and loud, Arlene. Tell them to crank it up."

Arlene's go-to-hell-I-don't-take-my-orders-from-you scowl

faded when Charles said, "Yes, Arlene. The band will distract them while we sort this out."

"Stay inside," Reagan told Charles, as he left to find Janelle. "You can't go out there. Not until we get in front of this, okay? We have to stay on message. And right now, you're persona non grata, Charles. You do know that, right?"

"Me?" Charles said. "I'm the victim here."

Just as Charles turned from Reagan, hiding his look of disgust, but shoring himself up for the task at hand, the horrible task—he would talk to Janelle first, but he had to restrain himself, he could not holler like a hound from hell, "See what that evil woman you called a friend did?" And then he could tell Mira that this was a mean-spirited attack—Mira's voice came from the top of the stairs.

"Daddy? Up here."

Charles climbed the stairway, following Mira's voice, his heart pounding along with his feet. At the top—Janelle. Burry too.

The three of them. An ambush.

"Janelle," Charles rasped, enraged again, for it was Janelle who let that monster in, "do you see what she did? I warned you she was dangerous."

Janelle did not look at him.

She was unhinged. Of course she was!

"We were just asking Mom about why her friend Lana would send this kind of thing out now," Mira said.

"I will ask," Janelle said.

"You're in touch with her?" Burry asked.

"She said she would come today."

"She's not coming, Janelle," Charles said. "Don't you see? She's gone. She…she absconded with your jewelry." He turned to Mira. "That criminal took all your mother's jewelry! Do you see what I've had to contend with? She still thinks that vile creature is her friend."

"Lana is my friend. She helped me remember things."

"Are these things true, Mom?" Mira said.

Silence, before an ear-splitting guitar riff squealed from outside.

Burry turned to his father. "Is it true?" he demanded. "Mom had the accident leaving Stan and Mary's?" Never had Charles felt such rage radiate from his son. Mira said, "Not now, Burry. Please."

"Yes," Charles found himself saying. "Yes, Janelle was leaving that night...she and I discussed that—"

"You 'discussed' that? When? Why in the hell did you say Mom had the accident on the way to Stan's?" Burry said. "What did you have to hide?"

"It was supposed to help your mother! She had an accident heading there, not leaving...not...rushing away after an argument, leaving in such a state. So people wouldn't draw the wrong conclusions."

"Daddy," Mira said. Charles couldn't meet her eyes, any of their eyes. "But people drew all sorts of conclusions about Mom."

"Yes, and now—this...thing!" he said. "The vicious smears—"

"Charles," Janelle said and he looked at her. "I was trying to leave you. That night."

"Yes, yes, fine! We had a spat." He looked at Mira, at Burry. "Your mother arrived at Stan and Mary's, yes." He turned back to Janelle. "You were there and then you... I tried to stop you...I tried to stop you from leaving because I knew it was dangerous. You were in no state of mind to drive." Charles, so desperate now his mind seized up like a frozen engine, and he couldn't say the right thing. And he had to say the right thing. He and Janelle could talk later, after the wedding, they could straighten it out, he would own his shame, lay his contrition at his wife's feet, but now—he couldn't let the grifter win. "That criminal, she...warped things, this movie of hers...she wanted to ruin us, she knew how to create a scandal... It's wrong, what she claimed. Tell them, Janelle."

But Janelle didn't see him. It was as if she were looking right through him.

"Mom," Burry said. "That night. Did Stan force himself on you?"

"No," Janelle said. "But he tried to."

"Stan admired your mother," Charles sputtered. "He respected her. Stan was always praising you, Janelle—"

"He pursued me."

"Stan thought you hung the moon. He was always telling me how lucky I was—"

"But it was getting out of hand. I told you, and you promised to tell him...to stop it."

Janelle's sage-green eyes darker now, cold too, she was pulling away from him—

"A man admires your wife...that's a good thing," Charles said.

"He sent me letters," Janelle said.

"He got carried away—"

"I set up the fax machine and he would...he would send love letters to me."

"Stan wanted you because he couldn't have you," Charles said, realizing it all over again.

"And you were proud of that?" Mira asked him.

Yes. He was proud of his wife! What was wrong with that?

"Your business partner harassed your wife and you were... flattered?" Burry said.

"And Stan humiliated her," Janelle said.

"Humiliated?" Charles repeated.

"Mary was through with it," Janelle said. "I was through with it."

When Spec parked the minivan at the farm, he was afraid he was in trouble. His mother would be looking for him. She might even find out he drove alone. She would tell him he was going dark, no devices for the rest of the summer.

But Grandmother would help him explain, wouldn't she?

He got out of the minivan, held the puppy's leash, picked up the aquarium. The hens had not wanted to get into the minivan so he told them he would come back later to get them. In the aquarium Shelly was tucked inside her shell.

On the way from the cabin Spec had stopped once, at the produce stand. He got out of the minivan to check the back seat. He made sure Shelly's aquarium stopped sliding around. Then he drove to the farm. It was easy now because he knew all the traffic laws.

Spec made his way across the lawn, carrying Shelly's aquarium while Biscuit walked on the leash. He looked around for the first time at all the people—they were not looking at him. They did not notice him. They were looking at their phones.

Inside the farmhouse it was cool. He set down the aquarium on a hallway table. Biscuit tugged the leash. His mother said, "Spec, baby, come here. I've been looking for you." She hugged him, pressed her face on his head, and did not even yell at him, not even about Biscuit. "There are some sad things going down here."

He pulled away and said, "I have a puppy. I need to look after this puppy." She would say no, he just knew it, but she didn't. She didn't.

She said, "Can you walk the puppy outside, baby? Burry and me, we need to be with Aunt Mira for a bit, okay?"

"Okay. I have a turtle too. To look after."

She didn't hear him. She was looking over his shoulder; there were people looking up, more and more people walking toward the porch. A lot of UPSET people.

45

THE SITUATION ROOM

They assembled in the farmhouse office, the "situation room," Reagan called it.

Mira in her wedding dress, a flower in her hair—rumpled but beautiful, so much like Janelle, really. Charles's heart began to sink.

"It's bad out there," Reagan announced, as she closed the door. "Seriously effed up."

"It's bad in here too," Burry said.

"Hey, okay if I see the bride all dressed up now?" Nelson said, holding up a hand as if Mira's presence blinded him. "Isn't it bad luck? Not that I'm superstitious."

"It's okay, Nels," Mira said.

"Bad luck?" Reagan said. "That train has left the station."

"I want you here," Mira told Nelson.

Charles, turning to them all now like the town crier, announced, "We've been attacked. Our family has been attacked. A criminal has…" Charles turned to Janelle. "Tell them…that woman Lana, she sent that video out to, to—" He looked over at Mira. "She embedded notions into your mother's—"

Burry sat down beside his mother, still furious on his mother's behalf. "Seriously, Dad? Is this about the sicko wife-swap thing?"

Charles looked around the room, seeking an ally, finding only astonishment and disgust, even…Teddy. Teddy! Did they hate him? All of them? Even…Janelle?

"Janelle, I need to hear it from you," Teddy said firmly, gently. "It's not true, right? About my mother and Charles?"

"Everyone?" Reagan said. She kicked off her heels and stood

up on the ottoman, peering down at them. "I need everyone's attention, okay? This is a crisis. And if there's one thing I know? It's managing a crisis."

Teddy said, "Can we assume the source…this, uh, criminal…is easy to discredit? I say ignore it for now, until we get a handle on—"

"Senator Rex is getting smeared every microsecond, Teddy. We have to offer some measured response." Reagan stepped off the ottoman. "Janelle," she said softly, and that got everyone's attention, Reagan's whispery, desperate plea. "Janelle, you can undo this. You hold the power. You were helping some actress or wannabe director with a project, right? Some film project or whatever, and she misled you. You can admit this is shocking and upsetting, right? That this clip has been edited and screwed up, and it's not true. That part about Stan? Not true. I've drafted a short statement; I'm going to read it to you, and then I want you to repeat it."

"Really?" Burry said.

Such a disappointment, Charles thought. His son the mama's boy, who did not care their family's good name was smeared.

"You're just going to gloss over this? We're not going stand here and let Mom get thrown under the bus again," Burry said, glaring at Charles. "That's not going to happen. Mom was there that night at Stan and Mary's house, let's start with that."

Teddy looked at Janelle. "You were there? That part is true?"

"Your mother was leaving Stan," Janelle told him.

"But…why didn't she?"

"You."

"Look," Reagan said. "This is devastating for all of us. It's disturbing, and there are understandably a lot of…complicated emotions to process. But let's pull together. We—all of us—we have to get on the same page. First step, Janelle and Charles. You walk back outside arm in arm, giggling, you dance and laugh and kiss, like one of those Viagra commercials—"

"No, no, we have to tell them…tell them, Janelle, how that grifter tricked you," Charles said. "I told her she was a con artist." Charles looked at Mira. "I told your mother she would bilk us. That she was out for our money—"

"Money?" Nelson said, turning to Mira. "That woman ripped off your mother?"

"Yes, yes, do you see? She fleeced your mother," Charles said eagerly. He turned to Janelle. "And now...you can't let her ruin Mira's wedding."

"There isn't going to be a wedding to ruin," Mira said with a rueful glance at Nelson. "Look, everyone. I think it's best if we call it off."

There was a beat of silence. Outside, the band screeched out another ear-splitting ragged song.

"What?" Reagan said.

"You can't cancel your wedding," Charles boomed.

"How will we get our deposits back?" Nelson asked.

"I'll cover it, Nelson, okay?" Mira said. "You won't have to spend a cent. Can't you see this...disaster unfolding around you, right in front of your eyes?"

"That sucky band isn't getting paid, is it?" Nelson said. "What kind of wedding band plays 'Cat Scratch Fever'?" He jabbed his thumb toward the curtained window as the singer screamed.

"Okay, that's a mistake, calling off your wedding," Reagan told Mira. "That screams shame. That gives this crazy thing legs. You can't give up."

"You can't let that criminal win!" Charles said. "Janelle, tell her, she can't call it off—"

"How about you and Nelson go through with the ceremony?" Reagan told Mira. "Just don't sign the paperwork or whatever."

"Reagan," Teddy said. "If Mira wants to call off her wedding, let her do it."

"I don't believe this."

"Reagan, chill."

"Chill? Chill? Teddy, I'm not going to stand by while your father's name—your name—is dragged through this swamp.

Wife swapping? Who came up with that seventies corn porn, anyway? The skinny is Janelle was pranked, okay? We have to go with that. And we have to, all of us, go out there and just… just carry on."

"Yes," Charles said. "Yes, that's right."

"I think we should go home, Mom," Mira said. "We'll slip out the back. Burry will get the car."

"No. No, that's so wrong," Reagan said. "Slinking away like that?"

"Go on, Mira," Teddy said. "You're doing the right thing."

"What in the…? I'm trying to mop up this hot mess," Reagan told him in a steely tone.

"I'm not hiding it anymore," Teddy told Mira. "Now that you called off the wedding."

"That's not why I called it off."

"You don't mean that."

"You can't," Janelle whispered to Mira, but they could all hear. "You can't love him."

When her mother walked in on her and Teddy—well, Mira liked to think it wasn't just the indignity—her mother's embarrassment, her look of sheer horror—that clarified things. Mira couldn't build a marriage on lies. She couldn't love Nelson enough—not enough to marry him, to take a vow for the rest of her life, raise a child with him. No way. She must have been insane. Trying to just patch things up and jump-start her best self…crock of shit. Now her mother stared hard at Teddy, and Mira thought, Okay, Mom, point taken, but don't lay this on Teddy, not all of it, not today…

"I know I can't, Mom," Mira said, not looking at Teddy, but feeling his eyes on her, his hurt.

Mira looked at Teddy. Teddy looked at Mira.

That look between them. The wind went out of Charles; he sank to the ottoman, onto something soft.

Mira told Teddy, "Don't. Please don't."

Then Teddy's hand. On Mira's shoulder. That's all it took. Teddy's wedding-ringed hand on Mira's bare, soft shoulder. The yearning. The tender intimacy. Everyone saw it then, everyone.

"What's...going on?" Reagan asked.

"Yeah, I'm wondering that myself," Nelson said.

Reagan searched Teddy's face. His eyes flashed with furtive excitement. He dropped his gaze.

"You and...Mira?" she said slowly, then gathering steam. "You and Mira were...all those nights you went to that bar," Reagan said in an odd, flat voice, "and I was working my ass off? And you and Mira—"

Teddy doesn't love Mira, Charles thought. Ridiculous. Teddy and Mira, Mira and Teddy. The words ringing in Charles's head, drowning out their rising voices, their accusations.

His arm went numb; he was going to be sick right here in front of everyone. Was there no end to his humiliation today? The floor spinning, coming closer. Janelle looked at him finally, saw his shame. Saw how sorry he was—a sorry husband!—the pain, the pain—his pangs of conscience. He couldn't breathe. Burry, big, soft, always too soft, but strong now, as Charles teetered, as the floor headed for him and Burry caught him...and then, nothing.

PART V

AUGUST 2015

46

CHARLES

He was supine, helpless. He did not know things. He did not know how long he had been here, tethered, surrounded by machines that chirped and fussed.

Charles drifted in and out. Strangers stuck him with needles, shined lights into his eyes, some of them talked to him, some did not, some were stern, one smiled. They looked at the machines. They looked at him.

The lady in blue who smiled asked him to describe his pain, on a scale from one to ten. He opened his mouth, he wanted to tell her the pain was there, hovering, a funnel cloud heading right for him, and he was stuck, tied to this—

"Hurrrr." Groaning sound, coming from somewhere, from him. It hurts. It hurts like a son of a bitch.

But then—thank you. Thank you. The lady in blue fiddled with the line attached to him. His veins sang. The warm thing happened, the wind picked him up, he could leave. Black wings so wide he just sailed, he circled up high, gliding over the land. He admired buzzards. He never knew that until now. The cleanup crew. No need to work too hard, you feasted on a bounty of leftovers. Freeloaders. Mostly you just glided in circles, over and over, the shadow underneath you a second dark bird.

Visitors arrived and departed. Charles was channel surfing, flipping through the noise, skipping over the flat screen, never lighting. Janelle. But she had on a baggy T-shirt? And Burry, frowning, Charles could see it…the anger around Burry. I did that, a thought dribbled slow and cold. I caused that pain. And Mira…that was Mira in the T-shirt…not Janelle.

Janelle. Where was she? Not here.

Then—Janelle. Here. She said, Charles, can you hear me?
He could.

She said, Squeeze my hand?
He couldn't.

He couldn't bear letting her win, that charlatan! That was
what was keeping him alive. Janelle had to understand—
Lies. Lies.

Sordid, appalling, disgraceful.

She's not coming. He tried to tell Janelle. I always took care
of you, of us. She ruined us, anyway. Do you see? Do you see?

Sometime later, when he came down out of the sky, when he
was trapped and tied again, Lana arrived.

Silent, glaring, ignored by the nurses who came in and out.
She sat underneath the mounted television in the corner; her
painted mouth sneered.

"Did you actually think you were rid of me?"

He groaned. "Not true…Your liessss—"

"Oh, the video. Your night of iniquity? Which part?"

The pictures floated around Charles now. His own movie.
Stan doted on Janelle. Charles didn't mind because Stan looked
up to Janelle, he trusted her judgment, and Charles looked up
to Stan.

"You didn't mind? Are you kidding me, Charles? You liked
it. You encouraged it. Stan licking his chops over your wife. Oh,
how it excited you."

Shut up. He couldn't say it. His mouth wouldn't move. He
screamed at her in his mind. Shut up. Get out.

"Admit it."

It excited him. Rekindled the passion, the thrill from the
night he stole Janelle away from the judge's iron fist, crashing
her debutante party, luring her away from that rich bow-tied
escort, when Charles won Janelle—

"Like a prize."

Shut up!

Stan smitten with Janelle, so Charles was too, again. Deep

affection is how Stan described it, nothing to worry about. Harmless.

Lana snorted her hoarse laugh. "Harmless. Good one, Charles."

Stan…yes, all right, yes, he got out of hand, brazen, that's what Janelle called it. The love notes, the moony-eyed gazes at Janelle. And Janelle said, Talk to him, tell him to stop or I will. Now Lana was making him watch the bad movie. Even when he closed his eyes, it was there. The night of Janelle's accident. Mary in the back bedroom crying, Stan in the living room, broken wine glasses glistening in the carpet, Stan livid— he'd never seen Stan so…out of control. She thinks she's going to leave me.

"What a shame," Lana whispered, "that Mary confided to Janelle. And Janelle made a big mistake. She told you. Trusted you to keep your piehole shut for a few hours. You promised Janelle you would not breathe a word to Stan. But you did. Of course."

Charles arrived and Stan said, My God, Charles, you have to go back there and talk to her. If I see her, I might kill her. Go calm her down. Mary threatening to take every penny Stan had, ruin their business, she'd already talked to a lawyer.

"That poor woman. Stan got his wife all turned around that night, didn't he?"

Charles wanted to tell the nurse in blue to come back, to make the vampire leave, she was sapping his strength, she was killing him.

"Let me take a wild guess, Charles. Stan claimed Janelle was late on purpose that night, didn't he? Yes, clever, how Stan Rex convinced his wife that Janelle had turned on her. He concocted quite a tale, didn't he? Claiming that it was Janelle who'd told him Mary's bags were packed, she was leaving on a jet plane— that Janelle had squealed, not you. And Stan had the balls to claim Janelle was the one throwing herself at him, making a fool of Mary."

We had to appease Mary, Charles tried to say, a flock of

words, flying, flying out of him. Mary would ruin the business—
"The business. That's all you two bastards cared about."
Talk to her, Stan had said. Calm her down.
"And you agreed. Such a sacrifice, Charles. A poke in the
sack to shut up Stan's wife."
Noooo. Charles grunted.
"And with Janelle due to arrive there any minute. See, Charles,
this just screams recklessness, or...maybe excitement?"
No, no! Stan said, By the way, Janelle called, she isn't com-
ing—
"The senator fibbed? To you? I'm shocked."
Mary lay across the wide, creamy bed, sobbing. He'd sat
beside her. Patted her leg. Mary, it's all right—
"It wasn't."
She said, I don't love him. He said, Now, now. You don't
mean that.
"She did."
Mary said, Do you know how long it's been since we...since
he held me?
"Because, well, his war injury, right?" The grifter grinned.
"To put it delicately. Stan's sacrifice for his country. He was
shooting blanks—and couldn't get it up half the time. Poor girl.
I bet Stan tormented her. Only Janelle could excite him, why
couldn't Mary be more like Janelle—on and on. Mary Rex was
starved for a little loving, huh? Enter Charles."
Get out! Get out!
The pain chugged, gathered steam. Charles tried to call the
smiling nurse—
"Then Janelle arrives, and nearly catches you in flagrante,
while Stan puts the moves on your wife in the living room."
The vampire cackled, but Charles would not look at her. "And
you have the nerve to claim my little movie exaggerates?"
The smiling nurse came in. She disregarded Lana with a
coldness that warmed Charles.
"You're spineless, Charles Wolf. Janelle saw it. She wanted
to leave her 'perfect' marriage. Even before your roll in the hay

with that poor snookered Mary, shackled to the sadist. You handed Janelle an excuse to leave you that night..."

The smiling nurse studied the chirping machines; she leaned over to him, said, One to ten, pain.

Ten, a voice croaked. Like a frog. Bullfrogs in a pond...oh, oh God, help him. From inside him. Ten. Ten.

All right, Mr. Wolf, hold on...relief is on the way.

She fiddled with the thing.

He flew.

47

TEDDY

Teddy hadn't slept all weekend.

He was wounded. Self-inflicted, yes, some of it. He had betrayed...but he had been betrayed too! By Charles. By his own mother, who'd never talked about the night of Janelle's accident, not to him. That was a hell of a blow, landing harder and harder. Why hadn't his own mother told him about Janelle arriving that night of the accident? Had his mother really planned to leave his father? Had she and Charles even...hooked up? Come on. No way. His mother would have come clean on her deathbed—about that. Right? Teddy puked, worse than any hangover.

Then out of the blue, Burry—of all people—texted him.

—It's all true. About Dad. Mom and Mira talked.

Oh yeah? Thanks for the FYI. As far as Teddy was concerned, denial was made for this kind of messed-up shit. Deny! Deny! Blaring in his head like a car alarm.

Teddy tried to call Mira; she didn't pick up. Well, fine. He was no longer obsessed with contacting Mira.

Teddy was now obsessed with seeing his wife. At least talking to her. He didn't even know where Reagan was staying, or who she was staying with. Was she heartbroken? Reagan had a lot of men who would love to comfort her... God, what an idiot he was. He couldn't lose Reagan! He wanted her.

Now that she didn't want him.

Get it together, Teddy told himself. Tend your own wounds, bro, or you are going down. Get to work. Wouldn't hurt to draft a little speech, a few salient points to tell clients.

At some point, he would have to go into Rex Wolf, address the staff, tell them Charles had suffered a heart attack.

"After they get him stabilized, he's going for surgery," Arlene had told Teddy Saturday night. She had called him just hours after Charles had been rushed to the hospital, and Teddy had never been so happy to hear that old bat's voice. In fact, after their numerous phone conversations over the weekend, he and Arlene had formed a strange alliance.

At first Arlene was beside herself, bawling, and Teddy was reminded of how protective she was of Charles, because, man, that toady had his back, and Teddy...well...he couldn't bring himself to think of Charles's face on Saturday, twisted in pain, falling...

"But he will pull through," Arlene told him. "Yes, Charles will pull through, stronger than ever, that's what you need to say. That's what everyone needs to hear."

But what else did Teddy need to say? Surely there would be questions, awkward inquiries, phone calls from clients, from potential clients, from all those wedding guests privy to that salacious video clip. Holy hell, he did not want to go to the offices of Rex Wolf. Not yet. He'd just make it worse. First do no harm, as the doctors say.

"Are you going to try to see Charles?" Arlene had asked. "Because they're only letting family in."

"Later," Teddy mumbled. "After he's stable."

Then Arlene had complained that Mira didn't call her every hour with an update as she'd promised. "Of course, what that girl went through, having to postpone the wedding and all, because her daddy—" Here comes the waterworks, Teddy thought.

Arlene sobbed.

Teddy wanted to.

In the wake of the wedding debacle—after the ambulance left, the guests lingering and asking what happened, what happened like some doomed Greek chorus—Teddy had been foolish enough to assume he and Reagan would drop by the hospital.

The look on Reagan's face then. Subzero. She'd turned and stomped off to the car, pausing only to take off her shoes and run the rest of the way. He'd followed, jumped into the car as she started it up.

The AC blasted, and the music too, the Lumineers—sunny lyrics, mocking, before Reagan turned it off. She looked straight ahead as he fastened his seat belt. "When it begins to dawn on you how stupid you've been? I don't want to hear your lame excuses."

"I think we—"

"Be quiet and listen." She still did not look at him, even when he let out a plaintive but manly sigh. "It's just like you to sneak around with some sad-sack poet who must have been so grateful for—"

"Reagan—"

"Shut it, Teddy."

He shut it.

She finally turned to him, her wide, gleaming forehead smooth, her eyes cool and exquisite, only her mouth made ugly with a blunt announcement. "I will drive us home. And then there will be no more *us*. I'm going to pack and then I'm leaving."

She held up a hand when he tried to speak. "And the other thing? If you say one word, just one word, you can get out of my car and hitchhike."

They drove home in silence. Inside, she went straight to their bedroom and threw things in a suitcase without her usual care. She grabbed some bottles in the bathroom and emptied out a drawer in another bag. He stood by helplessly watching, silent, wringing his hands like a grim mime. He wanted her to cry, expected her to lose it, because he could…comfort her. He could possibly explain. Find the words that now—two days later—were just occurring to him. It was a stupid crush. It didn't mean anything.

Reagan picked up her suitcases, headed out the front door, and only then did she turn to him. "Don't look for me. I'll contact you."

And so, he waited.

All weekend. Every twelve hours without any word from his wife, Teddy allowed himself to call her again. Just twice a day because he couldn't appear desperate. Reagan would hate that. How to apologize and sound strong, though? He hadn't got the hang of it. What would he say when she picked up? If she picked up. His texts and emails went unanswered, his calls went straight to voicemail. He hung up without leaving a message.

When Arlene called him on Sunday night, he agreed they had to do something about containing the fallout. How apt. The fallout. Radioactive and pulverizing. All of them in the same ash heap if this thing didn't get handled. By Teddy! Well, everything was on hold, as far as Teddy was concerned, though he didn't tell Arlene, of course. Taking over Rex Wolf? Not with Charles in the ICU. But that was some cover, wasn't it? Or at least, a freeze-framed pause? Until Charles recovered. Teddy wondered if Arlene had heard rumors, or maybe, oh please, God, yes—could she at least reassure Teddy he was exaggerating the impact of that viral video…surely written off as a prank?

Calamity? Or nothingburger?

Teddy had lost perspective.

"What that woman did to him," Arlene's demon voice croaked to Teddy.

Calamity, Teddy thought. Definitely calamity.

"May she burn in hell," Arlene said.

For a minute Teddy thought Arlene meant Janelle. Then Arlene said, "She tormented Charles. She's a witch, you know. The real kind, with big soup pots and gobbledygook spells. Got Janelle all worked up. And wasn't a thing Charles could do about it. And now people are saying the ugliest things."

Monday morning, after pacing for hours, he waited until sunrise to call Arlene. Her voice, thick with sleep, powered up fast. "Is it Charles? Oh Lord, is there news about Charles?"

"No, sorry. No news about Charles."

"Oh, you scared the stuffing out of me."

"I called you to let you know I won't be in the office today. I'll plan to come in tomorrow morning and address the staff."

"All right." Neutral, no disapproval, no approval, either.

"For now, you can tell everyone that Charles may need surgery but is expected to make a full recovery. Let them know—"

"I know what to say," she said, not angry but terse. In control. Teddy felt strangely relieved. Better to leave it in Arlene's hands for another day.

"And just let some asshole bring up what that witch did," she said. "No one is insulting Charles. Not when I'm around. Let them try. They won't know what hit them."

"Thank you."

"All right, hon, you rest," she added with more compassion than he'd heard from anyone in…days.

But he couldn't rest.

He was feeling a little peckish. Six-thirty in the morning, too early to order a pizza. He should get out of the house. Go… somewhere. The liquor store for starters. He was down to a bottle of chablis. Not his drink of choice, but, hey, he'd gone through the beer and most of the vodka—

Focus! Prepare today. Go into the office tomorrow. Get in front of this. Get on message. There was Reagan's voice in his head.

If he could just have the rest of her.

But his wife was gone. His career, in pieces. His life…in the sewer.

He could really use some goddamn crisis management.

48

MIRA

Her father was dying.

Then not. Holding on, stabilizing. Back and forth. In the hospital waiting room, her mother slept in a chair. Mira stood up, stretched, went down the hall for coffee. She wore Pansy's borrowed capris—stretchy, forgiving fabric—and Burry's baggy Pink Floyd T-shirt. Perfect leisurewear for sitting around in hospital waiting rooms. Because, other than a wedding dress, Mira didn't have clothes. She hadn't contacted Nelson about picking up her things, about…anything. She was too exhausted to agonize over the tone of a text. Finally tapped out, *can we talk later?* No response to that yet.

Also, she was bleeding.

Big old heavy period, like *here I am*! Yoo-hoo! Your uterus! Shedding away, cleaning house, flushing another egg. Fooled ya. Well, bring it on, the bloating, the cramps, the headaches, the hourly trips to the bathroom. A mortification of the flesh. Because, period. That was good news. So, there was that.

Of course, she knew it was on the way. She'd taken the pregnancy test, the wedding "gift" that Burry had left her, another temptation she couldn't resist.

At the hospital gift store now she bought salted almonds, M&Ms, Red Bull, crossword puzzle books. Burry would bring them dinner later. He'd apparently taken up smoking again. Giving myself a pass, he said. You should too. Take up a vice. Eat Krispy Kreme donuts. Read trashy tabloids. Watch *Real Housewives*. Go ahead.

Burry offered to spell her, but Mira insisted on staying at the hospital. It wasn't like she had a life to get back to.

In the waiting room now, her mother jolted awake when Mira sat down beside her, bearing provisions.

"Is it time?" her mother asked.

"Another half an hour."

Janelle would nod off, then startle awake, blurting out sentences, like one of those Disney World animated figures. She and her mother sat and mostly didn't talk. Every few hours, a nurse allowed one of them to see Charles. Mira begged the nurses to mute the blaring television in the waiting room. The nice ones did. Mira worked her crossword puzzles. Her mother wrote in a notebook.

Her father's condition was critical. Looked bad for a while there. When Mira relayed this to Arlene—who called her incessantly—the woman burst out crying.

Janelle hadn't shed a tear. Not in front of Mira. Not yet.

But she refused to leave the hospital. And Mira took that as a kind of loyalty, even in the face of those accusations…about Mira's father. Which she and her mother would eventually get around to discussing in detail. Why did that so-called friend of yours send out that video? Mira longed to ask her when the time was right.

Her mother took out her pen and notebook. Mira envied that, the ability to write anything now, especially now. That was incredible. Mira could barely write her name. She was fried.

"Is that…are you keeping a diary, Mom?" Her mother looked up from her notebook. "If you don't mind my asking."

"A diary? No, it's just all of this…it has come very fast, Mira."

Binge writing calmed her mother. Hypergraphia, which was a thing. A real symptom. Which Mira would like to have.

"I will need help sorting it all out," her mother continued. "When Lana gets here."

"When…what?" Mira shut her mouth and waited for her mother to discover how illogical this was. Her mother returned to her notebook.

"Mom, has it occurred to you that your friend is not coming

back? That she left, like Daddy said, and"—careful now, tread lightly—"maybe she is more foe than friend? That she could have…manipulated you into saying some of those things?" Mira's father, vilified, that wasn't right. Stan—sure. Throw his sorry ass under a freight train. But her own father? "Did you know your friend was recording your 'sessions'?" Mira, hopped up on Red Bull and chocolate, found herself blurting it out.

"Yes, of course there was a camera…it was how we fit it all together, the bits of things I remembered."

"But, Mom, why would she send something confidential… and so personal about you to everyone?"

"I'm going to ask her. When Lana gets here, we'll work it out."

"What do you mean work it out?"

"We'll clear it up. I'll start up sessions with Lana again."

Mira walked over to the window. What was that trick about calming yourself by staring at a tree? See that willow at the edge of the parking lot? How still and tranquil it is, roots blanketed with asphalt.

"I looked over her website." Mira sat back down beside her mother. "She wasn't a conventional counselor, that's for sure. What kind of methods did she use?"

"Methods? We were…friends. I wrote letters to her. And then I'd fill notebooks. Lana loves reading them. I write it all down. It pours out, and she…it's like a puzzle and we put it together—"

"But what about…the implications about Dad and Mary that night? Where did that come from?"

"Lana says we should stay open to even the most disturbing ideas and explore images—"

"Mom, look. Is it possible she distorted your memories? And maybe Lana fabricated…things?"

Her mother took off her reading glasses and capped her pen. "Sometimes we explore alternate truths because they reveal—"

"Alternate truths? Oh my God, Mom, that's gobbledygook for making stuff up." Mira should stop now; her own heartsick frustration was building, getting away from her. "It's just...I don't want Daddy to be remembered that way. Your friend had a perverse outlook. You may not realize it. She...she coaxed you, right? Maybe she twisted your story, Mom."

Mira was back at the window, counting the limbs on that willow tree. "I want to know the truth, Mom. Your truth. Dad claiming you never showed up that night, that your accident happened on the way—that's disgraceful. And Mary planning to divorce Stan, that's understandable. But Dad and Mary... together? Dad wanting to pawn you off on Stan for kicks? That's...we should clear it up." Diplomatic *we*, not accusatory *you*. Good catch. "When's the last time you talked to Lana, anyway?"

"Two weeks." Her mother sighed. "And it feels like forever."

"Burry said you and Spec visited her, your friend. At a cabin."

"Was that wrong? To take Spec?" Her mother sounded alarmed now, even rueful. Finally. "He liked to go—"

"Yeah, Burry said. But what did Spec do while you and Lana talked?"

"We would have a snack and then Spec played with the pets; he really does love animals—"

"Is she still staying there, at the cabin?"

"Lana had to leave to see to her other clients. All over the country. But she was planning to attend the wedding. In all the confusion...I fear I may have missed her."

Mira groaned. "She didn't show up at the wedding, Mom. And if she did? What kind of friend doesn't check in when her friend's husband has a heart attack? And, Mom, please don't say you're going to ask her."

"But I am."

"Look, just...will you promise me something? Promise me you'll tell me if Lana contacts you? Even if she tells you not to tell anyone? Tell me?"

"Of course I'll tell you, Mira."

Mira took her mother's hand. "Mom, will you let me in...tell me about this work you've done? Your remembering? You write things down for your friend, but I want to read your notebooks. I would really love to...sometime. I want to read all of them." She expected her mother to be defensive, even insulted, but she looked perplexed. "You do? I had no idea."

"I know your notebooks are private, and you might not want to share it all, but, Mom, I would love to know all this...all of you."

The nurse came in then and said one of them could see Charles for a few minutes. Janelle was up next.

"He's probably still out of it, Mom. He won't know you're there."

"He will," she said.

When Janelle left, Mira pulled out her mother's notebook. And read.

49

JANELLE

Are you close by, my friend? I think you are. I want to tell you this, all of it. I remembered something terrible.

When Mary visited me in my own living room, she brought her sorry flowers and her belly—jutting out at me. She did not say baby. She did not have to. But the fevered idea, how I glommed on to it, made it mine. Precious cargo inside of me, I gobbled it up.

And then I had to go back to the hospital.

All these years mourning that loss too. A baby. But there was no baby.

Not my baby. Do you see?

Mary said, I knew it would be hard for you. She said she was sorry. Sorry!

She thought I knew all along, you see.

I didn't.

You asked about Stan, if he spoke to me alone. After the accident.

Once. Years later.

One of his election celebrations. He always won. There were always celebrations.

An empty corridor. Stan sitting on a bench. His shoe off, dangling from his foot, he slid it back on. Too much pride to use a cane.

Janelle, he said. We have our own map of scars now, don't we?

Stan with his nimble shamble, war wounded, a landscape of humped scars on his calf, the enemy's sweet revenge.

You know how I've longed to find my love for Charles. But I can't find something I never lost.

There was no love to lose.

Janelle Before left Charles. She did not love him.

I do not love him.

I close my eyes and I see...her. Janelle Before. The water fills her gaping mouth, her hair Medusa wild, her lungs burn—I see her, drowning.

Janelle Before. I have swallowed her. We are one. Again. I AM her.

50

SPEC

Spec smuggled a spoon from the kitchen. In the backyard, in the shady part under leaves, that's where the juicy worms hid. Biscuit pawed the dirt as Spec dug up earthworms. Biscuit tried to help. Spec petted her head.

The worms were pink, segmented, and slick; they squirmed faster and faster when Spec held them, and they tickled the inside of his hand. He put them in a paper cup and called Biscuit and they went back into his room to feed Shelly. He told each worm he was sorry when he put them in Shelly's dish. They didn't have eyes or ears or a mouth, but they wriggled fast like they felt things. They were like pieces of a big body, stomachs or lungs, and he was sad they were scared, but Shelly poked her head out of her shell because she was getting used to Spec, and probably she was hungry.

Dad knocked, then pushed open Spec's door. "I'm bushed, little man. Gonna grab some Zs. You need anything?"

Spec shook his head. Shelly's feet had little claws and she had a tiny tail, too, and she was looking at the worms and starting to move toward them. Spec must have had a smile on his face because Dad said, "It's good to see you happy, Spec. You're taking good care of that turtle."

"She's a box turtle named Shelly."

"Shelly. Yeah. Look." Dad sat on Spec's bed and Biscuit grabbed the shoelaces on Dad's shoes.

"Biscuit likes shoes," Spec said.

Dad reached down to pet her. Then he cleared his throat and that made Spec's stomach hurt because when Dad cleared his throat it meant Spec might be in trouble. "I promised your mom that…" Dad stopped and he looked like he wanted to leave. Spec wanted him to leave. He wanted to feed Shelly and maybe sneak some banana out of the kitchen and see if she ate that too. Like a dessert. Like a turtle's banana pudding. She had a tomato for a salad and worms for meat and she might like a dessert too.

"We don't want you to get too attached to Biscuit and Shelly. We're going to keep looking for the owners." Dad and his mother kept asking where Biscuit and Shelly came from. No one at the farm knew, because Spec's mother had called and asked. But Dad said their owners might be looking for them.

"You know, we should think about releasing the turtle. Don't you think it would be happier in its natural habitat with other turtles?"

That made Spec sad, but he thought of releasing Shelly near the pond, imagined her sunning on a log with other turtles. Spec could take her there and see if she wanted to stay outside. Maybe her mom and dad were waiting for her. "When she gets bigger and stronger," Spec said.

"And we're going to need to return Biscuit to her owner. I just want you to be prepared to—"

"No. NO. NO. NO." Spec dropped to the floor. He felt Dad's hand on his arm and then he didn't feel him or hear him. He knocked his head on the floor and Biscuit barked, and Spec knew Biscuit was trying to help him again.

Dad's words came back in his head. "Stop, stop, please, come on, Spec, please."

Spec stopped. Biscuit's pink tongue was the only thing he could see, the only thing in his room, the only thing.

"Look. I promised your mom we'd talk about it. And, hey, we talked, right?" Dad stood up. "Screw it. I'm so tired I can't think."

Dad's phone rang. He pulled it out of his pocket and left Spec's room.

"Who?" Dad said. "What? What…happened…you freaking kidding me?" He was talking on the phone in the hallway about another bad thing, Spec could tell.

Spec closed his bedroom door. At least Dad would leave him alone now. And that was good.

51

TEDDY

Could you suffer from cabin fever in a contemporary two-story in the suburbs? Yes, apparently you could. Teddy didn't make it to the office all week, didn't go anywhere. He simply lost the will. Reagan would come home any minute and he couldn't take a chance on missing her. That's what he told himself. Teddy hadn't had a drink in days. Whenever he had a craving, he got on Reagan's treadmill like a hyperactive hamster. He'd start to yell at himself—you lazy bastard, pick it up, you loser—and he'd increase the speed and incline, his feet pounding, until he begged himself to stop.

Even with all the pizza and cereal, he was starting to lose a few pounds. It was the treadmill. And stress. Now when the pizza delivery guy rang the doorbell—a daily occurrence—his heart was in his throat. Reagan's silence screamed hostility, and for all he knew, she'd hired a lawyer. Maybe the next pizza guy would serve him divorce papers.

He wandered around the house a lot. He had no plans. No meeting-stuffed days, a cleared calendar, the month of squares no longer a grid for strategies, a chessboard of deliberations. For all he knew, he had no more marriage or career, or house, for that matter. Liberating, huh? he asked himself. No more pressure, too. He could call up some pals who had landed jobs in DC think tanks. Or maybe law school. Or travel on the cheap. Mexico. Or…move to LA. Write a screenplay. He could do anything he wanted to now. Isn't that what he really wanted? Freedom?

Then why did he feel as if he were falling down a mineshaft, pinwheeling?

Arlene seemed to take his calling out in stride. She didn't question him when he said he'd come down with a stomach virus, and all his meetings that week were canceled anyway, and she was doing such a stand-up job even when they were trying to just power through, to be brave…for Charles.

Arlene called him religiously.

Reagan didn't. She hadn't contacted him at all.

Teddy spent more and more time in Reagan's home office. Those pink five-pound barbells, a tower of labeled files on her desk, her left-behind belongings comforted him. She'd have to come back for it. Any day.

He got on her treadmill, fifth time that day. A little more aerobic therapy couldn't hurt. But it did. After twenty minutes, it hurt like hell. He was wheezing, his throat on fire… How did she stay on the thing for an hour and make calls too? Blow out the carbon, she called it, like tearing up the highway, the fast lane—

He got off the treadmill, sweating, took off his drenched shirt. Stood there, hands on his knees, recovering.

Crisis management.

He poked through her cabinet and found a file. Stood there reading it, his perspiration plunking on the pages.

Sticky note on top, her writing. *Suze, plz load in deck for presentation. Thx.*

Crisis Management=FANS

F=Full responsibility. Note: take responsibility for disaster. Your fault. Own it. Cathartic!!!

A=Address fallout. Note: Concede damage. You feel their pain!!!

N=Never again. Note: Reassure customers/stakeholders changes made so will not happen again.

S=Salvage goodwill. Note: Draw on trust already banked with customers/stakeholders and build goodwill going forward. Best crisis management happens BEFORE crisis.

He called Reagan. Voicemail. This time he left a message.

"Reagan, look, I take full responsibility for what I did. No excuses. You have every right to cut me off, to never talk to me again, I get that. I trashed our marriage. Even if it was just a ...flirtation, a harmless crush, really. Nothing...no. No, it was something. I take responsibility for it. I know you're royally pissed off. You have every right to be. But it won't happen again. Ever. With anyone else. I swear. I'll do anything to...earn back your trust. Anything. Because we are so good together, so good. And...I can't imagine life without you."

Then he got back on the treadmill.

Not a peep for hours.

He fell asleep on the couch, cradling his phone like a pet.

After midnight, a ding. A buzz.

A text. From Reagan! Oh, thank God...his exhausted, sore body flooded with relief.

She had texted him—

A link...

—Take a look, Teddybear. Enjoy!

52

CHARLES

"Charles?"

Arlene was here. That was good. They could talk about his calendar. Rex Wolf was stronger than ever, on the edge of a comeback—

"That woman is gone." She leaned in closer. He smelled cigarettes and those wintergreen Certs she ate, rolls and rolls of them, years of those little mints. Arlene's whisper tickled his ear, he could barely make out what she was saying—"not bother you again."

Lana sat in the corner. Arlene didn't see her.

Or maybe she did. Arlene giving that crazy bitch the cold shoulder.

He wanted to tell Arlene it wasn't safe. Don't turn your back on that vampire, not for a minute...

"They found her car in a pond, up near Pudding Swamp. They're dragging the pond, looking for her body, may she burn in hell. I wanted to tell you as fast as I could 'cause it will make you stronger knowing that evil witch got what was coming... so you get ready...walk out of this place...in no time. You hear me?"

He did hear her.

And Lana, too—laughing.

"Charles, I see your lips moving," Arlene said. "But you should rest. The docs got you on some good dope. You might as well enjoy it. Because you're gonna be back at work in no time."

It was nothing! Charles said. Tried to say. Just that once, there was no affair. Janelle was everything to me, she is everything—

"Right," Lana said, not even whispering now, announcing. "You did it all for Janelle. Only you put a bun in the oven that night. A bonus, huh? Bet the senator and his wife were thrilled. Mary finally knocked up after all those years. Did they even bother to thank you?"

Not a word from Mary or Stan, because their happiness swelled as his own drained, as he nearly lost Janelle and never got her back, not really.

Sometimes he would catch himself wondering. About Teddy. He had willed himself to forget the possibility, the truth of it, embedded like a sword to the hilt, but it pierced him now, clean and sharp. Teddy. Teddy...his son.

"Charles." A blast of wintergreen and cigarettes. "Nod if you understand what I told you, hear? Nod?"

He did not nod. He did not understand.

Because Lana was right over there, sitting in the corner, looking at him and he felt oddly...relieved.

She was here. Not in the pond—

He tried to say it.

The machines peeped and sang.

"What's...I can't understand," Arlene said. She squeezed his hand, she was loyal as a hunting dog, this woman. Always had been, and he'd once said she looked like a hedgehog, ugly as a hedgehog, loyal as a hunting dog; he hadn't said that, had he? About good ol' loyal Arlene?

Lana shifted, stood—

"Somebody fishing is how they found it. The car. They'll find her body anytime. But she's gone, Charles. Dead as a doornail. And good riddance. Now then...you rest, hon. You rest and get ready for the operation."

Arlene left.

Lana turned to watch her leave. Lana in profile, green in the pulsing lights of the chirping machines.

The back of her head...was gone.

53

MISSING WOMAN'S CAR FOUND SUBMERGED IN HAVEN COUNTY POND

HAVEN, SC—The Haven Police Department has requested the public's help in finding a missing woman after finding her vehicle in a pond.

Haven County Police Chief Sam Crum said a fisherman spotted a partially submerged tan 2009 Sebring convertible in Pudding Pond early Sunday and notified authorities. The vehicle was traced to a deceased Arizona woman, but Crum said paperwork recovered at the scene indicated the driver may have been Lana O'Shield, a Nevada resident, who investigators believe was vacationing in a nearby cabin.

When authorities arrived on the scene, they discovered O'Shield's rental cabin had been ransacked. Crum said officers found a broken window and disarray inside, including a mattress that had been "slit open" and an overturned refrigerator.

It's unclear if the alleged vandalism is connected to O'Shield's disappearance.

Law enforcement have dispatched tracking K-9 to the scene to search the area for the car's driver. Bloodhounds were working for hours trying to track O'Shield's path, but where she is remains a mystery, Crum said. O'Shield may have fled on foot from the cabin, he said, but the K-9 unit did not "pick up anything" beyond the pond. "Canines tracked her scent from the cabin, down toward the pond near her submerged car," he said.

Crum said divers are searching the pond and nearby Twin River along Horse Highway. He declined to say what investigators were looking for. "We are looking for evidence," he said. "That's all I can say."

Crum added that the authorities are treating O'Shield's case as a missing person/disappearance investigation. "We are looking at all angles and speaking with anyone who might have had contact with her [the missing woman]."

O'Shield's cabin had been leased through the summer, paid up front with cash, according to a Mountain Breeze Vacation Rentals spokesperson. O'Shield, a counselor whose website describes her services as "soul tending," had apparently little contact with nearby residents or businesses, Crum said. Investigators have attempted to contact the missing woman's next of kin but have not yet been successful.

The website for O'Shield's business was recently deactivated, so it's unclear if she was still running the business at the time of her disappearance.

O'Shield is white, about 150 pounds and 5-foot-10. The 40-year-old woman has reddish brown hair and brown eyes. She was last seen the evening of July 23 at the Starvin' Marvin gas station on Horse Highway wearing a burgundy shirt and cutoff jeans and carrying a red purse.

Anyone with information is asked to contact the Haven Police Department at (800) 555-2825. Anonymous tips, which may be eligible for a cash reward, should be directed to Crime Stoppers at (800) 555-6470.

54

SPEC

When his aunt Mira arrived, the house got loud again. They wouldn't let Spec stay in his room with Biscuit and Shelly; they made him come to the living room and sit down. They said they needed to talk to him. But they tried to make him talk.

"Why didn't you tell me the pets belong to Grandmother's friend?" Dad said.

Spec held his hands together in his lap. His fingers looked like separate people hugging each other.

"Spec, come on. This is really, really important. How did you get Lana's pets? Was she there at the farm on Saturday? Or did someone else give them to you?"

"Grandmother didn't know you were taking care of them," Aunt Mira said. "She doesn't know how you got the puppy—"

"Biscuit," Spec said.

"Did you name her that?" Dad said. "Biscuit?"

Biscuit heard her name and came over to Spec. She lay down near his feet.

Aunt Mira and Dad looked at each other. Spec felt a wall of glass surrounding him, a magic shield of ice. The cone of protection. That's what his counselor called it, where Spec went sometimes, to be alone and safe.

Dad asked Aunt Mira, "You're sure? Face it, Mom is not thinking straight now."

"I'm sure. Unfortunately."

Aunt Mira said Grandmother was "beside herself" and "inconsolable." Spec felt sad for Grandmother.

"Then, after the police investigator left, I asked Mom about the last time she'd seen her at that cabin, and she said something about Spec, she knew Spec would be upset because he was attached to Biscuit. And that's when I realized Spec had—" Aunt Mira lowered her voice, but Spec could hear her. "Lana's puppy. I freaked out."

"I've got to tell Pansy," Dad said. "Shit, I've got to call her at work."

The bottom of Biscuit's paws had pink pads, small soft cushions.

"Spec?" Dad said. "How did you get Biscuit and Shelly from Grandmother's friend?"

"Did Grandmother's friend come to the wedding?" Aunt Mira asked. "Did she give them to you then?"

"How many times did you go with Grandmother to her friend's house?" Dad asked. "When was the last time? It's important, Spec. Really important."

Spec looked out at them from the cone of protection. Biscuit was inside, too, so Spec wasn't alone.

"Don't...push...let's not panic. I'll ask Mom again later," Aunt Mira said. "But it's going to be a while."

"Jesus, Mira. How much Ambien did you give her?"

"Just one. I slipped it into her orange juice. I'm going over there. I'll stay in my old bedroom. She needs the sleep. Really."

"No kidding." Dad's voice sounded funny. He rubbed his face.

"Arlene is still at the hospital. She volunteered to stay as long as we need her to. Aunt Priscilla is there, too—I say we let Arlene hold down the fort for a while." Aunt Mira patted Dad's arm. "Burry, get some rest."

Dad laughed. A scary laugh. "Rest? I've got to call Pansy and I've got to do it now."

Spec stood up and Biscuit followed him into the bedroom. The house was quiet and good.

That was before the policemen came.

55

TEDDY

Reagan used SnapThat to document her revenge.

An app to send messages that disappeared after one view, vanishing into the digital ether, as Teddy discovered. Only the video Reagan sent him was seared into his memory. He couldn't forget it if he tried.

And he did try. For days he'd done nothing but try. Reagan's long, gorgeous legs wrapped around Nelson's lean back—rippling muscles and gleaming skin—wounded him like, well, radiation poison. Teddy puked his guts out. Next thing, he'd probably lose his hair.

Now when Arlene called, he didn't pick up.

He couldn't care less about her latest dispatches.

His capacity for making any decisions, businesswise? Zilch. He was awash in apathy, tormented by jealousy. The green-eyed monster had him in its jaws, all right, chomping down with a curved snout of jagged icicle teeth, and that son of a bitch hurt. That dumbass Nelson? Really?

Arlene called, the second time that morning. He ignored it.

He did get out of bed, however. And made himself take a shower. And tried to make himself not see Reagan's revenge, playing its endless loop in his mind.

Reagan's glorious face rising over that moron's shoulder like the sun peeking over a boulder, just enough to look into the camera to peer at him, at Teddy, before untangling and switching to another position—legs and arms knotting, this way and that, with the utility of a Swiss army knife.

Arlene called. Again. Teddy toweling himself off, nearly let the call go until the possibility occurred to him—a long shot but he'd take any shot right now—just maybe Reagan had talked to Arlene. Maybe Reagan was at the offices of Rex Wolf now, commandeering, calling a meeting this Friday morning, all hands on deck and she'd barked out an order to Arlene, call Teddy? Tell him to get his sorry ass down here? Teddy would take that. He would take furious Reagan. He would take that in a skinny minute—

"Arlene," he answered and there as a beat of silence as if she'd already hung up.

Then, "I went to see him," and something in her voice scared him.

"Charles, you mean? At the—"

"They wouldn't let me stay long. The nurses, I mean. But Mira was there and she told me…something bad."

Oh, sweet Jesus. Here it comes. Mira…what? Trying to self-immolate? And take him out too. Did she actually tell Arlene? That he, Teddy, was the real reason Mira called off the wedding? And just when he was getting in good with that old battle-ax. "Look, Arlene—"

"That woman. Janelle's crazy friend, the one who…you know who I'm talking about?"

Yeah. He knew. "I wish I didn't."

"I guess you saw it in the papers and all. She's missing."

"No. I haven't been keeping up with the news. I've been a little busy."

Arlene made a sound that could have been a snort of derision, or a sneeze. "Bless you," he said.

"Well, news flash. They say she's dead."

"Wait, who says she's dead?"

"—and the police are here," she hissed. "At the hospital. I'm in the bathroom. I'm fixing to leave soon, but I figured you need to know."

"What happened to her?"

"I got no idea. But it's suspicious or why else would the cops be here?"

"The police probably just want to talk to people who knew her."

"That woman was a demon. She tortured Charles. He doesn't deserve that. He hired me when no one else would even call me back. He paid me good and fair, he—you know coma people can hear things, it can seep in. The law is going to kill him, if they pester him with questions when he's hooked up to machines. It's the awfulest thing."

"How are Janelle and the rest of the family taking this?" he asked, oh so delicately.

"Mira flat out told the one policeman to get lost. Janelle is… I don't know. I'd say off her rocker, but what's new about that? Mira took her somewhere. Home, I reckon."

"Is Charles still scheduled for surgery?"

"Yes. Least there's that. Listen, Teddy. When they come to the office—I'm not talking to them."

"Them?"

"The law."

"Why would the police go to Rex Wolf?"

"I'm just not."

And she hung up.

It was after eleven that night when Arlene called him again.

"You watching the news?"

"No." He had been asleep, falling into bed from sheer exhaustion after another brutal treadmill session.

"Turn it on. Quick."

"I'll pull up the newscast online later. What's this about?"

Her breathing was heavy, ragged. "They've been dragging that pond. I bet they found it."

"Found what? Arlene? Hello? You there?"

"Her body. That witch. I heard Mira talking to Burry on the phone a while ago. She's having a conniption and no wonder. You know how the law don't say what they already know? Person of interest, a minor being questioned in connection to the disappearance, foul play. Like that? Turn on the news. You'll see."

"I'm not following."

"The news doesn't say nothing about his name, 'cause he's a kid and all. But I heard...the law is thinking Burry's boy done it. The stepkid. They think he killed her."

56

SPEC

Grandmother wanted to talk to Spec. She said it in a soft voice but no one heard. No one but Spec.

Spec's mother was crying. Dad said loud, UPSET words and so did Aunt Mira. They were in the living room. Spec was in his bedroom, but the door had to be open, that was the rule. He sat on the floor. Biscuit lay across his lap. She was sound asleep. Spec tried not to move, but his arms hurt from holding her so still, trying to cradle her like she was in a hammock on vacation, dreaming nice dog dreams.

Aunt Mira and Dad kept saying *lawyer.* They said that word over and over, so Spec knew it must be important.

Good lawyer.

Good lawyers cost money.

Spec was tired. His mother and dad kept asking him questions over and over all night.

Did he leave Aunt Mira's wedding? It was okay to tell them. If he did anything without permission they wanted to know. They wouldn't be angry.

They said a man saw Spec drive the minivan on Saturday during the wedding time. The man saw Spec get out and then get back into the minivan and drive away and Spec knew it was the grumpy man at the produce stand who did not like him.

They asked Spec if Grandmother's friend gave him Biscuit and Shelly. And when? They asked if he went to Grandmother's friend's house alone without Grandmother. They asked what he saw there.

Spec had put his hands over his ears and then he crawled under the bed with Biscuit. It was very late then. It was two twenty-five in the middle of the night.

Dad said, That's enough, baby, when Spec's mother cried. Dad said, Mom and Mira are coming first thing, we'll figure this thing out. They are not going to take Spec, over my dead body. Now it was morning. In twelve minutes it would be time to feed Shelly again. There were extra worms in a paper cup on Spec's dresser. After it rained, he found a lot of worms before the hot sun dried them up and the worms got stuck on the sidewalk. They turned stiff and crunchy. Shelly might eat the dried up, crispy worms for a snack, like chips.

"I want to talk to Spec." Grandmother's voice.

His mother was still crying. She was saying things to Grandmother.

"They are going to try to pin this thing on my boy, Janelle, and do you know what happens to boys like—like my Spec, locked up?"

"I want to talk to Spec." Grandmother said it again.

This time the talking stopped. Aunt Mira told Grandmother, "Here, this is what we need to find out, Mom. This is vital. Please, please…get Spec to tell you anything about that day, especially these questions."

Grandmother came into his room. Biscuit opened her eyes and stretched out her legs and got out of Spec's lap. Her tail thumped and she ran to Grandmother.

"Biscuit," Grandmother said and leaned down to hug the puppy, and Spec knew Grandmother was sad, but happy, too, that Biscuit was safe from the bullies. "And Shelly," Grandmother said, and looked over at Shelly's glass house on Spec's dresser.

"You rescued them." Grandmother's voice was quiet as a librarian, and Spec was glad it was not a question. Grandmother understood.

Spec said yes. Then he said the hens were still there, waiting for him. Grandmother said not to worry. She said hens can fly to avoid predators and they could roost together in trees to keep each other company and they could forage in the woods for grubs and worms.

Spec said the hens could live here, they could live in the backyard in a coop he and Dad could build.

Grandmother said that was a good idea. Then she said Spec had to promise her something. Spec had to tell her about the last time he saw Lana. Grandmother looked very sad then. She took out a tissue and blew her nose.

Grandmother said, "Spec, did you see Lana on the day of your aunt Mira's wedding?"

Spec shook his head.

"You rescued Biscuit and Shelly, but you didn't see Lana?"

He nodded.

"How did you know, Spec? How did you know to rescue them?"

When Spec didn't say anything, Grandmother said she couldn't believe that something might have happened to her friend, to their friend Lana. Because she was a missing person. Grandmother's eyes were watery but she did not cry and cry, like Spec's mother did.

"The bullies were after her," Spec said.

Grandmother said, "What bullies?"

"She had to run away."

Spec held on to Biscuit then, held her tightly, and Biscuit thought he was playing and she barked.

The bullies got Grandmother's friend. Maybe she tried to run away, but they got her. The bullies might come after Biscuit. They might come after Grandmother and him. The bad guys might be on their way right now.

"Lana would want you to tell me, Spec. She would want you to tell me what you saw. Did you drive there, over the bridge all by yourself to Lana's cabin? On the wedding day? Did you talk to her then?"

Spec stood up and walked over to his dresser and took the worms out of the cup. He put them into Shelly's aquarium. Grandmother stood behind him.

"You are taking such good care of Shelly and Biscuit, Spec.

Did Lana tell you to do that on that day you saw her, the wedding day?"

He shook his head.

Grandmother didn't say anything. Then she pressed the tissue on her right eye and her left eye.

"You didn't talk to her that day?"

He shook his head.

"Did you see her that day? When you rescued Shelly and Biscuit?"

"No."

"They don't understand what special times we had there, Spec. You and Lana and me and the puppy." Then Grandmother said she understood now, why Lana sent that ugly thing, the video. It was a cry for help. It was a message. Only Grandmother didn't know what to make of it. That's why she needed Spec to help her. "Were all her things there, Spec? All the work we did, at the kitchen table, you remember? In the cabin?"

"It was messy."

"It was messy when you went, you mean? And Lana wasn't there. But her things were? Her computer—"

"No. I used Mom's laptop."

Grandmother sucked in her breath as if she were scared. "For what?"

"For the Plan," Spec said. "Send the message. Then rescue Biscuit and Shelly."

"You sent out the…message?"

"In case the bullies came."

"You sent Lana's message…with the video. And it was on the wedding day." Grandmother spoke slowly. "And…and Lana wasn't there? She didn't leave a note, or…her car. Was her car there?"

He shook his head.

He was tired of talking.

Grandmother went back into the living room. She said soft words. Spec couldn't hear what she was saying. Then Burry and his mother and Aunt Mira raised their voices and it was very UPSETTING. Spec got up on the bed and Biscuit hopped up with him and Spec's eyes felt heavy, and as he started to fall asleep he heard Grandmother tell Mira to take her home, right now, and it was Grandmother's voice that was loud.

57

MIRA

Mira sat on her mother's bed after the shower started, listening to the splatter of water, to the sounds of her mother being okay.

The shower stopped. Mira knocked. "Need anything? A towel?"

"I'm fine, honey."

Her mother came out in a cloud of steam.

Janelle's insistence on coming home after she talked to Spec, well, it gave Mira hope—maybe her mother had to find something here, hidden. Some notes, maybe? Her calendar?

But no luck.

At home, her mother's sense of urgency disappeared.

Their appointment with the lawyer was at two. The best defense lawyer Mira could line up with such short notice, and with the cashier's check of ten grand, her "dowry" to hand over, to get things rolling.

And things had to roll.

Or stop rolling.

Her mother and Spec had to be protected. Lawyered up before they went in for questioning.

Janelle disappeared in the walk-in closet. There were the sounds of hangers scraping.

"Mom, look, for your sake and for Spec's, we need to go over everything again, the last time you saw Lana—"

"Lana is always disappearing. She comes and she goes."

The present tense. Not good.

Her mother came back into the bedroom wearing a slip, clutching a beige dress and sandals. Mira wanted to tell her it was too hot to wear a slip, no one had to wear slips or even pantyhose anymore, but never mind.

"Once the police find her body, there will be a coroner's statement and things could happen fast, Mom, bad things. It might be on the news, her connection to you and to... I just... I want to prepare you. Because you and Spec...we have to figure out things. We need to get your stories straight."

Mira's phone buzzed. She stepped out of the bedroom into the hallway. "Arlene?"

"Mira, your aunt Priscilla is trying to take over again."

Mira sighed. "I'm sorry."

"It's all right. She had a conniption because one of the nurses told her she had to wait an hour to see your daddy. But I got her calmed down."

"Thanks. For staying." Mira hadn't told Arlene about why she and her mother and Burry couldn't be at the hospital that afternoon, that they had an appointment with a lawyer. Arlene said they all must be running on fumes. And they were. Mira wondered how much Arlene knew, if the police had talked to her. Mira wouldn't ask yet, not now. She was grateful she could count on Arlene to guard her father. Also, Arlene had a cell phone. Her aunt Priscilla didn't.

"How's your mother?"

"She's...we're all just—" Mira said.

"You heard any more about that woman?"

"No," Mira lied.

"Uh-huh. Look, Mira, honey." Arlene's voice dropped and Mira had to press the phone to her ear.

"Those police don't need to be poking around trying to bother your daddy."

"They were there again?"

"No. No, just saying. They might. Because, well, you never know, especially when it comes to the law. They do whatever they want to."

"Call me first thing if something like that happens."

"In a skinny minute. No one is going in there to pester your daddy. He can hear what's going on, I know it, and he doesn't need to have the law sniffing around. Seeing as how he has to go under the knife tomorrow."

"I will be there this afternoon, by dinnertime—"

"Take your time. I got nothing better to do," Arlene said. "I'll go by the office, but I can be at the hospital in no time. T-Rex canceled everything; he's laying out like a bum. It's a disgrace. I'm just trying to keep your daddy's workers settled down."

"Canceled everything? You mean…it's closed? The business?"

"Not on my watch. You don't worry."

"Thank you," Mira managed.

"Now, don't you get all choked up, hon," Arlene said. "Charles needs y'all to be strong. Bye now."

Mira went back into her mother's bedroom. "That was Arlene. Nothing new to report."

Her mother nodded, but she looked disoriented, sitting there on the bed.

"I'm going to take a quick shower," Mira said.

Now that she had her own clothes. Thanks to Pansy and Burry who, before the real hell began, arranged with Nelson to pick up Mira's car, full of her things, and to inquire about her cat, Yeats, who was here now, at her parents' house, curled up on the sofa. The only communication she'd had from Nelson was "Thank God," after she'd texted him that she was not pregnant after all.

"Maybe you should rest, Mom. You're going to need your strength for this afternoon."

"I can't rest." Her mother fumbled with something in her lap. A notebook.

"If you think of anything, write it down. And maybe, maybe look through your old notebooks? Anything that will help us figure out how Spec ended up with those pets on Saturday and when he drove the minivan all the way there, or maybe met someone?"

"All right."

Her mother was restless, but there was a meek stealth about her.

Mira should have paid more attention to it.

Because after Mira showered and dressed—five minutes flat—and called to Janelle, her mother wasn't in her bedroom. Just a vague scent of powdery lilac, the mirror in the bathroom still steamy, a dress laid out on the bed, an empty outline.

Oh no.

"Mom?" She wasn't upstairs. She wasn't downstairs, not in the kitchen, or the living room. "Mom?" Silence. Mira's heart thumped hard. "Mom? Mom?"

She should have listened to her gut. The part of her that shouted, DON'T LEAVE YOUR MOTHER ALONE.

Mira opened the hallway door to the garage.

Her mother stood in her slip, beside her car.

"Oh my God, Mom. You scared me. I didn't know where you were."

Janelle turned to look at Mira, one hand on the hood of the car. "I didn't mean to scare you."

"You're not thinking of driving anywhere—"

"No."

Her mother dropped her hand from the car and walked to the corner of the garage.

"What are you doing?"

"I just, I need to check something." Her mother stood in front of a dented metal cabinet.

"Can't it wait? Please?"

Janelle reached for the cabinet handle, pulled it. It was locked. "Okay, well, that's that," Mira said. "Come on back inside."

Janelle held the combination, whirred, and clicked it. The lock snapped open.

"Mom?"

Jars of nails, old paint cans, tubes of grout—the usual depressing detritus of suburban garages. Mira sighed.

"What are you looking for?"

Her mother stood on her tiptoes, reaching up to the top of

the cabinet, her hands grasping, grasping at something out of reach.

"This." She took down a metal box.

Documents, maybe? For the hospital? "We've got all Dad's paperwork," Mira said. "Just bring it with us. We'll go through that stuff later."

The box had another lock. Another combination. Whirled, clicked. Opened.

Her mother pulled out a—

Mira screamed. Leaped across the garage, in front of her mother—"No! No, let me have it—" She put her hands over her mother's hand, the one holding the gun—

Her mother let go.

"Are you trying to give me a heart attack?"

"It's your father's service revolver."

Had her mother even held a firearm? No, Mira thought, no. Surely not. Her own hand shook as she put the gun back into the metal box.

"How long has this been out here?"

"Years and years."

"And you knew it was here?" Mira swallowed. Her throat hurt. "What were you planning on doing with it?"

"Don't you see? I didn't think it was here."

"No, I don't…what do you mean?"

"He thought I didn't know, but I did."

"Mom—I…I can't leave a firearm here. You know that, right?"

Mira cradled the box. Inside, the gun. And by the way, was it loaded? Were there bullets in there? "I can't leave it here, Mom," she said again, but what was she supposed to do with it? A possibly illegal firearm, and she didn't have a license—her father didn't either. Probably.

She coaxed her mother back inside, and then Mira slipped outside and put the box in the trunk of her own car, under the spare tire.

That would have to do for now.

Oh dear Lord. What would Mira do with her father's firearm in her car?

Mira's phone rang. Crying. Big hiccuping gulps—

"Arlene?"

"Y'all need to get over here," she wailed. "The nurse came and got me and said family needs to be here. Your daddy is... he's bad off, real bad."

58

CHARLES

"You want the TV on, Mr. Wolf?"

No. He tried to say no.

But the nurse turned on the television anyway. The evening news. Local. Live Breaking. Good evening and...investigating possible homicide...and our Fred Corely is live at the scene of Pudding Swamp—

No. Turn it off. Please...off. He didn't want to hear—

Authorities say they are questioning a minor identified by witnesses—

Lana stood at the foot of his bed. Most of her face smiled.

Make it stop. Make her stop.

"Mr. Wolf, calm down." The nurse's cool hand on his wrist. "You're safe. There's no one in this room but me and you."

Her, her, he groaned. "Her...go away."

"Auditory and visual hallucinations are side effects of your meds, okay? It's just a bad dream. Mr. Wolf, can you hear me?"

The Lana-thing beside his bed, clicking through the television stations, finding the most horrible pictures—

He closed his eyes, saw it anyway. The boy, Spec, in handcuffs. That strange fat kid. That he never liked. Embarrassing to have him around, but—

"They'll give that kid the chair," the Lana-thing said cheerfully.

No. Charles opened his mouth—he couldn't...breathe.

Two nurses looked at his machines, but not at him. And not at Lana. They still didn't see her!

He tried to talk. Tried to tell them to make that monster leave, she was tormenting him—

"Delirium noted," the nurse said.

Stupid. He was stupid and careless. Desperate enough that night to follow her. His hard-earned money in the trunk of her car! He couldn't bear it. Thinking—not thinking—pure impulse to tail her, because Red never could nail down an address. Maybe shacking up with trailer trash, he said, who knows? Charles assumed she'd take off, hit the highway or head to a bus station or airport...

So he had followed the vampire, watched her pull into that cabin, a mile from the river, the swampy almost putrid scent of the fishing pond at the bottom of the dirt road. That disgusting Svengali knocking around in a cabin—hiding out there, right under his nose.

He parked.

He shouldn't park. He should drive home.

This is a nightmare. Any minute he was going to wake up in his own bed, beside Janelle, a wife who still loved him. Wake up! He could stop this.

But he watched himself park up the road. Watched himself take off on foot, approach the cabin, and he saw—

"Mr. Wolf, please hold still? Your catheter is...we have to..."

He looked into the cabin window and it...infuriated him. All the lights on, loud music, and her traipsing around in jean shorts and a bikini top, holding the neck of a bottle. Celebrating. Because she'd won. She was basking in his suffering, and she laughed, talking to someone. He couldn't see who, for the life of him, who the hell was she talking to? And then she pulled up her shirt—*Shaking my ta-tas for you, Petya!* She really was repulsive, and—to a screen. A computer screen! That was who she was talking to. Not a person.

He moved to the back window and peered inside. There at the end of the bed by her suitcases, his bowling bag, his money—

Not twenty feet away.

A break-in, a robbery—she couldn't report it. Couldn't pin it on him. For taking back what was his! He felt around for a rotten sash and raised the window. Paused, but the music didn't stop, and he got a leg in, then the other, and took three steps and then he was holding it, his bowling bag and such a bright heat of hope, a little explosion of relief inside him—

Then a click.

Who would have thought she'd have a gun?

Pointing at him, in his general direction, wobbly because she was drunk. He could smell the liquor and his own fear, and pure instinct—he tried to grab the pistol, just to—it was self-defense—

"Yeah, right. You broke in and it's self-defense." The Lana-thing laughed and something dark and clotted oozed down her neck.

They'd wrestled. The worst grunting, the stink of his own sweat and the gun went off—

"I didn't shoot you!" On purpose.

And then she fell, hit her head on that big rock—

"Bashed in the ole' noggin. Want to see?"

She was on the floor. Smeared with blood. He took the blanket off the bed and covered her, so he wouldn't have to see her long, awful body.

His own ragged gasps were all he could hear until—

Barking. From somewhere near, another room. He ordered himself not to panic, it was a robbery, a botched robbery. Maybe they wouldn't find her, not for the longest time, fingerprints, and evidence gone, too...

He took his bowling bag and a pillowcase and wiped down the windows, all the time telling himself it was stupid and careless, stupid, stupid...but adrenaline took over, fight or flight, he grabbed the gun...left behind that hunk of rock with her blood—

"Hunk of rock? No, Charles. No, that was my prized rhyolite geode. It's volcanic rock. Rhyolite lava is very viscous. It flows...slowly...it burns and oozes and smothers."

He put the bowling bag back into his car trunk. Dropped the gun into a pillowcase, and set it beside him on the passenger seat. Drove away thinking, *What next?* What in the hell had he done?

The nurse now, not smiling. One to ten, pain, et cetera, et cetera.

The news droned on. He pictured the boy, handcuffed, crying.

Charles closed his eyes.

Lana's movie played. The boy. Spec. On death row...

"Can't tear yourself away, can you, Charles? From this preview of coming attractions?"

"Mr. Wolf? Your family is on the way. Hold on."

He held on.

"Daddy?"

Mira.

Where was—?

Janelle.

There. He had to tell Janelle he loved her, and he had wronged her, but he always wanted to spare her the worst of it and—

The machines screamed, they squawked, but he couldn't fly, not now, he couldn't—

More strangers in the room, moving fast...yelling.

Mira crying—

Charles said, Not boy. He tried hard to say, Not boy.

Mira and Janelle looking at him now, he—the pain—God, the pain. And where was Burry?

"NOT BOY...Mile M."

"What is it, Daddy?"

"Mile M—"

"He's not making sense."

"He's trying to tell us something."

The measure of his life, it was not good—the legacy, his legacy would be...murderer.

"Dad, who is Miles? Or Mark? Nod if you can—"

"M Mmmm twen fie."

"Who? Miles who?"

But better him, than the boy—

"Tweennnnyfv."

"Twenty-five?"

"Gnnnn."

Nurses looking at him, doctor looking at him. Somebody said, "Gun"?

Janelle leaned in close. "Not himmmmmm, not boy...gun MM twenty-five."

No pain, then. But...fear. Fear because he was not in pain— flying again, flying—away—

Below him, Mira crying. Janelle...not.

She understood. Janelle understood.

59

FIREARM FOUND NEAR HIGHWAY HAD FINGERPRINTS MATCHING MISSING WOMAN, SUSPECT

HAVEN, SC—Investigators revealed new evidence in the case of a missing Nevada woman. A loaded gun found after a sweep on Horse Highway had fingerprints and DNA matching those of Lana O'Shield, whose disappearance from a rental cabin two weeks ago remains a mystery.

Information about the firearm's location at Mile Marker 25 came from a primary person of interest whom Haven Police Chief Sam Crum declined to identify.

A source close to the investigation said DNA evidence recovered on the firearm as well as a large decorative rock in the rental cabin may be linked to a suspect, pending forensic testing. "It is unclear at this point who owned the gun," Crum said. "It was not registered."

O'Shield was last seen July 23 at a gas station. Her partially submerged car was discovered three days later. Authorities say someone ransacked her rented cabin and pushed her car into Pudding Pond. Investigators found "evidence of injury" inside the cabin, Crum said.

"The rock may have caused O'Shield's injury," he said. "And at some point we believe the (recovered) weapon discharged."

Crum declined to say if authorities were close to declaring the case a homicide investigation. "This remains a missing person investigation. Right now, we have more questions than answers. But we are going to continue working until we figure out what all happened. This evidence—we think it might lead to a break in the case."

A minor driving a minivan and spotted by a local store owner was previously questioned but is no longer a person of interest, Crum said. The 14-year-old boy, acquainted with the victim, stumbled upon the ransacked cabin to "check on her pets," but new evidence exonerates him, he said. Crum said a suspect in O'Shield's disappearance will likely be identified within several days.

60

THE FUNERAL

They decided the funeral should be small, much to the chagrin of the undertaker.

Surely this was no way to honor Mira's father, a town father, whose untimely death would bring out legions of acquaintances and friends? She would be surprised, the undertaker said, how many mourners someone of her father's stature drew, and the mortuary's small receiving room would be inadequate.

"We've talked it over," Mira told him.

"Your mother," he said. "Sometimes grieving widows aren't thinking clearly and it would be a shame—"

"My mother is the one who suggested it.

"Just an hour visitation open to the public?"

"Yes."

As if a curtailed funeral could condense their own mourning. With a sniff of disapproval, the undertaker nodded.

Mira assumed only a handful of people would show up. But the undertaker had been right. Unfortunately.

Throngs of people filed in, milled past the closed casket, crammed into the small room that smelled of lilies. No service, no music, no lamentations, no uplifting verses. A private graveside service would follow. Just for family. And Arlene.

Mira, her mother, and Burry sat on a prim velvet sofa, Aunt Priscilla in a wingback chair beside them, blowing through a box of tissues. Pansy and Spec stood for a while, until the room was so packed they went outside.

Bunch of old coots and gossipers flushed out from the rumors, Mira thought. Just a big old schadenfreude fest. How jaded of her. Uncharitable. But that didn't mean it wasn't true. They cupped her mother's hands, they hugged. They leaned into Mira, asked how her mother was holding up. Tina, her mother's neighbor, whispered, "Your mother seems to be taking all of this so well."

All of this. Meaning what, exactly? The salacious details of—well, take your pick. Her father dying of a broken heart after a video link circulated that cast aspersions, insinuated her father was a horny wife-swapper who'd lied about his wife's accident? Or the breaking news—the article or post or Tweet or whatever—that would hit the digital airwaves any day, any moment, identifying her father as a suspect in a homicide investigation.

He was dead. You couldn't convict a dead man. You could kill his memory, though. Label him as a lowlife crazed killer...

"She's doing as well as can be expected," Mira whispered over and over. "We all are." It was rote memory, the line she and Burry had decided on that morning.

So far, her mother seemed clearheaded. Detached. Disassociation, maybe? It was her mother, after all, who had insisted on calling the sheriff's deputy when they'd wheeled her father away for emergency surgery; well, he was on a crash cart by then, really...dying.

It was her mother who had told the deputy to check mile marker 25 on Horse Highway...her husband, Charles Wolf, had confessed—

Mira's aunt Priscilla was bawling now, collapsing into Tina's arms.

Burry looked lost. Last night Mira had told him she had their father's gun in the trunk of her car; it had apparently been in the garage for years. She didn't know what the hell to do with it. Burry said, Don't do anything. Not right now. Not until this case was closed, and her mother and Spec were safe from the focus of a capricious investigation that could take months. Not until they found a body. Lana's body. Not until she talked to a lawyer, if it came to that. Hence, Mira found herself driving around with a weapon in the trunk of her Kia. Not even the craziest thing to happen lately, not even close—

Burry was staring daggers across the room now, where people clogged the doorway.

Teddy.

Oh, T-Rex, you had to show up? He looked stiffly bereft in his dark pinstripes and silver tie, and hooked around the crook of his arm—a manicured, lovely hand. Reagan. Svelte and suave, in her midnight-blue wrap dress, on her tasteful but stunning four-inch black heels, her eyes sweeping over the crowd, pretending not to meet Mira, flashing triumph, taking a victory lap.

"They could spin this, you know," Reagan had told Teddy that morning over breakfast. Technically, brunch. Mimosas for her, Bloody Marys for him. A celebration of sorts, after a night of vigorous, reuniting make-up sex. And, yeah, it was a bitch trying to scrub that video out of his head, Reagan and that lunkhead, like a freaking hologram beaming in their bedroom all night—

But Teddy got his wife back. He won.

That's what he told himself as he'd reached for Reagan, and they'd go at it again.

Teddy said he'd do anything. He recited the right things, following along with the salient points of her crisis-management plan, and Reagan had smiled. "You can stop now. I'm impressed."

If she came back to him—

Just name it, he said. Anything.

Rex Wolf. Gone. They needed to step away and move on.

Yep.

No problem. No more Charles is like a father to me. Now that it was secretly, possibly true. Mira had called with that toxic tidbit. He hadn't picked up, of course, so she'd left a terse message. Teddy, Mom has indicated that my father and Mary were together and you, um, you are just maybe the product of that night. I thought you should know. Uh, no. Just no. He didn't need to know. And he certainly didn't need to wonder about the repulsive unspoken possibility, that he and Mira were possibly siblings. No thanks! Teddy reminded himself now that the question of his own paternity was contained. Aside from the Wolf family, he and Reagan, and maybe that shit-for-brains Nelson—no one had an overwhelming reason to suspect that Stan wasn't Teddy's father. Teddy had to believe that. Charles had been like a father to him all right, but not his father. No way. Charles was, well, a loser. And Stan was...not. Teddy was not.

A few nights before, Arlene had slipped up and told Teddy that the lawmen were blaming Charles; it had something to do with his last words. Or so he gathered from Arlene's hysterics. That was when Arlene was still talking to him, but now she wouldn't even look at him. Maybe Mira or Janelle had said something to rein her in?

Reagan had made some calls, got a few more crumbs about what was going down. And she was almost impressed. Almost.

"That took some balls," she told Teddy. "I mean, I didn't think Charles had it in him. He went over and took her on, that freak. Charles lost it, but he was defending his wife. That's how they should spin it. If they're smart."

Reagan had reached over and put her hand on his and a little thrill shot up his arm; he got her back. "We need to think about where we want to set up shop next, maybe Charlotte or Atlanta. Think big."

He was thinking big. So big he didn't want to come to the funeral today, but Reagan insisted. Of course they had to attend the funeral, even if they just kind of stood around on the periphery nodding sadly, not really talking to the Wolf family, no need for that, just show up so there was no talk of a rift. Just as long as Teddy didn't have to see Nelson, of whom there was no sign, thank God.

Did Mira know? How her douchebag of a fiancé had obviously been trying to put the moves on Teddy's wife? Teddy didn't know the details of how that revenge hook-up went down between Reagan and Nelson—didn't want to ever!—but that musclehead had no qualms about whipping it out for Reagan. It was clearly that lowlife's idea.

He glimpsed Mira now through the line of mourners, nodding to someone. She was pale as a candle in a black sleeveless dress. She looked drained and bewildered. A pang of sadness. What was this? Sympathy? The old pathetic Teddy—of last week—would have cut in line to hold Mira, just...hold her.

The old Teddy. Loser Teddy. Not T-Rex, who was coming back, roaring. Teddy had dodged a bullet; he could have come out of this disaster with nothing. No career, no Reagan, no future.

No Mira. He could live with that. Right? Technically an estrangement, since they were possibly family.

"Let's move over here, Teddybear," Reagan whispered to him now and they stepped out of line, hung back, because people were still queued up down the hall. "Maybe ease out before the waterworks start."

She was right, as usual. Where would he be without Reagan?

It was just, well, now that he'd won Reagan back, he had a fleeting doubt, a knife twist. One of those *Dear God, what have you done?* moments. You want this? The marriage? This power career? This...life?

Then Teddy told himself to shut the hell up.

A quick look at the guest book read like a who's who of Haven big shots. He signed the registry. Mr. and Mrs. Theodore Rex.

Spec stood between Grandmother and Dad at the grave. A man Spec didn't know read things from the Bible.

Aunt Mira wiped her face. She cried a lot for a grown-up.

There were a lot of flowers around Grandfather's grave. They were in circles like holiday wreaths and propped up on stands and they smelled good. There was a little tent set up with chairs underneath, but no one sat in the chairs except for an old lady, Grandfather's sister. They stood together and listened to the man who read from the Bible.

There was a bird singing in the bushes. A robin. It came out and looked at Spec and then flew away and Spec watched the bird until it turned into a dot in the sky. The mountains were far off but they looked close by, like construction paper cutouts. There were birds up there too. Big ones floating in circles, with wide black wings.

The man stopped reading. Aunt Mira blew her nose with a tissue.

But Spec was not sad. Maybe it was wrong not to feel sad when a dead body was right there getting ready to go into a hole in the dirt. Grandfather was in a fancy wooden box with flowers but soon he would be covered up. Then he and Grandmother could visit him here sometimes. That's what Grandmother told him.

Grandmother said Spec could come with her to the mountains, because she missed it up there on her daddy's land, and he asked if he could bring Biscuit and she said yes.

When Spec got home, he would take Biscuit for a walk. Then he would feed Shelly. Then he would do his chores. His mother and dad said he could keep Biscuit and they would all go and release Shelly when Spec decided Shelly was strong and big enough to live outside again. Biscuit and Shelly were his responsibility. He liked thinking about Biscuit, how she liked to bite her leash when they walked, like she was taking her own self for a walk, and that made him smile.

Grandmother looked sad now too. And Dad.

But Spec felt happy.

For the first time in a long time, Spec was happy.

PART VI

61

MOVING ON

After we bury Charles, my headaches start. I'm in bed for three days.

They decide I need to be looked after.

I lost my husband, I tell them. I have not lost sleep or my appetite or my mind. Not yet.

"How would you feel about me moving in?" Mira says. "For a while. Just until things blow over."

"You good with that?" Burry asks me.

I am. I am good with that.

"It's going to hit you hard, Mom," Mira says. "Grief at losing Dad. But also anger. Because he gaslighted you. Totally gaslighted you with Stan and…even Mary. All these years."

"Gaslighted?"

"When you remembered something," Burry says, "Dad convinced you that you were nuts." He looks at Mira, shrugs. "Harsh, but true."

"We'll hunker down here," Mira says. "Burry and Pansy will bring Spec over for dinner a lot. I'll drive you to errands and to the doctor. We'll get through this."

They look after me. The pain lets up, and I spend my days in the garden. It is peaceful.

Then—

Scandal breaks. One day the newspaper comes, with Charles on the front page.

The disgrace would have killed him if he weren't already dead.

But Teddy defends him, and Charles would have found some satisfaction in that.

Mira reads the article aloud to us, the quote from Teddy. *Charles Wolf was an honorable man who defended his wife and his family from a woman with a criminal past. When the evidence is in, I am confident Charles will come out of this heroic.*

Burry shakes his head.

Mira says, "I don't know whether to be pleased or skeptical."

"I vote for skeptical," Burry says. "T-Rex wouldn't spout that unless it benefits him. Nixon probably wrote it for him, right? Spin, Mira, spin, remember? All T-Rex cares about is his image."

Other parts of the article they don't discuss. Not in front of me. And I don't care to read it.

But I hear Burry on the phone later, whispering. Stalled investigation. Haven't found the body.

The body. Her. They're waiting to find Lana.

I am waiting too.

Teddy did not respond to Mira's email for the longest time. She thanked him for the kind words he'd said about Charles in those interviews for the newspaper. That meant a lot to her, Teddy's loyalty to Charles—

Who was possibly his father too. She didn't mention that. She didn't have to.

Not that he knew for sure. He did not want to know. No DNA test for him! He would go out of his way to never know. Let the toxic secret die with them—his parents and Charles— because it had already poisoned the next generation.

After all, this disaster could have been avoided in the first place if Teddy had known that Mira might possibly be…his sibling.

He finally emailed Mira back months later, from an internet café in Bangkok. He and Reagan had split, and he wasn't ever coming back to Haven. Ever.

And that was it. Brusque, yeah, but he had to get distance— temporally, geographically, emotionally, mentally—every way a human could extricate himself from the claws of the past.

Take care. Have a nice life. Sincerely, T-Rex.

Mira landed a decent gig: writer-in-residence for a year at a college in North Carolina. Two hundred miles away, though. She would have to move.

"Do it," Burry told her. "You have to move on."

Another family meeting in the kitchen.

Burry told their mother, "Pansy and me—we talked it over. We thought the three of us might move in with you, Mom. You good with that?"

Oh yes. She was good with that.

Burry and Spec helped Mira load up her car. Mira packed her mother's notebooks. Since the funeral her mother had been writing down her memories before they disappeared, she said. Mira had read the notebooks—over and over.

"Am I stepping on your toes, Mom? Am I invading your life? For some reason you and Dad, this open investigation about Lana. It's all I can think about."

"I'm sorry. How awful."

"No, it's not awful exactly. I'm feeling the energy, the curiosity. The questions."

Mira asked Spec to set up an email account for Janelle, so Mira could correspond with her mother.

Mira was committed to finding the truth.

"Your truth, Mom. Because you were lied to by Dad, by Lana, by everyone."

Spec's mom said she loved a man in uniform. She kissed Dad at the front door before he left.

Grandmother said Dad was handsome.

Dad was a forest ranger now. He worked at Haven State Park.

Spec and Mom and Dad lived with Grandmother because she needed to be looked after. Grandmother wanted the small bedroom downstairs near the kitchen. Mom and Dad took the big bedroom upstairs. Spec moved into Dad's old bedroom with Biscuit.

Spec went to a new school. He did not completely hate it. At Easter Aunt Mira came home for a family dinner. Spec said no ham, pigs are too smart to be eaten. They are sensitive beings. You mean sentient, little man? Dad asked. Sentient and sensitive, Spec said. Grandmother made deviled eggs and Aunt Mira made potato salad and Dad made spring peas with mint and asparagus and hollandaise and Spec and Mom made chocolate cake, and it was a good Easter.

Aunt Mira said she was writing a book. The book was about Grandmother. It was going to be a real book next year, the kind you could check out of libraries. She said she was dedicating it to Grandmother and to Spec.

62

VIVA VERLINDA

Verlinda Azure limped along, tapping the polished marble floor
with her cane, trying to keep up with Beatrice, who was eighty
if she was a day, spry and lithe, twice Verlinda's age and the
woman could run circles around her, with all the kale, tai chi
and yoga, the massages and facials, the wealth, the wealth, the
wealth.

"I'm so excited about our sessions," Beatrice said. "It's all I
can think about."

"You've made remarkable progress."

"What a lovely ring." Beatrice held Verlinda's hand, peered
closer.

"Thank you. A gift from a client."

"I'll just be a minute. Sofia can make you an espresso. Make
yourself at home."

The kitchen, what a world of pain. Overhead lights bright
enough for surgery, the wide gleaming patio windows, the tur-
quoise eye of the pool throwing excruciating spears of sunlight.

"Is there coffee?" Verlinda managed. Sofia stood at the sink
in her pink uniform, hand-drying the crystal sugar bowl, giving
her the stink eye. Fine, Verlinda would get it herself. Aspirin
and water too. A splash of rum, holy mother, what she would
give for a splash of rum in her coffee.

Verlinda took her coffee to Beatrice's plush office up the
hall, clicked on Beatrice's seldom used, gleaming computer for
the usual research.

Investigation at a dead end. Authorities frustrated.

It always made her feel better.

That time she'd stumbled upon the obituary for Charles

Wolf, hard to top that. She'd splurged on rum and oysters, threw herself a little celebration. But then, even better, she began to piece together the news, the quotes; and it dawned on her…

The video had gone out. Lana O'Shield's best work had been seen after all! That dopey kid had followed the contingency plan like a robot. Sent out that nasty family movie. Chaos ensued! Clearly the video killed Charles Wolf. Only fair.

Because Charles Wolf killed Lana O'Shield.

That woman was gone.

He'd left her for dead.

Then that woman woke up. Blood-caked face. Robbed…of her vision. Most of it. Shoulder bullet-knicked, a pitted, clotted wound. That woman couldn't see much. But she could hear.

Tires crunching on the gravel. Her instinct kicked in like a backup generator. Danger, get out. Take the jewels.

Later, it was one of the few things she congratulated herself for in a long string of screwups. Getting out of the cabin with the bag of jewels. She crawled out the back door and slinked away on her belly like some swamp creature, down toward the tall reeds near the pond. To hide.

They were loud. The sounds of breaking glass in the cabin, before they moved to her car with their knives, tearing up the seats, cursing. She oozed into the mud, trying not to think of snakes, but she'd take snakes compared to what they would do. Because those Russian goons couldn't find it. The loot.

Which Charles Wolf took. And she wanted to laugh in their stupid faces because…Charles Wolf! That loser had finally done something smart.

And then they were gone. It was black and dark in the shallows of Pudding Pond, and she was cold as death. When the sky began to lighten, he found her. He'd come to save her. Crying. Sobbing, the little pussy. Her rescuer, bawling like a baby.

Oh, my Lana, Lana, they come after.

Save it, she told him. We have to get the hell out of here.

Idiot Petya. He sold her out.

Oh, sure, he claimed he'd detoured on his way to their

rendezvous in Florida, to check on her. Bad feeling my Lana need help. Right. And she was born yesterday.

In more charitable moments, she told herself Luke and Vlad shook Petya down, those brutes roughed him up. But she didn't have many charitable moments.

At the pond she told Petya to push her car into the water. To cover her tracks. It would stall things, make it look like she was a goner. Goons might stop looking for her. Cops too.

Petya nursed her wounds when they made it to Florida. Attentive, too stupid to fake it. Thought she still had the funds stashed somewhere.

But starting over was hell. And she was wounded.

A stranger squinted back at her in the mirror. With her temple scar, her wonky vision, her pitted shoulder, her limp. Half-blind seer in shades, a gimp with a stick, clutching her antique cane with its clawed bauble, pinched from an antique store.

She didn't recognize herself, but neither did anyone else.

Verlinda pulled up today's new articles and began to scan the headlines.

She choked on her coffee. Fingerprints…FBI…ties to organized crime?

Luka and Vlad got sloppy. Left a fingerprint for the Feds to find in that cabin, in her car. Who knows what else they had on her? Evidence forever linking Lana O'Shield to those goons. Now the Feds would never stop looking.

Lana O'Shield would never be dead.

And just when things were picking up.

She had to deal with Petya.

Petya was a goner.

Tick tock, my pet.

Of course, it would be something…merciful. Something he wouldn't see coming. Bullet while sleeping. An opiate cocktail. The longer she waited, the harder it would be. The dumbass Ruski. She would miss him.

But he gave her up. Petya gave up Lana O'Shield once. He would do it again.

No choice.

Because, well, viva Verlinda. Verlinda Azure, soul tender, blind seer, survivor.

Time to hit the road, Verlinda.

Her instincts screamed, *Leave, leave, leave now!*

And Verlinda Azure's instincts were the only thing on this tired, old earth she trusted.

ACKNOWLEDGMENTS

I am immensely grateful to Judith Weber for her readings, suggestions, and encouragement. Additional thanks to the Edisto Writers Group for friendship, fun, and inspiration. Thank you Jaynie Royal and Pam Van Dyk, and everyone at Regal House, for bringing *Her Best Self* into the world.